Zimmermann
Mount Nemo
Tansley
Nelson
Appleby
RAILWAY
DUNDAS
GRAND
TRUNK
TORONTO AND NIAGARA POWER CO.
HAMILTON
Freeman
BURLINGTON JCT.
Port Nelson
Burlington
Aldershot
WATERDOWN STA.
BURLINGTON BEACH
CANAL
HAMILTON BEACH
BURLINGTON BAY
Hamilton Beach
Rock Bay
Carrolls Point
BEACH ROAD ST
HAMILTON

Other Books by Rachael Preston

Tent of Blue
The Fishers of Paradise
The Wind Seller

The Fishers *of* Paradise

RACHAEL PRESTON

James Street North Books is an imprint of Wolsak and Wynn Publishers.

Cover images: boathouses: "Around Dundas Marsh," by John Morris. Courtesy of Local History & Archives, Hamilton Public Library; skaters: iStock
Cover and interior design: Marijke Friesen
Map on endpapers: "*Topographic Map, Ontario, Hamilton Sheet*," 1909
Source: Library and Archives Canada/Department of Militia and Defence, Geographical Section/NMC-0079203
Author photograph: Christian TW Photography
Typeset in Goudy
Printed by Webcom, Canada

The publisher gratefully acknowledges the support of the Canada Council for the Arts, the Ontario Arts Council and the Canada Book Fund.

James Street North Books
280 James Street North
Hamilton, ON
Canada L8R 2L3

Originally self-published, in different format, as an eBook in 2012.

Library and Archives Canada Cataloguing in Publication

Preston, Rachael, author
The fishers of paradise / Rachael Preston.

Previously published: East Point Publishing, 2012.
ISBN 978-1-928088-16-5 (paperback)

I. Title.

PS8581.R449F57 2016 C813'.6 C2016-900681-6

For Mum and Dad

PART ONE

Chapter 1

The sledgehammers fall silent and the house shifts forward with a wooden groan. Like an aged swimmer anticipating the starter's pistol, it wavers a moment in the wind, knees creaking with the newly uneven weight, and then, in a slow choreography, the stilts fold under themselves and the house slides into the marsh. Water and birds explode into flight, squirrels leap from the bare trees. The sound, magnified by the geography of this enclave of lake and forest, by the stillness of the grey morning preceding it, ricochets a warning. The surface churns, and muskrats and beaver dive to the muddy bottom where carp and pike and bass huddle in the reeds. Water rushes over the porch of the two-storey home, washing against the door and windows as the house lurches drunkenly in its own wake.

No sooner has the lake settled than the thrum of an engine, expensive, throaty, cuts through the silence that has claimed the small crowd gathered on their docks and porches to say goodbye. A gleaming mahogany powerboat noses out from between a set of weathered boathouse stilts like some exotic, temperamental animal and guns into the marsh, leaving behind the heady scent of gasoline. The boat alone, a Grew recently confiscated from bootleggers who ran contraband liquor across Lake Ontario, is worth standing outside in the November cold to see.

Its current owner claims he can still smell the cordite along the three grooves carved portside by glancing bullets.

The driver circles the floating house, making it bob again, then eases back on the throttle and slows to an idle. His passenger turns in his seat to face the front door.

Everyone watches and waits.

Five minutes pass. Six.

Egypt Fisher stands at the shoreline, thinking her eyes might dry out from the wind if the door doesn't open soon.

"What are we waiting for?" Her young brother, Aidan, twirls a stick.

"For Ida to come out."

"Why is she in there?"

Why indeed? "She doesn't like boats."

"So why does she live in a boathouse?"

"Because."

"Because why?"

"Because, because." Egypt ruffles his hair and whistles for George, who materializes from a scrum of children and lopes towards her, licking his chops. He settles at her feet with his big-dog sigh and nuzzles the back of Aidan's legs.

"Stop it." Aidan wriggles and dances about but doesn't move from George's reach. Egypt keeps one eye on the stick.

"He's loving you."

"His nose is all cold and wet."

"That's a good thing."

Leaves rustle along the ground and a susurration of concern purls through the crowd. "Something's not right," someone whispers. "There's been an accident."

When Aidan spins around, Egypt puts her finger to the question on his lips and relieves him of the stick. She stares hard at the windows of the floating house for signs of movement, but they have become mirrors, revealing only the shifting reflections of water and trees. The air grows sticky with unease. What began as a wager has turned deadly. Someone should have dragged Ida Turnbull from her house before the sledgehammers started. Put her on the bus.

And then the door opens and Ida steps out with a smile and a wobbly curtsy for her neighbours. "I was having a nap," she kids, but she's rubbing her arm, and the sun, piercing the grey, catches sparkles on her clothing. Egypt pictures a shattered window, or, more ominously, the cloudy mirror that hangs above Ida's dresser.

"Having a drink more like," a voice mutters close to her ear.

Mick Long. Great. She braces for a barrage of Aidan questions, but her brother has slipped away. Then she spies the Mullins kids helping him onto someone's roof. The little monkey. If their mother catches him up there, Egypt will hear about it for the next week. She should give Mick a piece of her mind for distracting her, but turning around will mean greeting the lovesick Joey Payne, Mick's shadow, and today she just can't fashion her face into the necessary shape. George gets to his feet.

"Not speaking to us now, then? Uh-oh, Joey. You hear that? It's the sound of your girlfriend growing too good for the likes of us. Must be all that schooling."

Egypt rolls her eyes in case anyone is watching. Someone is always watching.

"Better take back that birthday present you got for her." Mick leans in so close she can feel his face part the curtain of her hair. "We'll buy some *li-quor* instead. Have ourselves a real party." His tongue darts out and grazes her skin. "Snob."

"I am not a snob," Egypt snaps, rubbing viciously at her neck. But when she looks around, her mouth stretched in a *Hi Joey* smile, the boys have disappeared.

When she faces front again, so has the dog.

Jacky Turnbull leaves the passenger seat to toss his wife two lines tied to the stern of the boat. Ida holds out her arms to catch them and ducks her head out of the way at the same time, causing laughter to ripple along the waterfront. When she secures the lines to the porch railing, a cheer breaks out. But it's a half-hearted hooray, one muted with sadness. Since plans for a new bridge were first announced, the community has been on edge. With the Turnbulls' leaving, it's as if the city has trespassed into paradise, marking it.

Ida curtsies again and disappears inside her house, emerging moments later with a wooden chair, a blanket to drape across her knees and a mug. As the Grew winches backwards on a long line, Ida seats herself on her lake-washed porch, the mug of tea – or something stronger – cradled in her hands, and, in a parody of Queen Mary, waves to her audience as she slowly begins to glide across the marsh and along the canal that cuts through the Heights. As if towing your home across the bay were an everyday occurrence.

Chapter 2

Boat and house pass under the fretwork of road and rail bridges that span the cut, and some of the spectators, unwilling to let the Turnbulls go just yet, stroll up the path that carves the brow of Burlington Heights to watch them emerge into the bay on the other side. Egypt hangs back until George returns, yipping at Aidan's heels and barking with the excitement in the air.

Up on the Heights, the wind is fierce, lifting Egypt's hair and blowing it across her face like a dark flag so that until she tames it in a loose twist of braid, she sees nothing of the bell-shaped expanse of harbour or the city and its dark mills sitting sentient at the water's edge.

"Goodbye, Ida. Goodbye, Jacky." Hands cupped to mouths.

"Make lots of new friends."

"Don't let those city folks push you around."

More waving, more farewells cast to the wind.

Egypt remains on the Heights long after the other well-wishers have dispersed, to fish or trap or play, to clean house or conjure the Sunday meal for their hungry families. The house passes the witch's finger of Carroll's Point and shrinks to a small, dark shape. She tugs at the collar of her coat. Ida is no doubt feeling seasick by now, listening to the chinking of plates in the cupboard and wishing she'd taken her neighbours' advice to pack her wares into boxes and ride up front in the boat. Egypt's own leave-taking won't be such a spectacle. She'll use the path. Chin held high. She shifts her gaze to the sickle sweep of bayside homes below her, almost a mirror image of the houses that hug the water's edge in Cootes Paradise, the marsh side of Burlington Heights where the Fishers live. A hundred or so dwellings in total. Less one as of today. There's a gash in the shoreline where the Turnbulls' house was ripped from its moorings. Tomorrow the neighbours will squabble over the garden fence, dismantle the privy. Over time, marsh reeds will gravitate to the sunny spot where the house used to sit, and come spring, the bindweed will reclaim Ida's potato patch.

She picks out the Turnbulls' convoy again, watching until it is barely visible, willing herself into the city, into next September, lessons tucked under her arm, the resounding clip of her heels in the school corridor signalling her authority, a hushed and expectant class of scrubbed and eager faces. *Good morning, Miss Fisher.*

George nudges her legs and she rests her hand on his shaggy head. "I know. You wouldn't last five minutes over there, would you? Fenced in, or worse, tied up." George pricks his ears, the whistle of a train sounding off in the distance. "No place to run. No rabbits or deer to chase." The dog's long, lean body tenses, every inch of him alert. He steps away from her and barks. "I'll miss you too, but you'll be fine here with Aidan." George barks again, a deeper and more menacing alarm, and Egypt at last turns to see the stranger who is making his way along the old ordnance road.

He crosses the railway tracks and approaches as close as George will allow. Hellos a greeting and lifts his hat. His hair, the colour of dried grass, is longer than it ought to be, ending just before his shoulders. Surprisingly, he's clean-shaven. A shade taller than average, and stringy – these days, who isn't? – he is good-looking in the way all newcomers to a small community are good-looking – their differences exciting and exotic. A girl could be attracted to someone simply because he doesn't look like all the males she's spent her life around.

"Nice dog."

George winds his long body between them, all hackles and rumbling throat, pushing Egypt so that she has to take a step backwards.

"He doesn't know you."

"True." He tips his head and shrugs his eyebrows, and though she keeps her face straight, she can feel a smile tugging at her mouth. George is the size of a small donkey.

"Stand down, killer."

George lowers his rear end and sits with his ears pricked, chest puffed out. The stranger's face creases in a laugh.

"What's his name?"

"George."

"How d'you do, George?" He holds out his hand for a paw, but George turns his head to watch Aidan digging at the edge of the embankment, lobbing stones and whooping when they hit the water. "Wolfhound?"

"Mostly." She scratches the back of George's neck. Lurcher. In George's case, part wolfhound, part bearded collie, part something else. Not a breed as such, but a type of dog. Fleet of foot. Bred by Irish gypsies and tinkers for poaching rabbits and hares. When Egypt finally understood that her father wasn't coming back and that George was his way of softening the blow, she'd gone to the library and looked up what she could find on the lineage of her new puppy, hoping for some kind of message. Her mother said that George had likely been plucked from a litter bound for the lake in a sack. Or some crony owed Egypt's dad a favour.

"He a good hunter?"

"He's fast."

"That your kid?"

"He's my brother." She juts out her hip and stands arms akimbo, flattered he thinks she's older than her nearly seventeen years. "He's five."

"Five and a half and a bit," Aidan, crouched in the dirt, calls over his shoulder. He jumps up and runs towards them, hands clasped together in front. "I have worms," he says, thrusting his hands towards the stranger.

"Let's see."

Aidan opens his hands a crack, and the stranger tips back his hat and stoops to peer inside.

"I reckon they're good for fishing with."

"You want them?"

"Sure."

Aidan releases his wriggling bounty into the young man's outstretched hands while Egypt regards his knapsack, his worn shoes and faded clothing. A drifter. But not like the blank-eyed tramps and hoboes that sometimes – more frequently since the stock market crash last year and the sharp rise in unemployment – jumped from the city-bound trains and wandered into the community to beg – or steal. He isn't so ground down. He doesn't smell so wretched. She almost changes her mind when he opens his jacket pocket and slips the worms inside.

"What are you going to do with them?"

"I understand there's some good fishing to be had round here." He winks at Aidan. "Thanks there, buddy."

"You can get fishing line from the flowers in the graveyard. Come, I'll show you." Aidan starts off in the direction of the road.

"Er, no roads or strangers, remember?" Egypt says. Aidan throws his arms up in the air and sighs dramatically.

The stranger laughs in an earthy, melodic register that thrums all the way down to her toes. "Your sister gives good advice." Then he levels his gaze at Egypt. "You two live round here?"

"That depends."

"On?"

"Who wants to know?"

"Matt Oakes." He sweeps his hat from his head and holds out his hand, which she takes, warm and dry. "Pleased to meet you."

Her brother pushes himself forward. "Aidan Fisher. Pleased to meet you too." But with the formality of shaking hands, Aidan is suddenly bashful.

"And what do they call your sister?"

"Egypt."

"Egypt." It catches him by surprise. Catches everyone by surprise.

"Ray's idea," she says.

"Ray?"

"My dad."

"You've got the look of an Egyptian about you."

She doesn't know if he intends this as a compliment or not, whether his eyes are smiling or laughing. "He was there during the war," she says, affecting a tone of indifference. She has to hurry because the train is on its way and she will lose his attention. "He was mesmerized by the great Sphinx in the desert." Matt Oakes lifts an eyebrow. *Little Sphinx* was always Ray's pet name for her, so she feels an affinity for the regal and lonely-looking statue in the desert. "And sickened when troops began chipping away at its face for keepsakes." A detail she's polished in her mind for so long – Mr. Mitchell mentioned it in class years ago as one of the theories behind the Sphinx's mutilated face – that it trips easily off her tongue. "When around the same time he learned that his wife – my mother – was pregnant, he wrote back telling her that if the child was a girl he wanted to call her Egypt." Egypt was born before the war started, but the story has always been too good to resist, and no one has called her on it yet. As to whether her father was in uniform during the war, let alone in North Africa, she doubts even her mother knows. And if he were, chances are he wouldn't have given a fig about any monument.

"It's a good story." Oakes crosses his eyes at Aidan, who bursts out laughing.

"She's telling porky pies. Egypt was the name of a horse that gave in when she was born."

"That came in, stupid." She bends to pick up a stick for George and hide her burning cheeks. Her words are lost as the train that's been approaching since their exchange began thunders onto its iron bridge, burying her discomfiture beneath the chest-thumping pump of mechanism. George turns up his nose at the stick, a soggy, crumbling specimen that she now feels obliged to hurl into the water. Airborne, it disintegrates. She lifts her chin, self-conscious under Matt Oakes' scrutiny and the realization that she's given away far more than she's gotten in return. While the train spews noise and soot on its way into the city, she composes a petition of piercing questions, but her brother is quicker off the mark.

"We live over there," he shouts as soon as the train has cleared the span and he can be heard. He points along the canal to the houses on the marsh side.

"Exactly where I was headed."

"How come? You looking for someone?" Egypt asks.

"I might be."

"Who?"

"Awfully young and good-looking for a gatekeeper, aren't you?" He winks at Aidan. "I was told to expect someone hairy and bent over."

Aidan laughs, points at his sister. "He thinks you're good-looking," he sing-songs, then pretends to retch.

Egypt blushes furiously. If her brother were within clouting distance, he'd be nursing his ears right now.

Matt Oakes sets down his pack and brushes the hair from his eyes, adjusts his hat.

"Either of you know anyone by the last name of Todd? Myrtle Todd?"

The marsh monster. Who flew on a broomstick and boiled children for breakfast. Egypt starts to laugh, then covers her mouth with her hand.

"Nope." Aidan spreads his arms out at his sides and spins like a top.

He does. Or did. But what kid ever bothered learning the monster's name?

"She passed away this July." Bloated in the heat for days before the stink finally rolled out and hit people. As offensive and vile in death as she was in life.

Aidan stops his spinning, eyes widened in horror, and for the second time today Egypt shushes him with her finger.

"I'm sorry. Did you know her well?"

He stares out across the bay, lost in thought. "I hadn't seen her in years. Not since I was a kid. She was my grandmother," he says after a pause.

"Oh." Egypt is at a loss for words. Squeezes Aidan's arm in warning.

"She used to write and tell me stories about this place."

The monster wrote letters? To a child? Egypt has already said she's sorry but wonders if she should apologize again. After all, being shackled with Myrtle Todd for a grandmother can't have been fun. Not that Egypt has any grandmothers – or grandfathers, for that matter – with whom to draw comparisons.

"Are you sad?" Aidan asks, wriggling out of Egypt's clutch.

"A little."

"Are you still coming to our house?"

"Who said he was coming to our house?" She rolls her eyes, but Matt Oakes only laughs his beautiful laugh again.

"How about you give me a guided tour of the area?"

"Only if I get to ride on your shoulders."

"Aidan!"

"Sounds like a deal to me." Matt crouches and helps Aidan find his balance before shrugging his knapsack into place and standing again. Egypt is captivated by his elegant hands, his long, square-tipped fingers gripped around her brother's skinny ankles.

"I can see our house," Aidan shouts.

"You could see it before," she gripes, "without acting like a monkey."

"It's not a problem," Matt assures her.

Until he falls, Egypt thinks, shaking her head at her brother's cheek, his *brass neck* in Ray's parlance. *Like father, like son*, her mother would say, though Aidan has never even met Ray.

"After you," Matt says. They cross over the tracks, and Egypt follows George down the incline, under first the High Level Bridge and then the second set of railway tracks, all the time keeping one eye out for her mother. Aidan caught perched on a stranger's shoulders will land Egypt in more trouble than her life is worth. By the time the path flattens out, she has made up her mind to take her brother home and leave Oakes to find his own way around. But then she turns to face him and already he's grown better looking. Aidan is yammering about the need to fetch his fishing pole, and when Matt lets him down, he runs for home.

"He's a sharp little man, your brother."

She smiles, knowing the minute Aidan steps over the threshold, her mother will want him to stay inside. And as long as he keeps his mouth shut about Matt Oakes, she won't come looking to drag Egypt back home too.

But now that she's alone with her handsome stranger, she finds herself tongue-tied. They stroll the path to where the cut opens into Cootes Paradise and a small sandbar forms a natural break in the line of jumbled homes. Matt steps down to the water's edge and toes at the mud with his scuffed boots. Hands in his pockets, he takes in the marsh and its islands, the grey forest stretched on either side. "That must be Rat Island." He nods towards Hickory.

"Rat's farther out, past that clump of trees on the right."

"So, where's Cockpit?"

"Over there," she says, waving her hand in the direction of Princess Point. "I'm not really sure."

"You've never been to Cockpit Island?"

"Never." She folds her arms across her chest.

"Bet your old man has." What cheek. She'd stomp off if only she could be certain he'd follow. Instead, she watches as he laughs with his perfect mouth, the curved lines that bracket his lips. Already she senses how dull and empty this day will feel once he's gone. Gesturing to indicate the stumps that outline the old Desjardins Canal, she brushes his arm with her fingertips as if by accident.

"When it freezes over you can skate all the way to Dundas." Her fingers tingle and pulse.

"How far?"

"A few miles."

"And is Dundas worth skating all the way to?"

"It was an important manufacturing centre and shipping port before they built the railway," she says. She's never been to Dundas, or even spoken to anyone who has. "The houses and mills are all built with local stone," she continues as he raises an eyebrow. "It's very beautiful."

"Sounds depressing. I prefer it here. This is beautiful." He holds out his hands in gesture. "And so peaceful. It's paradise."

She glances at his face to see if he's pulling her leg, and then scans the shoreline mix of rugged and weathered homes for evidence of this beauty. While it's true that some of the houses – tall and squat, narrow and wide – have been designed and built with obvious forethought, others edge precariously into the water on mismatched legs. Clumsy roofs balance on patchwork walls of corrugated iron in varying shades of decay. Some are little more than tin-roofed tarpaper shacks. Then there are the names, painted or burned on shingles nailed up over the doors: *Jakaloo*, *The Better Ole*, *UGOIGO*, *Kildare*, *Idle Some More*, *Seldom Inn*, *More Fun*. And the cringe-inducing moniker she has to duck under every time she enters her own house: *The Salty Mare*.

"People in the city think everyone here is inbred, only into drinking, gambling and blood sports."

"And are you?"

She rolls her eyes. "No."

"Then why do you care what they think?"

She lowers her voice, lest it carry across the water to one of the fish boats dotted about, or someone standing on their back porch jigging a line. "This place is full of small minds and busybodies with their noses in other people's business."

"Or maybe they're just looking out for each other. There are drawbacks to living anywhere. Depends on how you look at it."

She shrugs and points to a cabin three doors from her own. "Your grandmother's house is over there."

"Empty?"

She nods. The body was dripping when the men carried it out. Afterwards, they boarded the windows and nailed shut the door. "You're not thinking of staying there, are you?"

"A night or two. If no one minds."

People are more likely to lay bets on how long he'll last than to mind his staying. While he stares over at the marsh monster's old lair, Egypt commits every inch of him to memory: the breadth of his shoulders, the set of his hips, the squint lines around his eyes, his slender hands. Piano hands. "I don't mind," she hears herself saying.

"Mom said –" The scudding sounds of her brother running in gum boots. They turn to face the path. "Mom said you're in charge of the boat." Aidan is carrying two fishing poles, the ends of which are dragging on the ground. She's never been more disappointed to see him in her life.

"You have a boat?" Again the heart-stopping smile.

"A skiff."

Matt Oakes rubs his beautiful hands together. "I smell dinner."

"I told Mom you were taking me fishing," Aidan says to Egypt as he reaches them. He hands Matt the longer of the poles.

"That's my man." Matt squeezes his shoulder.

Egypt pulls her trembling mouth back in a smile. Her cheeks already ache. "Oh. That's good, buddy. And what did she say?"

"She said not to let George in the boat."

Chapter 3

Matt wakes to the sound of men's voices raised in argument. Not so close he can catch the words, but the intent is clear enough that he feels an undertow of anxiety. He breathes through his mouth, the smell on him and in him again – feral and faintly sweet, overtones of ammonia – reminding him where he is. The old woman must have died in here. He pulls the blanket over his head as the voices grow murderous, punctuated with the thud and splintering of a door being kicked in. Minutes later he hears a soft knocking just outside, lifts his head as the wiry silhouette of Laura Fisher appears in the doorway.

"It's Stan Byrd," she says, as if the man's name explained something. "They're going to beat him to a pulp." He knows what's coming next, and already he resents her for it. The lot of a man. He'll take the hunting part over the fighting any day. Hunting over being hunted.

"You have to go out there." She pulls the ends of her coat tighter around herself. The cloud of her breath dissipates in the air. She glances behind as if worried someone might have followed her. "You have to do something. You have to help him."

No, I don't, he thinks, fighting the downward pull his bed is exerting, the voice in his head almost a whine. Exhaustion has seeped into his bones, become a fog in his brain.

More dull thuds. More shouting. Threaded with a woman's keening.

"He's an old man. They'll kill him." Laura Fisher's voice rises in a panic. "Help him," she pleads. "You have to. Please."

Sleep. He craves sleep. Rubs his face. Whatever is going on outside will bring him either trouble with the police or a beating. She's standing so close he can hear her breathing; she's going nowhere until he plays hero. How did things come to this? He recalls the lamplight procession over here, the kids hovering at the threshold, as if afraid to step inside. Before that he'd been wrapped in a blanket in front of the Fishers' stove, his feet in a bowl of warm water. It's coming back. The way he'd leaned from the boat to help the dog, who seemed desperate to be onboard, and then been forced to jump out himself before the skiff tipped and dumped them all. The November water mercifully shallow but so frigid it made him gasp. He stumbled against the bottom, scratching his hands, and waded into shore, mud sucking at his boots. Mud and other horrors. The taste of it still with him. Christ. When the air hit his sodden trousers, he thought his knees might shatter. She'd given him a plate of fish and potato, a slice of stale bread. Food that heated him through. And now it's payback time.

Shaking the stupor from his head, he makes to climb from his bedroll, then hesitates.

"Sorry," she whispers, and turns her back while he pads naked across the room and grabs his clothes, laid out to dry in a flat, empty version of himself. They smell better than when he emerged from the lake, smell better than they have in weeks. But the pants are still damp, and he hops around with one foot stuck in a reluctant trouser leg. His balls, tender from the bruising water, slap about in a painful dance. Threads rip. By the time he buckles his belt, the skin of his ass is chafed and smarting.

Outside, the plaintive sounds of Stan Byrd's wife begging for his life echo across the water and cut through to something old and raw in Matt. Fists curled, he almost yells aloud as a creature rushes past him in the dark and disappears into the fields that separate the community from the road.

"Just George," Laura says, there at his elbow and hurrying him along the path.

The Byrds live three doors away. The yellow hue of their electric porch light illuminates the sad spectacle of Stan Byrd's beating and makes him an easy target for his three assailants. Though as Matt draws closer, it becomes clear that only one man is the aggressor. The other two stand guard and egg on the punching and kicking.

"Kid-killer. Scumbag," they snarl.

"Piece of shit," the man in the middle spits. Punches Byrd in the stomach. "Murderer. Murdering son of a whore."

Matt's legs grow heavy. Murderer. In trusting Laura Fisher, has he backed the wrong horse? She tugs on his jacket sleeve and he clenches his jaw against the urge to shake her off.

"You can't back out now."

Like hell I can't. "You hear what they're saying? *Murderer?*" He turns around, ready to head back to his borrowed cabin, stink and all. Back to his bedroll. "We shouldn't get involved."

"He's a harmless old man."

"You don't know that."

"I'd stake my life on it," she hisses, her face unrecognizable in the inky blue dead of night. "And how do you know they won't hurt Joanna, too?"

He looks again, and though it's clear the three attackers are focused only on the old man they've encircled, it doesn't matter anymore. Stan Byrd's wife stands on the stoop of her battered cabin, sobbing and wringing her hands, and Matt finds himself slammed up against his childhood again, paralyzed by the sounds of his own mother begging, her stunted cries. Hands trembling, he steers Laura into the Byrds' house and urges both women to stay inside.

A sickening thud as a fist lands square in the old man's face and he staggers backwards like a drunk. Now the hitting begins in earnest, as if the thickset man in the middle had been working himself up to this point, though it's obvious Matt's presence has nettled him. Again and again the assailant clocks Byrd, who doesn't even lift his hands to ward off the blows. *C'mon, c'mon, do something.* Matt paces at a remove, set to wade in, fists-a-fury, and send the hitter into next week. But there's something disquietingly familiar about Byrd's passivity, and the feeling grows in Matt that the old man not only expected this assault but also believes he deserves it. He searches the long shadows for an ally, someone who will watch his back if he comes to Byrd's rescue. But if other neighbours have stolen outside to gawk, they're staying well hidden.

Another punch to the mouth and a glistening tooth lands in the dirt and hoarfrost. Byrd drops to the ground clutching his bloodied face.

"No. One. Messes. With. My. Family. No. One." Every word sealed with a kick to the stomach.

"And this is from my old lady." Winding his stocky leg back, he drives his boot straight into Byrd's throat.

"That's enough," Matt growls, holding up his hands as he steps between the two men. He straddles Byrd with his feet. Byrd rolls over coughing and straining for air. His aggressor is winded, sweat running into his beard.

"That piece of shit" – chest heaving, bubbles at the corner of his lips – "that piece of shit killed my son. Pushed him in with a big stick. Like he was some lump of metal." When he makes to go after Byrd again, Matt first nods to the other two, then places his hands on the broader man's shoulders.

"You've made your point. No sense you getting done for murder. Too," he adds after a pause. He knows nothing about the story. His heart thumps wildly behind his breastbone.

"The fucking toe-rag deserves to die." And suddenly the stocky man is all snot and tears, the grief beneath his anger finally spewing to the surface.

"He was seventeen. He was just a kid," he yells at Byrd, who is inching along the ground towards his doorway.

"That's right, crawl back into the bog where you belong." He horks at the old man's bleeding head. "Fucking lowlife. Canal rats. Sooner the city runs you out of town, the better." He draws back his leg as if to deliver another kick, but Matt can sense the big man's energy is spent. His friends fold their arms around his sloped shoulders and pull him away.

"Better grow some eyes in the back of your head. You hear me?" he mumbles, slurring his words.

The three men stumble into the night, and Laura and Joanna rush out the door in a panic of grief and consternation. With Matt's help they haul the old man to his feet, into the cabin and onto the couch.

The room fills with the iron tang of blood. Matt snaps kindling for the stove while Laura fills the kettle and then fixes a cold compress for Stan's bruises. Joanna Byrd wrings out a cloth to gently wash blood from her husband's face.

Matt grows uncomfortable watching the women's ministrations; he feels like an intruder, a peeping Tom witnessing acts of tenderness between people he scarcely knows. His jaw throbs with tension. His shirt is damp. Already it's too warm in here. He wants to leave but even while handing him a mug of tea, Laura won't lift her gaze to meet his.

Pacing while the stove ticks out heat, he finds his eyes straying to the curve of her shoulders, the shape of her ears, behind which she continually tucks her flyaway hair. She must be too warm herself, still wearing her coat, the hem of her nightdress beneath it mud-stained from being trampled in the dark. With her defences down she seems far more approachable, vulnerable even, an impression heightened by her small, heart-shaped face and fine features, too small and fine almost for such large, expressive eyes – eyes that better fit the proportions of Egypt's face, her long and dramatic hair. He smiles when she catches him staring, and she glowers in return. Still angry over the incident with the skiff. Laura Fisher is somewhere in her mid-thirties, the age of his sisters, but life has used her differently. She wears her loneliness like a prickly mantle. Matt thinks it must be exhausting to be that tightly wound all the time. When did she last laugh?

He drains the lukewarm dregs of his tea and sets down his mug, wonders if and how Laura explained his presence tonight. The Byrds could have seen him out on the water earlier, heard him settling himself at his grandmother's place. *Grandmother.* That could come back to bite him. If he hangs around long enough. He should have hit the road again the minute he learned the old lady was dead. Cut his losses, his journey for nought. He can still smell it, absorbed into his skin and hair. He wonders if the others can smell it on him. Her. Death.

The old man groans and tries to sit up straight, clears his throat. Laura and his wife seat themselves on either side of him, like bolster pillows. Matt's eyes light on a wrinkle of wallpaper curling away from the wall. It's all he can do not to grab it and start pulling. He moves towards the door before he starts flicking his fingers at the knick-knacks.

"I killed that kid." Stan Byrd's voice is a ragged croak, the silence that follows as distorted and swollen as his battered face. Matt eyes the door. Oh, how he wants nothing more to do with this night, with this ruined man and his murder. Confession may be good for the soul, but beyond the fulfillment of base curiosity, there is no reward for the listener in such stories: only the confessor gets to unburden himself. He turns slowly back to the room. Laura's hands are stilled, folded in her lap.

"There was an accident," Stan begins again, and Joanna flashes Matt a look so beseeching that he finds himself back in front of the hearth and settled on a footstool.

It happened halfway through the night shift at the circlips mill where Byrd was foreman. Danny Farrell was a good worker, but cocky – too aware of his strength and agility, too reckless, too young to understand the vulnerability of his own body, how quickly accidents happen. He'd plunge the baskets into the vats faster than you were supposed to. The acid made the water roil and hiss, like a thousand angry serpents in a net bag. You had to duck or step back quickly in case it splattered out and caught you. But hell, they all did that. Familiarity – with the machines, the materials, the bubbling vats of sulphuric acid. They all got a bit cocky and less mindful. Stan should have put a stop to the boy's larking weeks ago. But with his wonky smile and his thatch of curly hair, his winks, his grins, the kid could make a Saturday night out of a Monday morning. He made them all laugh. And then he just slipped off the boards and into the acid. So fast. By the time Danny bobbed back up to the top, his skin was melting, peeling backwards from his skull. He came up with one arm in the air in supplication. A scream etched into his face, his mouth a darkened maw, voiceless. Stan Byrd acted quickly. Pushing him back down was the right thing to do. The kid never would have survived the acid burns. And if he had, he wouldn't have thanked Byrd for condemning him to some half-life stunted by pain. He didn't expect Farrell's family to be grateful, or even to understand.

Byrd's story leaves a sheen of cold sweat over Matt's skin. He tries blinking it away, but the image of a body rearing up from the acid, face in tatters, grinds at the base of his skull. The air in the cabin is suffocatingly claustrophobic, his limbs have grown weights. He has to get out of here. Just to walk, run, scream, anything. No chance he'll see sleep again tonight.

And then, as if she has heard his silent plea, Laura stands and straightens her coat. "You hungry?" she asks.

He nods. He's been hungry for months. Years.

"I think it's time everyone got some sleep," she says, hands on the Byrds' shoulders. "If you need anything, you know where I am."

Chapter 4

Laura stumbles in the dark, legs of treacle, as the night's adrenalin drains through her feet. She could curl up on the path and go to sleep. Whatever possessed her to offer the man food? Now instead of crawling back between her sheets, she must play hostess. She leans against the door to her cabin, nudges it open with her hip. Laura has never been one for small talk, the province of those more comfortable in their own skin.

She lights the lamp, and he sits at the kitchen table with a heavy sigh, rubbing his knuckles. The shadows are unkind, or he's older than she thought. She runs a hand across her cheek and over her hair, tucking it back behind her ears. "Do you think they'll come back? Farrell and his thugs."

"How would I know?"

Flushing, she bends to light the stove. Cuts two thick slices of bread, breaks eggs into a bowl and whisks in some milk.

"Anything I can do to help?"

"It'll be faster if I do it myself." She'd throw him a quick smile to cover the brusqueness of her reply, but the moment has already passed, and when she checks, he isn't looking anyway. Lost in his own exhaustion. Tonight's events on top of yesterday's drama. Plus the life of an itinerant: always on the move, sleeping rough. Maybe this was a bad idea. She's about to tell him as much, that he should just go back to his grandmother's cabin and get some sleep, when the legs of his chair scrape across the floor. She feels words gathering energy behind her. Her shoulders tense.

"The Byrds lost a son in the war about the same age as that boy," she says. "It can't have been easy for Stan. Having to –"

"Would you come back?"

"Me?"

"If it was your child who'd been killed. Would you want retribution?"

"I don't know." She feels scared by her answer. Her non-answer. The whisk hovers mid-air, dripping egg onto the countertop.

"You must have some idea. If you thought Egypt or Aidan could have been saved but someone else took it into their hands to play God."

She turns to find him leaned back in the chair, legs splayed in front, arms folded across his chest. "You blame Stan, don't you? You think he's responsible for the boy's death."

"That's not what I said. I just wonder if it crossed his mind at the time. How the boy's family would react. Whether he stopped to consider the full repercussions of what he was doing."

"I'm not sure any of us do that, Mr. Oakes. We'd be paralyzed by fear otherwise. We'd commit to nothing."

"Which is a commitment in itself."

"Oh, come on! We've all made rash decisions in our lives, decisions we later have cause to regret." Having delivered this homily, she turns back to the stove, fat sizzling in the pan.

"And you think we wouldn't make them if we knew the outcome?"

"No. No, I don't."

"Then we're agreed on something, Mrs. Fisher."

She reminds herself that tonight Matt Oakes put himself in harm's way to save a man he doesn't know. On her word. She cracks another egg into the bowl. She doesn't even know what happened out there.

"Those men, they didn't have weapons or anything?"

"Just their fists. But I wouldn't want to be Stan Byrd when he wakes up. Farrell had a mean punch on him. The old man's going to be one stiff and sore son of a gun."

"But it could have been much worse," she says over her shoulder. "If I haven't already said so, then thank you."

He yawns. Bones click as he stretches. "You didn't have to go to the trouble of cooking a meal at three in the morning."

"It's a little late for protests, Mr. Oakes. The eggs are already in the pan." Eggs. What is she thinking? She folds her arms across her chest and turns to face him.

"Would you like a drink?"

"Milk's fine."

"I mean a real drink." *How bold, Laura, offering a strange man a drink in your own home*. She feels reckless. And strangely free. Her shoulders opening out. *People are going to talk whatever transpires between these walls. May as well be hung for a sheep as a lamb.* This time when he looks up at her, she detects a glimmer of interest in his eyes. As if he were seeing her for the first time, or in a different light.

"Wouldn't say no."

She leaves the eggs to fish out a bottle from the back of the sideboard and places it on the table. "Elderberry wine," she says, and assumes her position at the stove, moving the wooden spoon in a circle around the edges of the cast-iron pan to keep the eggs from sticking.

"I'm sure it'll do the trick."

Trick? Danger prickles across her scalp. She sees her mother's disapproving mouth and banishes it. "I won it in a raffle. In the summer. The community has these big picnics on the long weekends. Everyone drags their tables outside and we line them up edge to edge. The women bake pies and cakes and sausage rolls and make mounds of sandwiches."

"And the men make wine."

"Something like that, yes." Does he find her provincial? She can't read the nuances in his voice. No doubt years of scrabbling out a living here, toiling at Hand & Company, and the flower stall before that, have worn down her finer edges. She splays her hands out in front of her, stiff and swollen, as if all the joints are gummed up. Mimes tinkling on piano keys, dismayed at how reddened her fingertips are from working with black powder, from scrubbing traces of it from her skin every night. When did her hands lose their fluidity? When did she lose her grace?

"And there's a raffle. There's always a raffle," she says, rolling her eyes because what else can she do? A useless gesture anyway because she has her back to him. "It raises money to help out some of the families around here that might be struggling. I've had it since August. The wine, that is. I was saving it." *More chatter, Laura?* It's as if she's already taken a draft or two, her lips loose, filling the air with words. "I've no idea what for. Or even why. Tonight seems as good a time as any." She rakes through the cutlery drawer. Throws out her arms and laughs at herself.

"But it would appear I have no way of opening it." And just as she was beginning to get the yen for a sip of its tart floweriness. A drop of forgetting to smooth the night and send her to a dreamless sleep.

He produces a pocket knife, as men invariably do. Flicks a small corkscrew and digs it into the cork. When it releases with a sharp pop, Laura puts her finger to her lips and Oakes holds himself still, bottle in one hand, knife and cork in the other.

She glances up at the ceiling, lets out her breath. "After today's excitement, I need Aidan to sleep through. He's so easily unsettled." She divides the eggs onto two plates. Outside, George barks once, scratches at the door.

"Do you mind?" She glances from Oakes to the door and back. "My hands are full."

The door scrapes along the threshold and George rushes in with the cold. He sniffs at the air and circles the kitchen once before settling himself beneath the table. Oakes seats himself sideways, allowing for the dog, and reaches down to stroke the animal's head. His eyes steal towards the staircase.

"No danger of Egypt waking, then?"

She nods to herself. Realizes she's been waiting all along for him to raise her daughter's name. Setting the pan back from the stove, she slowly opens the cutlery drawer. From the moment Egypt pulled Matt Oakes through the doorway yesterday, all dripping wet and stinking of the marsh, Laura sensed that his arrival marked the beginning of the end of her daughter's innocence; that no matter what his intentions, no matter what his game with Egypt – or with herself – it would end in heartache. Her fingers rest on the bone handles of the knives, one of Ray's surprise gifts. "If you're planning on taking advantage of my hospitality, Mr. Oakes" – she turns and meets his gaze dead on – "I should remind you, this is a very small community."

A thin smile. "I beg your pardon, ma'am. It was just an observation. A man sleeps light on the road. Force of habit."

She sits across from him and picks up her fork.

"I'm a light sleeper myself."

"I noticed."

"As long as we understand one another." She fills his mug with milk from the pitcher and, when he gestures with the bottle of elderberry, fetches two cordial glasses and nods at him to pour.

"To health."

"And happiness."

She grimaces. "To keeping the wolf from the door."

"Ask me, you're doing a fine job."

"I didn't."

He shrugs, curls his hand around his plate before eating. Another habit learned on the road, no doubt. The eggs disappear quickly. A draft of milk, a couple of bites and the bread is gone. He hardly chews. Milk again. Laura touches her hand to her throat as though she can feel the heartburn there. Oakes wipes his mouth with the back of his hand and reaches for the wine. Laura puckers her mouth and sips at hers.

"Egypt tells me you're from Winnipeg."

He nods.

"And you came here from there?"

"I've moved around a bit."

"Sloughing off the moss."

He stares hard at her and then lowers his gaze. "What about you? Have you always lived here?"

"The community isn't that old," she says, which earns her a small smile. "I came here as a young bride." Young. Impressionable. Naïve. It's hard to keep the vinegar from her voice. "Egypt's father won this house in an ice-race. Fair and square," she adds, with an edge of mimicry. Absurdly, she feels like laughing.

"Ice race?"

"Ice boats out on the bay. It's quite the spectacle."

"I'd like to see that."

"You plan on staying around then, to claim your inheritance?"

He shrugs. "Might not be much point."

"Sorry?"

"That man tonight, Farrell, the ringleader, he said something."

"Let me guess. *Squatters*. *Canal rats*. And those are the polite terms."

"Something about the city. They want you out of here?"

Laura leans her elbows on the table, rubs at her temples. "So they say. They've been squawking about it for years. A local politician has his mind set on some grandiose North West Entrance, and we're in the way."

"Entrance?"

"It's his big dream that Hamilton become part of the City Beautiful Movement."

Matt shakes his head. "Never heard of it."

"If we live surrounded by beautiful, man-made, surroundings – parks, boulevards, fountains and the such – we will become better and more worthy human beings. The wilderness needs managing, apparently. It's too wild, Mr. Oakes."

"They want to develop the area?"

"Strictly for our moral health. The city held a competition for the design a couple of years ago. The paper ran an artist's sketch of the winner. Picnic parks, bandstands. A zoo. It even had an art gallery."

"But you're not worried?"

"Can you imagine any city councillor announcing they were pushing over a hundred families from their homes for the sake of a bridge and a park? An art gallery? With factories closing everywhere and bread lines growing longer? Not if they wanted to keep their job. Besides, they don't have the money."

"They could make it a relief project."

Of course they could. They'd dug out the Rock Garden with relief labour. Some of the men from the community had signed on.

"Cheap labour. Other cities have done it. I've worked on a few road projects myself here and there."

"I'll believe it when I see it." She pushes her plate to one side and places her hand over her glass when he offers to pour her more wine. He refills his own glass to the top and drinks half.

"Egypt tells me you didn't know your grandmother had passed."

"No."

"It must have been a shock."

"You could say that." He drinks again. "I'm surprised no one razed the place, the way it stinks."

"People are much too superstitious around here. I think they were terrified she'd come back and cast one of her spells." He neither laughs nor smiles. Is she speaking out of turn? "You have to admit, she wasn't the easiest person to get along with. I know the children made her into a monster, which was perhaps unfair. All the stinky herbs she brewed for her tonics didn't help. Children have such wild imaginations." She should never have touched the wine. His face is unnervingly blank.

"Did you know her well?"

His eyes dart to his hands and back to her face, a fleeting movement, but it's enough. A tell. One of the things you learned being married to a gambler, listening to his tales. Laura can spot a bluff a mile off.

"She wasn't your grandmother, was she?"

He drains his glass. "No." Licks his lips while she waits for his explanation.

"Go on."

"She was the mother of someone I used to work with."

"Earl Todd."

"You knew him?"

"Knew?"

"He was killed in a logging accident."

"I see."

"I came to tell her."

"This just happened?"

"It was a while ago."

"Why did you lie?"

He lifts his shoulders in a shrug. "When Egypt told me she'd passed, I no longer had a reason for coming here. But he'd talked so much about the place – Cootes Paradise this, Cootes Paradise that – I just wanted to see it for myself. Way he went on, I couldn't understand why he wasn't living here."

"It's not much of a reason. Sure you're not hiding something else?"

"Such as?"

"Whatever's on your conscience, Mr. Oakes. If Oakes is even your real name."

"I'm sorry I've offended you."

"You'll be heading into the city tomorrow, I take it? That's where the relief rolls and soup kitchens are."

"I'm not looking for a handout."

"I'm not sure I'm comfortable with whatever it is you might be looking for."

The night has taken on a dangerous quality. She's harbouring a liar. Who knows what else he might be capable of? She pushes back her chair. "It's late. I have work in the morning." She rises and scoops up the dishes and puts them in the sink. Follows him to the door.

"Goodnight then."

"Goodnight."

He's still standing on the stoop as she closes the door behind him. Just as the latch is about to engage, he grasps the edge of the door.

"I'd come back." His voice low and soft in the dark. Laura swallows, not quite sure she's heard him properly.

"Sorry?"

"If it were my child who'd been killed, I'd come back."

Chapter 5

Laura shakes the rain from her headscarf, hangs her coat on an empty peg in the women's cloakroom and tucks her gloves inside one of the pockets.

"Someone wants to see you in his office." The dulcet tones of Peggy Parrish's tobacco-cured vocal chords. Laura pats at her nest of hair, wishing she'd had more time to make herself presentable this morning. Her skin prickles with the memory of inviting Matt Oakes into her house in the middle of the night, sharing a drink with the man, carrying on like some loose woman. And she's angry at herself for sleeping in. In seven years she has been late for work once, when Egypt had the mumps and she had to wait for the doctor. And while so far Hand & Company hasn't laid anyone off, that doesn't mean there aren't dozens, maybe hundreds, of jobless people only too eager to take Laura's job from her. And at a reduced wage. She licks a finger and runs it over her eyebrows.

"That's not going to help you this morning, darlin'." She meets Peggy Parrish's know-it-all glance in the mirror. "Not the mood he's in." Peggy produces a golden lipstick case from her pocket, pulls her mouth into a lipstick smile and begins reapplying pearly pink. She's the only woman who brings her cigarette habit to work, where her lipstick-kissed filters stand out like a scandal in the canteen ashtrays. "It's a war room in there," she says, smacking her lips at her reflection. "I just copped off for a loo break. You need a couple of Roman candles to cut the tension."

Laura's stomach lurches. She hasn't stepped foot inside Bob Watkins' office in nearly two years. Impressions from that afternoon, the memory of which she thought she'd blocked out, suddenly push their way to the front of her consciousness – the smell of Brylcreem in his hair, the desk edge biting the back of her thighs. She turns from the mirror and Peggy's probing stare. The woman is a gossip-hound. And Bob Watkins enjoys watching people squirm. He's probably less interested in why she's late than in the dressing down it means he can give her. Still, it would help to have a plausible excuse at her fingertips. If he puts her on probation, she'll offer to come in early and set up everyone's workbench. For three months. As long as it takes.

When she knocks at his door, he calls her in and hands her a letter folded in three.

"I need you to sit there and read this." He motions to a chair against the wall facing him, a couple of yards back from his desk. No mention of her tardiness. She glances at her name written in pencil on the outside. A form redundancy? He doesn't mess around. Must have been waiting for a chance like this ever since ... She sits, squeezing herself together against a sudden urge to pee.

Dear Employee,

Hand & Company. would like to take this opportunity ...

She scans the contents quickly. She isn't being fired. She is, however, losing her job. As is everyone else. The company will relocate to Cooksville in the new year. *We understand* – of course they do – *that in these hard times the loss of work will be difficult*. Difficult! She lifts her gaze to meet his, but Bob Watkins is busy studying the ledger on his desk. How will she pay Egypt's school fees? Buy food? How long before they're forced to join the gaunt-cheeked and glassy-eyed legions lined up outside the soup kitchens? Parading their humiliation in public. She pinches her leg fiercely. She will not cry in this man's office. She folds and refolds the letter on her knee and stands to leave. Watkins waves her back down, then clasps his hands together over his ledger and clears his throat.

"Hand & Company has recently acquired their major competition, Dominion Fireworks Company, and so have been looking for a larger site. Cooksville meets all their requirements." He has chosen a point on the wall behind her, about six inches right of her breast, at which to stare while he drills her with these details. She thinks of the eggs she cooked up in the middle of the night. If she's careful, she can put a little aside over the next two months, enough to tide them over the worst of the winter.

"In addition, Hamilton City Council has recently passed a bylaw prohibiting the manufacture of explosives within city limits."

She stares at the thinning patch of hair on his crown. Why is he telling her all this? Is he going with them? Selling his house and moving the wife and family out to sunny Cooksville? Or, like the trick with the chair, is he simply trying to prove he's better than the floor workers, more privy to company goings-on than the working grunts, the powder packers? Silly little man. He'll be bald in a few years. *Better rush the wife out to Cooksville now before she leaves you for someone with a full head of hair; something she can run her fingers through, something she can grab onto while she's yelling his name.*

"I need you to sign this form to say you have read and understand the letter. This plant will close at the end of January. On behalf of Hand & Company, I would like to thank you for your dedication and hard work." He holds out his hand. She ignores it, her gaze running along the edge of his desk.

"And what about the bump and grind here in this office?" She offers a thin smile. "The shag." One of Ray's expressions. Crude, oh, but the look on his face is well worth conjuring the ghost of her estranged husband. Standing, she brushes down her skirt. "Would you like to thank me for that, too?"

She's out the door before he can respond, laughing and shaking at the same time. A weight off her chest spitting out those words, despite the loose feeling in her bowels that her little act of rebellion has left her with. She winks at Peggy Parrish as she strides by and settles herself at her workstation.

Chapter 6

Monday morning: a smudgy rain on the classroom windows. The soot-stained edifice of the normal school across the road, hunched like some angry-shouldered beast, swallowing the thin morning light. Inside, electric lights hum overhead, casting students and teacher in a brassy incandescence. Surreptitiously, Egypt leans back against the classroom wall, hoping to draw some of the plaster and paint coolness through her spine and palms. Kids' artwork, crinkled and stiff with gouache, rustles behind her head. *My favourite place.* For the moment she'd forgotten about the paintings, though she helped the class thumbtack them to the wall just a week ago. A stern glance from Mr. Mitchell and she straightens quickly, which is just as well – the room is warm and Egypt had a restless night; leaning back, she might have closed her eyes and nodded off. As if sensing such possible treason, Mr. Mitchell draws himself up to his full five feet and seven inches, pulls back his shoulders and expands his chest.

". . . which prompted newspaperman William Lyon Mackenzie to denounce this ruling elite as corrupt and to coin the term *the Family Compact*. He demanded a more democratic government for British North America." The teacher's stentorian tones push back the pale green walls and roll across the curd-white ceiling. He stops beside the desk of Evelyn Hough, an average student with a tendency to chatter and who is easily distracted. The Junior II class stops fidgeting and leg swinging and sits straighter at their desks. And even though they are not, strictly speaking, under his supervision, the fifteen additional normal school students, spaced like fence posts around the edges of the classroom and there, like Egypt, to observe the day's lessons – lessons they will try to emulate on Thursday – adjust their posture. Mr. Mitchell brooks no lollygaggers or dissenters in his classroom.

"What did William Lyon Mackenzie advocate?"

"A more democratic government, Sir."

"And what term did he coin?"

"*The Family Compact*, Sir."

"Very good. *The Family Compact*." A glance in Egypt's direction. "At least someone was listening." The relief is palpable; Evelyn Hough is preening. Even King George relaxes a little in his gilt frame above the blackboard.

"Stay awake, would you?" Gloria Henry hisses once Mitchell has spun away from them and is striding back to his desk.

But staying awake is easier said than done. The subject is dull, the classroom crowded, and Egypt is positioned too far from the open window to receive the benefit of any fresh air. Standing in one spot for hours at a stretch, observing another teacher grinding out old school lessons – particularly Mr. Mitchell, with his monotone drone, his blackboards crammed with dizzying lines of cursive writing, and the stewed vinegar stink of his mouldering tweed jacket – can test the ardour of even the most enthusiastic student teacher. Egypt glances at Gloria Henry's beatific expression. Or not. Maybe it's just her. And the fact that Matt Oakes has set up camp in her head.

"Mitchell's got his eye on you." Paul McClusky, on Egypt's right, has perfected the skill of speaking without moving his lips.

She giggles. "Which one?"

The sinister left, of course. Because Mr. Mitchell's right eye is glass. Shrapnel from an explosion that killed the three men flanking him in the Passchendaele mud. Everyone knows this, in the way that students always know salient facts about their teachers. That Mr. Mitchell reeks is self-evident. That he has a glass eye is intrinsic to the gossip that is groomed and tweaked and dutifully passed on to each incoming year. No one can tell for sure which eye is glass because no one dares look at him directly for more than half a second, but it is said to be his right. Egypt suppresses a yawn before he turns back in her direction. Sleep was impossible while Matt Oakes lay tucked in his bedroll mere doors away, their spare blanket draped over him for extra warmth. She spent the night rerunning the day's events, examining every word and gesture that passed between them, polishing the details until they no longer resembled themselves. The way she'd ushered him through the door, fairly trembling with the excitement of having him there under the same roof, breathing the same air. Changing it. And the way, under her mother's baleful eye, Egypt had become someone she scarcely knew. *Let me*, she'd said, offering to launder his clothes, set the table, peel the potatoes, dice an onion.

As a consequence, she'd slept in this morning. Coincidentally, so had her mother. Upstairs is divided in two by a curtain, and Egypt must pass through her mother's half of the room, the room she shares with Aidan, to access the stairs. At the sight of Laura still asleep, unusual enough in itself, she had paused a moment. Her mother looked vulnerable rather than peaceful. Her jaw slack, hair mussed on the pillow, one arm flung behind her head in abandon. Or surrender.

Downstairs she discovered dishes in the sink, the musky scent of wine. Out of sorts, she rushed the porridge, which turned lumpy. Aidan whined and she snapped at him, relieved when he stomped off to school by himself in a sulk, as it left her free to seek out Matt's company.

But Matt wasn't alone. Joanna Byrd, of all people, was hovering in the doorway of Myrtle Todd's place, her matronly frame blocking it. Egypt could hardly stand behind her and listen in, nor could she wait around until the woman was finished with her asking and telling. Mrs. Byrd would want to know what she was doing, and why she wasn't on her way to school, and did her mother know where she was. And then, as if Egypt's morning weren't already marked by oddities, movement out on the water. A flickering shadow in her peripheral vision. She looked to see two men paddling by in a green canoe. She recognized the man in back, a birdwatcher who visited the marsh regularly. Usually alone. He doffed his cap and waved. Dutifully, she waved back, but it was his companion who drew her eye. The way he sat so utterly tall and straight in the bow, as if he were dressed in his Sunday best rather than a soft cap and jacket. A man more accustomed to suit and tie. And polished shoes. He handled the paddle stiffly, as if out of practice. The man in the stern sat lower in his seat, shoulders rounded.

"Friends of yours?" She startled to hear Joanna's voice just behind her.

"They're not from around here."

"No. They'll be from Lands and Forests, trying to catch someone hunting or trapping."

"Just birdwatching, I think."

The canoe moved slowly around the marsh. Every now and then the birdwatcher pointed his arm and said something to his companion, but the water picked up his words and cast them back at the sky, hollow and disjointed. As they approached the gap where the Turnbulls' house used to sit, the men shipped their paddles and stared. The canoe slowed as it drifted by.

Egypt was about to look away when the sun finally broke through the clouds and struck the side of the canoe, winking off the water. The men vanished.

"...when the governments of Upper and Lower Canada finally came together to discuss the bill before them..." A wave of acrid body odour snaps Egypt back into the room.

"I'm glad you find the history of our country so... thought-provoking, Miss Fisher. Perhaps you'll be able to impart that keen sense of study to your own students someday." The teacher's eyes inches from hers. Which one is glass? Difficult to tell even at this close range. "If you can recall enough of today's lesson to pass it on, that is."

Egypt's gaze slides sideways across the pale green walls, past the yellowing sheets of newsprint with their multiplication tables and the class-made timeline of Canadian history, to the clock on the wall. Forty-three minutes until recess.

By noon it has stopped raining. She volunteers to watch over the kids in the playground during dinner break and dons her coat, hoping the brisk air will snap her out of her sleepiness. Mr. Mitchell's class is still young enough that on hitting the playground, the kids divide immediately into groups of girls and boys. Skipping and cat's cradle along the sheltered east wall, teams of Red Rover and kick the can on the grassy, wide-open spaces of Victoria Park. By the time the students reach Senior I and II, the two sexes will begin circling each other and pairing off.

She turns into the wind and squeezes her eyes shut. Tears stream from between her lashes, across her temples and into her hairline. She could cut this afternoon's classes, offer up the skiff again. Just the two of them this time. No Aidan, no George, no tipping. That is if he isn't already breaking a sweat at some relief job in the city, or back aboard the train on his way to someplace else. Trust Mrs. Byrd to spoil things. Even Egypt's limited experience tells her men like Matt Oakes don't happen by often. What did Mrs. Byrd want anyway? And what of the plates in the sink this morning, with their traces of egg? The glasses redolent of wine?

"What is wrong with you today?" Gloria Henry. Egypt rolls her eyes to disguise the fact that she was startled and folds her arms across her chest. Takes a step back. Gloria can be ten feet away, but it always feels to Egypt like she's standing too close.

"I'm tired, Gloria."

"Tired or bored?"

"What is it to you what I am?" She stalks around to the front entrance of the school on Lamoreaux Street, hoping to shake her shadow and to spot Matt sauntering towards her, a come-spend-the-day-with-me grin on his face, but Gloria is right on her heels. "Leave me alone, Henry."

Gloria stops beside Egypt and folds her arms in parody. She has green gloves that match her expensive and warm-looking green coat. Green. No one can wear green like Gloria Henry can. Gloria with her extraordinary green eyes and her bumbling sense of virtuousness. She looks good in any shade. A cream-coloured tam and scarf set off her sleek strawberry-blond bob. "You know, you make it bad for everyone with your attitude. If you don't want to be a teacher, then why are you here?"

Egypt wishes the ground would open up and swallow Gloria the Good, or a hand reach down from the sky and pluck her away. She stares off across Victoria Park at the buildings on Locke Street. House after house, it's an imposing display of Hamilton red brick. Variations on a theme climbing the gradient of Locke. The hotel on the corner of Peter Street. Then, where the road flattens out, three in a row, nearly identical. A lane. And nestled against its weedy edges, the house with the arched second-floor windows at number 62. The house with eyes, as it has been dubbed by area kids for as long as Egypt can remember. Watching her now, watching Gloria Henry inch under her skin. "Who says I don't want to be a teacher?"

"You don't have to say anything; it's written all over your face. Anyone can see you don't care about what we're learning, or about the children."

Chil-dren. Gloria draws out the word, and Egypt, remembering Mr. Mitchell's terse scribble in her first-term Training Report, feels a stab of panicky guilt. *Not very accurate or thorough. Needs to speak with more authority. Classroom control is weak.* So she'd rather be someplace else today, with someone else. It doesn't mean she doesn't want to be a teacher. She cares about children, of course she does. She cares about Aidan. Aidan was the one she lunged for yesterday when the skiff threatened to tip. Handsome Matt Oakes could fend for himself, but her brother is just a little boy, and small for his age too. Of course, there are days when she would gladly toss him in the marsh, or dangle him from the nearest tree branch, days when she's convinced he was put on earth for the express purpose of getting on her nerves. Her nerves. She glances at Gloria's smug expression. It's Egypt's nerves that are the problem. Stage fright.

She doesn't know how the others do it. Just standing in front of a classroom filled with rambunctious nine- and ten-year-olds is enough to set her heart racing and tie her tongue.

"Even Miss Summers says so."

"Miss Summers?" Egypt is stung. And Gloria doesn't try hard enough to hide the smirk on her face. It's no secret Egypt is half in love with Miss Summers. If she could be anyone in the world, she would be her favourite teacher: slim and pretty, with a peaches-and-cream complexion and a bob of auburn hair that swings forward in a shine and tickles your face when she leans over your desk to answer a question or help with a problem. She smells of sugared almonds and matches her two grey skirts with a dozen differently coloured and styled blouses. In winter she adds a cardigan, navy blue or black, and recently showed up to school in a new soft-grey angora twinset that must have cost the earth. Egypt believes that since she stepped through the doors of normal school, Miss Summers has always and especially been there to help her, the girl from the edge of town determined to lift herself above the seamy elements of boathouse living.

"She's worried she might have to fail you."

Egypt walks away before Gloria sees the tears she's struggling to contain. She set her sights on teaching years ago: it is her rung up on the ladder of respectability, her path to a different kind of life from her mother's. If she doesn't even qualify for a second-class teaching certificate, then what? The thought of being yoked to the likes of Joey Payne for a lifetime, poaching muskrat and taking in other people's laundry, standing alongside her mother packing gunpowder makes her want to weep, or howl at the moon. When classes resume, Egypt makes sure she is standing on the opposite side of the room from Gloria.

Chapter 7

Matt has stayed in rooms like this before: rooms preserved like a shrine to the lost son, his scent faintly discernible in the weft of his bedclothes, amongst his clothing still jumbled in the closet, between the pages of his well-thumbed and dog-eared books. Often, a token of the absent boy's prowess is evident. A worn football sits askew on a desk or windowsill; or a paw-like baseball mitt, the leather scuffed, the lacing stiff and desiccated. A lacrosse or hockey stick leans up against a corner. Sometimes, as here in Neil Byrd's old room, every pennant and sports trophy, every rock and marble, every catapult and wind-up truck, every die-cast caboose – complete with miniature engine driver – is preserved and displayed like a pre-war photograph. As always, he is humbled by the magnitude of generosity and trust engendered in such offerings. And cowed by the long-armed reach of a war he'd been too young to fight in.

"Neil was a natural athlete; he could handle the puck like a professional." *Couldn't they all.* Matt moves aside as Joanna steps into the room. To cast one last dusting of herself among her son's things before relinquishing his room to the stranger. She looks wrung out, her iron-grey hair lank and oily, her face wearing the strain of the night's events. She shuffles to the window, with its fusty blue curtains, and looks out.

"And in the summer, you should have seen him swim. The kids would have these races, and he was always yards ahead of the rest of them." She turns to face him, her eyes shiny. "He always said it was because of his feet. *I got your feet, Ma,* he'd say, laughing." She holds a slippered foot aloft, inviting Matt to laugh with her. Which he does, knowing that this is part of the ritual, something that the mother of the boy slain overseas, fighting for his country, needs to hear. "See what clodhoppers they are? He said his feet made him fast in the water and fast on the ice. No one could catch him."

Matt keeps his knapsack slung over his shoulder. He's learned it's best not to put it down, not to lay claim to any corner of any room until the ritual is over.

"And you're welcome to stay here." Her voice folds in on itself and for a moment he thinks she might cry, but she pulls herself together. Waves his thanks away. It's the least they can do after what he's done for them.

"You'll be helping us too." There it is, the meaningful look. Confirmation of his role. The real reason she called on him this morning. Room and board in exchange for protection. In case Farrell and his thugs come back.

"You say you've done a bit of woodwork before." She places her hand on the banister, her question intended to draw him back downstairs. She's not yet ready to leave him up here by himself.

"Some."

"What kind of woodwork were you doing exactly?"

"I was building a house."

"And where was that?"

"Home. Winnipeg," he adds when she turns to look at him.

"This was your own house you built?"

"I built it for my mother."

"You're a good son. She must be proud of you."

He shrugs. "It burned down."

"Your mother –?"

"She's okay."

"That's a blessing."

Why did he bring the subject up? Now he's made her feel awkward. He follows her outside, struggles to pull the kicked-in door closed behind him, which doesn't quite close on account of the jamb being damaged. Compromised by damp and wood rot.

"Well, here it is," she says, opening the door to a small tool shed parked off to the side of the two-storey cabin. He peers inside. Even before his eyes have fully adjusted to the dimness, he can see that Stan Byrd is a methodical and organized craftsman. "He must have every woodworking tool known to mankind," Joanna says, sensing Matt's wonder. "Good with his hands is Stan."

Father and son. Hands and feet. Matt smiles. Which must make Joanna Byrd the brains of the family.

"You use whatever tools you need to get the job done. You have trouble finding anything, you let me know."

"I don't foresee a problem there."

"'A place for everything and everything in its place,' my Stan always says. You have hands just like his." She covers Matt's hand with her wrinkled fingers, her skin cool and surprisingly soft, like the onion-skin pages of his childhood Bible. "Like his used to be," she adds, squeezing his hand. "Speaking of which," her face softens, "I should get back to him."

"Don't worry about the door. It'll be like new again."

"New I don't need," she calls over her shoulder. "Just make sure it's good and strong."

Matt examines the fence board; certainly not the best lumber he has ever worked, but under the circumstances, it will do. He clamps the board into the bench vice, spinning the handle one way and then the other, and picks up a plane, reacquainting his hand to the shape of the handle, the wood warm and welcoming like a much-loved glove. He runs the blade along the edge of the board; the cut is a little too coarse. A turn of the dial and the plane shavings peel like licorice ribbons from the aged timber, the sweet smell of gumwood filling his nostrils. He pauses mid-task to take in the surroundings; pride bursts from every corner of the work shed. Small to large, a series of screwdrivers hang from clips on the pegboard above the workbench, like a panpipe. Saws arranged neatly. Mason jars with nails and screws, each carefully sized. He takes his time reminding himself how much he has missed the tools he hasn't seen or held in a long time.

Two boards to replace the panels Farrell and his heavies put their boots through last night. He could make a nicer job if he took the door off, but the suggestion seemed to make the Byrds nervous. And so he reassured them he could fix it in place. He chooses the right size nails and saw and goes outside to rip the board down to size.

At the house, he fits the boards in place. A fraction off one end, a quick file. Nails and a hammer to finish the job. His hands magically find their rhythm again, as if he never stopped working with them. A sense of peace and serenity overtakes Matt whenever he works a piece of wood, the calm spreading from his head down into his chest and arms and all the way to the ends of his fingers. His movements feel fluid and precise, like a dance he's known his whole life.

By the time he's back in the tool shed cleaning up after himself, determined to leave the place as he found it, he's whistling.

Chapter 8

The studio is a south-facing addition grafted to the back of the house on George Street. Egypt follows Gloria inside, blinking back both the afternoon light that pours through a sweep of floor-to-cathedral-ceiling windows and the caustic sting of turpentine and oil paints. An easel in the middle of the room supports a colossal canvas upon which paint appears to have been thrown. The floor is so spattered that in places the colours have muddied to a swamp green. High and low along the white walls hang another dozen or so bold and discordant canvasses. Mrs. Henry is no tidy and careful painter of still lifes. After the quiet elegance of the rest of the downstairs, it's like stepping into a carnival – all riotous colour and house-of-mirrors distortions. A prickling sensation runs up Egypt's spine. Modern art. These must be the kinds of images Miss Summers was referring to when she waxed on about the new way of seeing, about the shifting of light and colour and perspective. Egypt squints back at the easel. She wants to step closer and investigate, but her feet feel pinned to the linoleum, as if the paint spatters are some kind of glue holding her down.

"Impressive, isn't it?" Draped in a paint-smeared smock, Gloria's mother materializes from a wall, or the ceiling somewhere, wiping her hands on a filthy, turpentine-soaked rag. Egypt, light-headed with the fumes, nods mutely. The painting has impressed her, without a doubt. Does she like it? She couldn't say.

"*Man Walking a Dog*."

"I'm sorry?"

"*Man Walking a Dog*. That's the title."

Egypt stares but sees nothing resembling man or dog. A splash of red and orange pulls her eye to one section of a collage predominated by dark, angular shapes. She wonders if it's finished.

"Is it raining on them?" she asks, horribly aware that her throat has grown dry.

Gloria's mother narrows her eyes and stares at Egypt the way a prospective buyer might size up an object in a store. Egypt would normally find such close scrutiny discomfiting, but a streak of yellow paint across Mrs. Henry's cheek renders her harmless, even endearing. Suddenly, she reaches out and grasps Egypt's face, the skin on her hands as dry and coarse as that of a labourer.

"Gloria so rarely brings friends home," she murmurs, tilting Egypt's face one way then the other, and finally rearranging her long, dark curls across one shoulder. "Are they all as striking as you?"

What friends? Egypt thinks, flushing with the compliment. It's hard to believe this is Gloria's mother. Even the paisley scarf twisted through Mrs. Henry's hair to keep it off her face appears more exotic than practical. And she moves like no other woman Egypt has ever met. Confidence radiates from her. It takes Egypt a moment to understand that Mrs. Henry, without losing a trace of her femininity, holds herself more the way a man does.

"You should sit for me sometime." And she turns away to approach her canvas. "Gloria, tell your friend she should sit for me."

Egypt would sit for this woman just to soak up her presence, just to see how Mrs. Henry might translate her *striking* looks to the canvas. Boxy purple hair? A pyramidal body? Is she any good? She's certainly had a lot of practice. Dozens more unframed canvasses of varying sizes lean in stacks against the back wall. Egypt turns to look behind her and finally notices Gloria standing at a sink set in a nook at the west end of the studio, cleaning palettes and brushes by the looks of things. A small green girl in a big bold room. She's all but disappeared inside it.

"Egypt is busy with school."

Not so busy, Egypt wants to protest. But school is the reason she's standing here in Gloria's house in the first place.

"Would it be all right if Egypt stays to dinner?" Gloria is now arranging the brushes in Mason jars in order of size.

"I don't have a problem with it, but it's a little short notice, don't you think?" Egypt finds it fascinating how neither mother nor daughter looks at each other while speaking. In Laura's world, such insolence would be rewarded with a slap. "Remember, your brother's coming down from Montreal today. Have you checked with Martha? She's the one who'll be most put out. You know what she's like."

"Martha is fine."

Martha with the disapproving mouth? Martha in the severe and dark-grey button-down dress who took their coats at the front door? Egypt might want to check her meal for broken glass, or rat poison. Though she's less disconcerted by a hostile maid than she is surprised by the fact that Gloria lied. And not only lied to Egypt but to Miss Summers, too. *Supper and a sleepover*, Gloria said yesterday, roping their teacher into her scheme. She, Gloria, would spend Friday evening coaching Egypt through her lesson plans and building her classroom confidence. Something Egypt was sorely in need of following her abysmal performance at the model school yesterday when she blanked out in front of her class not once but several tongue-tying times. Gloria had run home in her dinner hour and checked with her mother – *She thinks it's a wonderful idea* – and so, with Miss Summers all smiles and relief on her pretty face, how could Egypt say no? Supper and a sleepover it would be. It meant doing homework on a Friday evening and passing up the chance of seeing Matt, or at least walking George by the Byrds' place several times, looking through the lighted windows for glimpses of him. But how could she turn down the opportunity to see inside Gloria's house? And what city folk served for dinner? Rich city folk. It would seem, however, that

Gloria has asked her mother nothing until now, and Egypt likes her a little better for her mendacity.

A sudden commotion of voices and laughter at the front door and Gloria grows large again. "Oh," she breathes, staring into the sink. When Egypt steps up behind her, she sees the broken Mason jar and Gloria's trembling hands.

"Did you cut yourself?"

"I don't think so." But she continues to stare at her wet hands as if expecting to see blood appear.

"Aren't you going to go and say hello?" Mrs. Henry sing-songs across the studio.

Gloria dries her hands and primps herself in the square of mirror on the wall above the sink. "Would you like to meet my brother?" she asks, a strained smile meeting Egypt's gaze in the mirror. "You'll like him. He's very handsome."

She leads the way from the studio to the front door, where the two Henry men, father and son, stand bantering with Martha as they remove their hats and shuck their coats into her waiting arms. They have brought with them the tang of whiskey and wintery air. The temperature outside plummeting. Egypt smells snow on the way.

"There you are. We were beginning to think we'd been abandoned. I found this dashing young man hanging about my office this afternoon. We would have been home earlier, but he insisted on taking me to the Hamilton Club."

"Then someone else insisted we stay later." A tenor version of his father's bass. Of a similar height and frame, father and son also share the same deep-cleft chin in a square jaw, but there all similarities end. For once, Gloria was not exaggerating: Philip Henry could be descended from the gods. The two men share a private joke.

Gloria pauses to collect herself before grabbing Egypt's hand and pulling her forward. "This is my friend from school, Egypt Fisher. Egypt, I'd like you to meet my father and my brother, Philip."

The older Mr. Henry gives a curt nod in her direction, but Philip thrusts out his hand and stares boldly at Egypt.

"They say a man should wait until a lady offers her hand to be shaken, but this is a rare and exciting moment, meeting a friend of Glo's. How do you do?"

"Fine," she says, his enthusiasm robbing her of any other response. His handshake is strong, his hand so warm that Egypt feels herself heating up. Philip Henry possesses the kind of strong, square jawline, smoky eyes and dark, wavy hair that women flock to the cinemas to swoon over. And everything about him – the way he inhabits his well-tailored clothing, the amusement playing at the corner of his mouth, his insouciant and suggestive slouch – broadcasts that he knows this.

"Did you visit the basilica when you were in Montreal?" Egypt asks, finally finding her tongue and anxious to show she knows something of the city. "It apparently boasts one of the world's largest domes."

Philip cocks his head and delivers a smile she has to take a step back from. "I'm at medical school there. McGill University."

"Oh."

"And on a scholarship, no less," Mr. Henry boasts as he strolls into the first room off the entrance hall, leaving Gloria standing in the shadow of her brother's brilliance. Little wonder she is such a brown-noser at school. Egypt almost feels sorry for her.

A tinkling of crystal is heard, followed by the sound of liquid being poured into a glass.

Philip pushes away from the wall. "I should go and join my father. If you'll excuse me, ladies." He tips an imaginary hat. "It's wonderful to see you again, Glo." He reaches out but doesn't quite touch her arm. "We have lots to catch up on."

"Why didn't you tell me this weekend was a family reunion?" Egypt whispers crossly as soon as he's out of sight. She has half a mind to leave Gloria to her lies and her supremely accomplished family. "We could have arranged this for another time."

Gloria reaches for her hand. "Please say you're not angry with me. You are still staying, aren't you? You have to now that everyone's gone to so much trouble."

Trouble? Gloria is so melodramatic. But already Egypt can feel herself being drawn into the Henry family performance, like a spectator at a play.

"Maybe you should look over my lesson plans before dinner. Tell me what I'm doing wrong."

Mrs. Henry is seated at one end of a dining table that could accommodate eight comfortably, ten at a squeeze. She has exchanged her paisley scarf for a shimmery green-and-gold affair that matches the exotic tablecloth she appears to be wearing. But it isn't only her clothes that are different; from her languorous posture to the vacant cast of her eyes, Mrs. Henry's entire manner has shifted. She's in the room and yet absent from it. Leaning back in her chair, legs crossed at the thigh, she swirls a goblet of viscous green liquid in front of her. Egypt smells licorice. As Egypt and Gloria approach the table, Mrs. Henry dabs her finger in her glass and runs it around the rim, making the crystal sing. When father and son enter the room, she barely gives them a glance. Philip finishes the remainder of his drink in one swallow and leaves the tumbler on the sideboard before taking a seat in the mid-stretch of table between his parents. Martha of the dark-grey dress wheels in a trolley loaded with steaming-hot serving dishes.

"I didn't realize you were staying for dinner, Egypt – such a striking name, by the way. I'm not sure Martha knew either, did you Martha?"

"No sir, I did not."

"FHB then." He winks at Egypt. "Family Hold Back. And the cutlery works from the outside in," he adds.

Egypt blushes furiously.

"But you already knew that, didn't you?" He leans towards her with a smile.

"Doesn't everyone?" Egypt laughs awkwardly, and everyone laughs with her, even Mrs. Henry.

"Egypt is also staying over tonight," Gloria announces.

"Well, then, Martha will be prepared for breakfast, won't you, Martha?"

"Yes, sir." Egypt fancies she even curtsies, but then brushes it off as a combination of her imagination and Martha's ungainliness.

Martha passes Mr. Henry the carving utensils and places a roast in front of him. Egypt can't tear her eyes from the meat. The only beef she's eaten is ground, which Laura fries up with an onion, smothers in lumpy mashed potatoes and calls one of her *dishes*. Gloria's father stands and carves with practised expertise. Slivers of meat, pinkish in the middle, fall from his knife and fan across the plate like a slow shuffle of playing cards. The loaded plate then makes its way around the table.

"And is Egypt staying all weekend?" Philip raps his plate with the serving spoon. Despite his call for FHB, most of the remaining potatoes are on his plate, leaving little more than a mouthful for Egypt. She opts to forgo the glistening trail of melted butter and pass over the dish as if it weren't there at all, rather than have everyone apologizing and making a fuss.

"Absolutely, she is." Mrs. Henry reaches an unsteady hand in the direction of her wineglass. "She's agreed to sit for me. We can't have all that lovely bone structure going to waste." Egypt didn't realize they had progressed so far in their negotiations. And from what she's seen of Mrs. Henry's artwork, she wouldn't have thought bone structure was something she paid much attention to.

"Actually, I have to be home tomorrow. My mother needs my help."

"Is she not well?"

"Philip!"

"I'm merely showing concern, Mother. Egypt's circumstances are clearly more strained than ours." He rolls his eyes at Egypt, drawing her into collusion with him against his mother's perceived foolishness. "Do you live around here, Egypt?"

"Could you pass the carrots, please?" Gloria reaches across the table towards her brother, knocking over the cruet set. In an instant Martha is at Philip's side, sweeping the spilled salt and pepper into her hand with a napkin. Philip never takes his eyes from Egypt. His rapt attention is almost disconcerting, but at the same time thrilling and heady. She has never experienced such intense interest from a male before – Joey Payne doesn't count – particularly one so striking. She senses that Philip is doing his best to make her feel safe, to make her feel that she can confide in him, in his whole family, without fear of judgement.

"No. Actually, I live in Cootes Paradise. In the boathouses there."

"Cootes Paradise!" Mrs. Henry claps her hands. "How utterly delightful. You must take me there, Egypt. When the warmer weather comes. I've always wanted to paint the area. Such rugged beauty. The weather-worn siding and the way it blends into its surroundings."

"Better hurry then, Mother, before Tommy McQuesten and the Parks Board huff and puff and blow them all down."

"And the people, too," Mrs. Henry continues. Mr. Henry taps a finger impatiently on his knife. Egypt can feel Gloria squirming beside her. Mrs. Henry is painting the air with her wineglass. "There's such a tenacious wilfulness about a group of people who would build their homes in the wilderness."

"I thought you'd washed your hands of the Romantic period, Mother. *Tenacious* indeed. It's basic survival instincts. The first primitive peoples built their settlements next to water. Egypt's people grasped a golden opportunity."

Her people?

"It isn't their fault the land they occupy is being coveted by the city's movers and shakers. Rotten bad luck, I'd say." He turns his gaze on Egypt again. "What will you do when the city starts issuing eviction orders? Where will you go?"

Eviction orders?

Mr. Henry clears his throat. "Philip, this is hardly the subject for dinner conversation."

But Philip pays not the slightest attention. Perhaps he's drunker than he seems. He indicates Martha should pour him some wine and then turns his attention back to Egypt. "Tommy McQuesten is the City Beautiful Movement. Of course you've heard of the City Beautiful Movement?"

"Of course." Egypt looks down at her plate to hide the tic in her cheek. Her stomach offers one long and plaintive rumble.

Mr. Henry sighs. "Let us say grace." He bows his head and clasps his hands before him. His children follow suit. "For what we are about to receive . . ."

Egypt can't resist peeking around the table. She spies Gloria's mother reaching for her drink.

". . . may the Lord make us truly thankful." Mrs. Henry catches Egypt's eye and winks.

"Amen."

"Amen."

After her first bite Egypt wants to weep, wants to pull the serving plate towards her and devour the whole roast, throw back her head and howl at the chandelier. Never has she tasted meat so tender, so exquisite. It isn't dark like wild hare or oily like duck or tough and gamey like most of the meat that has been placed before her over the years. She wills herself to eat slowly, to savour every bite. Still, compared to Gloria and Mrs. Henry – who spend more time rearranging the food on their plates than actually eating any of it – she appears to have the appetite of an ogre. The men tuck in with relish, but a full belly does nothing to slake Philip's interest in her.

"And what does your father do, Egypt?"

She angles her knife and fork together and pushes her plate away, and then, seeing that no one else has followed suit, pulls it back towards her again. It's hard to look Philip in the eye without feeling her soul is being laid bare. "He's dead," she says. She flinched hearing this lie from her mother's lips the first time. But how much simpler it is than admitting that he's gone. Missing. Absconded. In truth she has no idea if Ray is still alive, never mind what he might be doing for a living. She glances at Gloria, wondering what she's thinking, what she knows. Gloria's lack of popularity means she isn't privy to the school's malicious gossip mill.

"So your mother is raising you alone?" Mrs. Henry's voice like liquid.

"Yes." Not a lie. Though Egypt considers herself already raised. When her cheeks cool, she dares to lift her eyes to Mrs. Henry, who places a hand on her arm. Her face is tipped towards Egypt in an expression of sincerity, though her eyes are all surface.

"Then she's doing an admirable job. And on that positive note, I'll leave you all to your pudding," Mrs. Henry says, addressing the table in general and rising from her seat. She pauses, hands on the dining table, before pushing herself away from it and gliding from the room.

"You know, it's bad luck to wear an opal if it isn't your birthstone. Terrible things can happen to the wearer. Accidents, illness." Gloria pauses and Egypt realizes she's been pacing the length of Gloria's bedroom since they came up here over an hour ago. A headache has bloomed behind her eyes. She never knew a person could talk for so long about nothing. It's as if Gloria is making up for her silence throughout dinner. "People have died."

"Died?"

"From wearing opals."

"I'm safe then." Gloria frowns. Egypt spreads her hands in a shrug. "I don't have any opals."

"And this is the necklace I wore to my confirmation four years ago." Egypt squints at Gloria's flowery bedspread and the magpie's nest of jewellery winking in the centre. The rich girl parading her possessions before her poor friend. For whose benefit is this performance? If Egypt wasn't so bored –

Footsteps come to a halt on the landing outside Gloria's door. In the pause before the knock, Egypt watches as Gloria stills herself like an animal hiding in the undergrowth. The door opens before she can say come in.

"Well, this looks very cozy." Philip is glassy-eyed and a little unsteady on his feet. Suddenly it's as if there's too much furniture in the room, too many busy patterns – from the bedspread to the curtains to the wallpaper – all clashing with one another. Egypt retreats to the cushioned seat in the window, willing herself not to bolt from the room. She pulls a blanket around herself and pictures George and his loping gait, herself running across the fields beside him, the wind fanning her hair and blowing away all the Philip that clings to her.

"You're up late, Glo."

"Egypt and I have a lot to talk about."

"Girly chatter." He walks over to the dresser and picks up an atomizer; pushes at the pink ball with its impossibly tiny crochet stitches. A sickly sweet burst of violets fills the air. "Chitter chatter."

"We were discussing school, actually. Teaching strategies and curriculum." Chalk up a whopper for Gloria. "And could you leave my things alone, please? I don't go into your room and mess with your things."

"Maybe you should. You know what they say. All work and no play makes Glo a dull girl. And Egypt too." He looks over at Egypt for the first time since entering the room. "Interesting name. Egypt. Whose idea was that?"

Egypt launches into her explanation about her father and the Sphinx being target practice for the troops. But Philip Henry, drunkenness aside, is sharper than Matt Oakes. Or less mindful of her feelings.

"Napoleon's troops, actually. Or so the story goes. Whereas your version would make you only about fifteen." Without giving her a chance to respond – not that Egypt can think of much beyond the sudden pounding of her heart – he strides over to the window seat and sits down beside her. "North African operations didn't start until 1915. Besides, her nose – she is a she, don't you agree? I've always thought so – was missing well before either war. Or so it's documented." His smile says he's teasing, but Egypt feels skewered, like a butterfly trapped by a pin and a boy's spite. He squeezes her leg, just above her knee, and she almost leaps from her skin. Heat pours through her belly and she shifts about in her seat, wanting to fling his hand away and yet at the same time reluctant to do so. Philip smiles.

"Glo, have you shown your guest to her room yet? It's awfully late you know."

"Egypt is sleeping here, with me."

She is? Egypt was counting on the luxury of her own room; had even pictured brushing her hair in a mirrored vanity with a dressing table set backed with mother-of-pearl. Had been so counting on it in fact that she'd dashed out the door this morning before her mother could make sure she'd packed her own hairbrush, with its chipped painted handle, and her pilled and faded nightgown. Now she closes her eyes and wills these same items into her satchel. She eyes the width of Gloria's bed. And a roll of barbed wire to keep them apart.

"Well then, ladies, sleep tight. Don't let the bedbugs bite." He jumps up, and as he reaches the door, leans back into the room. "Oh, and Egypt, my little sister snores. If it gets too much, you can always snuggle in with me." He wanders off towards his room, leaving the door wide open.

"Here, I thought you might like to sleep in this. We can be like twins." Gloria pushes to the door and hands Egypt a nightgown, all ribbons and flowers. A pink version of the same yellow nightgown she has laid out for herself.

"Like twins," Egypt echoes. If Gloria isn't going to mention her brother's behaviour, then neither will she.

But when they climb into bed and Gloria clicks off her bedside lamp, Egypt's mind can't help but wander back through the evening's events. *Eviction notices*. The street lamp penetrates the curtains and she stares at shadows the unfamiliar furniture casts on the walls and ceiling. *Supper and a sleepover*. She considers the half-hearted effort Gloria put into the tutoring she made such a promise of. What was the real reason for inviting her over? To provide her mother with a model? Or her brother with a paramour? She dismisses this last thought as quickly as it came to her. *Paramour?* Where did that expression come from? Mr. Mitchell's history class, no doubt. As if the Henrys of George Street would ever embrace the likes of Egypt as a match for their radiant son. She's suddenly warm all over, blushing in the dark, embarrassed at having even entertained the idea. And something else she can't quite shake – the feeling that Philip's gallantry isn't altogether genuine, that while he's dazzling her with his charms, he is at the same time laughing at her. No, Matt is the man for Egypt. The Philip Henrys of this world should be courting movie starlets and society girls. She'd like to see him gut a fish, or split a cord of firewood.

The bed rocks as Gloria turns over and Egypt feels the moist warmth of Gloria's breath on her face.

"You awake?"

Panic slips inside her body. "Yeah."

A pause, and then, "Do you think people should marry for love?"

"I don't think there's any other reason to marry," Egypt gushes at the ceiling, thinking of Matt, pushing his face into her head. His strong, lean arms and capable hands. *Matt Matt Matt Matt Matt Matt Matt.*

"Do you think my brother is handsome?"

"Very." Her lips are dry and sticky. Gloria can't possibly know what she's been thinking.

"He's not really my brother."

"He isn't?"

"He's my half-brother."

Is Gloria expecting a response? Egypt says nothing.

"He dates a different girl each week in Montreal. I could ask him to take you on a date if you –"

"No."

"I thought you said you liked him." Gloria sounds peeved.

"It's not that. There's someone . . . um . . . I have –"

"You have a sweetheart!"

The blush is back, racing across her skin. She's smiling herself silly. "Yes. I have a sweetheart."

"Is he handsome?"

"Ruggedly handsome. A diamond in the rough," she adds, quoting her mother.

"Has he kissed you?"

"No."

"Do you think about it?"

"Yes."

Gloria falls silent and the room gradually fills with the ticking of the clock on her bedside table, the accumulated sighs of her teddy bears. She is silent so long that Egypt begins to wonder if she has fallen asleep. And then:

"Do you think about anything else? About him doing anything else?"

"Such as?" Egypt's throat is so dry she isn't sure she managed to squeeze the words out.

"Such as him touching you." Gloria's voice seems to be coming from some dark, cramped corner of Egypt's head.

"Touching?"

"Down there."

"I know what you mean, Gloria," she snaps. What she can't believe is that Gloria Henry knows what she means.

This time, the silence presses down on the bed. The bedcovers weigh the earth. Egypt pretends to fall asleep but is too aware of the rhythm of her breathing, feels suffocated by it. She draws a deep raggedy breath and turns over on her side. Gloria rescues the night.

"Someday a handsome prince will sweep me off my feet and carry me away."

"To Paris?"

"Paris isn't hot enough. Besides, that's my mother's dream."

Egypt rolls onto her back again. "She's very interesting, your mother. Your whole family is interesting."

"That's one way to describe them."

"They make you more interesting by association."

"Thanks. I think." Silence for a while and then Gloria starts giggling.

"What's so funny?"

"That's the nicest thing you've ever said to me." Another wave of giggles and Egypt joins in. She snorts into the soft, thick sheets.

"I have a confession to make," Egypt says.

"What's that?"

"I didn't want to bring clean underwear in my satchel in case I accidentally pulled them out in class and Paul McClusky got a hold of them."

"And made up one of his dreadful limericks."

"And organized a sing-song at recess."

"What are you saying, you want to borrow some clean underwear tomorrow?"

"Not necessary. I wore tomorrow's pair overtop of today's."

"You did not."

"Oh yes I did."

"And you wore them all day?"

"They kept me nice and warm."

Gloria's turn to snort with laughter. Faces buried in their pillows, the harder they try to stop themselves, the harder they laugh, and the more the bed shakes.

Chapter 9

It has begun snowing by the time Laura exits the factory. In the amber halo from the street lamp across the road, snowflakes whorl madly and then twist away into darkness. A leap of tension as her gaze is drawn from the hypnotic dance of snow down the shaft of the street lamp to the figure leaning against it. One leg crossed artlessly over the other in that loose-hipped Hamilton-gangster pose of his, a cigarette pinched between thumb and forefinger and cupped in his right hand.

Ray.

He remains motionless while she stands gathering her wits, knees locked against the tide of workers pouring towards the gates. They flow around her, like water around a rock caught in a riverbed, joining up again and then forming tributaries before they reach him, as if Ray were a larger object in their path – a dam or a dike. Laura and Ray, the only stationary figures in a moving landscape. Laura and Ray. Ray and Laura. *Laura loves Ray*. Gouged into the rock face at Devil's Punchbowl. *Loved.* She lifts a hand to her hair and discovers she is shaking. *Laura hates Ray*. She waits for the surge of anger she's practised feeling from his absence, the venom that will enable her to run across the road and slap his face. Punch him, kick him, beat on his chest. *Where the hell have you been?* Her throat is burned dry. His nonchalance is possibly staged, possibly not. Knowing Ray doesn't always help a person predict his behaviour, what he is capable of.

She considers walking off, pretending she hasn't seen him, but Ray sets his own agenda. He'll only follow her to the cabin. Or surprise her someplace else. *Oh Lord, Egypt. Aidan! What if he's tracked them down already?*

He lifts his cap as Laura hurries across the street towards him, a lazy smile pulling at his lips. A tic starts up in her cheek.

"What are you doing here?"

His eyes widen in mock surprise. "How you doing, Ray? Long-time no see, Ray? Where you been, Ray? Good to see you, Ray."

He's thinner, sharper looking. Lines fan from his eyes; those around his mouth are drawn a little deeper. Perhaps Ray's brand of charm has worn thin in his new home, wherever that is.

"You have some nerve."

He grinds his cigarette beneath the toe of his boot, shaking his head and smiling to himself as if she were the incorrigible one.

"'Night, Laura," someone calls. She raises her hand. She'll be the talk of the shop floor tomorrow.

"Lori-Lee, still as beautiful as ever."

"Ray Fisher. Still as infuriating as ever. And don't call me that."

"And especially beautiful when you're angry. My little firecracker." He lifts his hand to touch her cheek but she angles her head out of his reach.

"I'm not your little anything."

"I always said it suits you, working here." He nods at the factory sign behind her. *Hand & Company Fireworks.*

"It always suited you, you mean. Me working, you off to see a man about a horse."

"You've a smudge on your lip."

She wipes her glove across her mouth. Black powder. It clings to her skin and attacks the fibres of her clothing.

"You better be careful with that stuff. You don't want to blow a hole in that pretty face of yours."

Doesn't she? She could shake it from herself at night; sweep it into a pile, save up to make her own fireworks. Blast the cabin to smithereens. The bridge. How tempting to someday walk straight to her workbench without stopping at the entrance to tap the copper plate. Skin and hair sparking with static electricity. Take out the whole damned block. See what the city makes of that.

"What do you want, Ray?"

"I've missed you, girl." He reaches for her again but Laura folds her arms across her chest, feet planted apart, ready for whatever he might throw at her.

"You know, you can't do this, you can't just waltz back here after years of being away – six whole years, Ray! – and expect everything to be as it was before. Expect people to be who they were." *By the way, you have a son. We have a son. There's something I never told you. As I had no goddamned idea where you were, whether you were even alive ...*

"From where I'm standing, you look just the same as you always did: terrific." That sly sideways smile again, the one Egypt has inherited. On either, it is infuriating.

"Ray, I'm the least of your worries." *And if he decides to follow you home, Egypt is the least of yours, Laura Fisher.*

"Meaning?"

She glances at the darkening sky for courage. She should tell him right here and now. Get the drama over with.

"Egypt. Remember her? The daughter you left behind. A little girl with a lot of questions. Questions her mother couldn't answer."

Though not as many as Laura had steeled herself for. The questions had taken their time percolating before rising to the surface, and even then, Egypt seemed strangely at ease with both the situation and the half-truths her mother fed her, never pushing for more. At least not at the time. Later, when Laura was least expecting it, an earlier question might be revisited in a more oblique form. But from that first day, Laura marvelled at her daughter's composure and resilience. Egypt knew something was up the moment she was told to sit down. Possibly the tic in Laura's cheek gave her away, or her flattened-out voice. Looking older than her eleven years, Egypt had narrowed her eyes and set her face to blank. Laura was still trying to absorb the news herself, and the bitter fact that Ray hadn't been man enough to tell her himself but instead had left his wheezy old cohort Manny to do his dirty work for him. Every time the right words managed to collect themselves on the tip of her tongue, a wave of nausea would wash them away again, and so Laura waffled and stalled, filling Egypt in on the minutiae of her day and apologizing over and again for not having dinner ready. Meanwhile Egypt sat perched on the arm of the battered couch, staring someplace west of her mother's shell-shocked face and swinging her legs. Laura focused on Egypt's bony, sticking-out knees, scabbed and grubby from scaling trees and hurling herself from railway embankments and the roofs of mausoleums in the cemetery if you were to believe everything she told you. When Laura eventually mustered the courage to tell Egypt her father was gone, the girl tried valiantly to appear nonplussed. But lost and vulnerable weren't far beneath the surface. Laura wanted to scoop her up and rock her in her arms, but she hadn't held her daughter since – oh God, she couldn't remember when. Egypt was always so prickly, squirming to get away, or was it that Laura was simply too busy and preoccupied, too angry with Ray and his latest schemes and exploits that she could never reach out to her daughter? Either way, she had not been able to cross the divide between them that afternoon.

Ray's gaze wanders past Laura's shoulder. "What did you tell her?"

"That you were dead."

If he's hurt, he's careful not to let it show. Good old Ray. That much hasn't changed.

"So what do you think she's going to say when she sees I'm not dead?"

"What makes you think I'm going to let you see her?"

"You can't stop me seeing her."

Laura looks away, down King Street at the retreating backs of her workmates, wending their way home. No, she can't stop him doing anything. She never could. Wasn't that the root of all their problems? Still, her impulse is to throw herself between them, absorb some of the shock she knows is coming. The pain of betrayal. As for Aidan . . . perhaps if he saw him first. Her shoulders inch up her neck, an instant headache cleaving her face in two.

"So, you think she'll be pleased to see her old man?" For the first time he sounds less sure of himself.

"What do you think, Ray?"

"I'm asking you."

"Put yourself in her shoes."

"I never was much of a letter writer."

"I'm sure she'll appreciate that, if you explain it to her nicely."

"You reckon?"

"Oh Ray, for heaven's sakes, you abandoned the girl. You abandoned us. Take some responsibility for once in your life."

From his inside pocket he retrieves a tobacco pouch and rolling papers but then thinks better of it as a gust of wind threatens to blow the flat cap from his head. Stuffs them back and shrugs. "Sometimes these things just come on a man."

Cold creeps through her bones and the shadows deepen around them as, shed by shed, the factory lights extinguish. "And you think they don't just come on a woman? Or a child?"

"It's not the same though, is it?"

"You couldn't even find it in you to send a birthday card? A trinket at Christmas? You might as well have been dead."

"What are you saying?"

"You think it was easy for me? She hated me, you know. Not you. Blamed me for driving you away." Her voice shrill in the dark. She's turning into one of those women she's always detested – screaming in the street, airing their dirty laundry. But it's as if some other version of herself has taken over and the real Laura, the one who calmly picked up the pieces after he left and soldiered on – she had a child to raise, and another on the way, so best foot forward – is standing across the road, looking on in vague horror. She can't even derive any satisfaction from his discomfort, his searching the ground for an answer.

"So you didn't tell her I was dead."

"I told her you went away to find work, that it was difficult to write because you were on the move, and then that you were overseas. But you know there were only so many excuses I could come up with."

And one day Egypt stopped asking. Which in a way made Laura's life easier. Ray was simply a subject to be skirted around or skipped over, like a hole in the kitchen floor. But the longer they avoided talking about him, the harder it became to bring Ray's name back into the conversation. She didn't have the courage to ask, so Laura no longer knew how her daughter felt. She still doesn't. "I think eventually she just accepted that you weren't coming back."

"No real harm done, then," Ray says after a pause. Laura turns to face the dark and shakes her head. Blood pounds between her temples, dizzying. "It was probably better coming from you. In the long run. Daughters listen to their mothers."

"So why didn't I listen to mine?" She says it to herself, but loud enough so he hears her.

"Because you liked the excitement." His voice husky in her ear. She smiles ruefully in the dark.

And look where it got me.

"I brought you something special." He pulls a small parcel from his pocket, hands it to her. String tied around butcher's paper. She stares at it in disbelief and then wonders why she's surprised. This is Ray all over. "Pork chops. Loin cut," he adds, smacking his lips. "Should cook up a treat with some spuds and gravy."

And a side dish of heartburn. Heartache. At least the snow has eased off. A sampler for what's to come later, perhaps. She tucks the parcel under her arm and they set off in the direction of the boathouses.

A silent Ray is a brooding Ray, so Laura is grateful for the stream of banter he colours the air with during the walk home. She's half-listening. Where he's been – Detroit – why he left – some convoluted, cockamamie Ray-tale about a debt – her ears are pricked for these details, but the cronies, the deals and the get-rich-quick schemes, the he-never-saw-it-coming stories, she's heard them all before. Different backdrop, but a similar cast of ne'er-do-wells and the same old beginning, middle and end. Her indifference almost astounds her. As little input is required save the odd exclamation or affirmation, her mind is free to sift and winnow through all the possible reasons he might be back, and to fret over how long he plans on staying.

As they pass the cemetery and approach the High Level Bridge and the path to the boathouses, Laura's legs feel strangely inert, wooden; her knees creak with cold. The previous three days of solid rain have rendered the path a quagmire, mutable, treacherous. Halfway down, she slips and falls hard on her tailbone.

"Up you get." Ray grasps her by the elbows and has her back on her feet before she can register the full impact of the fall, which in the next instant robs her of breath. "I've got you," he coos, arm around her shoulder, pulling her close. The nicotine and woodsmoke smell of his jacket stirs an old yearning in her belly, and a brief distillation of memories leaks through. Carnival rides and ice boat races. Sitting in his rooms while he cooked up batches of *Marmaduke Firth's Most Excellent Elixir & Tonic*, singing music-hall medleys spliced with lyrics that poked fun of people they'd met that day. She would shrug him off, but the ground dips and sways, and just for a moment, leaning into his shoulder feels comfortable, familiar.

When the cabin draws into view, Laura tries to extricate herself from his embrace, but Ray only tightens his hold. As a consequence, exacerbated by the three inches in height she has on him, they shuffle clumsily through the backyard gate, looking more like a disgruntled puppeteer and his uncooperative marionette than Ray's vision of them as a newly reunited couple. And to crown the moment, there's young Matt Oakes, stacking wood against the side of the house. Laura's stomach twists like sheets in a fierce wind. Now she'd like to fling Ray's arm away but doesn't dare. Nor does she dare raise her eyes to either man. So she stares down at herself, dismayed by her dishevelled appearance, the filthy package in her hands, her torn stockings and muddied coat magnifying the picture she presents of a battered wife.

The longer Ray remains quiet, the more nervous she grows, stumbling as she reaches for the door handle. "I don't even know if she's home," she says. But lights blaze in the cabin, attesting to her lie. "Egypt," she calls out. "Egypt, there's someone here to see you." She closes the door behind her in time to watch Matt retreat, axe in hand, through the backyard gate.

"Someone, eh?" Ray says under his breath. "There was someone standing outside, missus. You could hardly miss him. Bigger than some fucking trees round here. You gonna tell me you didn't see him or something?"

"What's to see? He's a neighbour. He lodges with the Byrds."

"So who is he, then?"

"I told you, he's a lodger."

"Lodger. My steel-town ass he's a lodger." His vitriol pins her in the middle of the room. "I meant who is he to you?"

So that's why he's back. He must have cronies dotted across the city still, keeping tabs. Someone's tipped him off there's another man in the picture and Ray is back to keep an eye on his woman. He's practically foaming at the mouth.

"Standing outside my house with my bloody axe in his hands, chopping wood he must have hauled in here from yonder woods. No bugger grafts like that for free."

She pulls at his fingers where they're bruising the softer flesh on the inside of her elbow and he pushes her away in disgust. "There's enough out there for the whole damn neighbourhood. Build a bonfire, you'd see it from the bloody moon."

"He's been good to the Byrds. Like a son." Good to Laura and her family too, as if bent on proving his worth and wiping out the Myrtle Todd lie. What is surprising, for a household that has managed so well all these years without a man, is how easily they have reset the cadence and rhythm of their days this past month to accommodate him. Though not so difficult to understand, perhaps, given how uneven the arrangement, how squarely it falls in Laura's favour. But she could only protest so many times. If Matt wanted to haul water and wood and share the spoils of his fishing and trapping with them, then why should she stop him? How could she? Aidan would have asked too many questions. Egypt would have been sulky and uncooperative, and Laura would have been fighting a battle on several fronts. The Rays of this world didn't understand what it took to do everything; to be two parents at once, both breadwinner and moral guide. But now that Matt has flushed Ray Fisher out of hiding, she wishes she'd sent him packing that first day instead of bending to Egypt's manipulations.

Who knows how long Ray's been in town? She wouldn't put it past him to have been spying on her all week. Following her to work. Her and Matt. Innocent enough. Matt was on his way downtown anyway, he explained on Monday, running up behind her while she was hurrying along the path towards the bridge, walking quickly to ward off the cold and the prickly feeling of loneliness that always descended when she walked to work in the dark. Something about a line on a job, and would she mind some company? But maybe not so innocent filtered through Ray's imagination.

Now that she's thinking about it, Laura can even recall the echo of footsteps behind them this morning. *Ray. Stalking the usurper. Pathetic little man.* There have been no suitors in Ray's absence. A couple of mean gropes outside the Victoria Park Hotel. Bob Watkins, the shop floor manager whom she'd once let talk her into lifting up her skirt, thinking stupidly that it might get her extra hours, more shifts doing lighter work. And that he might leave his wife. Instead, she'd barely hung onto her job. Which makes them both pathetic.

Come on out, Egypt. Look who your pathetic mother has brought home: your pathetic father. And we're going to celebrate with some pork chops.

"A bit young for you, isn't he? Or does he like his meat seasoned?"

Laura would laugh in his face but for the thought of Egypt bounding down the stairs and catching her long-lost father cuffing her mother about the mouth.

And here she comes now, bounding down the stairs, all light and life. George beating her to the bottom, skidding on the rag rug placed at the foot of the stairs for precisely this reason. Already Laura's eyes are pricking with tears. Egypt has brushed her hair until it glistens, has pinched her cheeks for colour, and while she's wearing the same clothes she left in this morning for school – not that the girl has much choice otherwise – she has arranged herself a little more provocatively. Her shoulders are back and her chin up, accentuating the curve of her flawless neck. Balanced on the cusp of womanhood and believing herself to be in love, she is quite simply stunning. Poor Egypt.

On catching sight of her father, she falters. Laura's throat swells so painfully she can scarcely draw breath. All her daughter's grace and maturity disappears at once. She looks eleven again. Little else has changed in the cabin from that day six years ago. The furniture is shabbier, the floor scratched up from George's nails. Looking at her now, Laura tries to imagine the weight and substance of such long, sturdy limbs, whether Egypt would feel light or heavy in her arms. How soft the caress of her skin against her cheek. She wishes all over again that she knew how to reach out to her daughter but can sense from the heavy feeling in her belly that it's too late.

Ray takes off his cap, smoothes back his thinning hair. "How's my little Sphinx?"

Egypt remains mute, staring at her father as the air in the room turns to glass.

Not so little anymore, is she?

"Aren't you going to give your old man a hug, then?" He holds his arms out at his sides, part embrace, part shrug. A built-in mechanism for taking the sting out of rejection. Egypt glances at her mother, but Laura can manage only to pull her mouth into a crumpled line. More grimace than smile. There was a time when Egypt would have run full tilt and launched herself at her daddy's small frame. Flung her arms around his neck, all the time squealing like an excited pup. As a child, she would never sleep until he was home. And then she'd drum her heels on her bed and call him, over and over, *DaddyDaddyDaddyDaddyDaddyDaddy-Daddy*, the name a mantra, until he went to her room and sat on the edge of her bed and told her a story. Ray folds his cap in half and pushes his hands back inside his pockets.

"You look good. Better than good even, you look great. Beautiful." The timbre of his voice is returning; he's finding his stride again. "You look like that movie star, doll, you look like Greta Garbo." Egypt's eyes flash in the beginning of a coy smile, but it isn't clear whether it's in response to the compliment or because she recognizes he's trying to manipulate her.

"I'm back now, nothing to worry about, doll."

Egypt is twisting her fingers in her hair and Laura has to strain to hear her daughter's response.

"Back for how long? Back for good?" She shifts her weight from one foot to the other but doesn't move from her spot at the foot of the stairs. In part because George, tail down, ears back, is leaning against her legs, effectively pinning her to the banister.

"Back for however long you like. Yeah, back for good." He claps his hands and rubs them together, chuckles. "That all right with you, missus?"

Laura's eyes throb as she stares at the back wall. Already he's making promises she knows he can't keep. What insanity prompted her to walk back home with him and let him pick up where he took off? Why couldn't she have just stood up to him? Told him to clear off and leave them alone. She's let Egypt down. She's let them both down.

"You don't think that's a good idea?"

"Care now what I think, do you?" She has to unclench her teeth to answer him.

"I've always cared what you think," Ray growls under his breath. "You just weren't always listening." Rumbles issue from the back of George's throat. Laura prays for the dog's sake that he doesn't lunge for Ray.

"I think we should talk after we've all eaten something and had a chance to calm down."

"We'll talk in the morning," Ray rejoins, cementing a place for himself tonight.

The door opens and Laura wrings her hands. Ray's face darkens.

"Who the hell is this?"

Aidan looks from his mother to his sister. "I'm Aidan Fisher," he says. "I live here." And then he walks up to Ray with his hand extended. "Pleased to meet you."

Chapter 10

Ray Fisher exits the cabin – his cabin, won fair and square – and, leaving the door to bang in the wind behind him, strides into the night. *Damn bitch.* He makes his way towards the bridge, hands pushed deep inside his pockets, fingers rubbing a hole in the worn lining, worrying at his fingernails, the bumps and ridges. The urge is on him. An itch at the base of his skull, tightening his scalp. He heads for downtown. Someone must have a game on. Or a fight. Brain firing like a Gatling gun. Manny would know. He doubles back and makes his way down to the water's edge. Unties the skiff and rows quickly to the other side of the canal.

Manny's dozing in his chair. Ray flicks on the light and Manny blinks in the sudden glare from the naked bulb. His eyes red-rimmed and crusty, his face the grey of unfired clay. He rubs his thinning salt-and-pepper hair, and Ray's eye is drawn to the weeping sore on the back of Manny's hand. He's never been the cleanest or sharpest of guys, but the eye-watering stink that Ray has always associated with him – he hesitates to call Manny a friend – has been replaced by the heavier feral stench of rot. Already soaked into the walls. Manny's crummy mausoleum. Still, he rouses himself for the occasion.

"Ray? Ray Fisher? That you?" He pulls himself from his chair when he sees Ray standing in front of him. A small white cat leaps from his lap; shreds of food or dirt scatter in its wake. Ray grins to hide his irritation at the inevitable barrage of, "Where've you been? What you been up to?"

"Around, Manny, you know." A wink, a leer, a flexing of his fingers, and Manny's chuckling. A wet rattling in his old man's chest. Ray has to keep moving, shimmying a measured pace around Manny's cramped quarters. He twists his feet at the grit he can feel through the worn soles of his shoes, grinding it into the linoleum floor. If the cat were still in the room, he would have kicked it by now.

"Sit down, will you? You're giving me a headache with all your dancing around."

Ray spreads his arms and swivels his head. "You only got one chair, Manny."

"Look at you, geez. You haven't changed a bit. Still got ants in your pants."

"Still got the touch, too." He flips a coin inches from Manny's face, snatches it out of the air. "Hear of anything going on?" Breathing slowly through his nose, in and out. Raking his nails through his hair.

"Now you're talking." Manny cracks a grin, taps a forefinger against his nose.

He knew it. Good man. Manny was always the man in the know. Ray feels the night taking on shape, lustre. He turns down the flame on the kerosene heater, a rusted, jerry-built contraption from the last ice age. It's a wonder Manny hasn't set the place ablaze. When he turns around, Manny's still dithering, patting his pockets, shuffling his carpet-slippered feet on the filthy linoleum. Christ. What happened? He's been gone, what, six years? Hardly a lifetime. But just look at the guy. It's all Ray can do to stop himself from frogmarching him to the door.

Manny pulls items from his pockets, looks them over: matches, baccy, pipe.

Christ, he smokes a pipe now. "Need any help there, Manny? Sun'll be up soon at this rate."

"Where's the fire, Ray? Cripes. I'm doing as fast as I can."

Then Ray twigs. "You holding out on me, old man?"

"What?" Manny's jaw hangs slack, his grey eyes rheumy and lost-looking. It's a good act. "Holding out? Don't know what you're on about." His head's wobbling like an ill-fitting castor and Ray tries to follow his gaze. The bottle can't be too far.

"Where is it? Where you hiding it, Manny?" He's laughing now, a half-maniacal cackling that Manny's thin-timbered walls can't absorb. He checks behind the greasy cushion on Manny's chair. Nudges the chair with his foot and Manny's there, elbowing him aside.

"You can move when you want to, eh, Manny?"

"You talking shit again, Fishy boy." He straightens, bottle in hand, and spins the lid free. "I got something for us here. You and me." Lamb's Navy Rum. Manny lifts the bottle of dark liquid to his lips, drinks, takes a breath, drinks again, then wipes his mouth on the back of his sleeve. Ray takes the bottle from his outstretched hand, tips it back but keeps his eyes open, watching Manny watching the bottle and its contents. When the liquid hits his throat he almost spews it back out. The stuff scorches like battery acid. There's no Lamb in that bottle, no matter what the label says. Manny's either into moonshine or someone's ripped him off and he can't tell the difference anymore.

Eventually Ray shepherds Manny outside, but it's like taking a Sunday stroll with a cripple. Ray dribbles a rock down the path a ways, kicks it into the bushes, plucks flat stones from the shoulder of the road and skips them out between the darkened shapes of the boathouses, pauses to listen, setting odds on the number of skips each takes across the water. He can hear Manny wheezing behind him. Ray's been breathing Detroit air a long time, but he's too wound up to take in the fecund scent of bark resin and compost piles, of chicken runs and the packed-earth road, the boggy odour of the marsh shallows that fringe the head of this Great Lake. He's walking backwards, willing Manny's feet to move faster.

"You want me to go on ahead. Tell 'em you're on your way?"

"And have your blood on my hands?"

"Always did exaggerate your own importance. You're not my minder, remember that."

"Stateside air must've rotted your brain some. You left some bad-shit feelings round here. Feelings that've been festering these years since."

"I can take care of myself." But Ray's no fool. Manny's words have hit their mark, settled the blood humming through his veins. He left here with good reason. Stayed away for other ones. His fists tighten in his pockets. Anyone gives him trouble, he's ready. He takes a leak against the back of a shed and hears a rustling, the rapid chinking of uncoiling chain, the rush of a four-legged creature. Ray stands his ground, jaw set, calculating the length of the dog's chain, primed to kick if he's wrong. A thwuck as the chain runs out, a sharp whelp, and a dog starts up a bay so close Ray can feel the heat from its breath. He turns to put himself away and dribbles piss on his shoes. Manny is suddenly there at his shoulder, his voice a low hiss.

"You trying to wake the damn neighbourhood?"

Ray shakes his foot about. "Wake 'em up. We'll have a party."

"People going to want to know where you been."

"That's my business."

Manny's eyes shift away. "They might not see it that way. They got long memories round here."

"Red has a long memory, you mean. Fucking micks. Born hanging on tooth and nail to past grievances."

Manny steps from the dirt road onto a path that is but a trampling of longer grass winding through and around shrubs and small trees towards an old barn on the northernmost edge of the boathouse community.

"Carpenter's place."

"He drowned in the bay last winter, cutting ice. Slipped off the edge and was sucked under before anyone had the chance to realize what was happening let alone try to rescue him. Kids use it in the summer and that."

"And Red McMurray and his Murray men sneak inside during the witching hours."

"Brings a different crowd. And they can use the bridge. Not everyone wants ferrying to Cockpit, 'specially when the water's frigid. There's been late-night tippings."

Silhouetted against the inky sky, the barn shows no chinks of light between the boards, lets no voices echo across the water. But the air feels charged, and Ray fancies he can see the whole building vibrating. He hurries Manny along by his elbow, deaf to the old man's objections, his watery chest.

They are almost on the place before they spot the kid in short pants, a long graze down one shin, sitting on a box upturned against the outside wall. He's peeling bark from the limb of a tree but lifts his eyes at their approach, glances from Manny to Ray and back to Manny again, his face in the moonlight grubby and expressionless.

"He's a friend," Manny says. But the kid drops the stick and slips off the box anyway, disappears inside the barn. Probably felt the back of Red's thick farmer's hand too many times before. Manny follows the kid inside, Ray on his heels, every hair on his body lifting, his senses snapping into overdrive.

Heat. The hum of men's voices. *Five-to-four. Speckled. Six-to-five. Brown.* Air damp as the walls of an underground cave, a soup of piss-smelling sawdust, bird shit and rank sweat, in spite of the lake breeze he can feel pushing between the barn boards. He blinks till his eyes no longer smart, steps into the soft warm light of a hurricane lamp, then ducks sideways into the shadows again. Manny's back, even his silver-white hair, is gone, sucked into the darkness. Ray moves towards the scrum of men. Twenty, maybe thirty of them. Tension threading the cords of his muscles, pulling his nerves tight as piano wire. Circular rows of hay bales form makeshift bleachers, though most everyone on the outer rim is standing, pitched forward at an angle, eyes trained on the pit at the centre. If this were any other place in any other town, Ray would narrow his shoulders and slide his five-foot-six, 125-pound frame between the bigger men blocking his view, inch his way towards those crouched at the front. To smell the blood, brush the feathers from the back of his throat. But he sizes up the crowd first, counting the dimly lit faces, the rounded backs, the upraised hands. There's more than a few might come sniffing around, thinking he's back because he's flush and he owes them.

Pay-up time. Payback. Some new faces; could be kids who've grown up since he's been away. He spots a gentleman farmer from Stoney Creek. Recognizes a couple of coppers. *Always comforting to see Old Bill and some flush toff getting chicken shit on his cashmere coat. Rich and poor spitting in the same sawdust, squatting in the same outhouse. There's no event so egalitarian as a cockfight.*

Manny's an arm's reach away, trading hand signals across the place like he's the tic-tac man at a racecourse. A man steps out of the scrum, all piss and hunched shoulders, and heads in Ray's direction. Ray's hands curl to fists, he pushes out his chest. But the man's anger is directed at the creature in his hands, one bloodied eye swinging from its socket, tracking the ground, the other twitching upwards at its master's scowling face.

"Fucking useless piece of shit." The man whips the bird to the ground and kicks it into the darker edges of the barn. Sees Ray watching, horks up and spits at his feet. Ray's thinking he could send Egypt over in the morning to score the carcass for a meal and then remembers what a squeamish kid she was, wonders if she's grown some backbone at all. The man slumps onto one of the hay bales. Ray gives him a wide berth and slips between the punters on the outer rim.

A collective cry breaks out – half groan, half triumph. A bird lies in a stain of sawdust, its head almost cleaved from its body. The victor spins in dizzying circles before a kid not even old enough to shave scoops him up with a practised movement and tucks the bird's fighting blade out of harm's way. Ray's heart is jack hammering like he's just run the Around the Bay Race. He cranes to catch the bookie's eye.

Henry Stubbs steps into the pit, cradling a copper-bodied bird with blue-black plumage, a flush of white through the centre. Stubbs always handles his own birds, reckons he has a way with them, that they take a cue from his heartbeat, the calm in his hands. The way Ray figures it, a calm bird is the last thing a punter needs. Wired is better. He casts a long glance at the copper bird's opponent. Cream-coloured head and body, with blue-grey tail feathers. Comb and wattles trimmed close, this bird's strutting a strut. Draws a few whistles.

Stubbs steadies the creature while a kid fastens a gaff to the bird's right leg, the fighting blade, three inches of razor-sharp stainless steel. Ray crouches, inhaling sawdust and sweat. Betting on fighting cocks is all instinct. Sure, you can know the owners and what they feed the birds and how they keep and train them, but nothing beats that sure crawl through a person's belly. He's betting on the white fellow. There's a glint in his eye, and that's what Ray watches for. A manic look.

"Good-looking bird," someone says. Hands sign and deal around the ring, the bookie taking coins, bills, promissory notes; a pencil behind his ear, odds scrawled in a notebook. Ray fishes inside his shoe and slips another bill from the stash he filched from Laura's Russian nesting dolls, holds up his hand. The bookie nods. Ray has often thought he could be a bookie. He's quick with calculations – can do them in his head. And he's got a keen memory for faces. But the more successful bookies are bigger fellas or those who can hire a heavy or two to watch their backs. You carry that amount of cash in your pocket, you're a beacon for trouble.

Ray takes his stub and the air tightens around him, his skin cools. People talking, chattering in his ear. Why can't they just shut up? His brain is going to explode. Natter, natter. Owners and handlers talking up their birds. People shouting in each other's faces. Why can't they all just shut up and let the sport commence? Breathes in and out slowly. He wants to climb from his own skin. The only time Ray Fisher feels a measure of peace is when the cards are in his hand, the dogs are on the track, the cocks are in the pit.

The last bet is taken and, for a moment, the place falls still. The handlers approach each other, backs bent, birds held out before them, beak to beak. And then the birds are dropped. A split second contact with the ground before they're a blur of blood and flying feathers, a screech that could split your skull. Quickly, the white bird gains advantage, leaping into the air, wings spread to balance himself as he bucks and slashes at his opponent, kicking for all he's worth, one claw, one lethal foot. Claw, blade, claw, blade – then thrusting his head forward to peck at the copper bird's eyes, his throat, whenever he gets the chance. From the outset, Stubbs' bird is on the defensive and within seconds has fallen back, mortally wounded. Stubbs tries on the look of the resigned, but he's a lousy actor, too emotional for this business as far as Ray's concerned. Occasionally a bird will act submissive, or seem to give up, in which case the pair are picked up and held face to face again to egg the fighting on. *At least your bird fought back*, someone should tell him, *no shame in that*. But Stubbs would rather wallow in pity, hogging the stage a while longer, his shoulders slumped in defeat as he stoops to swing his copper pride by the feet, slack as a bag of weighted feathers. Another creature bound for the soup pot.

Ray stands and pockets his winnings. Limbering up. The next pair of handlers enters the ring, birds under their arms. The odds are set, the gaffs fastened. It's going to be a sweet night. Ray rubs his hands together.

"Well, well, well, look who it isn't."

Before Ray can place the voice, before he can turn to look the speaker in the eye, a brass-knuckled fist drives into the back of his skull and knocks him sprawling into the ring. His hat flies off. Shit and sawdust in his mouth. Birds squawk and flap their wings; claws scrabble at his bruised head.

"Wait till the pit's clear, asshole," someone grunts. A medley of jeering and curses follows as men chase down the birds, hoping to scoop them from harm's way. Ray's assailant crushes his hand beneath a heavy workboot; the pain threatens to loosen his bowels. A vile puddle of chewing tobacco phlegm hits him in the back of his head and slides, warm and viscous, around his ear and down the front of his neck.

"Didn't think you'd show your ugly face round here again." Red. Ray thinks of cracking a joke but knows better. There isn't a casual person in this building. Everyone's deadly serious.

"Thought it was about time you paid a visit to the wife and kids, did you?"

"Heard she was banging the drifter. Heard the girl was too." Adenoids. Or a mashed-up nose. Must be Red's goon. The keeper of the brass knuckles. The Mick never does his own dirty work.

Red leans in close. "No one likes a cut-and-run man, Fisher. This place is too small. But I'm guessing you already figured that. Where've you been hiding your skinny arse?" Ray tries shifting his nose out of range of Red's foul breath without making it seem like a rebuff. Red's a sensitive sort. Liable to break your teeth if he thinks you looked at him the wrong way.

"Been out of town on business, Red."

"Sure you have, Fisher. You got coin?" Ray indicates he needs his hand and the boot lifts off. Sliding his throbbing fingers into his pocket, he pulls out a roll. Red snatches it from him and peels the real notes from the outside. "Oldest con in the world," he says, tossing the roll of paper blanks at his head. "Thought you were smarter than that."

I am, Ray thinks, rubbing his toes against the rest of Laura's notes. *You'd think she'd have found a new hiding place. Dumb bitch.* The goon's hands rifle through his pockets and then jerk free his boots.

"Nice hiding place, in your shit-stinking socks. We'll call this a down payment, shall we?"

Fuck. What the fuck was he thinking? Lying here eating bird shit, nearly pissing his pants. Where the fuck is Manny when a fella needs a friend? Ray sucks in a breath as hands grab the back of his jacket and yank him to standing. He's a rag doll, knees of water, head light with fear. Pain radiates down his spine as he struggles to find his balance once his feet touch the ground. Catches a flash of iridescent feathers from the corner of his eye. Too late. He staggers into the man cradling his bird and bowls him over. The crowd backs away as the handler, unwilling to part with his prize, his pet, his means to the good life, topples like a pin. His hands shoot out too late to break his fall and he lands on the bird. The bird kicks out instinctively with his feet, gaff honed to the sharpness of a butcher's cleaver.

The cut is clean. And deep. Ray, on his hands and knees, swears he can hear it, like a soft puncture. A man with a slashed larynx can make no other kind of noise. The man's blood, dark and sluggish, empties into the sawdust, staining it black as oil. The barn throbs with the sounds of shallow breathing, shuffling feet. Even the murderous bird has fallen silent. Fear clogs the air, drips along the rough-hewn walls, condenses on the brows of the gathered men. Who will kick the pebble from the dike? Whoever makes the first move will set in motion the course of events to follow: reprisals, the law, the newspapers, jail, revenge. Seconds pass. A minute. Then a creak from the door rents the air, a ribbon of cold through the men's legs as the first to gather their wits take their leave. Probably the two off-duty chickenshit cops, protecting their reputations and their jobs. More men make for the door, and while others yell for order, Ray seizes his own opportunity and lunges for the squawking bird, rudderless in the pit. Recoils as pain sears the palm of his left hand. *Jesus-fuckingmarymotheroffuckingchrist.* Curled up in the sawdust, hand clamped under his armpit, he can feel the pump of blood from the wound, warm and wet through the lining of his jacket sleeve. Leans on his elbow, pukes pain in a thin stream of bile. Wipes his mouth on the back of his sleeve.

"He dead?"

"May as well be. By the time help gets here."

The bird man's legs twitch a response; his body convulses and then stills. Blood blooms around his head and shoulders, a dark poppy.

"Who's gonna fetch the police?"

"They just left, brother."

Someone laughs.

"Don't be a smart-ass. You want the goddamned police down here?"

"What were you planning on doing with him? Tying rocks to his legs and dumping him in the water?"

"Sounds like a plan."

"I said, you want the cops crawling all over this place?"

"Got a better idea, asshole?"

"Anyone got a boat?"

"Who is he, anyway?

"You mean who's likely to come looking for him?"

The men lapse into silence again. Ray unfurls his legs, rises in a fog of pain and begins backing away. Stumbles against a brick of a man. *Red.*

"Not back in the place five minutes and you've got everyone set against each other." Hissing in his ear.

"Wasn't my fault."

"Nothing's ever your fault, is it, Fisher?"

"Fuck you." Ray struggles to brush himself down.

"When you gonna learn you don't shit on your own doorstep?"

"Fuck the lot of you." That goon especially. Manny is nowhere in sight but Ray doesn't care. Shoeless, cradling his injured hand, he aims for the light by the door and staggers into the cold night.

To Ray's relief, the kid sitting outside has cleared off. Grabbing his abandoned stick, Ray slips down the opposite side of the barn. His hand is throbbing like the devil, the rest of him a fevered trembling. He pulls his shirt from his shoulders and with his teeth and his one good hand tears the soft cotton into strips and binds the cut tight. Head back against the side of the barn, he gulps air till the knocking in his chest subsides. A few others stumble outside into the frosty night, Cashmere Man amongst them, his long coat flapping at his legs as he hurries along the path. Two men approach and Ray presses himself against the barn wall as they unbutton themselves to take a leak into the bushes. He waits. Someone else leaves, weaving drunkenly into the dark. He waits some more until finally the door opens and Red's henchman appears.

Ray waits till the man has his dick out then creeps up behind him.

"Hey, peckerface," he whispers loudly. Ray takes aim as the goon turns, swinging the stick two-fisted in an arc that ends at a point beyond his thuggish face. His nose explodes with a wet crunch and he sails backwards to land in the mud. Ray straddles his chest and, squeezing his good hand around the man's greasy throat, leans in and growls all his pent-up rage – from the grim and bloody streets of Ancoats, Manchester, where he was dragged up, to the dark years in Detroit, to the disappointment on his wife's face. Spits in the goon's open mouth, shakes him, blood warm and sticky. So much blood. Shakes him again. It's a slow dawning.

Ray has been drinking, flush with winning, adrenalin has scorched his veins. He can't think through the noise in his head. *Shit. Shit. Shit.* Lowers his ear to a slack mouth, pushes his fingers against a still neck. Rears back and scrambles from the body. *Shit. How the hell? It was a tap.* He spins in a circle. What to do? Red will want his blood. His balls in a vice. His head over a chip pan. *Run.* Should he run? What about the body? Two bodies in one night. Red'll be out here any second. What to do? It's curtains for Ray Fisher. He doesn't know his own strength. The cut across his hand pounds.

The water is too far off, the ground too cold for a barefooted man with one hand and a dead weight to drag. The longest fifteen, twenty yards in Ray's memory. He dry retches halfway there, his stomach twisted inside out, and lies quivering face down in the hoarfrost every time men step outside to relieve themselves or reel towards home. Then the posse in charge of the bird-handler's body emerges. He hasn't the brains he was born with. What was he thinking? They'll be on him any second. For an agonizing quarter of an hour, he lies still as a rock as the ground sucks every shred of heat from his body, his ears strained for the sounds of Red's Belfast brogue. Manic whispers. Someone has a launch moored bayside. Ray's heart leaves his throat. The men shuffle slowly away.

At the water's edge, Ray pulls off the henchman's shoes, still warm, and slips his own sorry, cold feet inside them. Rifles through the dead man's clothes, empties his pockets – wallet, cigarette case, lighter, switchblade – and fills them with as many stones as will fit. Takes the blade, hands raised high, and brings it down hard just below the rib cage, pushes and grinds, listens for escaping air. Not everything you learn inside can get you killed. Sometimes it might just save your life. One last glance back at the barn before he rolls the body face down into the marsh and then pushes it out into the water with the stick. When it finally sinks out of sight, he hurls the stick into the bush and, nursing his throbbing hand, heads back to Manny's place.

Chapter 11

Egypt sits with her knees hugged to her chest, shins pressed against the table edge, and watches her mother from behind the veil of her hair. Blurred. Slamming cupboard doors, banging pots and dishes. Laura marches back to the wash basin and repeats her earlier scrabble through the mess of Russian dolls, lipstick tubes, envelopes, hair clips and pencils that sits on the odds-and-ends shelf below the mirror. Aidan watches Egypt pushing the cooling lumps of porridge around her bowl. She throws him a warning glance and then gathers a spoonful and dangles it beneath the table. George pads over to investigate, sniffs and flops down again by her feet. When Aidan giggles, she glares at him. Then at her mother's back.

"So did you kick him out or did he leave again?" Her words part the air and free-fall slowly, landing with such a force that she stares at the kitchen floor, expecting to see a small crater. Her mother leans across the table and pulls Egypt's hair back from her face.

"Your father has always marched to his own drummer." Egypt recoils from her sour breath, her ragged, chewed-on lips. "And if you believe anything I have ever done or said has any influence on whether he comes or goes, then you haven't been paying proper attention."

"I heard everything you said last night."

"No, you just think you heard everything. Aidan, go back upstairs while I talk to your sister."

"But –"

"But nothing. Go."

"But I can hear everything you're saying from upstairs anyway," he mumbles, dragging his feet towards the stairs.

"Now both my children talk back to me," she says when Aidan has finished thudding up the stairs. "I suppose I have you to thank for that?" She's back to searching drawers, inside the tea caddy, the pockets of jackets hanging by the door.

"And who do we thank for our absent father?"

"You're being unfair, Egypt. No one knows him like I do. No one has had to live with him year in and year out like I have."

"I've lived with him," Egypt mumbles to George, hunkered beneath the table, head buried between his long, shaggy paws.

"The man just swoops in here and everyone falls for his charm and his patter. *Oh, Ray's such a card. He could charm the birds from the trees, the notes from your billfold.* And as always, I'm expected to smile and pretend everything is normal while he runs around talking the talk and wreaking havoc with our lives."

"He only got here last night."

"Exactly."

"Now who's being unfair?"

"You have no idea what you're talking about."

"So why did you marry him if you hate him so much?"

"Because I was too damned young and naïve to know what I was getting myself into, that's why."

They retreat to their corners while Laura's cussing struts the room, a bird with its first flush of showy feathers. Egypt recovers first.

"Everything was fine at suppertime, and then you must have gone and ruined it somehow." Porridgeless, her insides cramp and whine.

"I ruined supper? You must have been sitting at a different table from the one I was at."

In a way she was, because while he looked and sounded like Ray, the man seated opposite her last night was not the same man she remembered as her father. But at this point, lashing out is easier than admitting her mother might be right. Ray ignored Aidan completely. With Egypt, he managed a perfunctory question or two about school – how did she like her teachers? Was she strict with her students? – but seemed too distracted and edgy to do much with her answers beyond lobbing the odd *When I was your age* rib about her still being a student. A brooding silence elbowed its way to the table. And then, out of the sky, he launched into an attack on councillors and aldermen and politicians who used their public position to protect and further their private interests. He'd heard about the plans for the new bridge – *how?* Egypt wanted to ask, when he didn't even know of Aidan's existence, or that she was in teacher training – and wanted to know if the city had been talking expropriation or evictions – questions no one could answer. It was like sitting with a dangerous animal. When, heart clenched, she dared to ask him about Detroit, he launched enthusiastically into a story about the salt mines tunneled out beneath the city, where he'd first worked, but within minutes had segued to some argument he'd had with a foreman or supervisor someplace else. The man with all the keys. *A cruel bastard*, he called him, eyes glittering dangerously. By the end of his tale he was stabbing at his dinner and muttering revenge threats about some man called Tommy and his boys. *Detroit thugs*. She could see the words dangling from her mother's lips.

Aidan sat pale and silent. Egypt couldn't eat: the pork chops her father had made such a big deal over like sawdust in her mouth. Complaining of stomach ache, she left the table for the balm of her room – her air, her belongings. Although even there, everything felt already transmuted, changed somehow by Ray's presence. As if with his reappearance her world had shifted onto an altered plane. Sometime after ten o'clock the door slammed, shaking the cabin. Egypt pressed herself against the window, hoping to see him leave, but the darkness swallowed his slight form as soon as he stepped through the gate.

She could have sworn she lay awake the whole night but must have fallen asleep before her mother ventured up the stairs to bed.

"Where did he go?"

"I have no idea, Egypt. You'll have to ask him when you see him. Just don't expect a straight answer."

"Where's he been all this time?"

"Again, I don't know. I don't want to know."

"Well, maybe I do."

"It's not that simple, Egypt. Sometimes we're better off not knowing."

"I'm going to ask him anyway," she says, watching her mother's face. But she won't. The way he was ranting about Detroit sent splinters of fear through her belly.

"I wish you wouldn't."

"So what were you arguing about?"

"I don't think that's any of your business."

"It is if you were arguing about me."

"We weren't arguing about you."

"Aidan. You were arguing about Aidan. Dad didn't even know about him until last night, did he?"

"Egypt, please, my head is pounding." She pinches the bridge of her nose. Her eyes are puffy, the pupils narrowed with pain – the same headache clawing at Egypt's temples: too much emotion, not enough sleep – and shadowed by dark circles that appear darker still because her mother looks so wan, so bleached out. "We'll talk about this when I get home."

No, we won't, Egypt thinks. They never do. It's just something her mother says but doesn't mean. A lie. They'll carry on as before, ignoring the elephant in the room.

"You should be getting yourself ready for school."

She can't face the place, feels pinned to her chair with inertia. Besides, it's Thursday, and in spite of the tips she's gleaned from Gloria over the past weeks, Egypt is once again woefully unprepared to stand in front of a classroom filled with bored and sniggering children. She feels hollowed out, as if everything she ever knew about teaching has been scraped from her head along with the set of responses she had to the people in her life and the pattern of her days. Bed beckons, and she longs to bury her aching head in the stale sheets.

"Get a move on. I'll walk you there."

"You'll be late for work."

"So hurry up."

When they reach the top of the footpath, Egypt's heart lifts. There's Ray, sitting on the boulder. Waiting for her? He jumps to his feet and Laura tightens her grip on Aidan's hand and picks up her pace. Egypt hangs back, glad to be free of her oppressive anger, the chance to talk to her father without the weight of her mother's solicitude bearing down. Still, she's unsure whether to be smiling or not as she approaches.

He pulls off his hat, waves it with a flourish and bows. "How's my beautiful little Sphinx this bright morning?"

"Good." She can't help but smile in response to his broad grin, his theatrics. He's larger than life this morning, more animated, as if he's grown a couple of inches in the night. Could be it's because her mother isn't around, spoiling things. Already Egypt likes this version of Ray a whole lot better. As father and daughter draw closer, however, a different picture emerges.

"You look tired." With his bloodshot eyes and wrinkled clothes, he looks like he's been in a fight, or slept rough. Or both. A barnyard stench of piss and wet sawdust seeps from his clothing, pushing her back a step. His skin is sallow and waxy looking, the stubble on his chin flecked with grey. He stuffs his hands in his jacket pockets, but not before she spots a makeshift bandage peeking from the cuff of his left sleeve. Questions prickle the back of her throat. Her toes curl in her shoes.

"You okay?"

"All the better for basking in your beauty, kiddo." She wants to smile again. Does he really think she's beautiful? That she looks like Greta Garbo? Does Matt see the resemblance? Should she ask him? If her mother hadn't marched her out the door this morning, she might have spent some time before the mirror, trying on her lipstick, arranging her hair with the part to the side.

"I didn't hear you leave last night," she lies.

"That's because I'm light on my feet, my sweet." But the lie is on his feet, his shoes – different from yesterday's boots – several sizes too big. Egypt's cheeks blaze. A palpable awkwardness settles between them.

"What are you doing here?"

"Waiting for you, of course." Though it's what she wants to hear, the words elicit no warm, fuzzy glow inside. Is he lying, or has her mother poisoned her mind?

"I'll walk you to school if you like."

Egypt fashions her most grown-up face. "I was thinking of giving it a miss."

"You're halfway there already."

"Not halfway. Less than a quarter, probably."

"Miss Exact. You were always correcting your friends. You remember that?"

"They were always correcting me."

He pulls out his pouch of tobacco and papers. "Know how to roll one of these?"

"No."

"Right." He tucks the pouch back inside his pocket, stamps his clown feet in the cold.

"Anyway," she says, "I was wondering if maybe we could do something together. Today. Now, I mean." But even as the words are leaving her mouth, Egypt isn't convinced it's what she wants. Dinner was challenge enough; a whole morning and afternoon with Ray, watching what she says, trying not to trip his temper, would be exhausting. Far easier just to stay home in bed and daydream the ideal day. And yet a part of her wants to reach out to him, include him, make him feel that she needs and wants him around, especially as her mother clearly doesn't. "We could take the James Street Incline, walk along the mountain. It's clear, the view will be spectacular."

His mouth twists in a crooked line as if he's thinking long and hard on her offer. "It sounds like a right good idea, lass, but I'm a bit tied up at the moment." He has to see a man about a dog. That's something she remembers. Also, that his Manchester accent is strongest when he is caught off guard and trying to squirm out of something. She's tempted to remind him, but from the pressure building at the base of her throat, she knows that her voice will betray her.

"Look at her." Ray is staring at her mother hurrying past the cemetery on her way to work, her tight-hipped steps. "She can't get away from me quickly enough."

"She's mad at you for showing up after all these years."

"Are you mad at me?"

"Of course not." Egypt glances back at him and smiles, but when her cheeks begin to quiver, she glares at her feet and blinks a lot.

"That's good to know, kiddo." He gives her a playful thump on her shoulder. She wants to take his arm for reassurance, thinks about it, but can't seem to lift her own arm – numb or heavy or both – from her side.

A whistling from the footpath and she turns to see Mick Long and, as ever, slouched two steps behind him, Joey Payne.

"Morning, Egypt." Mick's eyes slide over Egypt like oil, while Joey's, in utter hopefulness, rest a little longer. Mick nods in her dad's general direction. "Ray."

Egypt can't decide whether to laugh out loud or slap his face. Mick Long was still in short pants the last time he saw her dad, still lining up games of conkers and marbles. And suddenly he thinks he's the big man.

"What about your education?" Ray continues, as if he hadn't sidetracked their earlier conversation, as if the boys weren't even present. "That fancy teaching job you're after." In other words, *no*. The Incline Railway isn't a part of today's plans.

"You want to get yourself off to school." Mick's parting shot, in startling imitation not only of Ray's accent but also his gravelly drinking-

and-smoking-the-night-away timbre, and softened only by Joey's one-shouldered shrug, his wry smile.

They walk in silence a while past the cemetery, Egypt shuffling until she matches her footsteps to her father's, hobbled by his odd and unexplained footwear.

"I used to work at the Anderson's Hotel here when you were small." He waves at a section of empty green space where some trees have grown and a few headstones now lie.

"I know, you've told me before."

"Your old man's getting boring is he?"

"Never," she says, shaking her head.

"Hey," he nudges her with his elbow, "remember Leo the Lion?" He chins towards Dundurn Castle where the zoo used to be. "We'd hear him roar in the mornings sometimes and you'd be so scared." His laugh turns into a chesty cough. "You used to ask me if I'd wrestle him if he escaped and came looking for little girls to eat."

What Egypt remembers is Ray telling this story over and over. In her memory, Leo, who died when she was eight years old, always looked flea-bitten and bored; nothing at all like the majestic creatures she'd seen in picture books at the library, and hardly the stuff of nightmares.

"Remember? Remember how scared you were?"

"Yeah, I remember."

They turn down Dundurn Street, and as they draw closer to the school, Egypt feels a growing petulance. Why couldn't they take someone's boat out on the bay? It isn't *that* cold. Or spend the day at Dundurn Castle? She hasn't seen the aviary, though it's been there over two years. And yet . . . and yet, though she has missed him fiercely at times and believes she would gladly march into school and parade him before all those who have scorned her in the past – whether to her face or behind her back – for being fatherless, for being abandoned, a part of her can't help but wish that he were taller, more successful looking, and that he didn't stink of last night's revelry.

On Lamoreaux Street she slows her pace, willing the bell to ring before school comes into view.

Ray leans back against the gatepost on the edge of the school grounds and pulls a crushed packet of Murad Turkish cigarettes from his coat pocket and lights one. She bats at clouds of foreign, oily smoke. They smell so much worse than the ones he usually rolls. He's wound his way back to last night's story about the man who had it in for him, but she lost the thread a while ago. She scuffs her already scuffed shoes in the dirt. It's all she can do to nod and smile in the right places. Without turning her head or appearing obvious, she strains to see whether anyone she knows is watching them. The effort blurs her vision, and the back of her throat contracts in a painful urge to cry. How can she both want him here and wish him as far away as possible? Her mother can make her cringe in embarrassment with the things that come out of her mouth, the way she still shepherds Egypt across streets as if she were Aidan's age. But the level of shame she feels in Ray's presence is entirely new. And disturbing.

Egypt has imagined her father's return for so long now that it's nearly impossible to reconcile his dishevelled and twitchy reality with her daydreaming. He would show up outside school waiting for her; Laura would be the one surprised at home as they arrived together, laughing over an earlier joke or a shared understanding. He'd be leaning against a shiny new truck, sometimes a car. He even nosed up to the cabin deck a few times in a sleek mahogany racing boat. Clean-shaven, he was smartly, if not sharply, dressed. But above all, he was contrite; he smothered her with hugs and kisses, pulled out a crisp white cotton handkerchief, dabbed at her eyes and held her fast, rocking her slowly from side to side and crooning her favourite lullaby until her tears dried. Her eyes slide over the figure her father cuts. The idea of Ray hugging her – the dirt crusted around his fingernails could well be dried blood – leaves her faintly repulsed.

Egypt spends the morning in a fog, only vaguely aware of Miss Summers' displeasure – a sharpened tone here and there, a general reprimand of the class. She breaks the chalk dotting her i's and crossing her t's. At morning recess, Egypt steps outside both hoping to see Ray and planning to chase him off if she does. After circling the block, she crosses the road to stroll the edge of the park. Within moments, as if she's been awaiting her reappearance, Gloria is walking beside her. Despite the sharp morning air, Gloria pulls off her gloves. A silver charm bracelet hangs loosely about her left wrist. Jewellery is forbidden at school, and while she seems too conscious of the way she holds her hand – *too show-offy*, Egypt's mother would say – once again Gloria rises a little in Egypt's estimation. Gloria shakes her wrist so that the bracelet spins around; she smiles in a self-satisfied way, as if soaking up a compliment.

"Did you see my new charm?" She holds her wrist before Egypt's face, jiggles it.

"Which one's that, then?" Gloria's done it again, roped her into a conversation about jewellery. She must be a master of manipulation.

"The entwined hearts. Philip gave it to me. Pretty, isn't it?"

"He's in town again?"

"No. He sent it by mail." She turns an earnest gaze on Egypt. "He's getting engaged. He's bringing Cassandra home to meet us at Christmas."

Cassandra. A society girl's name. If the charm is a birthday gift, Egypt would rather not know. She cannot muster the bonhomie to sing "Happy Birthday." The effort required for small talk is already draining her. Over Gloria's shoulder, she spots a clutch of model-school kids approaching. They saunter onto the path in front of the girls and form a semicircle, blocking their way. In spite of their diminutive size, they feel menacing.

"That your old man at the school gates this morning?" the one in the middle says.

Egypt scans their prepubescent faces, pale and angular. The ringleader has pouty, dark red lips, as if someone's been sucking on them.

"What if it was?" Now she has to answer to eleven-year-olds? Worse, eleven-year-olds she's supposed to be standing in front of this afternoon for a peer teaching evaluation. Mick Long is probably behind this. She wouldn't be surprised if he were hiding behind a tree, watching.

"You know how he got that cut on his hand?"

"Sure I do." Sawdust in her mouth.

"Sure you do." The kid with the bee-stung lips looks back at his friends for encouragement and on cue, they start laughing. "Got his ass kicked at a fight. A *cock*fight."

They move off in a whooping, back-slapping bunch.

Before Gloria can weigh in on her father's resurrection from the dead, Egypt holds up her hand. "Don't say anything. Please." She strides away along the circumference of the park, Gloria following behind, the crunch of her smart shoes on the cinder track an echo of Egypt's shabby pair. And then Egypt veers for home.

Chapter 12

Either Ray Fisher likes to take an early morning constitutional or Laura kicked him out and he spent the night elsewhere. Matt's betting it's the latter, and smirks at the figure Fisher cuts, jouncing along the path like he's walking on the balls of his feet. *He probably thinks it makes him look taller.* Suddenly, Fisher stops and turns to stare up at where Matt is standing in the window of Neil Byrd's old room. He ducks behind the curtain, but Fisher saw him for sure. *What manner of beast has eyes in the back of its head?*

Joanna calls up the staircase; his breakfast is ready.

"Coming!" He shuffles his feet so she thinks he's getting ready and approaches the window again.

"What are you doing up there?"

"Nothing." *Spying on your neighbours.* Fisher is nowhere to be seen and yet still he can feel the man's hostility prickling under his skin. Staring over at the cabin for signs of Laura, for Egypt and the boy, Matt counts off the seconds. Two minutes. Four. Has he missed them? Five.

"It's getting cold!"

"Just finding my socks!"

He can't tear himself away from the window. Ever since he crossed paths with Ray Fisher in the dark last night, Matt has felt uneasy, his insides coiled.

And there they are at last, mother and children leaving, unusually, together, Aidan running in front, tripping over his too-big gumboots. He smiles, relief flooding through him, along with something else: a frisson of excitement that he brushes off as sleep deprivation, an overactive imagination. A side effect of being on the road a long time. By the middle of last night, he'd managed to convince himself that Fisher had committed some act of evil – threatened his family, made prisoners of them. Or worse. The three Fishers grow smaller as he follows the path they climb under the steel frets of first the rail and then the road bridges to York Street. Just as he's about to turn away, a fourth figure joins them. Fisher. Lying in wait, having hidden out in a shallow grave somewhere.

So what? A man should be allowed to talk to his own family without other people interfering, thinking they know better. It's no business of yours, he tells himself. *Go eat your breakfast*. Maybe it's time he was moving on.

"There you are. I was ready to send out a search party." Joanna is standing at the stove, mashing the tea. The kitchen window is filled with condensation from the boiling kettle. He's about to respond with something glib when she turns to face him. The strain behind her smile is palpable. And it hits him. The inquest. His eyes flick to the clock on the sideboard. Less than two hours away. How could it have slipped his mind? Stan's chair is empty. No surprise. He's probably been holed up in his shed since before dawn, sharpening his chisels and drill bits, sizing all his screws and whatever else he can find to get up to out there.

"I baked you some biscuits. And there's a soft-boiled egg which has probably gone hard by now." Her voice scolds but he senses she's more relieved to have his company than she is angry with him.

"You sound just like my mom, Mrs. B."

"She was a good woman, your mother."

"The best."

"She must have been proud of you."

"As a peacock, Mrs. B." She doesn't know how right she is. All his mother's pride is past. Joanna's hands shake as she pours tea into two mugs.

"You sleep okay?" he asks.

"I'm fine. Don't you go fretting over me."

"It's going to be okay, you know." He takes a draft of scalding tea to punish his patronizing tongue. She deserves better from him. He should have been downstairs an hour ago, entertaining her with stories of his travels, making her laugh. Now when she most needs it, he can't conjure a single tale to distract her with. He's kidding himself if he thinks he can move on. Not yet, not while he's still in her debt.

The first couple of nights with the Byrds, Matt had been on guard, wound up from being on the road and worried Farrell and his thugs would show up again. And then he fell ill. It must have been that stupid stunt in the water. Not the first time he'd been waylaid by a pretty face. Or an overexcited dog. It felt like something from the lake had crawled inside his bones and set them on fire. At first he was barely conscious of his surroundings. Every now and then Joanna's voice would filter through, but his mind would set her words in the mouths of any number of women he'd met along the way. Sometimes his sisters. His mother. Vaguely he was aware of the cool washcloths Joanna placed on his forehead, the teas and broths she made him drink. Then she'd leave and he'd fall at once into a bizarre hallucinatory state – images from his childhood jostled alongside the dismal and cramped insides of boxcars. He was convinced that Buddy, the scrappy black-and-white terrier he'd had as a kid and whom he hadn't thought of in years, was standing on his chest, tail wagging, barking hot breath in his face. Buddy could hear Matt's eyelids open. His sisters, four strong and capable women, stood huddled at the foot of his bed, talking in hushed voices.

When the fever broke, he woke to the smell of sick air and carbolic soap laid over the rank smell of his own unwashed body. Joanna leaned out of an overstuffed armchair towards him – had it been there before? A blanket lay over her legs, a Bible in her hands.

"You're awake."

She sounded so relieved, so filled with gratitude, that he was embarrassed by the sudden intimacy of the situation. He tried to sit up but his limbs, spongy and useless, would have none of it. He fell into a spate of apologies, trying to work out how long he'd been lying there, how long she'd been playing nursemaid to two invalids – was Stan still laid up? – but his mind was as rubbery and uncooperative as his body. He was at a loss how to respond to her, to the closeness she had assumed in his illness. He'd been delirious, she told him, leaning forward to check his temperature, the back of her hand grazing his brow. *How delirious? Loose-lipped delirious?* Matt searched her face for how much he might have revealed, worried he might have mentioned Earl Todd, exposed the shady details of their log-salvage business. Log theft. Or worse, talked about the day Earl went missing. He'd admitted to Laura Fisher he wasn't Myrtle Todd's grandson, but how much did Joanna know? When he stirred again that evening, she fed him soup and then plucked *The Wind in the Willows* from her son's bookshelf, opened to a third of the way and began reading. He felt awkward at first, embarrassed to be listening to a children's story, and a little sad, thinking of her son who was just a kid when he'd been conscripted to die overseas. But Joanna read well, her voice so melodious, so impassioned and clear, that he soon found himself caught up in the antics of Rat and Mole, messing about in boats. And in her act he sensed Joanna's need to hang onto her son's childhood, to keep at bay visions of him torn to pieces in Flanders mud, impaled on barbed wire in no man's land. Rat and Mole's antics made it easier for Matt to play ailing son to her doting mother.

She hands him a plate piled high with fried scones and the over-cooked egg, now peeled and quartered.

"What about Stan?"

"Don't worry yourself. There's plenty extra. Not that I can get him to eat a thing this morning anyhow. These headaches of his, you know," she says, stirring sugar into her tea, a luxury Matt has long since lost the taste for. "He says he can't get a wink's sleep. Not to mention he had another rough night with his breathing."

Matt nods in part sympathy. Stan's battered nose will never sit straight on his face again, and the old man's snoring saws through his dreams at night, leaving him tense and frayed by morning. Sometimes,

Matt believes the snoring is a form of retribution, Stan's way of evening the score between them. Around the time Matt emerged from his fever, all fuzzy-headed and weak, someone from the company showed up at the door to tell Stan that he'd been suspended from his duties pending the inquest. "Fired, you mean?" Stan shot back, but the official busied himself shuffling papers in his briefcase and wouldn't meet the old man's burning stare. Stan had told him the story himself when he first left his sickbed, back when it looked like the two of them might become friends.

As soon as he felt strong enough, Matt was outside trapping rabbits and catching fish to supplement the dinner table. He even took down a deer with the old man's rifle, which, skinned and butchered, Joanna used to barter for staples and pay Stan's doctor's bill. But his contributions received at best a grumbling thanks. His virility underscored the old man's weakness, and as Stan's face healed, so too did his pride. Now Matt catches the odd surly glance cast his way, hears Stan griping about freeloaders and handouts. Every time he leaves the house he expects to find his bag packed and waiting for him on his return.

Suddenly he wishes his sisters were here with their inimitable good cheer, their chattiness, the air of excitement they always carry with them into a room. They would round up Joanna's gloom and send it packing. She doesn't even know he has sisters. And he can't tell her now. He's spent so long resisting any woman's attempts to draw out the pieces of his past that it's become a habit he doesn't know how to break.

Joanna fills the sink with soapy hot water and lowers her hands into the suds. Matt reaches for another scone.

"I feel for the mother, you know," she says, catching him off guard. "Mrs. Farrell."

"Of course you do," Matt says, though he's surprised by the turn of conversation.

"It's hard to lose a son."

"It's hard to lose any child. I would think," he adds into her silence.

"When we lost Neil, when the telegram arrived, I thought the whole neighbourhood could hear my heart breaking." Matt shifts in his chair.

"When you lose a child, all your hope goes with him. I didn't get out of bed for a month. Wasted away to nothing. So did Stan." She lifts the cookie sheet from the water and gives it a quick wipe with the dishcloth. "He had no one to cook for him." *Was that a joke?* He wishes she'd turn and look at him so he could get a better gauge of her mood. Of how he should react.

"But you survived, right? You're here now, talking with me." He glances towards the door. Stan is going to step inside any minute and tell her it's time they were going.

"Depends on what you mean by survived. You know, I often wish it was me who'd been taken instead, just so my Neil could have married and had children of his own; so he could have watched them grow up and have their own children. The way things are supposed to be."

When she faces him, there's a softness about her expression that he's learned to recognize. He girds himself.

"Seems everyone's lost someone in the war." She pulls her mouth into an upside-down smile and folds the tea towel against her belly. It's his cue to speak, to fill her in on the terrible tragedies the war visited upon the Oakes family. But life has shaped Matt differently. Though it twisted his father so that he was barely recognizable, it's a long stretch to blame the war for Matt's troubles. War is amorphous, a huge machinery with ill-defined edges. Hardly the same as blaming a person. Not at all the same as blaming yourself. She reaches for the plate he's finished with and turns back to her dishes.

"And some families make wars of their own," she offers, with more prescience than she knows, and then asks him if he misses his.

"It's been a while," he says non-committally.

"Everyone who comes here is either running to or running from something," she says, wiping down the table, keeping her eyes averted.

A buzzing sound has started up in the back of Matt's head. "I like the water," he says eventually, when her back is to him again. He licks at his lips, his tongue dry. The taste of the river. Something he thought he'd never be rid of. And for a time, he believed he'd never be able to go near water again, but it drew him all the same. The water here, lapping at the stilts of this straggle of homes in the calm and shallow end of a protected bay, he can live with. And some mornings, standing at the shoreline, staring at the glass-like surface, the colours of the rising sun reflected there, he can almost believe it isn't the same element.

His snares are empty. Maybe the rabbits around here have grown wise to his loops of wire; they smell his human stink, little rabbit minds peppered with images of their writhing, twitching brethren. Maybe they've moved on, though he knows this isn't likely. He kneels to set them again. Trapping with a snare is less an art form than it is sheer luck, and half the daylight is gone already. He might have to take the Fishers' skiff and see if the fish are biting. It's important there's a hearty meal on the Byrds' dinner table tonight; he could be in for a long night of consoling.

He opens the door, intending only to reach in for his rod, leaned up against the wall by the coat rack, but the air inside feels charged, raises the hair on the back of his neck. He steps inside. Ray Fisher. Leaning back in one of the pressboard chairs – Stan's chair as a matter of fact – his face a blank menace. He must have been watching the house. Waiting for the Byrds to leave. A gear switches in Matt's head. This skinny shit's been spying on him. Matt's fists are clenched so tight he thinks his skin might split. In three strides he's crossed the room, ready to lunge for Fisher's grubby neck when he spots a switchblade sticking out of the tabletop, its point buried deep in the grain. No prizes for guessing who emptied his snares. Fisher works the handle of the knife back and forth, gouging the polished wooden surface some more.

"What are you doing here?" Matt struggles to keep his voice even, the muscles in his throat clenched like a straining winch.

"Passing on a message."

A bloody Brit. One of his brothers-in-law had trained with the British at Salisbury and hated every minute of it, said he would have rather spent his time with Krauts. The English personality, he was fond of saying, was as abrasive as the stewed tea they served in the mess, distilled over years of lousy weather, lousy food and a buck-stupid class system.

"What's that then?"

With the backs of his fingers, Fisher strokes the handle of the blade, like it was a cat. "I wouldn't plan on settling down here."

"I haven't decided what I'm doing yet."

"Then let's just say I decided for you."

"What if I don't give a shit?" The air pinches and cracks. He can feel it pushing at his face and throat.

"There's nothing for you here."

"I wouldn't be so sure about that. I've made friends." He pauses a beat, knowing he shouldn't say any more, that baiting a man like Fisher is like sticking a wounded bear, but his mouth is already shaping the words. "Your wife and kids for a start."

Fisher jolts the table as he leaps to his feet, veins popping, face stretched into ugliness. Sweat beads across his brow as the colour leaks from his skin. Matt's eyes slide to the hand Fisher has been nursing in his lap, now splayed on the table, and the knife corralled between them. A dark stain appears between the bandaged fingers of his left hand. The sweet stink of blood rises between them.

"You'd best get that stitched." With one last glance at the knife, Matt turns and walks away. When he reaches the door, he calls over his shoulder. "And you can let yourself out."

Chapter 13

There's a light on in Stan Byrd's tool shed. Egypt approaches cautiously. She avoids the old man if she can. Seeing him no longer turns her stomach – his face is almost what it used to be before the beating – but his temper has devolved into one mean dog. What a thrill to find Matt instead. Egypt stands at the threshold, waving her arms about to stave off the cold. She stamps her feet and cranes her neck to peer up at the grey skies, heavy with snow. Matt is hunched over the workbench, sharpening his hunting knife. Eventually she clears her throat.

"For someone who claims to have been living by his wits the past few years, you're pretty easy to sneak up on. I've been watching you for ages."

"I knew you were there," he says without looking up. He tests the blade on a piece of wood, then picks up a smaller skinning knife.

"How?"

"You're wearing enough scent to knock out a small army; plus, you're blocking the light." Egypt faces the marsh to hide the flush rising on her cheeks, pretends to be interested in the Hewitt kids with their rocks and sticks, shattering the forming ice. When she spins back on her heel, he's fussing with his snares.

"You seem busy."

"Yup."

"Anything I can help with?"

"Shouldn't you be in school?"

"I thought you didn't care about school."

"I didn't tell you to cut class, did I?"

"No, but . . ."

Wind slashes across the lake and through her thin coat. She blows on her reddened hands and shoves them back in her pockets.

"But?"

She's not known him to be so short before. She would step inside the shed and out of the cold, but his testiness pins her at the doorway. Her eyes begin to water. What has she done wrong? She can't bear his being angry with her, not today of all days.

"My dad showed up yesterday. Completely out of the blue." Making her voice sound more detached than she feels summons a prickle of sweat between her shoulder blades. "As if he'd only been to the store and back, and not living it up in Detroit for the better part of six years."

"How do you know he was living it up?"

"I don't, I guess. I just –"

"Dammit!" He yanks his hand away, but the wire only pulls tighter around his trapped finger. Egypt gasps and steps into the shed to help, but he throws her such a withering look that she presses herself against the wall, tries to make herself as small as possible. Patiently, he cuts himself free with a pair of wire cutters and then proceeds to cut two-foot lengths from a reel of wire on the workbench. An angry purple groove now circles his finger below the nail. Egypt wishes George were here to sniff around the dusty floor, rub his face against her legs, whip the sourness from this cramped space with his happy tail.

"Is that why you didn't stay for dinner?"

"What?"

"Because of my dad."

Matt hangs the tinsnips back on the pegboard and reaches for a small pile of sticks at the far end of the workbench. "If you want to help, you can thread these wires for me, through the holes I drilled in the tops of these stakes." Shoving aside the rusted mess he was trying to unsnarl, he grabs a stake and shows her how. Egypt's eyes stray to the tangle of old wire with its traces of fur and dried blood. The air in the shed feels oppressive in spite of the open door, and the machine-shop smell is making her queasy and light-headed. She tells herself to get a grip but wonders at the same time if she can't also smell blood, dead rabbit.

"Why do you need so many?" she asks as he hands her a stake and a length of wire.

"Gives me better odds."

Better odds. It bothers her that he sounds like her dad. She wonders if the rabbits are always dead when he checks his snares, and what he does if they're still alive, but decides against asking, as she'd rather not know. She struggles for a while to catch the wire in the tiny hole, her frozen fingers nearly numb.

"You must be glad to have your dad home."

"Yes." She rests her arms on the workbench, leans in close enough to breech the invisible wall between them, but not so close as to declare herself loose. Breathes in the dizzying scent of him. "And no." A coy glance, which he misses. "I mean, I think I am, and I know I should be, but there's a part of me thinks it might have been easier if he'd just stayed away." Matt hasn't shaved, and in his day's growth already she can pick out shades of brown and blond and red. "Does that sound awful?"

"Not to me. How's your mother taking it?" He's speaking through the ends of wire he's set between his teeth, his voice all gruff and muffled.

"She seemed okay last night, but this morning she was in a foul mood."

"She's had time to sleep on it."

Or not. To Egypt it felt like she'd been nursing her venom all night. How else to explain this morning's reaction?

After Ray left, her mother spoke of him only when Egypt brought the subject up. Which happened less as months and then years passed with no word from Ray, no news of his whereabouts or whether he was still alive or had been found down some alley with his throat slit – her mother's dire prediction, offered only once and recanted immediately on seeing Egypt's ashen face.

"I don't think she wants anything to do with him."

"What about Aidan?"

"He's a little quiet."

Matt frowns. "It must have been a shock, meeting his father for the first time."

"I suppose." When Aidan was old enough to start asking, Laura told him much the same as she'd first told Egypt, that Ray was away working in the States. But Aidan was less content with this as an answer. He was small for his age, and when the Mullins brothers weren't around, the other kids teased him mercilessly. When the taunting grew too much, Laura switched tactics and, exacting Egypt's complicity first, urged her son to hold his head high. *Sticks and stones*, she said, explaining that his father was not a well man, that travel was difficult for him these days and the journey to Canada just about impossible, but that he'd send word eventually. Aidan just had to be patient. Egypt shrugs. "He'll be fine. Aidan is Aidan, he takes everything in his stride. As long as he gets to fish and play out all day, what does he care?"

"So you think your dad will stick around?"

"That's what he says. But who knows? My mother doesn't trust much of what comes out of his mouth." Finally, she can feel the tip of the wire through the other end of the stake.

"Do you believe him?"

How to explain the mess of feelings that Ray's reappearance has churned up? She wants to confide in Matt but needs to be sure any confession on her part will earn a reward – an arm around her shoulder, a hug. A soft, lingering kiss. Her mouth is so dry her lips are sticking to her teeth, her fingers so cold they're beginning to burn; she should have stopped off at home first for a pair of mittens.

"I want to. But I guess there's a part of me that holds back, that can't let myself trust him." She offers a wobbly smile, willing him to look at her, but his gaze is fixed on the task before him, deft fingers knotting the wires into long loops. She startles as the hinges on the shed door let out a long, groaning protest.

"Skipping school, Fisher? How you ever going to get yourself a fancy teaching job if you don't go to class?"

Mick Long. The stake leaps from her fingers, the wire slips free and scuttles into hiding. What's he doing here? Following her around? Mick and his shadow, Joey Payne. Mick and Joey. Jick and Moey. She crouches and pretends to scrabble around on the dusty floor for the lost apparatus. How long have they been standing outside? How much have they heard?

"I wonder what Ray would think if he knew his precious Sphinx was cutting class, was going to turn into a loser like her old man. Or does having rich-bitch friends and hanging out in a posh house make you too good for us now?"

"Leave her alone, will ya?" A half-hearted protest from Joey.

When Egypt stands and faces her tormentor, Mick is swinging on the shed door. He pulls his lips back in a sneer or a smile; his broken front teeth make it difficult to tell which.

"Aw! He's sticking up for his girlfriend. Looks to me like you've got competition," he says, indicating Matt behind her with a nod of his head. Egypt's eyes sting with humiliation.

"You might have to fight for her." Mick body checks his friend, then throws an arm around his neck and jerks him off balance. "What d'you say? Think you can beat him. Big boy like you?" Joey pretends to fight back. It's completely absurd, a Keystone Cops episode in close-up, not to mention that Joey has nearly a foot on Mick if he ever dared pull himself up to his full height, and could, if not overpower Mick's bullish body, at least stand his ground. But Joey would never upset the balance of power between them. Mick knows this, uses and abuses it. Joey gives Mick a mock shove, his big hand almost obscuring the side of Mick's head, but is careful to check any strength there might be behind it. Mick will lash out, especially the mood he's in today. He's broken Joey's nose before.

Behind her, Egypt can hear drawers opening and closing, Matt cleaning up after himself. "Aren't you going to introduce me to your friends,

Egypt?" There's a hint of amusement in his voice. Immediately, Mick stops his clowning, and Egypt senses this whole act has been orchestrated to get Matt's attention. Now he has it.

"Mick Long." He pushes past Egypt into the shed, holding out his stubby, nail-bitten hand. "Anything you need, you just come see me." Matt shakes the proffered hand and Egypt rolls her eyes at the shed roof. "And this here's Joey, Egypt's boyfriend."

"He's not my boyfriend," Egypt protests. From the corner of her eye she sees Joey's face fall. She would kick Mick Long if she wasn't so sure he'd kick her back. And harder. She wants to comfort Joey somehow, take the sting out of her denial, but has to be careful what she says. Indulge him too much and he'll misread the situation, and she'll be forced to let him down again. And despite the distance between them now, Egypt and Joey – friends long before Mick and his family moved to the community – were once close. They grew up together swimming and playing shinny, walking to school. *Peas in a pod* was how Joey's mother described them.

But things changed the summer Joey turned thirteen, the summer she smelled a man's sweat on him instead of a boy's: acrid, less innocent. His voice broke and a soft line of fuzz appeared on his upper lip. He grew ungainly, tripping over his giant feet, which seemed out of proportion to the rest of him. Most of all, the way he looked at Egypt changed. She let him kiss her once, and she really did try to lose herself in the moment, but all the while she was too conscious to enjoy it at all: the wetness of his mouth, the potatoes-and-bacon taste of his last meal, the hard and slick feel of his teeth. She had outgrown their childhood friendship, while Joey's feelings were developing into something altogether more serious. Egypt began distancing herself, and Joey turned to Mick for company.

"How've you been, Egypt?"

"Fine." She folds her arms across her chest and stares out over his shoulder. Why does he have to do this to her? Make her be mean to him. Why can't he just sense she'd rather he cleared off?

"I haven't seen you around much lately."

"You know, school does take up a lot of my time, despite what your friend may think."

Joey stares at his shuffling feet, flicks his eyes over Egypt and clears his throat. "*Anna Christie*'s playing at the Locke Street cinema. Greta Garbo's in it. You had such a crush on her, remember?" He blushes at the word *crush* and Egypt feels the blood shrinking from her skin. "I've got tickets for tomorrow night. Or I could change them for Saturday if that suits you better?"

If Joey's flush, it probably means he's been helping out his uncle, a scrap metal merchant down on Barton Street. Could be, too, why Mick is flashing cigarettes around. When Egypt glances behind her, he's leaning over to offer the open pack to Matt, flicking his head from side to side as he does so, making the bones in his neck click. She watches as Matt tucks his acquisition behind his ear, saving it for later. She's never seen Matt smoke.

"I don't think so, Joey." She shifts her stance so she can keep one eye on Matt, but in the confines of the shed it's difficult to see around Mick, who is suddenly bobbing around like a jack-in-the-box, apparently re-enacting the beating Matt saved Stan Byrd from a month ago. There's something scrappy about Mick that reminds Egypt of her dad. Something unsettled and angry. His shoulder blades sprout from his back like stunted wings. He's demonstrating a few choice moves, kicks and punches Matt could have used to take down Stan's assailants without breaking a sweat. Matt laughs as Mick ducks and feints, squinting against the smoke from the cigarette propped in the corner of his mouth. At times like this she can almost understand why Joey is so enamoured of his bully friend, but not to the point that he lets Mick push him around. And the smokes are only fuelling her irritation. To Egypt's knowledge Mick Long has yet to find work. He shouldn't have the money for rolling tobacco, never mind store-bought cigarettes.

"I'm off movies at the moment." Joey's eyes look scalded. Egypt can't believe she ever let him kiss her.

"Okay, everyone, show's over, I have things to do." Matt shoos everyone from the shed, pulls the door shut behind him. Egypt hangs about expectantly, hoping for an invitation to accompany him, even if it means helping him set his rabbit snares again, but Matt walks away without so much as a glance in her direction.

"You coming, Fisher?" Mick and Joey are heading towards the Owls' clubhouse. "We have smokes and a couple of beers. Could have ourselves a little party."

"I don't think so, boys," she says, and turns for home.

She regrets her choice the minute she opens her own door to find Ray pacing the breadth of the cabin and back, chafing at the world. George trots over to greet her, his head low, tail tucked between his legs.

The air is so rancid she stoops to bury her face in the smoky comfort of the dog's fur. The smell is coming from Ray. He draws on a cigarette and she stares at his hand, the black that has seeped through the grubby bandage. "Your hand," she says, straightening, but he barely glances at her. Egypt's throat tightens. Something has changed since this morning. The blood isn't running, but it has at some point seeped through the bandage and down between his middle and forefinger, dried like tears of treacle.

Ray stares at his hand as if in half a mind to cut it off for troubling him so much. He tugs at the dressing, cursing as a burst of red fans the edges of the black stain.

"Shit. Piss. Fuck." Spittle flying as he yanks the dressing free. Egypt, toes clenched, amazes herself by approaching him, reaching for his wounded hand and gently taking it in both of hers.

"It needs washing, Daddy." Her motions, plus the steady coolness of her fingers on his, calm him. The look he gives her is so tender that the back of her throat aches with a sudden urge to cry. A spasm of coughing overtakes him and he pulls his hand away.

She pours water into the washing-up bowl and then lowers her father's hand into it. Icy. The water shocks at first, hammering at her bones. Ray never utters a sound; the water swirls red then brown as she rubs at the grime in his skin as gently as she can. She dumps the dirty water by the back door, pours more water from the kettle to rinse the wound, then pats his hand dry with a towel. Standing this close, the bitter smell of his sweat stings her eyes. His blood flows freely, the wound having found its voice. The cut is deep, the surrounding skin inflamed. She glances at his face. Pain has dulled his eyes, rimmed them red.

A cockfight. The wound weeps beyond her abilities and she feels dismayed by the amount of blood that wells up when she lifts the bloody towel away, the way the edges refuse to knit. Ray breathes through clenched teeth. She recalls one of his old jokes, *You should see the other guy*, and understands that her dad is always in some scrape or another. Not like Gloria's father, who wears a dark suit and carries a briefcase. His shoulders aren't forever hunched in pique. Gloria's father never limps home bloody and bruised from scrapping with people at work.

"Bet the other guy looks worse," she says, then lowers her eyes before the dark cloud that is now Ray's face. His free hand fishes in his jacket pocket, pulls out a flask. Trapping it under his left arm, he unscrews it with his right hand and tips it to his lips.

"You get your old man a needle and thread, there's a good girl." His tone says he'll brook no argument. Egypt turns on wobbly legs and approaches the tin candy box where her mother keeps needles, scissors and bits of thread she's stashed over the years, some of it picked free of worn garments. In the fading light she dithers over what colour he might want, scrabbling amongst the buff, the white, the robin's egg blue, searching for a black or navy. Threading the needle proves tricky as her hands tremble and her vision blurs. She walks to the window in order to see better. Ray has sunk into the shadows, but she hears him at intervals swallow long and hard from his flask, sniff and wipe his nose on his sleeve. Swallow again and cough. When she moves to light the kerosene lamp, he waves her away.

"Put the needle there." He nods at the palm of his hand. Egypt does as she's told and backs away. He picks up the flask again and, with a surprisingly steady hand, pours a few drops of whiskey over both the needle and the cut. Resting the wounded hand on his left leg, now crossed tightly over his right, he sets his jaw and begins sewing.

Egypt turns her head and drifts away. Ray's progress she measures by the sucking in of breath through his teeth and the series of *shits* and *fucks* he spits back out. She feels hot despite the cold and has to grasp the seat of her chair as the darkening room swells and dips, pitching on its axis. He took her trapping with him once when she was younger and the three of them were a normal family. A girl on an adventure with her dad. They punted out into the marsh in the skiff, and he hauled up a chain at the end of which dangled a beaver he'd trapped. She held herself perfectly still as he dragged the wriggling creature into the skiff, terrified of its size, its nearness, and yet drawn, fascinated by the beaver's own terror, its high-pitched cries. She saw herself taking the creature in her arms and stroking its sleek fur, soothing it. When her dad cracked the beaver's head on the gunwale, she vomited all over herself and the bottom of the skiff, which earned her a sharp clip around the ear. He never took her trapping again.

"Now you can give us some light." His voice gravelly. Egypt reaches for the hurricane lamp. The yellow glow darkens the windows, reveals Ray's glassy eyes, his sickly pallor and the wounded hand he offers her.

"Not bad, eh? For a navvy." He's giddy with the pain, with the task he's just completed. Egypt wonders how her mouth can feel so dry when her body is literally dripping. The wound looks wretched and inflamed, but at least the blood has stopped running. She dresses his hand in clean rags and ties the flattest reef knot she can manage. He leans back in the chair, closes his eyes and drifts for a minute or two. Egypt contemplates leaving, or getting up to start the fire, but when she moves to stand, his eyes fly open and dart at her. He straightens in his chair, takes a wad of tobacco from a pouch in his inside jacket pocket and a paper from a packet of RIZLA+. She watches him struggle to negotiate the tobacco in an even line across the paper that refuses to lie flat, keeps her hands in her lap against the urge to extend them across the table to help. Using his injured hand, he bats the tobacco into line at one end, then picks up the paper and tobacco and, with practised dexterity, rolls a neat and tight cigarette, pops one end in his mouth, twists the other, then strikes a match and lights it. He smokes greedily, sucking all the pain from his hand deep into his lungs and pushing it out again in a long and troubled sigh that steals around Egypt's shoulders. George is restless, fidgeting at her feet when he would normally stretch and pace the room. She wants to flee, run through the cemetery with her dog, put some distance between herself and the fluttering in her belly that won't quit. But she wants to stay too; scared if she does leave that when she comes back, her dad will be gone again. For good.

"There's a man staying round here. Tall piece of work, lazy look about his mouth."

Matt. Egypt glances at Ray's face but he's squinting against the smoke of his cigarette. What is she supposed to say? She twists her fingers in the longer hairs of George's coat.

"Know who I'm talking about? The man your mother's been sniffing around, the one lodging with the Byrds," he continues, before she can even nod yes to the first question.

"What's his game?"

"His game?" She pushes her voice up at the end, forcing it into a question.

"His game, you know, his story. How much has he told anyone about himself? You can't trust someone who wanders in from the back of beyond and flashes you a smile, you know. Where's he from? And when's he going back? – that's what I'm more interested in." It's like he's talking to himself, like he's already forgotten Egypt is in the room. "Who does he think he is, throwing his weight around here like he belongs, flexing his muscles, thinking he can –"

"Winnipeg."

"Eh?" He snaps back into the room, refocusing on his daughter sitting across the table.

"He's from Winnipeg. Or somewhere just outside of there."

"So what brings him here? And why's he staying? How long's he been here?"

Egypt answers the only question she can: "He arrived at the beginning of November."

"And he and your mother . . . ?"

"What?" she says, too sharply. Ray's eyes narrow again.

"They been . . . what's going on between them? They *close* at all?" The word drips from the ugly curl that is now his mouth.

"No." *Close. Why would they be? She's way too old for him. She's married. She has a grown-up daughter. It isn't possible.* Egypt casts her mind back over moments where she's come upon them together, revisits the tension between them, picks at images she'd thought innocent. An uneasiness flutters in her chest.

"That's not what people've been saying."

"What people?"

"Round here. They say she's been going with him. That right? He been getting his feet under the table?" He leans across and lowers his voice. "In *my* house?"

"He was having his meals with *us*. He was not coming to see *her*." Egypt can feel her father's sourness infecting her. Nausea rising in her throat.

"You know what they say about women like that."

"Like what?"

"Like your mother."

The conversation has sidled down a dark and sordid alley. Egypt pushes her chair back. George shifts his weight evenly over the floor, head resting on his shaggy front paws, but Egypt can sense the tension in him. She rises to leave. Ray leans across the table to crush his cigarette in the ashtray.

"She ever mention your grandparents?"

A blast of December air rocks the cabin. Egypt stares at his thinning crown, the lock of greasy hair swept back in a younger man's fashion. His eyes are focused on the tabletop, his lips turned upwards in a serpent's smile. George is on his feet too, and Egypt's hand rests on the dog's big, bony head, his wiry fur. He leans against her legs, his reassuring weight laying claim, protecting. It hasn't escaped Egypt's notice that George keeps Ray at a distance. And that while her dad is very much aware of the dog, he makes a conscious effort to ignore him.

"She told me you ran away from home when you were a boy," Egypt says. The words seem to come from someplace outside herself. *He isn't talking about his parents*. Egypt doesn't understand how she knows this, but her face has grown heavy and it's becoming difficult to work her mouth.

"That orphan story she's been feeding you is a load of codswallop." He picks a piece of tobacco from his teeth, rolls it between his fingers and flicks it to the floor.

"I don't know what you're talking about."

"Course you don't. I just thought it were about time you did know, you being so grown up and all now." He squints up at her through the smoke of the cigarette end still burning in the ashtray, watching her face change. "Your mother's no more an orphan than I am the King of Siam. Her mam and dad are both alive and kicking. I even took a wander past their place today, just to check."

Egypt's ears are ringing. She has grandparents. Family she's never met. Could this be one of his tall tales? Doubt hovers a moment and then disappears; some part of her knows he's telling the truth. Her legs don't feel strong enough to hold her up and she sinks back into her chair.

"And before you start, it was your mother's idea."

"What was?" Her world has shrunk to this small space inside the cabin. Inside her head, which weighs a thousand pounds.

"To hide you from them and them from you."

She blinks at the floor.

"They live on Robinson Street in a posh white house."

Twisting her hair into tight ringlets, twisting until the hair pinches at her scalp, twisting until she feels it breaking at the roots.

"Must be something in that Presbyterian blood of theirs." He tips his chair onto its back legs, his voice grown more expansive. "They threatened to cast her out if she didn't stop seeing me, so it was either live over the brush – which wouldn't have suited your mother – or elope to Niagara Falls and say our *I do's* standing next to one of the world's natural wonders. The old folks disowned her after that." He's pushed back his sleeves and is rubbing his arm above the wound in an unconscious gesture. When he sees her looking, he quickly tugs his jacket back in place, but not before Egypt has glimpsed the dark markings on the inside of his arm.

"So they don't know about me either?" She isn't sure if she's spoken aloud. Ray doesn't move to answer, so perhaps the words just echoed in her head. She stares at the part of his arm that was just exposed. *A tattoo? Tattoos are for criminals and gang members.* The room is damp and cold. Her mother will be home from work soon, complaining that dinner isn't started, the fire isn't lit; angry because Ray is here. Egypt stands. *And maybe angry because Matt isn't?* She can't face her, and she doesn't know how to be with this man who is her father. He seems to be both here and not here, and the way his attention glances off items around the room is making her nervous and jumpy. George shakes himself and pads to the door. Egypt follows.

"It's her you should be mad at."

Egypt listens as he settles the chair back on four legs, spins the lid on his flask.

"You going to get a fire going for your old man, Little Sphinx?"

She glances back and he nods at the injured hand cradled in his lap. Egypt leans her head against the door, her throat so full and sore she couldn't utter a protest if she tried.

"There's a good girl."

Chapter 14

He checks his customary gait, slows himself to a lazy Sunday stroll, despite the fact that it is Monday. To anyone out and about this morning, to anyone stationed at their window, Ray Fisher is out stretching his legs, a dreamer; a man drinking in the natural beauty of the head of the lake. For once his fingers are motionless, those on his left hand swollen to a hook and pulling his jacket pocket further out of shape, those on his right stilled in sympathy. But his mind twitches and strums. His restive eyes scan the surface of the grey water. For a bloated stomach. A blue and busted face.

His breath whorls steamy curlicues in front of him. Bodies stay down longer in the cold. So he's heard. Though what he's counting on is the temperature staying down long enough for the marsh to freeze over. Give the carp time to take care of the carcass. Carp eat anything. Eyeballs. Fingers. Won't be the first human flesh they've dined on.

He traces the perimeter one more time, then heads off downtown to the library on Main Street. Clutches of men huddle on street corners, backs to the wind, collars upturned against the edges of their flat caps, sharing a smoke. Or a hard-luck tale. It's the same story all over. Poverty fashions pretty much the same complexion no matter what city you're in.

When Ray skipped town six years ago, Detroit had sparkle and glamour. The whole romance of the car industry. Gleaming automobiles lined up in rows outside the Highland Park plant, where Ray had first gone for a job. He hadn't been taken on, the plant in the process of closing for a bigger facility at Dearborn. But Detroit wasn't a one-industry town. There were the Kellogg's and Post cereal companies to try his hand at, as well as hundreds of smaller industries. His first job was underground in the salt mines, living out a subnormal existence among the eerily white underground roads, the otherworldly room-and-pillar labyrinth of glittering rock salt. He left the day one of the donkeys died. Not because he'd grown attached to it or any of the other donkeys that were lowered into the shafts to toil, trapped underground until they died. But because he'd seen his fate as tied to theirs. It was time to move back up to the surface. Which is where the real trouble started.

Now the lines between the cities have blurred. He recognizes the same sets of jackets with patched or threadbare elbows falling shapeless from gaunt shoulders; pants shiny and thin with age bunched around lean haunches, held up with rope. He strides by these men with purpose, aware of their haunted eyes fastened on his progress, the grim set of their lips. Where's he going? What does he know that they don't? Some leave their posts and set off after him. Ray quickens his pace, ducks down side streets. One determined sort follows him right up the steps and into the library, the sighs of his ragged breathing keeping time with the pounding in Ray's swollen hand. Once inside, Ray's shadow loses heart. Could be the sharp tang of desperation in the air, the sour metallic breath of the hungry. The tables and chairs occupied by men as broken and weary as himself. Men with little or no work and too much time to fill. *See*, he wants to turn to the man who was following him and say, *I was going no place special, after all. I know no more about the next job or meal than any other hard-luck case in town*. Instead, he unclenches his jaw, relaxes his shoulders.

He wanders among the stacks awhile, but never aimlessly, always with one eye trained on the progress of the newspaper, its grubby hierarchy of readers. There's a few more waiting their turn today than there were on the weekend, or even last Friday when he'd wandered down here after walking Egypt to school, stalling. Wired. Having not slept a wink the night before. An eternal night. Jerking awake each time he'd drifted off, reliving the heavy's skull giving way beneath the stick in his hand, the warm stickiness of blood, the drag of dead weight towards the water. Last Friday, Ray hadn't expected to find anything written up about his man – it was too soon. But the ritual of going to the library and reading the newspaper had given him something to focus on. A way to kill time.

More than an hour passes before it's his turn. He shakes the paper out, turns the pages. Nothing. Another day's grace. He relaxes a shade, turns back to the beginning and starts again, glancing over the headlines, the classifieds, the ads for liver pills and men's worsted jackets on sale. The shuffle of scruffy men grows impatient. *There are no jobs*, he wants to tell them, stick a pin in their hopes, watch their faces fall. The library is warm. He feels sleepy and restless at the same time. He scratches at his throat, and the paper flutters from the useless hook that is his left hand. He grasps wildly at it with his right, punching a hole through the page. The librarian glares at him over the rims of her glasses. When he tries to roll a couple of cigarettes, she leaves her post to stand over his table and glower. Ray heads for the exit.

He's almost at King when he spots Doyle, another of Red's heavies. *Shit. Nothing to do but keep on walking towards him. No place to hide anyway. And if Red's looking for you, you might as well show yourself – you'll be found sooner rather than later.* He wishes he had a cigarette to suck on. But with his hand buggered up the way it is, rolling is no longer something he can do while walking. Doyle's scowling like he hasn't taken a shit in a week.

"Boss wants to see you."

"You don't say."

"Don't get smart, Fisher. Just get in the car."

"Or what?"

Doyle grabs him by the elbow and frogmarches him across the road towards a fancy black McLaughlin-Buick idling on King Street outside the hospice and in full view of the front entrance to the Scottish Rite. Red is sitting in the passenger seat, wearing a camel coat, an unlit cigar between his teeth. Ray wants to laugh at his pretensions. Who does he think he is? Some big gangster type? One of Rocco Perri's men? *You got the wrong blood in your veins; you're a bloody mick,* he wants to tell him. But the bloody mick'll probably break his nose. Or his legs.

"Fisher," he says without turning around when Ray climbs into the back of the car. Ray makes a show of getting settled, straightening his jacket, patting down the plump leather seats, then stares at the back of Red's head, the ginger hairs sprouting from his stubbled, ruddy neck, the paler ones on his thinning crown, speckled with red. Like some of his roosters.

"Nice day for a drive."

"Something you want to tell me?"

"Can't think of anything."

"Let me jog your memory for you. You had a bit of a run-in with a colleague of mine."

"Colleague?"

"A certain James Edward Fitzpatrick."

"Nice Irish Catholic name, that."

"I believe he was wanting to borrow your boots."

Red tilts the rear-view mirror towards him, and Ray meets his eyes. The skin around them crinkles, and the car fills with Red's forced belly laugh. Doyle heaves his shoulders in tandem, as would any heavy worth his weight in moonshine and stolen cigars. Red's laughter brings on a coughing fit. When it passes, he takes out a silver case and lights a cigarette. Ready-made. Ray's nose prickles as the sharp smell of sulphur occludes the heady scent of leather. Notes of rich toasted Virginian lick the back of his throat. He takes a deep breath, hauling the smoke through his nose and into his lungs. He could smash a rock against the back of Red's head for one of those fags.

"Nice try, Fisher, but you're a lying piece of scouse shit."

"I'm not a scouse." *You dumb fucking mick.*

"The armpit of the arsehole. Same difference."

Ray stares out the window and wonders when Red is going to get on with it, or whether he's going to keep him here all day, batting him around like a cat with a mouse.

"Cigarette?" Red leans partway over the back of his seat, proffering the open cigarette case. Ray hears himself say *no thanks* but watches his fingers pull three from the case. He slips two into his top pocket and the third in his mouth. Red snaps the case shut but doesn't pull his hand away. Eventually, Ray looks down, knows what he's going to see even before he reads the engraved initials: *J. E. F.*

"Amazing the things you can find in a pawn shop these days," Red says, his voice all brass knuckles and lead boots. He turns to face front. Doyle strikes another match, holds it out for Ray. Ray leans forward. Only when he raises his hand to cup the flame does he realize how badly his hands are shaking.

The smoke makes him dizzy. And careless. He's forgotten to eat. That would explain the hand trembling. Can't remember the last drink he took. The last flutter.

"Now I'll ask you again. Anything you want to tell me about last Wednesday evening?"

Nicotine thuds through Ray's temples. He could lie down on Red's plump leather seats and catch himself a nap.

"You owe me, you little piece of Northern scumbag. I've a good mind to feed your balls to the pit bulls."

Ray's head clears a fraction, his heartbeat settles to a steady thump-thwump. "There was an accident."

The air stills, even the smoke stops in its swirling tracks. Red's eyes in the rear-view mirror have lost their humour.

"*There was an accident.* You hear that, Doyle? There was a bloody accident. Jimmy Jar must've been off his fecking head to walk right into the big stick Fisher was swinging. That right? That how it happened?"

Ray sniffs and hocks up a ball of phlegm, rolls it around his mouth, sorely tempted to deposit it on the carpet between his feet, or on the back of Red's head. Instead, he swallows the warm, viscous lump.

"What stick? I don't know what you're talking about."

"You were seen, scumbag. Shitting on your own doorstep again." Ray can feel Red's ire scorching the already stuffy air. He continues to stare at the sun glancing off the windows of the hospice. It was possible a patient might be standing at one of the windows, staring out at them. Or were terminal cases all confined to their beds?

"Must've been someone else."

"Then how come you're wearing his shoes, you feckless little git."

The colour drains from Ray's features. Not such a dumb fucking mick after all.

"So, now that we've got that little matter straightened out, I'll be needing a small favour from you."

"Favour." It isn't even a question. The time for opening the door and walking away has passed. If it ever existed.

"We'll call it interest on a loan. Doyle will contact you. You'll go with him. You'll do as he tells you, when he tells you. Now get out, you're stinking up my leather seats."

Ray is left standing on the sidewalk as Doyle shifts the car into gear and pulls out into the King Street traffic.

Chapter 15

Feet sliding in Jimmy Jar's shoes, sliding push-glide, as if this were a January afternoon's adventure on the ice, playing shinny, skating figures, couples arm in arm. Except it's the dead of night in mid-December when the lake may or may not be frozen through, at least not enough to take a man's weight. The waning moon's no more than a thumbnail clipping in the charcoal sky.

Hands out for balance, hands numb, bones in his fingers burning. Wind whipping salty water from his eyes. The ice squeaks and groans, its voice louder, more insistent, the closer he push-glides into the middle. Water slops over the tops of Jimmy Jar's too-big shoes, burning his feet with cold. Now Ray can't feel where they begin or end. Or his hands. His head. The ice shifts and bows beneath him, more freezing water around his heels, the toes he doesn't own anymore. How long before it takes his knees, his backside; how long before his bones snap like icicles, the lake swallows him up, tips him into darkness, takes him to a peaceful place where he can no longer see or hear or feel or smell.

The street lamp hissed orange as Ray walked by, heels ringing off the pavement. Hot and cold in his too-thin clothes, his ill-fitting dead-man's shoes. Jimmy Jar's shoes. Two sizes too big, the shoes blister his heels; with every step his toes jam up against the wads of newspaper he's stuffed in the ends, his knee bones scour his shin bones, thigh bones grind down his hip sockets. *Watch the cracks in the sidewalk in case you trip, watch the shadows, watch for Doyle watching, waiting for the mark.*

A hand reaches from the dark and grabs his arm. He leaps as if scorched, spins around to face a stranger in an overcoat that pulls at the buttons across his front. A hat that looks like it's been knocked from his head a few times.

"You look spooked. Ray, isn't it? Ray Fisher? Didn't mean to scare you." The man's voice, familiar and strident in the heavy night air. Lewis Randall, or Brindell, something like that. Heavier than Ray remembers him, ponderous girth, slack around the jowls, eyes hooded, aging face sliding towards his neck. Lewis acts like they're old army buddies, greets him with a fondness Ray doesn't share, a slap on the back of his shoulder blade that resounds through his hollow chest. "Long time, no see." Ray grits his teeth against the urge to thump the man back, flail at his fat stupid face, lest the anger he's been coddling all afternoon be spent on the wrong person.

"You live around here now?"

"Nope."

Lewis's head bobs forward as if he's suddenly lost the will or strength to keep it up. He staggers off balance, then rolls his jowls towards Ray. "Listen – *lishen* – you couldn't spot an old friend a buck or two could you?"

"Wish I could, fella," Rays responds, sensing his chance to escape and sounding more generous than he feels, an itchy feeling at the back of his brain that he might in fact owe Lewis Randall. Though it was years ago. "Just got cleaned out at the track."

"Damned left-footed nags got me too," Lewis mumbles, no longer as interested in Ray as he was. Across the road the hulking shadow of Red's McLaughlin-Buick nudges to a stop against the curb. Doyle steps out the passenger side and stands, arms folded, watching. Ray wipes the sweat at his temples, wills Lewis on his way.

Doyle lurches towards him once Ray is alone. "It's not a social engagement, Fisher," he growls, careful to stay in the shadows.

"That bloke was half-cut. Won't remember a thing tomorrow." Ray's half-running to keep up with Doyle's long strides. Turns down a side street and then into the criss-cross of laneways and alleys, emerging back onto the lighted street only steps behind Ray's old racetrack buddy. Before Ray can summon the words to protest, Doyle grabs the back of Lewis's collar and pulls him into the alley.

"You'll just have to make sure of that, won't you?" he says, as a sawn-off shotgun materializes from under his coat. Doyle cocks the triggers and fires both cartridges point blank at the man's feet. Lewis hits the ground roaring like a gelded bull. Ray's ears are ringing; his teeth taste burned where they're grinding against each other.

"C'mere, Fisher."

Ray wills Jimmy Jar's shoes to move him closer to Doyle and Lewis Randall/Brindell, footless, writhing in blood and torment. The spill of streetlight between the houses picks out slivers of bone amongst the litter of leather and flesh. Doyle magics a steel rod from thin air, hands it to Ray who, dazed, takes it from his outstretched hand, almost losing his balance with the unexpected weight.

"You can finish him off."

Head buzzing, legs filled with ice water.

"Didn't you know? Randall's your mark." The shadow of his hat obscures Doyle's face, but it's as if Ray can feel the henchman's toothy grin pressing into his skull, smell the flint in his laughter.

"Word is it's your weapon of choice." The alley fills with whimpering and begging from the man on the ground. Lights flick on in the windows of nearby houses. There's an unmistakable odour of shit. Ray sets his face away from the man's pleading eyes. No one he knows anymore. Hands grab at his pant leg.

"Please, please, please . . . no . . . no, no, please no, please, please . . . mercy . . . please, no."

"Shut the fuck up," Doyle growls, driving his foot into the man's face, sending him backwards into silence. "I can't fucking think straight with all that racket." Several neighbourhood dogs have set up barking and Ray struggles to keep one eye on the shotgun Doyle is waving about, like he's some menacing cowboy who's off his trolley. Ray readjusts his grip on the steel rod; he's running out of time. There's too much noise in his head; he tries flipping the station in his brain. *The lodger. Picture him. Sitting at your table, eating your food, groping your wife*. His mouth floods with saliva, touching off his sore teeth. He pulls his arms back, the rod a golf club or hockey stick, curls his lip, squints to focus his aim, then closes his eyes and swings the rod down and through, arms jolting as the rod makes contact. Draws back again, eyes still closed, and misses, catches something hard on the return swing and steps back, breathing heavily, stumbles on the remains of Lewis Randall's feet.

He's bent over, hands on knees, dry-retching, listening to the cinder crunch of Doyle's impatience. Dogs barking, voices shouting, the distant wail of a siren.

"Get a grip, Fisher." With a fistful of jacket, Doyle pull-pushes Ray back to the main road, the heady cigar and leather reek of the McLaughlin-Buick. The car roars and squeals away.

"Not bad for your first time," Doyle says, calmly reloading the shotgun in the passenger seat as Ray reels in the back. "The first is your worst. Helped that you knew each other. Breaking the ice and all that." Ray can't tell whether it's better or worse that Doyle doesn't laugh at his own joke.

He's aged a decade by the time the driver slows to turn down Dundurn Street and Doyle barks at him to get out. He trudges along York, braces himself for the slippery descent to the boathouses, aware he isn't carrying the steel rod anymore though he can't say where he lost it, threw it away, set it down. The lumpy scab across his palm pulses, remembering the rod's cold weight. He walks past his house, black as pitch. Steps out onto the ice.

Ray turns back so he faces the shore. Home is a dark, ragged line of tar-paper shacks and rough-hewn cabins, a wife who no longer wants him, the look of bewildered hurt in his daughter's eyes, a son who may or may not be his. The ice groans and tips as the lake yawns, suddenly greedy, reaching for his ankles. His bowels loosen, a memory of bile flooding his mouth. Staggering in the dark, feet fumbling, knees lifting, something hammering at his shins, and then, just as panic locks its fingers around his throat, the treachery beneath him shifts, suddenly more stable. He runs, or tries to. One foot push-gliding while the other scrabbles for purchase on the ice. Push-glide, scramble. Push-glide, scramble. He falls several times, but the line of homes grows closer, rooftops fingering the night sky. He doesn't stop until he's thrown himself on the shore.

Chapter 16

"It's not so special, being painted. You'll soon see. Sitting still for hours with nothing to do. You'll be bored to tears."

Egypt's eyes close in a smile wide against the intemperance of yellow roses – on the wallpaper, comforter, nightdress-case, pillows and shams. *Shams! – what a scream of a word!* There is no way on earth being painted by Gloria's extraordinary mother can be half as claustrophobically boring as watching Gloria colour a block graph for her model school class. *Bored schmored. Flattered more like. Immensely so.* Yesterday, Gloria had caught her sleeve as she was leaving school just ahead of the bell and invited her to stay the weekend. "My mother would like to paint you," she announced archly. How did Gloria manage to be one creature at school and quite another at home? Egypt wondered if Philip would be around, whether after negotiating emotional potholes at home all week she had the energy or the inclination to stand in the range of his sophisticated teasing. But she can't pretend there isn't a part of her that isn't excited by the idea of seeing him again, if only to soak up his Douglas Fairbanks good looks.

As far as home goes, she doesn't trust herself not to snap around Laura. *She ever mention your grandparents?* Not a word. *Quite the feat when you think about it, keeping your parents from your daughter, your daughter from her grandparents. A virtuoso performance. Bravo, Mother.* Egypt swallows a needle of rage. Ray presents another set of problems: years of pining over her father's absence, of remembering and reconstructing her childhood in obsessive detail, and now that he's here, in the flesh, Egypt finds herself chafing at the invasion of her home. He swings between a tetchy abrasiveness and protracted bouts of grim silence. Impossible to ignore, his moods, like tainted water, affect everyone who comes into contact with him, bar the bleary-eyed and leering friends he collects like stray dogs, and whom Egypt often finds (or hears) snoring on their couch in the morning. He can dismantle a room – and its occupants – just by standing in the doorway. A blue pall of cigarette smoke hangs in the air even when he isn't around. It's as if half a dozen people have moved in with them. And he's beginning to scare her. Having woken at the crack of dawn yesterday, she was first downstairs. Ray was sitting at the kitchen table, red-eyed and muttering to himself. His cot hadn't been slept in. He looked hunted, cadaverous. The flesh had shrunk from his face in the night.

And yet, like the pricking wax and wane of nausea, Egypt senses the devastation she would feel if he left again. Ray Fisher is her dad, her family, and though he wielded the news as a weapon – to hurt her or to make her stay and listen, she can't decide which – he has brought more family in his wake. A month ago, Egypt's family numbered three. Now it stands at six.

Resting one knee on the edge of the window-seat cushion, she stares out at the leaden skies, the drifts of brown leaves in the gutters. Gloria's room feels cold, and just as Egypt is wondering why Gloria would choose the cold north side of the house over the sunny south, she sees him. Ray. Walking down George Street with feigned nonchalance, nursing his injured hand in his jacket pocket. She steps back, waits a moment and then cranes her head to see, hoping he hasn't noticed any movement in the window. This time he's looking. He's facing forward, but even from this distance she can feel his eyes straining sideways, feel the heat and intensity of his gaze. Ray can't know it's her; his daughter's features would be impossible to make out from the street. Unless he's been shadowing her. Though she can't think why he would. It's a bit late to be exhibiting fatherly concern. And anyway, her dog would surely have flushed him out. She pictures Gloria's father with his hat and suit, his woollen overcoat and shiny shoes, and she shrinks a little inside her skin. Ray's George Street business can only be funny business.

"See something interesting?"

"Oh, nothing." Egypt's voice leaves her as a strangled bark. "Just a squirrel with a funny tail," she adds, sensing Gloria right behind her.

"Where?"

"It's gone now." Trapped at the window, Egypt watches Ray stroll across her field of vision and disappear stage left.

"A squirrel!" Gloria gives Egypt a mock shove. "That's the funniest squirrel I ever saw. And the biggest. Open the window and call him over."

"Who?" *Gloria, meet Ray. You may have to stand back because he's a little ripe. But don't let the shadows beneath his eyes, the greying whiskers on his face, put you off. Or that red, lumpy scar that snakes the width of his hand – he got knifed at a cockfight, remember?* This is a bad dream and she's going to wake up any minute.

"Your dog."

"George?" And there he is, trotting down the other side of the street. *Tracking Ray?*

"That's George," she says, relieved Gloria's attention is taken up by the dog and not her dad casing the neighbourhood.

"I've always wanted a dog," Gloria gushes. "You should call him in. Mother can paint him, too. George of George Street! Go on, call him in."

"In where? In here?" Just the idea of George trotting through the Henry household, shedding hair and clumps of dirt, sniffing in every corner, lifting his leg at one of the towering potted ferns or aspidistras that dot the main floor or, horror of horrors, digging through the mound of gaily wrapped presents beneath the Christmas tree. Then she imagines the look on Martha Misery's face.

The moment Egypt lowers the cloak, every sense is heightened, her skin a different, more thrilling animal. Air warm and cool plays over her breasts, heat licks up her spine from the fire crackling in the Quebec stove, the dense velvet pile of the chaise caresses her legs. Mrs. Henry's paintings seem brighter and bolder, less threatening. The scratching of charcoal against paper, the spill of light through the cathedral windows, the accumulated scents of past models trapped in the folds of the cape cleverly draped to kiss her curves. It's all so heady.

"You truly are a beautiful girl."

She is. The embodiment of bountifulness and fecundity. Her hair, her skin, her curves are lush, flawless. *Heady, heady*. Mrs. Henry can hardly contain herself. The words pound through Egypt's bloodstream, making her dizzy. What would Matt think if he saw her now? She imagines him standing at the French windows looking in, his breathing shallow, his throat dry. She blushes as he steps inside and moves towards her and then, arrested by the vision before him, lingers beside a stack of Mrs. Henry's canvasses, his gaze adoring and besotted.

"Exquisite. Hold that look, those perfect shoulders."

Egypt squeals as George's wet nose touches her bare skin. He burrows his long nose under her arm and flicks it away from her lap.

"Sorry. He's looking for attention." And something else, she thinks, as the air around her fills with the stink of bad eggs.

"Aren't we all," Mrs. Henry mutters, and Egypt flushes. She resents having to apologize for George. It wasn't her idea to bring him inside.

"Gloria? The dog. Please. He needs to go out."

Gloria sighs dramatically, places her book face down on the floor and lets George out into the garden through the French doors. She'd been hand-feeding him kitchen scraps until she grew bored. Egypt suspects Gloria's enthusiasm wore thin once the heat from the stove began releasing the secrets of George's coat – running with coyotes, rolling in eviscerated rabbit and fish guts. She flounces back into the oversized armchair with a dramatic sigh and picks up her book again.

"Ready, Egypt?"

"Ready."

"Remember what I said. Beauty radiates from within." A smile. More words of praise, a little cajoling. "Feel all the muscles in your neck relax, all the way down your spine and into your hips. There you go, that's lovely." Mrs. Henry's voice, smooth and seductive, makes her feel that she is the most beautiful girl in the world, that painting her is not only natural and right, but ordained.

"Breathing beauty."

Egypt's spine softens, a rope of silk. Her shoulders melt into the fabric. Beautiful. She is the most beautiful girl in the world – far more beautiful than her wraith-like mother, with her bony knees and elbows, her protruding hip bones, her belly lined with stretch marks. *They say she's been going with him*. A hundred times she's been over the conversation with Ray in her head. He's delusional. Paranoid. Why would Matt want Laura when Egypt is the more obvious romantic heroine? *Young* romantic heroine. Her mother is thirty-six at least. Ancient. Her hands are always red and chapped, even in summer, and she wears a perpetual frown. She's a nag: *Have you done this? Don't forget that.*

She ever mention your grandparents?

"Breathing. In and out."

So many times this past week Egypt has been tempted to shock her mother by telling her how much she knows. But life with Laura and Ray, mainly Laura and sometimes Ray, has taught her there's a power to be mined in keeping secrets. She will bide her time. Meanwhile, how intoxicating to know something she isn't supposed to. In the dead of night, though, hatred consumes her, blocks up her throat and squeezes her temples. She lies rigid, fists clenched at her sides. Sometimes she thinks if it wasn't for Aidan tucked up beside their mother, or sprawled over most of the mattress in boyhood dreams, she would ambush Laura in bed, wrap her hands about her mother's scrawny neck. *Why? Why did you keep them from me? Who was that supposed to help? Me? Them? Or –*

"Egypt, Egypt!" Mrs. Henry swoops towards her, waving her sooty fingers. "Such a sour face." She kneels at Egypt's feet, wipes her fingers on her smock and reaches out to brush a hair from Egypt's face. Softens her voice. "Whatever it is, try to strike it from your mind. Think only happy thoughts." She squeezes Egypt's hand. "Think beauty and grace, and you become beauty and grace. Think of love. Think of the happiest moment of your life. Could you do that for me?" Egypt nods mutely. "Good girl," she says and begins to rise. Then she touches the folds of the cloak. "Perhaps we could try a pose without this, yes?" She stops in the motion of pulling the cloak away. "You are a magnificently beautiful girl, Egypt, and you shouldn't be ashamed of your beauty. Gloria, come here and take this from me, would you?"

Gloria sets down her book and takes the cloak from her mother's outstretched hand. Though Gloria seems nonplussed by her schoolmate's nudity, Egypt feels her face flush as Mrs. Henry gently lifts her hair from her shoulders, twists it in a loose knot and quickly pins it in place. Goosebumps travel her skin as the sleeves of Mrs. Henry's dress, also sooty with charcoal, brush her neck and breasts. When Mrs. Henry steps back to assess the now naked Egypt, her mouth and eyes all smiles and benevolence, Egypt lifts a hand as if to ward off the prickling at the back of her neck.

"Are you warm enough?"

She nods though she's close to shivering. She tries to hold Mrs. Henry's gaze, take comfort from her intelligent hazel eyes. *Think beauty. Become beauty. Imagine Matt –*

The front door slams, truncating her thoughts. Seconds later a waft of cooler air reaches the studio. Mrs. Henry looks cross. Egypt wishes she had the cloak to pull over herself, but Gloria has thrown it over the back of the armchair she's curled up in.

"Gloria, would you mind going out there and telling Martha that I really can't do with her slamming in and out the front door. It's playing havoc with my nerves. She's to use the back door."

Before Gloria can mark her page, the studio door swings open and in strides Philip. Egypt struggles to cover herself with one arm and free the pins from her hair with the other.

He stops dead in the doorway. "Well, well, Egypt, you are a sight for sore eyes."

Egypt wills the faraway cloak over her, but Gloria has left her seat and is standing by the window, staring out at the sleet that is starting to coat the backyard. Quickly, Egypt arranges her hair in front, crosses her legs and tucks them under herself.

Philip sweeps the area before him with his arm and folds his upper body over in a deep bow. "Lady Godiva, I presume. I must have missed your trusty steed, or is he perhaps grazing in the garden?"

"Philip! Don't be so cheeky." Mrs. Henry retrieves the cloak from the back of Gloria's chair and hands it to Egypt before leaning towards her son for a kiss. "You're home for the holidays already?"

"Finished my exams, Mother. I'm celebrating."

"Is Cassandra with you?" Gloria asks, turning from the window. "I'm curious to meet the girl who managed to capture my brother's heart. And all his attention."

"The winsome and delightful Cassandra is spending Christmas with her family in Westmount. She's coming down on the train for New Year's." He waves his hands like a conductor. "You can spend all the time you need getting to know her then."

He catches sight of George.

"Oh, don't tell me," he laughs, crossing to the window. "Poor Egypt. You rode in on that shaggy grey hound out there. What the hell is that anyway?"

"A lurcher. And his name is George." Egypt is aware of the absurdity of trying to sound indignant while wrapped in a cloak and perched on the edge of this most suggestive piece of furniture. To think she'd never heard of a chaise longue before today.

"George the Lurcher. Sounds creepy." He directs his wolfish gaze at

Egypt. "But I'm sure he's absolutely lovable. And loyal to a fault. You'd be safe walking down any street with George by your side."

"You should have called or sent a telegram to let us know you were coming. Your father would have met you at the station, you know."

"Surprise is the tactic of all great generals, isn't that right, Egypt?"

She nods, biting back tears. Why can't he direct his attention elsewhere, or simply leave so she can get changed into her clothes? Instead he beams his full-wattage smile her way. She scrunches herself tighter. She wouldn't be surprised if he could see right through the cloak.

"Egypt has been modelling for me," Mrs. Henry says, pointlessly.

"And believe me when I say how grateful I am. You have no idea what a balm your beauty was to me when I opened that door."

"Do behave, Philip."

"Oh, come on, Mother, you can't blame a man for commenting on something so . . . arresting. Not after the gruesome-looking stiffs he's spent the past few weeks buggering about in. I can't tell you, I've been up to the elbows in all manner of ugliness."

Egypt's mind can't quite take her to where Philip's words want to go, but she feels her face burn regardless.

"You're embarrassing the girl."

Egypt winces. She's managed to tiptoe halfway to the curtained-off corner where she first changed clothes, and now Mrs. Henry has directed Philip's attention her way again.

"My apologies." He comes towards her and she smells alcohol atop something more antiseptic and medicinal that her mind processes as cadavers.

"I expect you to be more professional." To Egypt she adds, "He's grown up with my models and is entirely used to the female form."

"And still highly appreciative of it."

Egypt has reached her clothes. She whips the curtain closed and lets out her breath.

"You're going to be a doctor soon, young man. You need to learn a little respect; you'll be taking the Hippocratic oath soon."

Philip strides across the studio, his heavy footfalls shaking the floor. "You know, there's all sorts of gossip down at the club."

"So you found time to go to the club before you came home to your family?" A little pique has crept into Mrs. Henry's voice.

"Word is there's a killer about town."

"The shotgun murders, you mean." Gloria. Her voice set to melodrama.

"Murder, Gloria," Mrs. Henry cautions. "Singular."

"But Mr. Atkinson from two doors down has gone missing," Gloria says. "His wife suspects foul play, as do the papers."

"Another gambler. The plot thickens."

Egypt's skin prickles.

"And how would you know that, young man?"

Philip doesn't answer. Quickly, Egypt finishes fastening her skirt and steps out of the change room.

"I bet it's that Italian gangster, Rocco Perri."

"Perri's too clever for the police. They can never pin anything on him."

Mrs. Henry snaps the giant pages of her sketchpad in the air as she flips back through her day's work. Murmurs of approval issue from the back of her throat.

"May I see?" Egypt asks, but Mrs. Henry doesn't even glance her way; it's her children's attention she seeks. She folds up her easel and drags the legs across the floor. Gloria simply raises her voice to compete.

"No one gets away with murder, Philip."

"Yes they do. Smart people get away with it all the time."

"But there's no body, Gloria," Mrs. Henry says, exasperated. The easel has grown a mind of its own and refuses to lie quietly against the wall. "No body, no murder." She gives the legs a sharp kick with her pointed boot. Egypt hears snapping wood. "And I think the pair of you are being altogether too facetious. We're talking about a good neighbour. A good man." She unties her smock and hangs it on a coat hook by the sink. "Your father and I have known the Atkinsons for nearly twenty years."

"Good or bad, he's been done in. They're searching the fields around here and the woods on the side of the mountain. And if they don't find anything there, they're going to start dragging the lake."

"What a pair of overactive imaginations. I really don't know where you get your wild ideas from." She raises her eyebrows at Egypt. "People go missing all the time, don't they?"

People like Ray disappear for days on end. Weeks. Months. Years. But what does Mrs. Henry know about people like Ray?

"It doesn't mean they've been murdered. They may have gone off on a jaunt for a few days. Stepped away from their lives. Nothing permanent. I can't say it hasn't crossed my mind from time to time. To flit off somewhere for a few days, disappear into anonymity." She plucks a lipstick from her shelf of oils and brushes. Smooths her lips together after applying the colour. Finger-combs her hair. "But you know what your father's like, he'd have more than a little to say on the matter."

"Mother, I can't think of two people more unalike than you and Mr. Atkinson. That man would walk a crooked mile for a shot at a craps table. Or a cockfight."

"Whereas I . . . ?" A glass and a decanter have now appeared from the wash-up area.

"Whereas you, Mother dear, are a complex and utterly charming caricature of yourself."

"Less of the charming if you don't mind," she says, raising a glass of amber.

Egypt's stomach is dancing. *Cockfight.* "When did he go missing?" She's trying not to think about Ray. How much he might know.

"He never came home on Tuesday night. And no one has seen him since." Gloria's eyes round in the telling. "Reporters have been hanging around their house and asking the neighbours all kinds of questions."

"Cockfights and murders." Philip glances at Egypt. "Those sorts of things must go on all the time where you live."

"I don't think so."

"That's not what that boathouse chap was telling me last night."

"You were here last night?"

"Some of the chaps got together for a game. Ended up at Murdoch's place. Don't fuss, Mother." He turns his attention back to Egypt. "Scrawny runt of a chap. Likes the cards. Has trouble holding his liquor. Thick English accent."

Egypt's face aches from the strain of trying not to let her feelings show. She's had enough. Even Ray and Laura aren't this exhausting. "I won't be staying for dinner," she calls over her shoulder, heading out of the studio.

But as she reaches the front door she hears Gloria, her voice all sweet and slightly frantic, calling her name. She rushes up behind her and takes Egypt's coat from a hanger in the closet, holds it up for her to slip her arms in the sleeves. The nap of the coat lies even and smooth, as if it's been brushed. Her worn shoes glisten with polish. Miserable Martha must be fresh out of elbow grease. Egypt wraps her muffler about her face while she sorts out which expression to wear.

"I suppose that now your father's home you'll be playing happy family for Christmas?" Gloria says.

And what does that picture look like, exactly? Holly pinned over the door, the smell of mulled cider on the stove, the cabin festooned with streamers, glittery paper angels and snowmen, crafted at school when she was younger, hanging from a tree. Ray presiding over a glistening ham. Memories, or just pictures she's willed into existence? The hands holding the carving utensils look like her mother's.

"I haven't given it much thought to be honest."

"But Christmas Eve is less than two weeks away. I was planning to ask if you wanted to spend the holidays here, with us. We have Christmas carols and mince pies and a big turkey, and there'll be lots of presents under the tree. And presents for you, too. Lots of presents."

And indigestion. And quite possibly a trip afterwards to the Hamilton Asylum for the Insane up on the edge of the escarpment.

"Martha's dinner is the best you've ever tasted, and there's always too much for everyone."

Egypt tries to imagine Christmas at the cabin. Baking mince pies, chopping down a Christmas tree, stringing popcorn and cutting out paper snowmen. Ray twitching and snarling. Her grandparents showing up at the door. Laura's face. Kissing Matt under the mistletoe. All the things that make Christmas so special.

She steps from the house onto the front porch. "You're right, Gloria. I will be spending the holidays with my family."

She takes the first step, hears George deliver three sharp barks and then throw back his head in a keening howl. She can hardly bring herself to look at Gloria. How can she have forgotten her dog?

"He sounds like a wolf."

"He's part wolfhound, Gloria, not wolf. And he doesn't like being penned in."

"Shall I fetch him for you?"

A rustling of bushes and snapping of twigs tells her there's no need. George bounds into the front garden from the side of the house, stops and shakes himself, scattering dead leaves and cedar fronds.

"Good boy." He crouches and barks. Spins in a circle before clearing the brick wall that runs along the front edge of the Henry property. "Show off," Egypt yells, taking the steps two at a time.

The front door clicks behind her. From the corner of her eye, Egypt takes in the George-sized hole in the cedar hedge. She drags the toes of her polished shoes along the sidewalk, hoping Martha is stationed at a window, watching.

Chapter 17

A fist of sparks lunges for the roof as Ray lifts the lid free of the pot-bellied stove, pokes at the blazing logs inside. Egypt flicks her eyes at her mother darning furiously at the edge of the blasting heat.

"Stop playing with it, will you?" Her needle dives in and out of the sock. She tugs at the wool, bites off the end with her eye tooth, tosses it on the done pile. Egypt can't remember ever seeing the bottom of her mother's darning basket before.

"Wouldn't want it to go out."

"Not much chance of that, is there?" She's practically sitting in the kitchen. And Egypt has pushed her own chair back against the windowless north wall. Even the Christmas tree smells scorched. The crown has drooped and the branches have been shedding clumps of needles all evening. Half a dozen times, George has scratched at the back door, in and out, to cool his belly in the hardened snow. Egypt is poised to leap when he rises again, as she senses Ray's patience is stretched to breaking.

Tonight Ray is playing happy family. Or trying to. The fire is his penance. His way of making up for dragging Manny home with him last night, the pair of them lurching into the kitchen well past bedtime, rummaging for food. And then Manny dozing by the stove, the air curling green and foul with his sulphuric farts, while Ray strutted the length of the cabin and back, chuntering on about the friends a man can count on and the ones who shit all over him. "*I've a wife and kids to feed*, I said. *And it's Christmas. Have a heart. Have a bloody conscience.*" Egypt could almost hear her mother's eyeballs rolling in their sockets. Laura swept by his dramatic arm-waving as if he were invisible, filled her hot water bottle from the kettle on the stove and took herself off to bed, leaving behind Ray's cussing and the rotting-carcass redolence of Manny's expulsions.

The brutal cold snap that has ushered in this Christmas season and Ray's frenzied fire-feeding means the wood Matt cut and split is rapidly disappearing. Even the logs he stacked against the outhouse, claiming they would act as insulation – *You'll be thanking me when you're sitting there mid-January with your drawers around your ankles*. Egypt had turned her back to the flush that had fingered her mother's throat and neck. She wonders if Matt will be by to chop more wood for them. Or if instead they'll be made to endure Ray's crowing and posturing with the axe, his cronies gathered to witness him sweating for his family. Laura glances at the clock on the wall.

"You off to bed soon, Mother?"

"I'm not your mother."

"Wife."

"Hardly that either," she growls under her breath. "Why don't you just go on out. Anyone can see –"

What? That Christmas is a strain? That they are all as twitchy as starved rats in a cage? That there are no gifts to open? That Ray is bored with making amends and would rather be out on the prowl again, or whatever he gets up to in an evening. Egypt tried following him once, but he veered suddenly between two summer properties, dark and empty, and vanished like a phantom into the pitch of shadows, leaving her alone and weirdly spooked. Eyes in the dark, tracking her movements. Manny's eyes. Manny gives Egypt the creeps. She hurried back to the comfort of the path and the light from people's candles and hurricane lamps flickering in the windows.

From behind her curtain of hair, Egypt watches him stroll to the darkened windows, twitch the popcorn strings on his way past the Christmas tree – a patter of dried needles hits the floor – and circle back to the fire. Hands clasped loosely behind his back, he might start whistling any minute. She would laugh but can't be sure whether he'd laugh with her or drive the poker through the wall.

The wind whistles around the chimney outside, a reminder that MacNab Street is a daunting walk when the mercury hovers below twenty and the wind straddles the lake and street corners alike, an icy-toothed monster, ready to do battle. But the reward of her grandparents waits. And the neighbourly get-together in the church basement afterwards, which the minister promised last Sunday, along with a cup of hot mulled apple cider and Christmas cookies. She squints towards the clock on the wall. A little after nine.

"What is this, a conspiracy?"

"What?" Egypt scowls. Her mother's lips move silently as if in prayer. She's hemming dust cloths from a summer dress Egypt grew out of four years ago. *Aren't her fingers tired?*

"Staring at the clock every five minutes. You two have plans? Something else you'd rather be doing?"

Sitting in church. She mouths the words behind her hand. No one would believe her. But church, Egypt has discovered, is the best place to spy on her grandparents. She rearranges herself in the chair; wishes Ray would give up his staying-in-by-the-hearth farce and leave. Wishes her mother would go to bed. Egypt stifles another yawn; the tension between her parents is consuming her. The Christmas Carol Service begins at ten thirty and is one of the busiest services of the year, the church jammed to the rafters with seasonal attendees. She needs to arrive early to secure herself a seat. *Come on, Ray. Time to go.*

It hadn't taken Egypt more than half an hour in the library to track her grandparents down. She stared at the city directory and the address on Robinson Street and wondered how something like this, finding family members who had been unknown to her all her life, could be so easy. Too easy. It didn't seem right somehow. She should have had to struggle more to find something, someone, some two people, so important.

Two people who indeed live in a large white house on a posh street. Not so grand a house as Gloria's, but looking at it made her dizzy. Her grandparents lived behind those walls. Her own flesh and blood. The house has a wraparound verandah, a place to sit and survey the expanse of garden that slopes steeply in front and gently to one side; a garden dominated by an immense weeping willow with lacy branches that arch gracefully to sweep the ground. How majestic it will be in summer. She pictures herself ensconced in the protective embrace of the tree's feathery leaves, the private green space in the centre, cool and shady, her grandmother pouring glasses of iced tea decorated with sprigs of mint, reaching out to stroke Egypt's cheek and coax tales from her of all the years they missed. How long had her grandparents lived at this address? Had they always lived in Hamilton? From where did their families hail?

What Egypt didn't know gnawed at her. For several days she kept the house under surveillance, but she could only glide by their windows so many times without arousing the neighbours' suspicions. So she followed them. Now she knows their routines. Her grandmother shops at the York Street market every Tuesday and Saturday morning. Her grandfather works at the Hamilton Foundry offices on Bay Street North. The plaque inside the doorway declares he is the senior accountant. On Sundays, her grandparents leave their home on Robinson Street at precisely nine thirty a.m. and walk to the Presbyterian Church on MacNab Street, arriving before the arched wooden doors about twelve minutes later, depending on the weather and the condition of the sidewalks. Her grandmother walks with a slight limp, and when, two weeks ago, freezing rain left a layer of treacherous ice along the sidewalk, she wore flat, rubber-soled shoes and held her husband's arm, leaned on him. Egypt follows half a block behind and times her entrance just as the pealing bells heralding the ten a.m. service are silenced. She sits several rows behind them on the opposite side of the church, close to the centre aisle, which affords her an oblique view. Enough to take in their common features – she has her grandmother's nose, she's decided, and her grandfather's prominent chin, his squared shoulders. His height, too.

She glances at her mother, jaw set, squinting over her sewing; sees little evidence of either grandparent in her cross features. Some traits must skip a generation.

"You'll ruin your eyes in this light," she says. Not because she cares, but because of the scream building in the back of her throat. Because there's a gratification in tossing her mother's aphorisms back in her face. It's enough to snap Laura from her trance. The fabric is folded and put away, along with needle, thread, scissors and the tin candy box.

The moment Laura disappears up the stairs to her bed, Ray brightens. "You tired, Little Sphinx?"

Egypt shakes her head. Ray stops his pacing and shoots her a sideways glance before pulling on his coat. He makes to leave, then changes his mind, returns to the stove and feeds two more logs into its fiery maw.

"That should keep you going," he says. Egypt shrugs.

"Bye, Ray," she whispers as the wind wrestles him for the door. "Merry Christmas and all that." The spitting logs make her eyes and nose sting.

Gloves, muffler, hat and coat. She pushes George back from the door and, hand on the latch, takes a deep breath to calm her fluttery stomach.

"Where are you going?"

Aidan. She turns to find him standing halfway down the stairs. "Hey, buddy, you should be in bed. Big night tonight."

"She's snoring."

"Then go in my bed."

"I wanna go with you."

"You can't."

"Why not?"

"You have to sleep, Aid, or Santa won't come and visit."

He sits on the bottom stair. "Santa's a load of old bull."

Uh oh. This already. How old was she when Anne Ashcroft dashed her pleasure in Santa? Scoffed at the scarf she was knitting for his helpers. Eight? Nine?

"Says who?" She decides to let the cussing go. He must hear a lot worse out of Ray's mouth these days.

"Andy Dummican." *Andy Dummican.* The name means nothing to her. "He said Santa only stops for kids who live in proper houses, not marsh rats who live in shacks." A townie then.

"That's not true."

"It's okay, Egypt. I know he isn't real." He sighs and places his chin in his cupped hands. "You don't have to keep pretending for my sake."

How old is this kid? George, sprawled under the kitchen table, sighs in concert.

"I can't take you with me."

"Then I'm yelling for Mom."

"Okay, get your coat."

Aidan is at the door in under a second, pulling on his boots and cap; George winds his way around and between them, nudging at their legs, the door, play-biting at their coats.

"Where are we going?"

"It's a surprise." She points at the dog and he thumps back to the floor again.

"No George?"

"No George. And no telling. Deal?"

Aidan grins and thrusts out a mittened hand. "Deal."

Light from the church vestibule spills from the arched doorway, flooding the pathway of snow turned to slush beneath the trampling of boots and snow covers. The pews are filled to bursting and the spot Egypt has come to think of as hers is taken. She glances about for her grandfather's tall, thin profile, her grandmother's navy blue hat, smiling when she spots the sprig of holly that has replaced the little brown-and-white feather that usually adorns the brim. She grips Aidan's hand and weaves her way through the confusion of neighbourly greetings and wet-wool-smelling winter coats to the row immediately behind them. Pushes Aidan in front of her with an apologetic smile and a *Merry Christmas*. Obligingly, everyone shuffles over to make room.

"Not a peep," she says when he cranes his head around, brow furrowed and mouth open in a question.

"This is the surprise?" he whispers.

"The surprise is later. But only if you're quiet." She pulls off his cap and then sits on her hands to warm them and stop them from trembling. She has never been so close.

So close she could reach out and touch them. She studies the backs of their heads, the set of their shoulders, trying to read their pasts, the events that have marked their lives, shaped their personalities. Her grandmother turns to whisper something to her grandfather, and Egypt notes the strong lines about her mouth, possibly from years spent pursed in disapproval. But Egypt aches to see only the good. She can't decide which grandparent she is more drawn towards. Her matronly grandmother, shoulders rounded in the beginning of a dowager's hump, pearly-white hair pulled back in a tight chignon, or her grandfather with his ramrod-straight back, his mutton chop whiskers, the neatly brushed hat that sits on his knees. Egypt leans forward as if to adjust her stockings, her face warm with the thrill of proximity, and pulls in the scent of their skin, their hair, their overcoats – heavy with the Christmassy smell of cloves and oranges, an underlying tincture of lavender. Her grandmother must hang sachets of it in their closets. Melted snow still clings to the woollen fibres of her grandfather's dark grey overcoat. Egypt has never seen him remove his coat in church. He is as thin as a rail, his skin so pale it is almost translucent. She leans left a hair, watches as he picks up the *Book of Common Worship* and leafs through the pages, mesmerized by the blue tracery of veins on the backs of his hands, how delicate his wrists are when shucked free of sleeves and cuffs and cufflinks, how long and elegant his fingers, clasped in the act of praying. She wishes she could pass through the back of the pew, sit between them, lean against them, melt herself into these strange new people who share her blood and lineage.

All rise.

A hymn or two. A prayer or three. A sermon on giving. Aidan mugs for the family seated along the pew. They smile, which only encourages him.

Even her grandmother looks back once, though Egypt doesn't catch her expression. During a passage from the Gospel according to Luke, she has to pull Aidan off the kneeling bench he is pretending to ride and, when he is seated again, hold onto his boots to still his feet. All this just to avoid an interrogation from Laura. She should have let him yell his head off. Finally, he quiets down, and when everyone rises to sing the collection hymn, he's barely able to stand. Collection. For the love of... How can she have forgotten? Sundays she's been bringing the coin destined for the coffers of All Saints Anglican, which she would otherwise attend as part of her normal school obligations. But tonight? Tonight? Words tumble past her and then a shadow blocks her periphery. Egypt slides her eyes right. One of the churchwardens: bulbous, plum-stained nose, wheezy chest labouring to expel his minty breath. Egypt stares at the heavy brass collection plate in his hand. She's never seen it so full. The congregation is wealthy and filled with Christmas spirit. The mound of coins must total twenty-five dollars. Fifty. As Wheezy turns to her, she braces herself for the heft of the plate and its riches, the coolness of the metal. Her mouth dries. Aidan reaches up a hand, scratches on the backs of his knuckles, dirt wedged beneath his fingernails, and strokes the mound.

"We give, we don't take," she hisses, lifting the plate out of his reach and passing it along.

"I wasn't taking anything, I just wanted to feel it," he says, throwing her a wounded look. Her grandmother turns around and Egypt reaches for the hymn book to hide her face. And then a miracle happens. Warm, dry skin touching hers. She lifts her gaze. Such a surprise, her grandmother's eyes, the grey-blue of the lake in late September, young eyes for such a lined and worn face. Egypt, too bewildered to resist, lets her grandmother take her clammy hand between her smooth, dry ones. She drops a coin into her palm and does the same again for Aidan. Egypt presses the coin, a whole quarter, hard into her skin, hoping to leave something of her grandmother behind. The plate returns; reluctantly, she drops the coin, taps Aidan's hand until he lets go of his treasure, too.

Wheezy clears his throat and Egypt grasps her hymn book again, elbows locked against her sides, chin held high, and blinks to clear her vision.

Warm and spicy-sweet, the mulled cider slips down her throat like nectar. Aidan grins as he shoves first a Christmas bell, then a tree and then a reindeer-shaped cookie in his mouth.

"Good surprise, huh?" He nods and giggles, spraying cookie crumbs down his front. Grabs another fistful of cookies and a cup of cider and vanishes into the knots of chattering people.

"You better take one yourself, dear," someone says in her ear, "before they're all gone." Egypt obliges, closing her eyes as she bites into the sugary confection, her mouth flooded with butter and sweetness.

The sugar jolts her from the sleepiness she was beginning to succumb to in church. She looks around for her grandparents, spots them speaking with another elderly couple. She edges towards them, waiting for a chance to break into the conversation, but it's a tedious catalogue of old peoples' complaints – of aching bones and stubborn furnaces and Christmas cards that didn't get mailed in time. She wants to thank her grandmother for her generosity. Her Christmas spirit. *I'd like to pay you back if I could. Perhaps I could come over sometime and clear the snow from your front steps. Tend your garden. Clean your house.*

Her grandparents drift away from the Christmas card complainers and Egypt follows in their wake. A family materialises in their path: a tall greying man flanked by his mother, sisters, possibly a wife. And a step or two behind him, standing in his shadow, is the birdwatcher from the marsh. The man with the green canoe.

"Mr. and Mrs. Aiken, a pleasure as always," the tall man says in a low, rich voice; the rumble of a distant freight train; the kind of voice that makes people turn their heads to see who's talking.

"Mr. McQuesten," her grandfather intones, shaking hands with first the tall man and then his mother, the other women and finally, the birdwatcher hovering in the back. Egypt considers sloping off in case the birdwatcher recognizes her, wants to know what she's doing here half-way across the city, so far from Shacktown, but she can't make her feet move. *McQuesten. McQuesten?* Where has she heard that name before?

"It was a beautiful service," her grandmother says.

Mrs. McQuesten tips her head and smiles beatifically. "But that we all had the trust and faith of Mary, to humbly accept what was put upon her."

They seem to glow, this family. An energy pulses between them and spreads outward, simultaneously drawing others in and pinning them on the outside, like some centrifugal force at work. Egypt senses her grand-parents rapt under their spell.

"My heartfelt congratulations on the new leader," her grandfather says, addressing Mr. McQuesten. "Mr. Hepburn is quite the wit, I understand."

"Dynamic and forward-thinking. Exactly the kind of new man the party needs to front its progressive platform. The Liberal Party's fortunes are on the rise, Mr. Aiken, and Hamilton's fortunes with it."

McQuesten is accustomed to public speaking, Egypt thinks, not only for the melodious qualities of his voice but also the officious manner in which he bends towards her grandparents and then steps back to allow the others access, but not so far back that he isn't still front and centre of this tableau. The women nod and weave as one. Egypt's eyes flick from one to the other, but always back to the tall man at the centre. Mr. McQuesten. There's something vaguely familiar and oddly disturb-ing about him. And then, having murmured all their thanks and good wishes, they move away in concert towards the door, like some many-legged animal. Just as they reach the doorway, McQuesten lifts his hat to his head and Egypt recognizes his silhouette, remembers him as the man sitting in the front of the birdwatcher's canoe the morning after the Sunday the Turnbulls floated their house away and Matt Oakes walked into her life.

Chapter 18

"What's with the Christmas tree?"

Laura flicks her duster across the windowsill, sending dust motes scrambling. "It's a fire hazard, I threw it out."

"I can see you threw it out, woman. It's sitting in the bloody snowbank for all the neighbourhood to gawk at and wonder what it's doing there on Boxing Day already."

"So it's what the neighbours think that you care about?" He grinds his jaw slowly, and her gut clenches in anticipation. She'd wrestled the tree outside to get a reaction. Unwound the popcorn strings and made a game of balancing the chewy kernels on the end of George's nose, praising him when he flipped them into the air and caught them in his mouth. The orange Ray presented her with on Christmas morning she hurled from the door. Someone has probably already found it or he'd be waving it in her face. Her arms are a mess of red scratches and welts from the dried-out tree. Her skin itches from the resin.

"We all know you don't. Slinking around with that drifter."

"She is not."

"Don't you start." He wags his finger at Egypt, who is curled up on the couch with George. "I'm sick of the two of you ganging up on me. And get that damned dog off the furniture."

"He's cold."

"My Manchester backside he's cold. Off. Now."

Egypt flounces to the door and grabs her coat.

"Where are you going?" Laura calls, her voice more brittle than she intended.

"Out." A grumble under her breath, "What do you care?"

"Out where? Of course I care."

"Taking George for a walk." And she leaves, George bolting ahead as soon as the door opens. Laura's heart tiptoes out after her. As a child, Egypt was always itching to play outside, or mooning by the window, willing the weather to change, her friends to happen by so she could drop the book she'd been pretending to read and race outside and join them. Laura couldn't wait for her to shed her tomboy ways and begin hankering for hair ribbons and white ankle socks. She fantasized about having a little girl who wanted to play dress-up with her mother's clothes, who asked her mother to wrap her hair at night so that it would fall into soft ringlets come morning – not that Egypt's hair ever needed any help in that direction. Instead she'd found herself tasked with the perpetually scraped knees and dirty fingernails of a rough-and-tumble girl who would rather be one of the boys she was so fiercely proud of her ability to keep up with. Boys are still the concern, but Laura's worries have shifted to a more troublesome plane, and she longs for the days when the only battles were over trying to get Egypt into a dress.

"Fine. Leave, then," Ray shouts at the slammed door, the waft of crisp cold air it has ushered inside. "I get no respect around here."

Then we're in the same boat, aren't we? Laura casts her eye along the edges where the walls meet the ceiling. Dust-clogged threads of spiderwebs sway in the draft. She should fetch the broom, climb up on the stool. In fact, the whole place needs a good top-to-bottoming. A fresh start to a new – almost – year. But her shoulders ache with tension and the low-grade headache that has plagued her since Ray's return, and the effort required feels oppressively monumental, Laura herself too ground down and worn out. She stuffs the duster into her pocket. *How can a man who is barely around be so draining?*

"You just gonna let her leave like that?" he says.

"What do you suggest? That I chain her to her room?" *Build a wall between the girl and Matt Oakes? But it's too late for any of that, anyway.*

"You could try putting your foot down. She's going to get a name for herself."

"Didn't you hear what she said? She's taking her dog for a walk."

"She's getting into trouble."

"Then she's a chip off the old block, isn't she?" Laura could just crumple to the floor and put her head in her hands and weep.

Ray feeds the stove, then brushes dog hair – real and imaginary – from the cushions before settling his skinny haunches on the couch. Yawns, shakes himself and plumps the cushions. Reaches for his tobacco, then changes his mind. Fighting the lure of sleep, wearing himself to a shadow. Last night was just one more in a succession spent pacing the cabin and talking to himself. Dead but he won't lie down.

His restlessness isn't new, but it's tainted with a desperation Laura hasn't seen or felt before.

It was Ray's spirit, his moxie, which had first attracted her. Or was it the roguish wink he sent her way? A warm Saturday morning in May, and Laura had just entered the market two beats behind her mother's bustling efficiency. She felt the heat of his gaze before she noticed his eyes fastened on her: milky blue and framed with lashes so dark they appeared rimmed with kohl. Her blood quickened, casting her senses aflutter. She could scarcely tell which foot to set in front of the other. The small crowd gathered in front of his stall, *Fisher's Fixes*, was all smiles and smatterings of laughter. She shakes her head at the memory of the young girl she was then. Swept off her feet by a roguishly handsome hawker of quack medicines and cure-alls. Had it really taken so little to seduce her? Or had her motivation been more desperate – to escape the strictures of her mother's prudence and ambition? Heartache is myopic, and experience a great reviser of the truth. Dapper Ray was perched on an orange crate and wearing a snappy three-piece suit with cuffs and a bowler hat cocked at an outrageous angle. He waved jars of ointment and bottles of magical elixir, painting the air with his hands and twizzling his hat. The stories he wooed the crowd with were outrageous and patently untrue. Cleopatra and the Queen of Sheba both swore by this unguent to keep their skin soft and lily-white. The Iron Duke of Wellington's troops swallowed tablespoons of that potion before trouncing Napoleon at the Battle of Waterloo.

Her mother, engrossed in fingering the radishes and watercress and cross-examining the vegetable sellers and unaware of the alchemy taking place in her daughter's heart, believed her when Laura feigned a sudden splitting headache and begged to be allowed to return home.

Zigzagging her way back through the market stalls, her plan was to happen upon the handsome hawker on a break from his patter. But Ray anticipated her move and slipped around the flower stall behind his soapbox set-up to surprise her with first a posy of lilies of the valley in his right hand, and then a clutch of leggy yellow tulips hidden behind his back in his left. After entreaties and bars of song, he coaxed her into joining him for tea in a nearby café where the waiters wore long white aprons and bustled coolly between stately potted ferns.

Laura's sheltered upbringing had ill-prepared her to resist the flash and showmanship of the Ray Fishers of the world. Every encounter was a performance for Ray, who charmed the grizzly waiter into bringing them extra cakes, and had the ladies at nearby tables simpering and smiling behind their hands with his quips and on-the-spot revisions of popular refrains. While he courted and flattered and talked a blue streak about his plans to travel the world and build a business empire, Laura simply dissolved in his boundless and infectious energy. Her feet didn't touch the ground again until later that evening. She should have known better than to confide in her fourteen-year-old sister, who promptly apprised their parents of every detail of Laura's budding courtship.

Their rage was immediate and vitriolic. She had no business entertaining a low-class huckster and charlatan. A quack. But Laura was already lost to them. For her, Ray Fisher embodied the modern age, while her parents were quite literally from another century – the gulf between them as wide as between ragtime and the Viennese waltz.

She used to wonder if the flowers and song would have continued forever if not for her pregnancy. But it was only ever a matter of time before the real Ray Fisher would have made himself known. Her swollen ankles and the push of her tight, round belly didn't help; the mind-numbing fatigue that pregnancy dragged in its wake. Nor did the struggle for money. Ray began coming home late and sometimes not at all. And though her heart still tripped both when he left and when he returned, Laura didn't like the wife she was becoming: shrill and petulant, her mouth turned down, lips shaped in a nag. The more she changed, the more distant Ray grew. Pleasing her was no longer his number one priority.

Prodigal Ray is jittery and brittle and even quicker to temper. Gambling again. If he ever stopped. *Better than drink*, everyone is fond of saying. Though Laura isn't so sure where the differences lie, beyond the obvious physical imbibing of a substance that can knock you senseless and make you vomit. Like drink, gambling took a man by degrees. These days Laura finds herself dreading an unfamiliar knock on the door. Men pushing their way in to take her few sticks of furniture, her paltry possessions. Her children. She should have told him to clear off as soon as she discovered the housekeeping money and savings missing, because now that he has inveigled himself back into their lives, asking him to leave is nearly impossible. Laura has always felt powerless standing in the gale that is Ray's personality. And, not a small part of all this, he is the man for whom she forsook her family; he is her husband, for better or for worse, for richer and for poorer – *mainly poorer*, she thinks without irony. Somewhere deep inside, Laura believes she owes allegiance to that younger, more reckless part of herself.

As Ray's face slackens and his body relaxes into sleep, Laura grows restless. He twitches, troubled, still fighting. What demons chase him behind those eyelids? She moves to the window, stares out at the bright winter sunshine reflecting off the iced-over marsh, the crust of snow that blankets the area. She could go for a walk, cast off the yoke of Ray and his obsessive badgering. Pass the time of day with some of her neighbours. How refreshing to have a conversation with someone outside this claustrophobic family circle, a conversation not fraught with past hurts. Or crippled by the idea of future ones.

She brushes her hair, pinches her cheeks and reaches into her chest for a silk blue-and-gold scarf. One she never wears, always saving it for best. Which never comes. *So why not now?* The silk is at first cool to the touch and then warm around her throat. The scarf lends colour to her eyes and even brightens her hair, she thinks, tilting her face in the mirror.

Laura's eyes begin to stream the moment she steps out into the achingly bright sunshine. The cold air bites at her throat and clouds of vapour rush from her mouth, escaping into the sky. She pulls the scarf up over her nose, tiny beads of ice already tugging at her nostril hairs. January weather. Winter getting ahead of itself. There'll be ice-cutting in the bay soon if this keeps up. She glances at the Byrds' chimney. Stan and Joanna are away visiting her sister in Stoney Creek. The absence of chimney smoke signals their lodger isn't around, either. She pulls back her shoulders and lengthens her stride.

With every lungful of air, with every step she takes, the strain of being cooped up over Christmas loosens from her shoulders, aided by the welcoming sun. The Turners' goat, masticating old hay and vegetable peelings, turns to track her progress as she crunches by, her boots punching loudly through the skin of ice that has formed over the snow. Someone else's dog starts baying. A dozen or so blank windows watch her, scarf bright blue and gold against the chaste white snow, making her way to – why the hell should she care where everyone thinks she's going? Didn't she just accuse Ray of worrying too much about the neighbours? She's out for a walk. What's so unusual about that?

Around the path that hugs the curve of the marsh, to the farthest reach of the community. From here, her house is well out of sight. Out of mind. As is the Byrds' place. It's a while since she's walked this far. She doesn't have more than a nodding acquaintance with many of the people who live out here; she doesn't know their children's names. Some of the dwellings seem if not new, then at least newly constructed. Brave, or foolhardy, in light of the threat from the city. But with the numbers of jobless and homeless growing at an alarming rate, people are taking all kinds of chances. Perhaps they aren't so crazy after all. Why not believe in the benevolence and goodness of the city's councillors? Surely no one will pursue throwing people from their homes with soup-kitchen lines stretching two and three city blocks.

As she reaches the end of the path, a figure emerges from the woods at Princess Point and steps onto the ice, begins walking towards her. Halfway across and he's close enough she recognizes his gait. She's about to turn away when he waves. She waves back; it would seem unmannerly if she left now. Downright rude. Matt picks up his pace, sliding a little as he tries to balance the game in his left hand. Pheasants, from the length of the tail feathers brushing the frozen ground.

"I thought it was you," he says, long legs climbing the bank alongside the end house.

"From all the way over there?" She nods at the frozen water behind him, her face creasing in a smile.

He lays the birds in the snow by his feet, as if he means to stop awhile and chat. His eyes are electric with cold; his cheeks two ruby coins of fresh air. He shakes his hands and then claps them together, the sound muted by his fingerless gloves. "Your scarf caught my eye." He reaches out and touches the fabric, surprising them both. "A Christmas present?"

She's blushing. At his attention, the melody that is his voice carrying in the cold air. They've barely exchanged a word since Ray's return. Blades scratch the ice, and she glances over his shoulder. Kids have started a game of shinny. Her scarf is no doubt visible from their makeshift goalposts.

"I've had it for years."

"You should wear it more often; it brings out your eyes."

"Don't you just know all the right things to say?"

"Comes from being raised in a house full of women," he says, then quickly, "Did you have a good Christmas?" before she can frame a question about the house full of women.

"You could say it was an interesting Christmas." Instantly she feels guilty, as if she has betrayed her children and Ray and, by extension, herself. "It's the first time we've all sat down to Christmas dinner together." Though Ray more hovered about the table, unable to bring himself to pull up a chair and be seated. He picked at the chicken whose neck she'd wrung that morning, but whether any of the meat passed his lips she'd be hard-pressed to say. Egypt didn't eat much. Lovesick. And over this man. Laura closes her eyes to brush a strand of wind-whipped hair from her face. If it wasn't for Aidan, she wouldn't have bothered preparing an elaborate dinner; they'd have been just as happy with beans on toast. Which is all she'll be able to afford soon. No use counting on Ray. She'll be out of a job. Her stomach flip-flops every time she recalls that moment sitting in Bob Watkins' office, reading her redundancy notice.

"I haven't seen anyone for days. The Byrds are away visiting Joanna's sister."

"So you spent Christmas alone?" Her face warms with her lie. She already knows this. She wonders if he misses the house full of women.

"Just me and a plate of fried potatoes. Which is why I thought I'd go all out today." He nods towards the birds at his feet. Steam rises from their still-warm bodies; a smear of blood has feathered down through the snow. "You wouldn't care to join me, would you?"

"I couldn't, really. I have to . . ." Her heart is rattling like the lid on a boiling kettle. *Prepare dinner, do the dishes, sweep the floor, wash out my smalls – mine and everyone else's – pull out my fingernails, rig up a noose, torch the cabin.*

"Of course you do." He stoops to pick up his birds, looks up at her from under the brim of his battered hat. "Could I tempt you with a cup of hot chocolate?"

Could he? What a devil. But what harm in a cup of hot chocolate? Her cheeks tingle. She's grateful for the bright blue sky, the plunging mercury, the crystal-laden wind off the frozen lake.

"It'll warm you up."

Oh, it'll do that all right.

He falls into step beside her, and Laura resists the urge to glance at the windows of the boathouses they pass, at the spies stationed behind them. Once she's standing at the Byrds' refashioned door, however, she can't resist flicking her eyes over at her own place. *Slinking around with that drifter.*

"I can only stay a minute or so," she says, wishing she were already gone, that whatever game or collusion she has ventured into by saying yes to hot chocolate was already done and gone. Arms folded across her chest, she follows him inside.

"Let me at least get the stove going. Won't be a jiffy." He lifts the lid and strikes a match. "I set it earlier," he says as the fire catches at once. "Didn't know how long I'd be out there, how cold I'd be when I got back."

Laura stands awkwardly by the table in the kitchen, arms still crossed. She'd lean against it but can't be sure it would take her weight. She hasn't been in here since the night of Stan's beating. It looks different. Brighter, more exposed, winter sunshine pouring through windows that appear much bigger than she remembers. She feels ridiculous standing up, like a semaphore or a target; a goalpost for the boys playing shinny out on the marsh. But to sit would invite a different feeling altogether. This way, she's primed to flee at the first instance, though she can't think why she might need to flee a harmless cup of cocoa. Of course she can. Her stomach dances. She takes a step towards the door. And another. *It'll end in tears*. Years since her mother's voice has grated in her ears. Still stirring his cocoa, hot water and milk concoction, Matt turns from the stove, eyebrows raised.

"It's a good idea," her voice pitched too high. "To set the fire," she adds, gesturing at the stove as if there were some doubt to which idea she was referring. "I've often thought I should do it myself in the morning, before work. That way Egypt doesn't have an excuse when I come home and the fire's not lit." She's babbling, and dismayed that she's introduced her daughter's name into the room. "Completely impervious to the cold, that one. Like her dog. The two of them could sleep in a snowbank." Another step-and-a-half. Laura tastes blood where she's bitten the inside of her lips. "Of course, sometimes the ashes are still warm, so then it's not a good idea." Four more steps – three giant strides – and she'd be at the door. A cheery wave goodbye, a lighthearted *see you later* would set her free; her skin could unflush, her heart stand down.

"I've made it pretty sweet, that okay with you?" He pours the steaming cocoa into two mugs and sets them on the table.

"That's perfect." She stares at his mouth, imagining the feel of his lips crushing hers. Her legs have deserted her; it's as if she's standing on shanks of wet wool. She's hot. She can't do this; she can't sit and make small talk over this most dangerous cup of cocoa.

"It's getting warm in here now." He steps behind her, close enough he must be able to hear how heavy her breathing has grown.

"Let me take your coat."

Take me, she thinks, loosening the scarf at her throat. Tears sting the backs of her eyes. *Oh God, just take me*. His hands cup her shoulders and she fumbles with the buttons until his fingers close over hers. His knuckles graze her shoulder blades as he gently pulls the garment free. Her legs won't hold her up much longer. She has to remind herself to breathe.

"I –" she starts, though it escapes her lips as more a low moan, and his mouth closes on her neck. A darting tongue – so hot! – and the teasing edge of teeth send gooseflesh down her arms. Heat between her legs, her nipples so hard they ache. Another guttural sound, whether from him or her she can no longer tell. She leans into him, feeling the length of his body, lean and muscle-hard, against her back.

Sure and sinewy, his hands slide around her hips to her belly, to trail up over her ribs and along the curve of her breasts. The ache in her groin robs her of breath and sense. How long since a man touched her so deliberately? Aroused her this way? How long since Ray moved her like this? Matt groans in her ear and she turns to face him, lips bruising, teeth knocking. Fingers through his hair, pulling him closer, pushing her face into his. The animal in her could devour him. He tugs at her dress as she pulls down her stockings and underwear, and they stumble over the heap of her coat towards the couch. She's impatient, reaching for the buttons on his twilled cotton pants, reaching for him, excited by the chafe of his clothing against her naked skin. When he enters her, she arches towards him wanting every moment, every sensation inscribed on her skin. *How long, how long, how good, how good.* Laura hasn't felt like this in close to – has she ever felt this way? With Ray, even in the beginning, drunk on love and rebellion, there was always an edge, like a cliff she was walking, never sure of her footing, never knowing when one wrong step would send her tumbling below. Matt Oakes, with his long limbs and broad shoulders, is a different kind of creature altogether. She nestles her chin into his neck. Trickles of heat run past her ear. When did she start crying? As if sensing the shift in her need, his kisses soften and grow tender; he pulls back to undress and then folds himself into her again, this time to execute a slower, more deliberate dance.

Laura opens her eyes to darkness, arms and legs wrapped around the drifter from Winnipeg, her neighbours' lodger, a stranger but seven weeks ago, the man her daughter believes herself in love with. She squeezes her eyes shut. What has she done? What time is it? How could she have slept? She wants to rise and dress, run home. Skip the awkward post-coital exchange, pretend nothing happened. As soon as she lifts his arm he shifts, curling himself further around her.

"Where're you going?" His sleepy voice rumbles through her neck.

"Home."

"Do you have to go right this minute?"

"They're going to wonder where I am."

He makes no motion to let her go.

"What are you going to tell them?"

"I don't know. I'll think of something."

"Then stay here and think of it. I'll help you." His fingers begin circling her belly.

She tries to muster her indignation while fighting the urge to slap his hand away. "I think you've helped enough already."

Matt rolls onto his back, laughing.

"I don't see what's so funny about all this."

"I'm not laughing at you." He strokes her cheek, leans to kiss her.

"Neither of us will be laughing much if Ray finds out."

"He won't."

"How do you know?"

"I'll make sure he doesn't."

"How? No, don't answer that. I don't want to know." She closes her eyes. "Can I ask you something?"

The tiniest pause. "Sure."

"Why me? I must be ten years older than you."

"Not quite."

"Still."

He sighs. "Why do women always want to complicate everything?"

"Don't flatter yourself." Now her indignation is well and truly roused. "I just want to be sure that now you've had the mother you aren't going to try for the daughter."

Into the stillness of the silence that follows, Laura's face pulses with uncomfortable heat. "I'm sorry. That was a terrible thing to say." Oh, for the dignity of her clothes. She sits and pulls her knees to her chest, dismayed when he doesn't reach out to comfort her. Already he means something to her. Or she's weaving meaning into what happened here this afternoon. A long minute passes. She senses he is gone someplace else, and then he turns on his side to face her. She feels the back of his finger stroke her arm.

"Hey. Come on. Sticks and stones." She tries to smile. "You're a beautiful woman. And you could use some looking after."

Looking after? But before she can respond, a knock at the door startles them both.

Laura grabs for the afghan. "Who's that?" she whispers.

"No one. Ignore it." But his voice is as low and anxious as her own, his body tense.

When the door bangs again, Laura lunges for the floor and begins scrabbling for her clothes.

"What if it's Ray? What if he saw me come in here?"

"He didn't."

"How do you know?" Sometimes she thinks Ray can see around corners, through walls. She was insane to have come here. Who knows what he'll do.

The knock comes sharper, more urgent this time. "Matt? Matt, are you there? It's me."

Egypt. Oh my God. On her hands and knees, Laura crawls behind the couch. If her daughter . . . she tries to catch the breath stuck in her throat, tries to make herself small.

"What is she doing here?"

"How should I know?" Rustling sounds as he pulls on his clothes, pads over to the door.

"You're not going to let her in?"

"She'll just let herself in if I don't."

Oh God, he's sleeping with her daughter. *Who the hell does he think he is?* She clamps her hand over her mouth to stop herself from hurling curses and insults. A raw and naked insecurity slithers inside her head. How does her boyish figure compare to her daughter's voluptuous curves? Egypt's satiny skin, free of stretch marks.

The latch turns, the door is opening. "Can I come in?"

"Looks to me like you already are." Nails tapping along the floor. Panting.

George.

"What's wrong? Were you sleeping?"

"I might have been."

George makes a beeline for Laura behind the couch, wet nose sniffing her naked behind, tail thumping the furniture. *Please, please don't bark*. It's an awkward reach to scratch his chest and her elbow cracks. *I'll give you my dinner for a week if you don't bark, don't drop to your belly, don't think this is a game*. Her chest hurts from holding her breath.

Catching the scent of something else, George deserts her. Laura's head spins as she tries letting out the air from her lungs slowly.

Matt rushes to the kitchen. "He's after my birds."

"You were out hunting. I came looking for you earlier."

Take the birds away and George will be back sniffing behind the couch again. Luckily, Matt senses the same dilemma. "I have a soup bone if he wants, but he has to eat it outside."

"He's a dog. He'll eat beaver scat."

The door opens and closes. *One down, one to go. What could Matt throw into the snow that Egypt would run after?*

"So? Aren't you going to make me one of your amazing hot chocolates?"

Laura nearly cries out picturing the two cups still sitting on the table. Untouched. Cold.

"I have something to tell you."

"Oh?"

"Yeah. I was just waiting for the right time."

"Sounds ominous."

Why is he being so blessed patient with her? Send her on her way. *Goodbye Egypt*, and close the door. Cold air pinches at Laura's backside. Why can't he be more forceful? She's seventeen. She needs a guiding hand on her back, not the subtlety of prevarication.

Too late. She's making her way over to the couch, her flat-footed stomp shaking the floor, jarring her mother's spine. The door closes and she flounces gracelessly onto the couch. Laura has always been so light on her feet. She would have made the perfect thief.

"You have candles or a lamp or something?" Egypt laughs nervously. "Or are we going to sit here in the dark?" Her voice wobbles; she sounds less assured now. Has she noticed how rumpled the couch is? A certain musky odour with its illicit undertones rising from the cushions.

"We're going for a walk."

"But I have something to tell you." The couch creaks and Laura pictures Egypt folding her legs under herself like a crane. "It's pretty unbelievable," she says, her voice flattening out. Listen to the girl. Little Miss Melodrama. "It's about my mother. You won't believe what she's done."

Laura's heart thuds into the silence.

"Tell me outside. Come on, move it."

Laura waits, still crouched behind the couch for some time after the door closes behind them, long enough that her legs begin to cramp and her feet grow numb. She has no idea what time it is. As she straightens her stiff limbs and bends to retrieve her underwear, the salt-cod smell of him rises from her and she wrinkles her nose, suddenly afraid she might cry. How vulnerable she feels standing naked in the near dark of her neighbours' cabin. Why isn't she Rosie Swales or her friend Edna Jenkins, both of whom have been hopping in and out of different beds since they were fifteen, utterly unconcerned with who witnesses their comings and goings? Why is she condemned to be Laura Fisher, barely able to bring herself to glance at the Byrds' couch and ruing the intimacy that took place there just this afternoon? With every item of clothing she dons, Laura grows angrier with herself. She's acted like some love-struck girl. She's too old for such behaviour, too old for Matt Oakes. Where is her self-respect for goodness' sake?

She buries her head in her chapped hands, suddenly weighted down with the realization that she threw that away almost twenty years ago.

Chapter 19

Ray sometimes has to look down at himself to see whether his skin hasn't slid from his flesh and puddled around his feet. Songs come into his head, but they're discordant and off-key. Whispers scuttle down alleyways.

He kneels on the ice and brushes at the snow. The ice is clear in some places and he stares down at the water underneath. When Egypt was little, he'd walk with her over the ice to see if they could see the carp and the muskrats swimming under their feet. Now he's looking for Jimmy Jar's face, half-eaten by those same carp and muskrats, or their descendants.

It's not a face he wants to see. He doesn't want to see the others either, but they sneak up on him unawares. Something never quite makes sense: how they can stand on shattered leg stumps. A man carried his feet, wrapped in newspaper. He offered them to Ray to look after. Like he was handing him a baby. The feet were pale as the underside of a slug; they smelled of gasoline. Ray never knew a person could smell smells in their dreams. Strangely, he never dreams of Red, or even Doyle, whose work he's seen up close. It's the dead who haunt him.

This is the place where Jimmy Jar went down, by Carpenter's barn, but maybe he's travelled around the bay. Could be by now he's out front of Ray's place. That's why Ray hears him at night. Knocking. The sound reverberating across the ice, shaking the cabin and creeping through his feet. Sometimes Jimmy Jar puts his ragged, fish-chewed lips to the underside of the ice and howls like a demon, startling Ray awake.

Chapter 20

Egypt stares out the window. The January sky hangs sullen and headachy; snow whips sideways bearing pellets of ice. Fog lingers till noon when leaden storm clouds take over. Stalking is out. She is destined for hot climates, surely; it's written in her name. With no Matt and no grandparents, her world shrinks to a week-long tedium of bored kids, mind-numbing lesson plans and Gloria with her hand up in class. "Put your face straight," Laura snaps at her most every morning, "or else the wind will change and you'll stay that way."

Then, one chilly Sunday, the minister at MacNab Presbyterian announces that Mrs. Lily Aiken requires an assistant to help her with floral arrangements for the church. Anyone interested should wait after the service to speak with her.

Interested? In flowers? Not until this moment – but the power of suggestion! She can learn. She will learn. She will be the most apt and attentive pupil. She will be her grandmother's right hand.

She stands in the vestibule of the church after the service, her toes pushing against the salt-and-snow-stiffened tops of her shoes. She eyes potential flower arrangers, holds her breath as they pause to shake hands with the minister, exchange pleasantries with their neighbours. Breathes out as they exit down the church steps.

Three ladies remain besides herself. Two are close to her grandmother's age, the third maybe ten years younger. The kinds of people Mrs. Lily Aiken would rather have assisting her with the flower arranging. Egypt hovers at the edge of this group while her grandmother asks in turn after their families and then casts a pithy remark about the weather that Egypt only half catches and at which everyone else laughs. What was she thinking? There is no place for her here. She buttons up her coat, winds her scarf about her neck. Takes a step towards the doors.

"And you, young lady, you're interested in flowers?"

I was. Feeling the group's eyes on her, Egypt bites her tongue. "Yes."

"You can't possibly know anything about them." This from the lady with fussy silver-grey curls and an enormous mole by her bottom lip.

"You're right," she says, her voice edging into irritation. "I don't."

"What is your name, young lady?"

Egypt glances at her grandmother. Those startling blue eyes of hers.

"Evelyn," she says, surprised at herself. "Evelyn Summers."

"Evelyn Summers. Do I know you?"

She blanches under her grandmother's scrutiny. *Why the made-up name?* She promised herself no lies. "No ma'am."

"And you know nothing about flowers?"

Egypt shakes her head.

"Then she'll be no use."

"Thank you, Mrs. Hardcastle, I think I can conduct this interview by myself."

"I take instruction well."

"You do, do you?" Her grandmother takes her hands and inspects her nails, turns them over and runs her cool thumbs across Egypt's palms.

"Come on, Lily. You can't be serious. She's too young. She'll be utterly unreliable. I wouldn't be surprised if she tried to steal the candlesticks and drink the communion wine."

"Is that true, Evelyn? Would you try to steal the candlesticks and drink the communion wine?"

"Sorry?"

"Mrs. Hardcastle doubts your interest in flowers; she seems to be suggesting you're a thief and a drunkard. Are you?"

Egypt glares at Mrs. Hardcastle. She wants her hands back. "No."

"I didn't think so."

She squeezes Egypt's hands and releases them. Egypt, close to tears, pulls on her gloves and strides off. Quick, quick down the steps and she's making her way home. George materializes from a nearby yard and falls into step, trotting by her side. Egypt has crossed MacNab Street and passed two houses before she hears someone calling.

"Evelyn Summers!"

She turns to see her grandmother waving at the top of the church steps, beckoning her back.

"Evelyn Summers and her dog," she says when Egypt draws closer, a smile warming her eyes. "You make quite the pair."

"Yes ma'am," Egypt says, unable to think of any other response.

"Handsome fellow, isn't he?"

Egypt's eyes wander the scruffy terrain of George's grey and wiry coat. His too-small eyes, his droll expression. *Handsome? At a distance, perhaps.* George has his own charm and a regal gait, on account of the length of his legs, but the compliment brings a smile to her lips.

"Does he follow you everywhere?

"Most everywhere, yes."

"And is he well behaved?

"He doesn't make himself a nuisance. Not if you like dogs at least." She's thinking of Ray.

"Well, I don't allow dogs in the house, but he's more than welcome to wait in the mud room for you."

"The house. Your house? You mean I got the job?"

Her grandmother's eyes narrow. "This isn't a paid position you know. It's entirely voluntary."

"Yes ma'am." Egypt is grinning so hard her grandmother breaks into laughter.

"I was impressed with the way you handled yourself back there, Evelyn. And besides, your not knowing anything is a perfect boon as far as I can see. No bad habits for me to drill out of you. And I won't have any of your own fancy ideas to contend with."

Egypt is trying to keep her feet on the ground. She's going to her grandmother's house.

"And as for Angela Wright and Mary Hardcastle, what they know about flower arranging I could write on the back of my hand. No, you'll do perfectly well, my dear. Do you have time now?"

All the time in the world. Without waiting for an answer, her grandmother begins walking down the steps.

"Come along now, we have lots to do."

Up the pathway and along the side of the house to the back, where they stand for a moment and survey the garden. Egypt can't understand what they're going to be doing. Snow still covers the ground, which will be frozen fast for at least another month, and the first snowdrops won't push their way through the earth until late March.

Her grandmother tells her to wait where she is and steps inside, returning moments later with a pair of odd-looking scissors.

"Pruning shears. I want you to cut some branches from the forsythia. Over there," she responds when Egypt looks askance, and points to a bush as tall as herself with a spray of bare branches bending at the waist to touch the ground.

"How much do you want?" She fingers a branch about halfway. "I mean, where do I cut them?"

"Oh, from the ground. Yes, that's it. Take a few – eight or nine will do. Nine is a good number."

Egypt follows her grandmother through the back door, which opens into a tidy window-lined room off the kitchen.

"The mud room," her grandmother announces, "where we work our magic."

"Magic?"

"That's right, Evelyn. The magical act of forcing nature to do our bidding before she's ready." Egypt feels her eyebrows creeping up her forehead. "And we achieve that how?" Her grandmother fingers the soil in all the plant pots arranged along the windowsill, and Egypt realizes she's waiting for an answer. Wonders if her grandmother was ever a teacher.

"I have no idea."

"With warmth and light, that's how. By bringing bulbs inside, we trick them into thinking spring is here, and so they break their dormancy and flower earlier."

"It's that simple?"

"*Simple*. Indeed, it is that: simple." Her grandmother smiles. "I think we're going to get along just fine, Evelyn, don't you?"

Chapter 21

The uppermost branches of the blue spruce the Radcliffes planted when Laura was a girl now graze the eaves of their two-and-a-half-storey brick home. As her mother predicted, trowel in hand, one eyebrow arched wryly, the Gothic brickwork facade is completely obscured, and the lower branches, which push through and over the iron railing that lines the edge of the property, have created a prickly sidewalk bower of sorts that Laura hopes provides her some camouflage as she stands not quite across the road from the house she grew up in. Her parents' house looks different, smaller, on account of all the trees in the area that have thrust upwards and out, dwarfing it. Someone – her father or, if her mother had her way, a tradesman – has painted the stucco a more appealing creamy white than the flat, dull grey Laura remembers, and the green shutters that she and her sister had used to monitor whether their mother was having one of her headache days have been softened with a coat of Wedgwood blue. But even in the fast-approaching twilight, the effect is no less formidable. The phalanx of stone steps leading to the oversized arched door, perhaps. Or the two people who dwell inside.

She leans back against the Radcliffes' railing. Spruce needles snag her muffler and scratch the back of her head. It's madness to be standing here after all this time. A measure of her desperation, how dire things have become. Her feet burn from walking. Close on four weeks of pounding the pavement, looking for work. She should go home, rethink her strategy. Maybe there's another way, someone else's mercy she can fall on? At least she should come back bright and early on a Saturday morning, say, when she isn't so tired, so at the end of her rope. She hasn't the patience for her parents' tight little world, and they won't have changed, will no doubt be worse with age.

She can feel her resolve crumbling, but then imagines having to face her children.

Front door or back? Is it better to face her mother first, or her father?

As Laura approaches the house, the illusion of Fortress Aiken begins to crumble. On the lowermost step, the iron handrail has rusted loose at its footing; the Wedgwood paint is peeling from the shutters and sills. Perhaps her parents have fallen on lean times. It's possible her father has been laid off too – though she watched from a distance as he walked home, briefcase in one hand, umbrella in the other. Unless he's playing the same game she is, leaving in the morning and staying away all day, hiding the truth from those at home. In which case her appeal may be hopeless.

She mounts the steps, lifts the polished brass knocker, raps four times in a confident, upbeat rhythm and then turns to face the street. The knocker rattles as the door catches briefly on the sill as it opens. Laura counts to five, blood surging to her cheeks. When she turns to face her father he is, as ever, the picture of equanimity.

"Laura! It's been a while. To what do we owe the pleasure?" Out of her mother's mouth such words would carry a sting, but his eyes offer the hint of a smile and Laura feels her shoulders edge a fraction lower.

"Aren't you going to let me in?"

"Of course. Of course." He steps back, pulling the door wider. "It's good to see you."

"I didn't –" She stops herself, afraid her face will crumple. Her father pushes the door shut with a gentle click behind her, leaving them standing together in the semi-gloom of the unlighted foyer. He reaches out a hand to touch her arm, but her tight smile, or else all the nails, the jagged pieces of glass pushing out through her skin, stop him.

"May I take your coat?"

"No, thank you." She doesn't remember crossing her arms, now pulled tightly against her chest. "I'm not staying long."

"I see." He folds his long hands together under his chin and then changes his mind and lets them dangle at his sides. He's lost weight. "Your mother is in the dining room."

Laura fakes a sneeze to cover the giddy laughter that threatens to burst from her. She's lightheaded, wants to steady herself against the wall but hesitates to touch the flocked wallpaper lest the velvety flowers turn to dust beneath her fingers. So many smells flood her senses – Brasso and floor wax and soap flakes and elbow grease. The tincture of ammonia overlaid with lavender – sachets of which her mother hangs in every closet and slips in every drawer. Even the faintly rotten stink of their dinner – cabbage with overdone chops and boiled potatoes, no doubt – has her careening backwards into childhood.

Out of habit, she slips off her shoes and follows her father – toe before heel – down the carpeted hallway; a breath to steady her racing heart as he pushes open the door to the dining room. She glances at the piano first, a mahogany upright with turned legs and an ornately carved fallboard she was once so proud of, and then steps into the room and stands at the opposite end of the dining-room table from where her mother is seated. Laura reaches for the back of the chair. How old her mother looks. How lined and fierce. Someone could run a hoe between the scowl lines on her forehead. She glances back at her father. Harsh incandescent light from the chandelier reveals the aging in his face, how drawn he looks: the lines around his eyes have deepened and his hair is grey at the temples. But he looks positively youthful beside her mother's snow-white mane, her gnarled and misshapen fingers, the dowager's hump that pushes her face forwards in a permanent state of questioning. Or submission. *Don't be fooled by appearances*. Anne-Marie's adage. A sudden keen longing for her sister makes her eyes prickle. Though the room hasn't changed, her sister's absence feels palpable. What would she make of their mother now, all thick through the middle and curled over like a comma? Or a witch. Unconsciously, Laura straightens her back. A tiny muscle spasm in her mother's cheek gives away the effort this meeting is requiring of her.

"Mother."

"Laura. Hands off the back of that chair, please. You'll take the polish off." Laura buries them in her coat pockets.

"You're looking well."

"Don't be disingenuous, it doesn't become you. I look old. Old age comes fast on those who've been neglected by their families."

The self-pitying isn't new.

"I'd tell you that you look well, but we both know that would be stretching the truth." Her fingers close around her teacup, then open again. "You look dreadful. Did you cut your hair yourself?"

"Yes, I –" Laura tugs self-consciously at her dry, fly-away locks before remembering her resolve not to let her mother trick her into defending herself. She pats down her coat and forces herself to hold that watery grey-blue gaze.

"If you're going to wear it short, then you should have someone who knows what they're doing cut it for you – a professional."

"I didn't come here to trade insults."

"What did you come for then, pray tell? To ask forgiveness perhaps?"

Laura raises an eyebrow and is immediately struck by how like both her daughter and her adolescent self the gesture is.

"Or perhaps you'd like your old room back? The piano, then? Heaven knows no one else has touched those keys in all these years."

Then you should have gotten rid of it, she wants to say, wants to lean across the table and spit the words in her mother's face. Instead she fixes on the dinner table, the half-moon-shaped dent in the middle where Anne-Marie dropped the silver-plate candelabra one Thanksgiving dinner. And though she begged to be forgiven and promised to clean all the silver every week for the rest of the year, and the year after that, and every year until she left home to be married – Anne-Marie couldn't have been more than seven at the time – their mother punished her by making her sit at the table with an empty plate and watch while the three of them ate ham dinner and pumpkin pie.

"I need a loan."

"Money! I knew it."

"These are tough times," her father says, stepping around so that he is standing behind her mother, his hands cupping her shoulders. "We've had to make sacrifices ourselves."

"I've lost my job."

"Your job! You had a job? What kind of a job? Teaching? I take it that no-good scoundrel you married hasn't been living up to his promise to look after you? Which I predicted."

Her mother has one very long white hair – grey at the tip – sprouting from her chin. Laura focuses on that. *Why on earth wouldn't she pluck it?*

"You did get married, didn't you? You haven't been ..." She looks down at herself and brushes at her dress, unable to utter such unspeakable sin.

"Of course!"

"Ran off, did he? I always said that would happen, didn't I, Father? Do you have any idea where he is?"

"He's here, actually, at home as we speak, preparing dinner." *Drinking. Pacing. Muttering under his breath. Scrounging for a bet or robbing old ladies*. Why on God's green earth is she covering for him? To placate the nasty old crone posing as her mother?

"Don't take us for fools, dear."

Laura looks away, back to the dent in the dining-room table, the sterling silver cruet set with its lacy filigree she longed for years to run her childish fingers over.

"Where were you working?" her father asks, as if it matters now. "I hear there's still a demand for decent typists."

"I wasn't working in an office. I was at Hand & Company."

"Hand Fireworks. Oh my, Laura." Her mother pulls a handkerchief from her sleeve and covers her mouth. Laura is at pains not to roll her eyes. "You had so much promise. There was a time when I thought you would be a concert pianist. You were so talented."

"I was never anywhere near as talented as you wanted me to be."

"What about your teacher training? You could have married a nice man from a respectable family, a man with prospects. A lawyer or a politician. Thomas McQuesten was practically waiting for you to grow up so he could propose."

Laura almost laughs out loud. "Only in your imagination."

"You know you broke our hearts when you ran away."

"When I ran away?" Is that what they've been telling themselves all these years? What about the letter? She wishes she'd taken off her coat; her blouse is beginning to feel damp.

Laura had slept late the morning following the argument over her announcement she was getting engaged. When she came downstairs, the letter was waiting for her on the dining-room table, propped between the coveted cruet set and the silver toast rack. An envelope with her name underlined in her mother's elegant handwriting. The letter had been written by her father. They were sharing their disapproval the way they shared household tasks. She wasn't to use one against the other, this joint missive declared. Their decision was final. *In all good conscience*. What in heaven's name did that mean? That they felt good about throwing her out on the street? That this was a good decision? The right decision? They disapproved of her engagement, so they were throwing her out, leaving her no choice but to marry at once or live in sin. *In all good conscience*. Because where else was she to go?

Instead of feeling giddy and celebratory as she had the day before when Ray slipped a worn ring on her finger – his mother's, or so he said – she felt all shaky inside, like parts of herself had disappeared and the bits that were left were sloshing around inside the shell of her skin. Not so very thick after all. The house was empty. Her first clue should have been how quiet it was when she woke. But the silence felt so welcome, such a reprieve from the shouting and crying of the night before. Her father was at work, of course. But her mother and Anne-Marie were gone too. Their hats, gloves and mufflers missing from the front-hall closet. Her mother's town shoes and best coat. She was probably wearing the carpets thin in the department stores downtown, giving all the shopgirls the sharp end of her tongue.

No idle threat on their part, her father had pulled down the trap-door ladder to the attic and retrieved her travel trunk. It was sitting next to the piano. He must have tiptoed past her bedroom door carrying it on his thin shoulders – this morning or late last night – and she hadn't heard a thing.

Wanting to be gone before her mother and Anne-Marie returned, she packed quickly, inefficiently. Her best clothes because it was important to be pretty, the matryoshka dolls because they were important to her mother.

"You broke our hearts, Laura. Ask your father. And you brought shame on this family. We couldn't hold our heads up in the street. You spoiled your sister's prospects for marriage."

Laura shakes her head. It isn't fair, bringing Anne-Marie into the equation. But since when has her mother played fair? She glances at the window, at the heavy brocade curtains yet to be drawn and the darkness beyond the full, lacy sheers, the pale orange of the newly lighted street lamp. Shutters were never enough for their mother. Anne-Marie would spend hours at the window, peeking out at the world. *At all those men she would never marry?* Who knew what went on in her head? She played her cards so much closer to her chest than Laura ever did. "I rather think the war did that."

"She would never have gone over there if she'd been happily married."

"You don't know that."

"I know that what she wanted more than anything was her own family."

Laura can taste bile in the back of her throat. "I wouldn't be here if I wasn't desperate. The money isn't for me."

"It's for him! Have you taken complete leave of your senses? You can turn around. Go on, get out!"

"Mother." Her father places a quieting hand on his wife's shoulder and addresses his daughter. "There must be children involved, or you wouldn't be here."

Laura nods at her feet, unable to look either parent in the face. "A son and a daughter."

"How old are they?"

"Egypt just turned seventeen, and Aidan will be six at the beginning of March."

"Just a baby."

Her mother looks blanched, but it is no salve to Laura's irritation. "He's hardly a baby," she spits.

"What kind of a name is Egypt?"

"Does it matter, Mother?" She turns to her father, hands spread in appeal, then flinches at the hurt in his eyes.

"Aidan," he says. "It sounds a lot like Aiken."

"It wasn't intentional," she says, wishing immediately that she hadn't. "Look, I don't have the money for Egypt's term fees. She's studying to be a teacher. It's only until I get on my feet. A loan. Until I can find something else."

"That might be difficult, Laura. There are precious few jobs out there."

"Don't you think I know that?" Her feet throb in response.

"Well," her father clears his throat, "then why not move in here with us? You and the children, I mean."

"A loan, that's all I'm asking for. I'll pay you back."

"Move in with us." Her father steps towards her. "Raise your children here."

"Yes, yes, raise your children here, away from that man. It's the perfect solution."

Laura shakes her head. "That isn't possible."

"Be sensible, Laura. If you don't have a job, and from the looks of the rags on your back you're living hand-to-mouth, then you can't afford to pay us back."

"Stubborn." Her mother purses her lips. Lines of disapproval deepen around her mouth. "You always were a stubborn child. Stubborn baby. Wouldn't eat when I fed you, wouldn't sleep when I put you down."

"Move here and let you control our lives. No, thank you. We're happy where we are."

"Do the children have their own rooms?" her mother asks.

"That's your measurement of a child's happiness?"

"Hot, nourishing meals, warm clothes on their backs, good shoes on their feet."

"They're happy where they are."

"Which is where? Some slum in the east end no doubt?"

She could kill Ray for taking her nest egg. She's so angry her eyes feel hot. She could knock the dining table clean of its bloody cruet set. Smash all the flowery china and cut crystal trapped behind the cabinet glass. Instead, she stands where she is, fighting a furious urge to pee, while her mother has her fill of gloating.

"You could have come to us before."

"You think so, do you? Look at us here, now. We haven't spoken in eighteen years and we can barely keep things civil."

"She's kept my grandchildren from me." More theatrics with the handkerchief. Laura has to bite down on the urge to wrench it from her fingers and shove it down her throat. "Imagine the wickedness."

"That's enough now, Mother." Again, her father's long, bony hand on her mother's shoulder, silencing her.

He tries again. "There are two empty rooms upstairs. You could give piano lessons."

Laura pinches the bridge of her nose, warding off the headache that lurks behind her eyes. "I haven't touched the keys in over eighteen years. I doubt I can even play anymore."

"Nonsense. It isn't something you forget. You'd be a bit rusty, that's all."

"I should never have come." She turns and moves towards the door. Her face is burning. She has to get out before Fortress Aiken closes in around her.

"It's beginning to rain. Let me at least get you an umbrella." Her father disappears into the hallway, leaving mother and daughter to face each other alone.

"Your sister would never have treated us like this, you know."

"You have no more idea than I do what she would have done."

"Well, we never got the chance to find out did we?"

"And that's my fault, is it?" She closes her eyes, could slap herself. The monster has done it, dragged her in. *Why do you fall for it, every time? Why?*

"She went away because of you. She died because of your selfishness."

"She died from influenza. If you remember, it was a worldwide epidemic. She could have met the same end if she'd stayed here. And *that* is what we'll never get the chance to find out."

Her father meets her at the door holding an umbrella, which Laura refuses to take. She walks away grinding her jaw. *Stupid.* She was stupid for going there, for thinking that she could ask them one favour, one thing they could do for their grandchildren in all these years. To be humiliated and upbraided like that for nothing.

Head bent against the stinging sleet, Laura hurries home. But the wind impedes her progress. At times it's all she can do to stay where she is, leaning into the fury, eyes screwed shut, and pull air into her lungs. Tears prick at her eyes. The hell with them and their overbearing concern, their carping criticism of everything she is, everything she's done. Who are they to judge?

All she wants is to be home in front of the fire with a scalding hot cup of tea. No nonsense from Ray, no backtalk from Egypt. She doesn't have the strength.

Closing the door behind her, she slides her hands inside her pockets before removing her coat, and there they are, neatly folded. Two crisp five-dollar notes.

Chapter 22

Ray must have passed out somewhere. He spreads his hands, pushes his fingers along the rough weave of the fabric beneath his cheek. Rats have been scratching about in his head, have clawed their way out through his eyes. Throat flayed from liquor, muscles like lead, bones sore and tender. Last night refuses to resolve into a clear picture. Just as well. There are whole pieces of his head he'd like to cut out. Throw away. Burn. His fingers travel south, reach the floor. Linoleum and grit. Dog hair. He must be face down on the couch at home. He's fully clothed. He tries squeezing his toes; even his new boots are still on his feet. But how the hell did he get here? He shudders to think of Doyle shouldering him to the door, his murdering hands on the latch that keeps Ray's two worlds separate.

When he opens his eyes, his hat jigs by in a blur. And back again. A tuneless humming breaks through the skin of his hangover. It's the kid. The kid is wearing Ray's hat, tipped way back on his head so he can see where he's going, where's he's pacing. Strutting the length of the cabin and back, not humming but muttering under his breath. Ray tries lifting his head but someone must have glued it to the couch. He sinks back down. When the pounding abates, he understands it isn't words the kid is spitting out, but angry noises. Ray noises. He'd smile if it didn't hurt so much. The kid's a good mimic.

When he wakes again, Aidan is sitting cross-legged on the floor, staring at him. The hat is by his side.

"Haven't you got anything better to do?" Needles through his eyes.

Aidan picks up the hat and places it on his head. He flares his nostrils. "Haven't you got anything better to do?"

If he weren't such a comedian, he'd give the mouthy little git a whack.

Ray and Malcolm on the rob. Meandering through the damp cobblestoned streets. Waiting under the bridge on Canal Street or ducking behind a loaded dray until some poor unsuspecting mark, having drunk his troubles away, staggers by. Malcolm always the one swaggering up in front. *Hey guv'nor, got the time? Got some change? Got a pencil? Got a minute?* Ray, smaller, more nimble and dextrous, faster on his feet, always coming up from behind. Fingers sliding into pockets, lifting wallets, bills, change, switchblades, pocket watches. Rosaries, lint, ticket stubs, crispy handkerchiefs, shards of glass, slivers of metal. Sometimes he held a butcher's knife in their backs, at the skin of their necks. Malcolm jumping up to swat at the street lamps, the tinkle of breaking glass, shadows disappearing, smoke at the end of his stick. Ray's stomach grinding as his brother teased him with the ends of his saveloy, the remains of his chips, swimming soggy and cold in a bath of malt vinegar. His voice singing out, echoing off the cobblestones, the smokestacks, the sootied factory walls. *Keep yer fucking trap shut.* Malcolm bloodied in the gutter, eyes swelled closed, cheekbones smashed, his jaw hanging loose.

The first is your worst. Doyle's mirthless gapped grin.

His ma's face just before his dad knocked her across the room.

And then she was getting on his nerves. Nagging at him. He just saw her mouth moving and heard the noises coming out of her but couldn't connect the two. Noise and her mouth. So he slapped her. A backhander. No, a punch. She was asking him something. Asking him for something. So he hit her. Knocked her across the room. The kitchen. Small galley kitchen, like something in a ship. Except she hit her head going down. He didn't like the sound coming out of her mouth then, so he caught the trolley into town and then the train to Liverpool. Where he boarded a ship.

This time the light is sharper. Noonish. The cabin is empty. The kid has left his hat perched on the back of the couch. When Ray pulls himself to sitting, his clothes release a sour unwashed smell, along with something more corrupt. Grabbing the hat, he pushes his face inside the crown, catching the faint whiff of childhood. When he places it on his head, it almost hums.

Ray has lost his taste for nights. For days too, with their bruising light shining into the corners of his soul. The flint that is his wife's face. The welling in Egypt's eyes as she turns away from him. The kid. The way he's just wormed his way into . . . Last week, Ray took the stairs in his stocking feet and watched him sleeping. He wasn't planning on watching anything.

Tonight they'll put pressure on the wives. *And last night?* He doesn't like it, but it's better than the killings. He lets Doyle do most of the work. Doyle enjoys it better. Some harsh words, toss a plate or two to the floor, smash a clock, a mirror, dangle the cat by the tail, it never takes much. Even those foolish enough to protest back down quickly once Doyle starts with his steel-capped boots.

Are the killings over? *What happened last night?* The bodies seemed to pile up and then, these past few weeks, nothing beyond putting the wind up some folks. The four dead men lie cold and stiff beside him. Ray thinks he can run away from them, but they find him; wherever he lays his head, there they are, like the walls of a box. Three for the price of one. Is that the going rate? Three welshers for one stooge. Is he off the hook now? Has he paid Red back in full? The bird-handler is there too. That wasn't Ray's fault, but it wouldn't have happened if Ray hadn't been there, hadn't been picked on by Red's henchman. And so he lies alongside them too, along with the pool of blood around his head, like a bloody halo.

Ray checks his hands to see if there isn't blood on them. Dried down the back of his nails, worked into the calluses in his hands. Is he done? Each day that passes without a sign or word from Doyle or Red, Ray dares to imagine he's free again, but then night closes in and the demons start, the voices, the whispering in the walls. He can't risk asking them outright; the answer is sure to be no.

If he could get enough money together, he'd take them away. Laura, Egypt, Aidan. His family. His son. Take them way far away from the likes of Red and Doyle and that long-legged poison from Winnipeg with his big mouth and his hands on Ray's wife.

The Russian nesting dolls explode against the far wall, splinters of red-painted wood underfoot. If she has any money, she's found a new hiding place. He has to grit his teeth until the anger sweeps through him and out, leaves him shaking to the core. Blood in his mouth, the vein at his temple pulsing. The scar across his palm throbs in time to his counting. He fingers the knife in his pocket, pushes his thumb against the blade until he feels his skin puncture. His head a screeching wreck of grinding gears and twisted metal. He could smash the place with his bare hands. Grabs a cupboard door and yanks it from the frame, slams it over the counter. He could set the place on fire and watch it burn. If the dog were here, he'd rip it limb from limb. If he had a gun.

He slams the door so hard on his way out that the glass falls from the window.

Chapter 23

"That too tight?"

"It's good."

"You sure?"

Egypt rechecks the buckles on the straps of Aidan's bobskates. His feet have grown two buckle holes since last year. The straps are probably cutting off his circulation, but she knows he'd rather that than wipe out in front of the bigger boys because they're too loose.

"Mittens. Hat," she calls as he scrambles off the back porch and onto the ice. She brushes at the loose edges of hardened snow before sitting to pull on her own skates.

The sun, shining high in a cloudless sky, gives off little warmth, but the reflection off the frozen marsh is so dazzling that her eyes water the moment she looks up.

"Don't go too far." She cups her hand over her brow, but already Aidan is a blur between her lashes. Headed for the scrum of boys chasing a puck by Princess Point. She isn't worried; they'll tell him to get lost and he'll be back with a sulk on his face. She scans the white countryside for a bounding grey dog, chasing rabbits or running with coyotes. George has been missing since breakfast.

Hockey isn't the only activity on the ice. After a wearying month of grey skies and fog, driving snow and ice storms, the sunshine has drawn everyone from their homes and Cootes Paradise is busy with skaters: families and couples and clutches of giggling girls, children on bob-skates, even a group of curlers. All bundled up against a wind off the lake so crisp and raw it hurts the lungs.

The door to the porch opens.

"Are you keeping an eye on him?"

"He's fine."

"Any monkey business today and you bring him right back, do you hear?"

"Monkey business?"

"If your father starts showing him card tricks, penny-ante games, cheating signals, any silly talk about people who owe him or getting his own back. You know what he can get like."

She drives the heel of her blade into the icy snow until it bites, yanks at her laces. "Ray doesn't have any other kind of conversation."

"You know what I mean."

"Okay." Egypt winds the long laces around the ankle on her skate and knots a double bow in front. "Only sugar and spice and all things nice." She glances up at Laura standing in the open doorway, all spiky elbows and shoulder bones, pulling her cardigan tighter and biting her lip. Her mother is slowly disappearing. Worn woollen stockings bag around her ankles; her wrists look like they'd snap in a wind. She no longer sits with them at the table to eat but stands at the stove and picks.

"I'm not very hungry," she says when Aidan asks or Ray barks.

Egypt can't remember when her mother last grumbled about work, or passed on a scandalous Peggy Parrish story. She pushes the thought away.

"You know you're letting all the heat out," she says, parroting her mother.

Instead of disappearing back inside, Laura steps out onto the porch and closes the door behind her. "Your father's a little troubled at the moment."

"I know; you've told me a hundred times. He's come to us for help and kindness, he had a hard time as a kid, he didn't have a normal home or loving parents." She drives the spike of her second skate harder; the ice chips and splinters.

Laura sighs and rolls her eyes.

"I don't know why you agreed to today in the first place if you're so worried."

"Because I have you to keep an eye out, don't I?"

"Look at him." Egypt nods towards the shinny players swirling like a school of fish in front of their makeshift net, and the smaller figure skating by himself up and down the line of imaginary boards. "He'd rather play hockey than ice-fish."

"For pity's sake, the man is finally taking an interest in his own son. It's the least I can do. Anyway, it doesn't look like Aidan's having much fun over there."

"That's because Darius and Efron have one pair of skates between them. They get mean on the ice. It doesn't help that he's small for his age."

"You're a good sister to him. I couldn't have wished for better." Laura crouches at her daughter's side and, pulling a pin from her own hair, slides it through Egypt's locks by her temple. "There, now you'll be able to see where you're going." She's shielding her eyes with her hand, her skin stretched so translucent between bones and tendons that the sun seems to shine right through her. As Egypt shimmies from the porch onto the ice Laura adds, "You're a smart girl. Use your judgment."

Aidan is already skating back towards his sister, leaning out over his knees, scissoring his arms to help propel him forward. Like most of the boathouse boys, he's taken to the ice as if born with blades sprouting from his feet, but when it comes to hockey, his size counts against him. As he draws closer, Egypt can see from his fierce little face that the boys gave him a razzing. She slows and falls into line beside him, one stroke for every two or three of his.

"They're bigger than you, Aid, you'd only get hurt."

"I can keep up with any of them."

"I'll play with you if you like."

Aidan rolls his head and his eyes, pushes out an exaggerated sigh. "You're a girl. And girls are for cooking and cleaning. Hockey is for men."

"You cheeky monkey."

She's too surprised to be mad at him, by how much he sounds like Ray. Looks like him, too. As they glide into the canal that cuts through the Heights, she stares down at her brother frowning in concentration, squinting into the sun. He carries his father's slight build and mousy colouring. And his nose has grown straighter and more pointed, his face more heart-shaped since Ray's arrival, as if Mother Nature decided to step in and help: *see him? He's yours.*

"I'm asking Dad."

"He can't even skate."

She deserves the wounded look Aidan throws her, but she can't help it sometimes. *Dad.* How easily the word spills from his lips. *I'll ask Dad.* As if the man has been a presence in his life, there for all his birthdays and Christmases, and not some stranger who just turned up out of the blue one day. *Dad.* Egypt tries sounding it out when she's alone, but whether shouted into the seclusion of the forest or muttered at her ceiling, whispered inside the lid of her desk at school or chanted under her breath as she walks home, it sounds false and feels worse. Like her tongue is in the wrong mouth.

She pulls her muffler over her nose and ears and pushes her legs out in long easy strokes, feeling muscles and tendons lengthen in a glorious stretch. Scratch, scrape, the sounds of Aidan carving the ice behind her fade, his little legs unable to keep up. Her speed builds and with it, the urge to charge alone down the stretch of ice before her. Instead she executes a stiff spin and skates backwards past him and into Cootes again. A sharp turnabout and then, "Get ready," she shouts, speeding up. "Hold out your hand." She folds herself into a tuck as she draws close and reaches for him, gripping his arm above his wrist and pulling him along. Now she straightens and they're flying together down the length of the canal, flickers of light and shadow as they pass under the iron fretwork of the rail and High Level bridges, and then the oblong of cool cast by the stone abutments of the second rail bridge. As she warms up, Egypt's strokes grow longer, her speed increases.

"Bend your knees," she calls to him as they skate out into the bay where the ice, studded with dozens of fishing huts, is rough with gouges and frozen footsteps trampled into the surface. Tears stream from her eyes to freeze on her cheeks and lashes. How wonderful to be outside after being cooped up for so long. Everyone growling and snapping at each other. She pulls her muffler free to laugh out loud. Aidan's giggles dart between the ice huts and bounce around the bay as they wind S shapes up and down, back and forth and around the huts, occasionally dodging the odd shelterless fisherman sitting crouched by his hole in the ice. One man opens his door. "You're scaring the fish," he yells. But as long as the air rings with Aidan's laughter, Egypt continues to skate, pushing past the burning in her lungs and her legs and keeping one eye peeled along the shore for signs of Matt. If he's around, he's almost sure to be watching by now.

Some of the ice huts have names painted or scratched above the door to match those of the boathouses they belong to. But even nameless, Manny's hut bears its owner's shabby stamp. Whatever he touches grows mould or falls to pieces. Nails work their way loose from siding, mortar chips from bricks and windows crack. Tiles peel from his roof even when the wind isn't blowing.

The door starts to come off in her hand so that she has to shuffle it back into place, the bottom hinge rusted away or missing altogether. A fug of smoke and stale sweat streams into the atmosphere, revealing four men crammed inside an ice hut built for two at the most. Seated on upturned apple baskets and crushed buckets, knees to their chin, cards in their hands, they blink and squint in the sudden brightness. Egypt stares at the men, and then down at the piles of cards and coins on their makeshift table, a scorched piece of timber laid over the fishing hole and supported by bricks on either side. There's no room inside, so she stands in the doorway with Aidan, her stomach tightened to a small, hard knot.

Ray, seated nearest the door on the left, slides his eyes towards his children and then back to the cards in his hand. Manny, next to him, begins a chuckle that ends up in a wet, choking cough. The thickset fellow is Mick Long's dad, Bill. Though Egypt recognizes the fourth man, she can't put a name to his face.

"Looks like you're busy," she says.

"Won't be long." Ray's eyes don't leave his cards.

"You promised Aidan you'd teach him how to ice-fish."

"What d'you think we're doing, kid," Bill Long rumbles out of one side of his mouth, then shoots a stream of shit-brown tobacco juice out the other. He nods towards the fishing pole trapped under his foot. Now that her eyes have adjusted, Egypt can see the other three have rigged up similar devices. Aidan crouches and then shimmies forward on his belly, trying to see into the hole beneath the poker game.

"I don't think this is what Mom had in mind."

"She's not here, is she?" Bill mugs, leaning forward to ruffle Aidan's hair as if he were a dog. Manny tries to laugh again. Egypt stares at Ray but then has to step out of the way as another jet of Bill Long's tobacco juice sails out the door, staining the ice with an oily plop.

"Do you want us to come back, or should we wait here for you?" Egypt rolls her eyes. "Maybe we could make ourselves useful; we could check to see if anyone's cheating."

Bill Long horks up again. "You were my daughter you'd feel the back of my hand, sassing your old man like that."

"She's all right," Ray mutters. "Leave her."

Is that why your wife isn't around anymore? Egypt wants to say but doesn't. The more vicious rumours have Long bludgeoning his wife to death with the back of his axe eighteen months ago; that she's buried out back of the McKittrick property or under a giant rock below their feet. That she fed the bay catfish for a while. Those more sympathetic say she packed her bags and left when Bill lost his job as a stone carver. Egypt stares at his thick, bruising hands. She's heard Mick yelling and threatening his mother more than once. Apples never rot far from their trees.

"We'll just finish this hand."

"And then?"

"And then I'm all yours."

"I'm out anyway." Manny lays his cards on the table and Bill Long throws his down with a snort of disgust. He rises stiffly, knees clicking, and pushes his way outside.

"Here kid," says the man whose name she doesn't know. "Want to hold the pole?" He lifts it up and when Aidan steps forward, he scoops him up under his arms and settles him on his knee, pressing the pole into his hands. Ray picks up the piles of coins and pockets them. Manny dismantles the table and Egypt stares into the black of the fishing hole.

"You move the rod up and down like this," the man with no name says. "It's called jigging. The fish sees something moving and thinks it's another smaller fish to eat."

"I know how to do this. We did it last winter. In Cootes."

"We did not," Egypt says.

"You weren't with us."

"He's making it up."

"Am not."

"You catch anything?" No Name asks.

"A rope."

"No sign of the neck it was wrapped around, eh?" Manny laughs and Egypt steps back as he launches into another round of hacking.

No Name repositions Aidan's hands on the pole. "People throw all sorts in these waters. Junk. Stuff that's broken."

"Bodies."

"Shut it," Ray growls.

"Careful you don't pull up a finger. Or an eyeball."

"I said shut it. You're frightening the kid." Ray slaps at the rim of Manny's hat, knocking it from his head.

Aidan looks at his father, then down at the fishing pole in his hands. "Dead bodies don't frighten me."

"They should."

"We found a dead dog once. It must of fell in the water 'cause of its short legs. We thought it was a brown bag at first. Then a piglet. It was all swolled up and there was a round, flat rock leaning against the dog's head. Darius said someone had smashed the dog's head in with the rock, but me and Efron said someone put it there to hide the dog's face."

But for the soughing of the wind outside, the hut is dead silent. Aidan swings his legs until No Name grasps him roughly by the ankles, stilling them.

"Speaking of dogs," Egypt says, forcing a smile. "I should go. I have to find George. He took off this morning and I haven't seen him since."

"Got the scent of jackrabbit."

"Or deer." Manny leers and Egypt crosses her arms over her chest, wishing her muffler were a cape. A sack. A metal strongbox.

"It was a sausage dog. Except it didn't look like a dog anymore." Aidan intones, as if to himself. "It was all swolled up and frozen. Like a block of ice. Like it was a great big sausage-dog ice block."

"You ought to train him to bring them back whole." Egypt is frowning at her brother. It takes her a second or two to realize No Name is addressing her. "You eat first and give him the gizzards."

"George?" she says, pulling herself back to the present. "He's too set in his ways. You can't teach a dog new tricks."

"Like hell you can't." Ray cracks his fingers. "You got a big enough stick, you can teach a dog anything." Egypt glowers at Ray and hopes Aidan isn't paying attention.

"You could teach me hockey."

"What you want to play hockey for? Wait till the snow clears, son, and I'll teach you all about footie, a real man's game."

"You should be on stage, Fisher," Manny says with his wet cackle of a voice. "You make a great comedian."

Egypt shuffles around, making more leaving noises. A part of her wants them to protest, to keep her here in this fuggy dark place with them, with her brother, stop her from humiliating herself by skating back and forth in front of the Byrds' place, hoping for a glimpse of Matt, a wave, an invitation to tea. He's been avoiding her. Or perhaps he's been busy. With her luck, she'll bump into Joey.

"I'm off now."

They barely look up. She leaves the door swinging in the wind behind her.

Back across the choppy ice to the smoother stretch of canal, Egypt lengthens her stride and bears down to ward off the chill in her muscles. She could cramp up. Aidan could be getting cold too. Picturing him perched on No Name's knee, she thinks about turning back, even switches edges on her skates, leans into a turn, but then tells herself he's fine. He's a big boy. He can take care of himself.

Gliding aimlessly at the furthermost edge of the marsh properties, she spies first George and then Matt emerging from a thicket of spindly trees at the shoreline. George bounds onto the ice. Behind him, Matt steps cautiously, balancing a brace of kill over one arm. Her heart lifts and she pushes towards him in long, sweeping arcs, scoring the ice with her edges. Waves hello and proceeds to grapevine in front and behind him, cutting so close at times she can smell the woodsmoke in his jacket, the sweet stink of the rabbit flesh he carries.

"Don't mind me," he says as she swoops by again, missing his boots by inches.

"No need to be nervous," she calls over her shoulder. "I know what I'm doing."

"I can see that."

"Beautiful day."

"Where'd you learn to skate like that?"

"Like what?"

"Like a hockey player."

Her laughter rings out across the frozen lake. She's impressed him. Heat blooms from her chest all the way down to her knees. She stands taller in her skates and executes a short spin, arching her back and raising her left leg behind her. Beams when he breaks into applause.

"And she figure skates too. Nicely done, Miss Fisher."

"I played hockey with the boys as a kid. Don't say anything to Aidan," she adds, "it'll hurt his pride."

"My lips are sealed."

She pictures his lips, puckered, leaning in towards hers. Circles him at a remove until the blush fades from her skin.

"See you around," he calls when he reaches the shore where George is standing, wagging his tail.

Not so fast, Egypt thinks. Matt has been recalcitrant for weeks; her progress this afternoon has been hard won. She will not be brushed off so easily. She speeds towards him.

"Help me up, would you?" she calls once she reaches the shore, daring to stretch her hand out to him.

"You can walk in those?"

"It's not as if I'm going far." She could run in them if she had to but affects an air of helplessness, which he falls for: leans down to give her a hand while she takes mincing sideways steps up the snow-clogged bank and, once they are standing on the path, offers his free arm for assistance. Egypt leans a little harder than necessary, nursing the heat in her hand where she has grasped his arm.

"Can you make it from here?" he asks when they reach the Byrds' place.

"I was going to come in and say hello to Mrs. Byrd."

"She's at the market."

"Mind if I hang around awhile?"

"I have to finish dressing these." He indicates the rabbit carcasses, looping one of a series of ropes attached to the side of the shed around a hind leg.

"Mother's in such a foul mood," she adds into the silence that has followed his evasion. "I'd rather stay out of her way."

He fumbles reaching for the second rope. She can feel George watching intently. "What seems to be troubling your mother?"

"Ray. Same as ever."

"They not getting along?"

The rabbits spin in the wind and Egypt sees they have been field dressed, their cavities packed with snow, which is melting, staining the ground a pale pink. "They're barely civil with each other."

"Can't be easy to live with."

He pulls a long knife from a sheath strapped to his leg and slices through the necks in quick succession.

Her pulse quickens. "Can you keep a secret?" The two rabbit heads lie where they have fallen, eyes vacant, noses pointed in different directions.

"Girls and their secrets," he says, his mouth pulled in a wry smile.

"What do you mean by that?"

"Four sisters, remember?" He parts the slits and scoops out the bloody snow. Before either of them can stop him, George darts between their legs, snatches up the two heads and lopes away. In seconds, he's a small dark shape disappearing into the bushes.

"That's one smart dog." Matt stares after him, shakes his head and laughs. Egypt is still busy mulling over the sudden existence of Matt's sisters. Four of them. How could she possibly remember when he never said anything about them before? At least not to her. Not that she ever thought to ask. His four sisters must be something he and her mother have chatted about. "He already had the entrails."

George was with Matt this morning. She's surrounded by backstabbers.

"So you don't have any secrets?"

"Everyone has secrets." He cuts off the feet and hands one to her. "Lucky rabbit's foot?"

She takes it from him, still warm, and slips it inside her coat pocket. It thrums there, a life of its own. "But this is huge. Dangerous."

"Dangerous?" He chuckles. "You sure you want to tell me?"

"More than sure. You can't say anything, of course."

"Now you want me to keep it for you, too?" Taking his knife to the first rabbit, he cuts the skin around the hock joints of the legs and then slices across the lower part of the body between these two points. He looks at her. "Maybe I don't want that kind of responsibility." Removing the tail, he pulls the skin down and forward over the body like a sweater the animal was wearing, leaving behind a greyish, vein-mapped carcass.

"Don't look if it's making you squeamish."

"I'm fine."

He repeats the procedure with the second rabbit. Egypt stares at the skins crumpled on the ground. Pictures the trim around the hood of Gloria's expensive green coat.

Deep breath.

"I met my grandparents," she blurts out before he can block her from confessing. "My mother's parents. It's a long story, but they didn't know about me and I didn't know about them, but I found out because Ray told me and so I went and looked them up and found out where they live and where they go to church and now I've met them." Her voice is shaking; she's shaking. Her feet are numb. She buries her cold hands in her armpits. Matt throws his knife, stabbing the icy ground.

"Your mother's parents?"

She nods.

"And you didn't know they existed?"

"And they didn't know about me."

"But now they do?"

She blows on her hands and buries them in her armpits again. "Not exactly."

"Meaning?"

"They don't know I'm their granddaughter. I'm biding my time, waiting for the right moment to tell them about myself. See, they kicked my mother out when she married Ray and wanted nothing more to do with her." She gives Matt a doleful look. "If they know who I am, they may not want to know me, either."

"So who do they think you are?"

"Evelyn Summers."

"A name you made up?"

She nods. There's no point trying to explain about her teacher.

"How does Aidan feel about this?

She pinches her lips together and stares at the ground, at George's trail of pink, following it until she's gazing out at the marsh. Her eyes drift to the bay, where Manny's foul hut is crouched on the rugged ice. She can smell the fourth man suddenly, as if he were sitting beside them, Aidan perched on his lap. Nausea wells up the back of her throat. If only she could fly over there, scoop him up.

"You haven't told him, have you?"

"I could kill her for this, you know, for lying to me all these years."

"Egypt, you're lying yourself."

"I might have known you'd take her side."

"It isn't a question of taking sides. If you want an honest relationship with these people, you should be above board and honest with them."

"They kicked my mother out."

"So you're punishing them?"

"No. I don't . . . What are you saying?"

"The longer you leave it, the worse it'll get." He bends to pick up his knife.

"I wish I'd never told you."

"Me too." He sighs. "What did you think I'd say, Egypt?"

I thought you'd hate my mother. She's going to cry. She bites down hard on the inside of her lip; tastes blood.

"And what about your brother? Doesn't he count?"

"I was going to tell him, eventually," she says, looking away. "I just didn't want him blabbing to everyone."

"Don't you think he'd like to know he has grandparents? I can't believe the mess you've made of this, Egypt."

"It wasn't my fault. I didn't lie to me all these years. I didn't tell me suddenly out of the blue that I had grandparents I never knew about. You're getting mad at me and I don't understand. Why aren't you mad at her?"

"It's not that simple, is it? It was a mess before, but now it's a bigger mess."

"This is about you and her, isn't it?"

"I don't know what you're talking about."

"Are you having an honest relationship?"

"We're not having a relationship, Egypt."

"And Myrtle Todd was never your grandmother."

He stoops to pick up the skins, his mouth tight.

"I saw you. The day after Christmas. I saw you both go into the house here. And she didn't come out. And . . ." she doesn't want to say the words anymore but they've built their own momentum. "And so I came over. I was going to tell you then, about finding my grandparents."

His hands have stilled, and she shivers in the bright sunshine. "Was she here?" Her voice has shrunk inside itself, sounds like it's coming from some tinny, faraway box. "Was she hiding?"

He frowns and shakes his head. "She was long gone. Drank her cocoa and left."

"So what was she doing here?"

"Why is that any of your business?"

"Because she's my mother."

"And she's my friend."

"My mother doesn't have friends."

"Maybe you don't know everything about your mother."

"Does my dad? I'm sure he'd be interested in knowing you two are friends."

"What is that, Egypt, a threat?"

"Are you in love with her?"

"Don't be ridiculous." He lays the skins against his leg, insides facing, and rolls them up together.

"So you just like spending time with older women. Older *married* women."

"You're behaving like a child."

"Right. I'm too young, is that it?"

He levels his gaze so that she feels it burning clear through every layer of her, exposing every uneven shred of her being. Then he waves a hand, covered in gore. "Go home, Egypt."

Chapter 24

Egypt's fingers hover over the playing cards sprawled face down in the centre of the dining-room table. She's memorized half a dozen cards or more and could easily win, but hesitates; it's more fun watching her grandmother pluck a card from the pile to make a pair, the way her face lights up and she laughs, revealing a row of small, yellow teeth. But her grandmother's conquests are few and far between, and at this rate, the game could last all afternoon. Several times, Egypt has placed her fingers on key cards, trying to lead her, but her grandmother's memory is terrible. She picks a card: the wrong one. "Hard lines," her grandmother crows. Egypt flashes a fake disappointed look and clicks the butterscotch candy she's sucking on against her back teeth, sweeps it to the other side of her mouth. For such a sour-looking woman – on more than one occasion, Egypt has caught a glimpse of her grandmother's face, unarranged and unaware, her expression bitter, the lines that frame her mouth and cross-hatch her brow conspiring to draw her as miserable as possible – she eats a lot of sweets. Every Sunday afternoon, when Egypt leaves her grandparents' house, her pockets are stuffed with hard-boiled candies and gaily wrapped chocolates. In addition to the mysteries behind forced bulbs and flower arrangements, she's learning a whole new, sweet lexicon: sherbet and licorice and nougat, humbugs and butterscotches and pear sours and chocolate limes (her favourite), and chocolate éclairs (her other favourite), as well as aniseed balls – a nasty licorice concoction that she spat out once she turned the corner at the end of her grandmother's street. She plans to save whatever she leaves with today (hopefully not aniseed balls) for Aidan's birthday this coming Tuesday. If anyone asks, she'll say she got them from Gloria.

Her grandmother lines up her captured pairs, runs her fingers over their backs as if feeling for some secret message there. She plucks a sherbet lemon from the glass candy bowl on the table.

"Mr. Aiken and I were having a little talk this morning, and we decided it would be nice if you brought your brother with you next Sunday."

Nice for whom? "My brother?" Serves her right for even thinking about him.

"The little boy who was with you at the Carol Service on Christmas Eve. He is your brother, isn't he?" She pops the candy in her mouth.

Not such a bad memory after all. Briefly, Egypt considers discarding Aidan: a neighbour's kid. A nephew. But she's learning how quickly lies take on a life of their own, require elaborate histories and family trees. The butterscotch has grown sickly sweet; she wants to spit it out, but her grandmother has fastened her with her blue-grey eyes.

"He and Mr. Aiken could do boy things together while we see to the flowers."

"He's a menace. You need eyes in your elbows when he's around."

"He's house-trained, surely?" Her grandmother is smiling.

"Barely. You'd have to move all your nice things out of his reach." No way is she bringing him here to steal her grandparents' attentions, their candy. Besides, he'd be bored stiff. After church, her grandfather loses himself in the newspaper, or his books. He dozes. Forcing bulbs and embroidery and crocheting, her grandmother's activities, would hardly keep a young boy amused. He has the patience to sit with a fishing rod, but a card game would have him barking like a dog under the table or tying his grandfather's laces together. Odd times he's content to curl up and be read to and have his head stroked, but it's never long before he's off again, a bullet in the shape of a small boy, careening about the place.

He would wear them out, test their old-people patience. She's saving them an Aidan-sized headache.

"Well, if you feel like bringing him along one Sunday, he's more than welcome."

"Sundays he plays hockey."

"All day?"

"More or less."

"Maybe when the weather warms up he'd be more inclined."

"Maybe."

"Well, that's me done. I have to see to dinner. Why don't you play a nice game of solitaire?"

"I could fold some of those for you if you like." She indicates a box filled with palm fronds and a small pile of Palm Sunday crosses on top. "I'd like to," she adds when her grandmother hesitates.

"Try one or two then, and we'll see how you do."

Egypt plucks a greenish palm frond from the box on her left. Folds it in half, folds, twists, folds and folds again. She slips the tail through the back of the loop. Sets it down on the table to her right. Soon a small pile accumulates. It grows into a mound. Heat tick-ticks from the radiator beneath the dining-room window and the room grows warm. She sheds the slippers her grandmother has lent her. Her old pair, the ones she slips on to see to the laundry during the drying-outside months. Winter and rainy-day laundry is dried on a creel that lets down from the kitchen ceiling on a nifty system of ropes and pulleys.

Fold, fold, twist, fold, fold. The heat coaxes accumulated smells from the carpet, upholstery and curtains, odours that years of cooking, eating and living have left behind. Sweet and stale. The smell of dusty curtains and floor wax, lavender and mothballs. Nothing she can conjure her mother from. In fact, there's little if anything in this house to suggest her mother ever lived here, at least the parts of the house that she's been allowed to see. No photographs or pictures. Nothing atop the piano or the mantle, nothing gracing the walls. Not here in the dining room, nor in the living room into which she was briefly allowed that first Sunday.

"This is where we entertain guests," her grandmother said, and Egypt glanced around, opening her eyes wide and then snapping them shut, as though she were a camera, taking in every detail possible to be pored over and analyzed later. Stiff-looking chairs in nubby brocade with fussy cross-stitched cushions designed not to tuck into the smalls of backs but rather to be read and admired: *A Stitch in Time Saves Nine. A tidy home reflects a tidy mind.* Her grandmother's version of *out of sight, out of mind,* perhaps.

Upstairs remains a mystery.

Egypt has tried to imagine her mother seated at this dining-room table, pen poised over her homework, ringlets and ribbons bouncing, waving her knife and fork in the air as she regales her parents with stories of her day. Unwrapping Christmas and birthday presents. But the pictures refuse to come. It's just too hard to imagine her mother as anything other than her mother, with her chapped hands and chewed cuticles, her furrowed brow, her fly-away hair.

Her grandmother bustles in from the kitchen, and the smells of Sunday dinner trail behind her: roast beef and Yorkshire pudding, Brussels sprouts and gravy. She stops to peer over Egypt's shoulder.

"How nimble you are." There's a smile in her grandmother's voice. Egypt smiles in return. She's pleasantly surprised at her own dexterity. Years of believing herself to be clumsy and tomboyish, too big and awkward for delicate tasks, only to sit here now and watch her fingers fly, having quickly memorized this set of movements. The tapered ends of the fronds are already dry and unyielding. By the time they are needed, four weeks from now, the crosses will have turned golden and lost most of their sharp greenish scent.

"My hands can't move so fast anymore. Arthritis." Her grandmother rubs at her swollen and misshapen fingers.

"Do they hurt?"

"They ache, and they're stiff in the morning, particularly if the weather is damp and cold. Or if I've been doing a lot of gardening."

Egypt glances at the piano. "Do you still play?"

"Oh, goodness me, no, I was never any good at music. I like to sing the hymns at church, but the piano was always beyond me." Her grandfather lowers his newspaper, and Egypt senses his sudden attention.

"Our daughter played," he says. "She was very talented." Egypt's heart blooms in her chest. *So soon?* She should have prepared herself better. Is she ready for this moment of revelation?

"You have a daughter?" She's focussed on her hands: Fold, fold, twist, fold, fold.

"She died," her grandmother says.

"She –" Egypt can't formulate the rest of her sentence for the pounding of words in her head. Her lips are parted. Did she say anything?

"The Spanish influenza."

"The Spanish influenza." Her hands are paused mid-task. Since Ray's revelation, she's been wondering how her mother could dismiss her own family, sweep them under the rug. Her grandmother gathers the crosses, stacks them back inside the box from which the fronds were taken. The box is whisked out of sight.

"Would you like to set the table?"

And that's it; the moment has slipped away. Her grandmother is at the sideboard counting cutlery. Her mother is dismissed. No more talk about the lost daughter. Lost to the Spanish influenza. Lost to a lie.

All through dessert – apple crisp and custard – Egypt eyes the fourth pudding. Is curious when her grandmother rises from the table and sets about making up a plate of food, a slice of beef, some potatoes and sprouts, the Yorkshire pudding sitting on top like a puffy golden lid. A care package for later? She covers it with parchment paper and, when she sees Egypt watching, explains how it's for an infirm neighbour. Egypt is disappointed. Mrs. Pendlebury can't fend for herself, and her son lives in the States. A woman comes weekdays and Saturday mornings to take care of her and her house. Cooks and cleans, bathes her, changes the bed. On Sundays Mrs. Pendlebury becomes Egypt's grandmother's duty.

"I just take her over some Sunday dinner. A plate of what we had. Wash her hands and face; tell her about her friends at church. Who was there, who wasn't. Read to her if I have time. I'll tell you what, we can walk together. She lives on Caroline Street. It isn't out of your way."

But Egypt isn't ready to go home, would stay the night if asked. She can't bear the idea of running into Matt, can't wipe the look of disgust on his face from her mind. "I don't have to leave yet. I could stay and do the dishes for you. Or some ironing." She's never wielded an iron in her life. If her mother could hear her, she'd be after getting her head examined.

"What about your own family? Won't they be missing you?"

Egypt stands and begins clearing and stacking the plates. "They'll hardly notice I'm gone."

"Oh, I doubt that very much."

"I'll be very careful," she adds.

Her grandmother smiles. "I know you will." She unties her apron and hangs it on a hook inside the pantry door.

Her grandfather is asleep in his chair. His lips parted slightly to emit a soft snoring sound, his glasses pushed askew on his face by the wing of his chair, newspaper slipping from his lap. She could clear her throat and wake him, but would rather not. Her grandfather isn't as easy to talk to as her grandmother. Sometimes she catches him staring at her, puzzling, and she worries he's seen through her lies, that he suspects she lives nowhere near Charlton Street, that her name isn't Evelyn Summers. Egypt tiptoes back out and closes the door behind her. At the foot of the stairs she pauses, one hand on the newel post, one slipper rocking the bottom tread. Over the knocking in her chest, she can still make out the long, raspy intakes and short, puffy exhales of her grandfather's breathing. Shifts her weight onto the first step. Pause. Climbs to the second. Pause. The radiator clanks, cooling down. Egypt's foot hovers – *up or back down?* – until gradually, the air fills with the rhythmic sounds of his breathing and she takes the third step. Which creaks. Her heart booms again. Warm in spite of the unheated air in the hallway, the cold penetrating the soles of her borrowed footwear. Faintly, she can see the moisture from her breath. The fourth step creaks, as does the fifth. Her rib cage feels bruised; a light sweat has broken out across her face.

Upstairs is starker than she expected, but then, in the realm of the wealthy – or at least wealthier than her own immediate family – she only has Gloria's household to compare to. The bedroom has linoleum on the floor, though newer and in better shape than the stuff that covers the floor of the cabin. Two twin beds separated by a braided oval rug. She runs her fingers over the matching pale yellow candlewick bedspreads. Each bed also has a matching bedside table and lamp, and a picture hanging above it. Pictures of mountains and valleys in dull colours – different yet the same somehow – that feel like they were painted a long time ago. Egypt gets no sense of a personality behind these pictures. Not like the artwork in Gloria's house, which has Mrs. Henry stamped all over it.

Whether she hugs the walls or ventures out into the middle of the room, the floors creak. There isn't a safe place to walk. On the dresser, Egypt finds the silver hair set she was seeking but never found at Gloria's. She sits on the padded stool before it and picks up the brush, pulls it through her hair, mixing her dark hair with her grandmother's white ones.

The bedroom door opens. Her grandfather stands in the doorway.

Egypt leaps from her skin, the brush clatters to the floor.

"I think I know what you're doing here."

"I wasn't stealing anything." Her face in the mirror is pale, her eyes wet. How had she not heard him on the stairs?

He steps into the room and approaches her. "Your name isn't Evelyn Summers, is it?"

"I'm not a thief. I've never taken anything. I never will." Let him think anything but that she's a thief.

"I've had my suspicions for some time now."

Egypt struggles to her feet; her legs feel disconnected. Backing against the wall, she inches her way to the door. A choking sob is building in her chest, making it difficult to breathe. It's the disappointment in his voice that is unravelling her.

"I think it would be better if you waited downstairs until Mrs. Aiken returned, don't you? Then the three of us could have a talk."

Why isn't he shouting? She could shout back then, throw it in his face who she is, what she's doing here. But to open herself up to this tall spectre of a man now, with shame burning her face. She can't even bring herself to raise her eyes. She bolts from the room and down the stairs. At the door, she flings off her grandmother's warm slippers and rams her feet into her damp shoes.

"There's a storm picking up," he says from the top of the stairs.

She grabs her coat from the stand, yanks at the sticky door and steps out into the slush of wet snow already clogging the porch. One, two, three stairs, she hurries into the swirl of thickening snowflakes, not wanting to hear the door close behind her.

Chapter 25

Egypt parks her hands between the boys' two sets of longer hands. Cold gnaws at her wrists. Her elbows ache. They angle themselves like arrows, right knees bent, left legs stretched behind them, arms out in front.

"One, two, three, together." They heave with all their might. Nothing. It is like pushing at a mountain. The granite won't budge. Mick curses. "Put your shoulders into it." He sounds like his dad, a burl of a man with a voice that belongs to someone twice his height.

They push again. Nothing. And again. Egypt's feet slip continuously on the icy grass, giving her the impression she is walking against this mountainous headstone. Mick begins chanting under his breath and she tries pushing to his rhythm. Sweat tickles at her temples despite the wind and the frost, the burning cold essence of the granite seeping into her bones. She straightens and shakes the tension from her legs, hand cupped in the small of her back. What is the point? They're only here for a laugh. Aren't they?

"Get your hands back here and push, Fisher. We need all the help we can get. Even girl help." Mick is taking this too seriously. "The fucker's got to move sometime. You always give up on the first try?" This time Egypt leans her left shoulder into the stone, facing away from Mick and the grim set of his rat-like face. Mick's theory is, as his dad helped the stone into place back when he had a job, his son should be able to move it now and get him his job back. Egypt believes he is only half serious. Mick is here because he likes to be out causing mischief, and knocking down a few headstones in the cemetery is his idea of a good time. Except now that they're out here, Egypt realizes any one of them can be recognized by the light of the three-quarter moon. Even in silhouette. Mick because he is broad and thickset, like his dad; Joey because of his thin sloping shoulders, and the stoop he has already acquired disguising his height around Mick; and Egypt because, well, if not by the muscle of her hair, which even when braided still sweeps the small of her back, then because as always, George is loping around the periphery, keeping an eye on all her doings. A girl and her dog.

Egypt is not having fun anymore. The evening started out on a much lighter note, the three of them cracking up when Egypt spotted this scolding epithet on a headstone: *I told you I was ill.* But now her shoulder muscles have knotted, her hands are numb and her head pounds in the beginning of a headache. Two more pushes. One more and she will make her excuses and leave. And then she feels it. The tiniest shift; a give in the stone's obduracy. A small flicker of triumph. Joey collapses against the stone in laughter.

"Keep it together," Mick snorts, his breath ragged. And they do. Together, they master a rhythm of rocking that sets the great stone to cracking as the supports holding it to the base strain and eventually snap. *One, two, three, rock; one, two, three, rock.* A dull scrape of granite on granite, like the entrance to a cavern grinding open, and the stone leaves its bed and hangs suspended for a moment before crashing to earth with a dull thud.

"That'll wake the spirits," Joey says and laughs again. Unrestrained. A high-pitched sound that makes Egypt squirm a little, embarrassed for him. Still, it isn't enough to spoil her exhilaration, her blood pounding, leaving her wide-eyed and trembling. *What a feeling.* But Mick is all business. No time to gloat or revel in the glory of downing a mighty stone. On to the next target. A soapstone cross atop a sandstone base. Tall and slim. An easier target than the heft and weight of granite. It shifts at the second push, topples on the fourth. A thud and a snap.

"We broke it," Mick yips, all piss and vinegar now. Fists pumping imaginary bags. Or opponents.

Egypt hangs back as he shadowboxes towards their next conquest, Joey hunched in the same dance. The cross is in one piece, slumped against its base like a fallen soldier waiting for his comrades to come pick him up. Mick circles a granite obelisk, rubs his hands together, pushes at the night air, weighing up his approach. His mood has warped; now he seems bent on not only knocking them over but also breaking them. Whereas Joey is giddy with triumph, Mick's anger has distilled into a smouldering rage, heating the air around him. Even the snowflakes, falling thicker and faster, appear to melt before they can touch him.

"The more the better, right gang?" The more work there will be for his dad, he means. *For other people's dads*, he is always quick to add. Which is what makes Egypt doubt his motives. Mick is a vandal. He's made wrecking public property the habit of a lifetime, is forever borrowing other people's things and destroying them if he thinks they've done him or his family wrong. *He's two short steps from a prison cell*, as Egypt's mother likes to say. She'd be beside herself if she knew Egypt was out in the middle of the night with Mick and Joey. Jick and Moey. Her dad would laugh his wheezy smoker's laugh and pat her on the back. Matt would – she squeezes her eyes shut, clenches her whole body as if to expel him. Matt Oakes is no one she has ever cared about. He is a hollow ache in her chest. Ditto her grandparents. Two hollow aches. Three.

Another headstone topples.

"One more," Mick eggs them on. "You're not turning chicken on me, are you?"

"No chickens here," Joey bleats, nudging Egypt with his elbow.

"No chickens here either," Egypt says, sounding more enthusiastic than she feels. One more. Two more. She can't face being alone, trapped inside her head, and if she stops moving now she'll catch cold.

"This one next," Joey declares, lunging towards the obelisk with a drop kick.

"Keep your fucking voice down, Payne, you want the cops out here?" Mick spits under his breath. Egypt squints at the engraving on the base, searching for more levity, though the grandeur of the obelisk would seem to rule out any but the gravest of sentiments.

"Not this one." Egypt has caught a glimpse of the name. *Aiken*. Her mother's maiden name. Common enough, but still.

"We'll smash the fucker," Mick says, as if she hasn't spoken.

"I said, not this one."

"What's so special about this one?"

Anne-Marie Aiken. 1897-1918. Beloved daughter of Stephan and Lily. Taken from us too soon. A dead aunt. *She died. . . . The Spanish influenza*. How many other Stephan and Lily Aikens can there be?

"Fisher. I'm talking to you."

She can't tell them. Words ash in her mouth.

"Let's get a bigger one. Something that'll smash into a hundred pieces." Can he hear the pitch of her voice climbing the night sky?

"No, come on, Fisher. You tell me. What's so fucking special about this headstone? Why should this rich fucker be let off any more than any other in here?"

"Tall and pointy, giving God the finger. There's a shitload of them in here. Half of Hamilton's money telling God to eff off. Like they've a right to be pissed."

"Shut up, Joey."

"Yeah, shut the fuck up, Payne. I was asking Fisher here a question."

"Not this one. I don't know why. Just a feeling, that's all."

"Just a feeling, that's all," he mocks, his face inches from hers.

"You're taking this too personally."

"I am, am I?" He smirks, as if he's just caught the measure of her. "This *personal* to you, is it?" He horks up and spits on the engraving. "Anne fucking Marie fucking Aiken. *Taken from us too soon*. Why the fuck would you care about the stupid bitch. You know her? She's been dead since you were a kid. And now she's sleeping under some fucking stone that cost more than all the meals my brothers and me have ever ate. And you're wetting your pants here."

"It was supposed to be just a laugh." George nudges at her legs, his shoulders just under her hand. The change in Mick's voice has brought him back from deer chasing or running with the coyotes, or whatever it is George gets up to when he slips away in the dark.

"I'm still laughing, Fisher. Me and Payne here, we're still laughing our fucking heads off." But Mick has stepped back, George's head poised before his belly. And then Mick disappears. Cold fishes through Egypt's stomach. He disappears into the night so quickly. She waits without moving, staring at the piece of darkness that has swallowed him. She can feel Joey closing the space between them, tenses against his reaching out and touching her, her ears blocked in case he whispers her name. She taps her fingers against her leg, calling George back, willing him to slip his long, furry body between them. *Where is he? Has he followed Mick?* The wind cuts through her coat, and the sweat soaked into her clothing turns icy. Where the hell has Mick got to? Should she go home? She starts in the direction of the bay and suddenly, Mick is standing in front of her, short of breath.

"Going somewhere, Fisher?"

"Where've you been?"

"To see the Queen, where d'you fucking think?" Joey giggles again and Egypt risks a glance at Mick's hands. Empty.

"Frightened you, did I, Fisher?"

"No. I'm just cold."

"Then get back to work." He releases a guttural howl and charges at the Aiken monument, bellowing for them to follow. Frenzied, he hammers at the base with both his feet and his fists, and Egypt finally registers that the thwuck of stone-on-stone reverberating through her skull is coming from a rock in his hand. Mick is fired up on something other than mischief and residual anger over his dad's loss of work. It is like a cable has snapped inside him. He is drunk on the power of his own violence.

Egypt wants to exchange glances with Joey, get his take on the situation, but is still reluctant to make any sort of sign towards him. He'll take it the wrong way and she'll be forced to hurt him again. Also, she worries that turning her back on Mick's mood will shift the focus of his violence onto her.

The rock smashes into the granite base again. "Fuck, oh fuck," Mick spits between clenched teeth. The rock slips from his grasp as he rubs at his arm. Then he turns to face them and the moonlight falls on his face, his twisted features. "Am I going to get any goddamned help around here?" Voice raw as flayed flesh.

Egypt squeezes her eyes shut as the three of them heave and push against the base of the obelisk. It takes less physical effort than the others to topple, the monument's stability disadvantaged by the very grace of its tapered height. When it comes crashing to earth, it cracks both lengthwise and across its width in several sad pieces. Mick wades into the destruction and grabs for a piece, flails it around, pulverizing the remains.

nne M r Aike 1897-19 . Beloved daughter o St ly. Taken fro on, the base now reads. Egypt pictures her grandmother's face turning to stone and then crumbling, a face she is only just getting to know, a face she is still learning to read.

"Take that, you fucking cunt." Mick's voice is surely carrying across the graveyard towards the road and the houses on Jones and Woodbine. Egypt has had enough.

"George," she calls, and begins walking away, towards home. She doesn't realize she's crying until she feels Joey's arm around her shoulder.

They cross between stones, Egypt careful not to step on anyone, Joey not minding where he puts his feet. They walk until Mick's curses fade to murmurs on the wind. Egypt leans her head on Joey's shoulder, and Joey holds her tighter. They walk across the grass towards the path that winds through the cemetery.

"You want to go home?"

To Laura and Ray and their poison? She shakes her head.

"To Tucketts'?"

She hesitates.

"I have something to warm us up." He pats his jacket pocket and she lets him lead her past the gardeners' shed and to the right, where the path climbs the former ramparts from the War of 1812, into the side where some of the city's wealthiest patrons and businessmen have embedded their families' crypts. At the gate of the Tucketts' crypt, the one that dozens of boathouse kids have hidden out in over the years – smoking and drinking hooch, gambling – Joey stops and turns to wrap his arms around Egypt, pulling her close. She closes her eyes, wishing she were someplace else and Joey was a different kind of man. He holds her until he feels her resistance give.

"You want to go inside?" The words sound dried in his throat and she pulls back and watches as he licks his lips, unsure. In the dark, it's easier to pretend. She can't really see his acne and his stained teeth, and the smell that comes from his skin isn't altogether unpleasant.

She nods before she can change her mind.

Afterwards, Egypt brushes roughly at the grit that has stuck to her skin and pulls on her clothes. If he says one word to her, if he even opens his mouth – that boyish fuzz on his upper lip, those long, discoloured eye teeth – she'll shout or cry or slap his face. There's a scream rolling inside her head, ugly, purple, pushing against the inside of her face. *Why doesn't he hurry up?* If he leaves first, she won't have to say anything, won't have to push him away, recoil from his touch. Clumsy. Clumsy. He can't get his sneakered foot inside his pant leg. He's dancing around, a strange laugh gurgling in his throat. She wants to hit him for still wearing his sneakers, for never having taken them off, for wearing ugly socks, for having been born.

She pulls open the heavy crypt door.

"Hey, wait up," she hears as she slips into the moonlight and begins running across the graveyard, zigzagging between the headstones. She's running and there's George, running in front of her, looking over his shaggy shoulder to make sure she's with him. They run to where the trees thicken, then dart for the road, the bridge, the path to home.

Chapter 26

A grey, silent day; falling snow muffling the sounds of commerce, of pedestrians, of the car that draws close to the curb. Laura tucks her chin inside the upturned collar of her coat. The car doesn't stop but instead rolls on behind her, a menacing shadow keeping pace. Her skin prickles. Ray trouble? Or the police and that business with the shattered gravestones again. As if boathouse kids are the only ones capable of vandalism.

She tries walking faster, driving her heels into the soft snow, packing it for purchase. Her feet slip out from behind her. She's one step from falling on her face, imagines a hand grabbing her from behind. Faster. Stumbles, then rights herself. She fixes her gaze straight ahead but from the corner of her eye sees the car drawing level with her, the driver leaning over. Suddenly, the passenger door swings out.

"Get in," a voice calls. Familiar, yet out of place somehow. She tries running, her leg muscles pinched and screaming as she struggles to keep her balance.

"Laura, it's your father. Get in the car."

Her father. She stops and stares. Brushes a gloved hand across the front of her hat. The snow is falling thicker and heavier.

"I was hoping we could have a little chat."

"About what?"

"Hop in." He pats the seat beside him.

Hop in?

"I didn't know you owned a car. I didn't even know you could drive." She's staring down York Street, eyes screwed up against the swirling snow. How can the light be so grey and glaring at the same time? "That day I came to see you. I waited down the road until you came home. You were walking."

"I used to use it more before things got so difficult. The steel company has laid a lot of people off in the past year and a half. I didn't think driving around in a car would send the right message."

"Solidarity with the worker. Or ex-worker."

"Laura, if you'd just get in, I have a proposition for you."

"How long have you been following me?"

She feels small and vulnerable. Her life laid out before him in all its patheticness. She hasn't done so well for herself after all. He knows where she lives. *Has he seen the children?* She's been found out and is overcome by a wave of exhaustion. However the next part of her life is going to shape up, things have already been set in motion. It's almost a relief.

"You're going to freeze standing out there."

"Why the car?" Her skin prickling from the light coating of sweat.

"I thought we could talk, privately."

"You're scared of her too."

"Don't be facetious, Laura, it doesn't suit you."

"You even sound like her, you know."

"Just hear me out."

She climbs into the car, removes her gloves and places them in her lap. She's never sat inside an automobile before. When he pulls away from the curb, she places her hands on the seat on either side of her legs, feeling a little uncertain. Heat blows from a vent by her knees. The snow she's brought in on her boots melts, a small puddle forming at her feet.

"Where are we going?"

"To visit someone."

"Who?"

"Mrs. Pendlebury. She lives on Caroline Street."

"And Mrs. Pendlebury is who to me?" She's doing it again, sounding like Egypt. It's almost frightening.

"I've lined up a job for you."

"A job. If this is about piano lessons . . ." Irritation creeps through her veins, but she bites her tongue. Any job would do at this point; she hasn't been able to secure so much as a hint of work herself.

"I don't expect you to thank me, Laura. Gratitude was never your style."

"I don't even know what you're proposing. I told you, I'm not secretarial material." She would have thanked him. Honestly, she would. The words were right there on the tip of her tongue. But then he had to pull that bloody sanctimonious attitude, and now her shoulders are up past her ears. Good job they're not stopped at a traffic light. It's all she can do to stay inside the car.

"It's a nurse-and-maid position."

Visions of soiled bedpans and foul-smelling dressings. "I'm neither a maid nor a nurse."

"Mrs. Pendlebury is almost eighty, almost blind and largely confined to her bed."

"Why?"

"Her hips."

"Then why isn't she in hospital?

"Old age isn't a disease. You'll realize that when you get there. She just doesn't have anyone to look after her. Her son lives and works in the States. He can only make it up for a visit once a month or so."

"So why doesn't she move down there?"

"The point is she needs someone to cook and clean. To read to her. Make sure she gets her medications on time."

It's on the tip of her tongue to say, *I thought you said she wasn't sick*, but she knows how petulant this would sound.

"I have to think about it."

"I don't think you can afford to be picky."

"You don't have to do this for me."

"Believe it or not, Laura, I'm not doing it for you, I'm doing it for your children. My grandchildren. So they don't suffer."

She pulls a handkerchief from her coat pocket, sniffs and dabs at her nose. She needs to compose herself. "You followed me home."

"Would you not have done the same in my shoes?"

She can feel her scalp tightening in the beginning of a headache. "And I can just imagine what my mother had to say about everything."

"She wasn't with me."

"More dissembling, Father? You'll be running with criminals next."

"Facetiousness isn't getting us anywhere, Laura."

"But spying on me is?"

"The boy, Aidan –"

"He's small for his age."

"He looks like a good boy."

"Looks can be deceiving."

"You don't mean that."

"You're right. He is a good boy. In spite of having Ray's blood running through his veins."

"Your mother and I, we'd like to meet them, to get to know them."

"Now? After all this time?"

"Be fair, Laura. We didn't even know of their existence until a couple of weeks ago."

"How difficult would it have been to find out, if you'd only taken the trouble to make inquiries?"

"So we were supposed to chase after you, was that it? You made your choice when you ran off to marry that man."

"No, you made it for me and then turned your backs. Do you have any idea what it took for me to finally approach you? How hard it was to stand in your dining room with my hand out while she crowed and carried on?"

He is silent awhile, intent on his driving, a series of stops and turns now that he's left the main road. "I can only imagine," he says eventually.

Laura stares down at her lap, at her hands, twisting the handkerchief, trying to stop herself from crying.

"Do you regret it?"

"That remains to be seen, doesn't it?"

"Because, despite your mother's behaviour that day, I can say for both of us that your coming back into our lives is the best thing that has happened since your sister . . . since she passed."

Has she come back into their lives? That was never her intention. What heartache has she let herself in for?

"Why don't you bring them over on Sunday?"

"I can't." She shakes her head, raises her hand to ward off even the idea of it. "I can't be in the same room as her."

"Then why not let them come over by themselves? I could pick them up and drop them off. Your mother could feed them up with one of her roast dinners."

"Now you're saying I don't feed them properly?"

"I'm saying nothing of the sort. Why do you have to be so touchy all the time? Not everything we say or do is a challenge to your authority, Laura. We'd just like a relationship with our grandchildren."

"I can take care of my children, you know."

"Without a job?"

He pulls up outside a three-storey red-brick house on Caroline Street. Stained glass panels along the tops of the front windows, a circular window by the front door. He turns off the engine.

"So which is it going to be?"

Laura leans her burning forehead against the cold of the passenger-side window, closes her eyes and takes a deep breath to ease the tightness in her chest.

"Mrs. Pendlebury, you said?"

PART TWO

Chapter 27

Egypt isn't sure if the shadows flickering on the ceiling have woken her, or the noise. A muted hiss and snap. Voices shouting. Downstairs, George whimpers, scratches at the door. She sits bolt upright, pulling the covers with her. Behind the curtain partition, her mother stirs.

"What is it?

"You smell that?"

"What?"

"Smoke."

Laura's bed creaks. "Fire." Her voice sounds oddly disconnected, or maybe it's the static in Egypt's head, like an off-frequency radio. Outside, a discordant clanging of metal on metal – someone sounding the alarm. More voices shouting.

"Fire!"

"Fire!"

Egypt scrambles from her bed and pulls back the curtain that divides the upstairs. Aidan is already out of bed though he looks bewildered, as if his mind hasn't quite caught up to his body, standing there, shivering in the cold. Laura tugs her shawl around her shoulders and fishes under the bed for her slippers; Egypt and Aidan follow her downstairs. A dance of orange on the water, reflections of the flames.

"Ray," she calls, all glass and vinegar.

Egypt makes out her father's gaunt silhouette by the window. She tastes dirt at the back of her throat. *How long has he been standing there? Why is he not outside already?* It's too dark to see if he's wearing his boots.

"It's the Byrds' place," he says, as if he were announcing the weather.

"The Byrds'?" Laura rushes to the window.

Matt. Matt could be in danger. Could already be dead. The words swim through Egypt's head without touching the sides.

Men thunder past the door, shouting authority. As she stares at the light display in the window, Egypt's eyes sting. Her nose and throat burn. She grabs at the wall to stop her world from shaking. How can she be so cold and hot at the same time?

"There goes the shed," Ray announces.

"*There goes the shed?*" Her mother's voice thrums through her chest, theatrically low and chilling. "Is that all you have to say for yourself?" She's by the door, pulling on her boots, her coat. "It isn't some bloody Christmas store window, you know."

Egypt's legs have grown numb. Aidan's hand finds hers. Their mother's tone has breached a wall. *Bloody*. Even Ray has turned from the window to stare at this new Laura.

"What are you saying?"

"I'm saying nothing."

"Didn't sound like nothing. Sounded to me like you think you know something."

She's shrugging Aidan into his coat, tugging him this way and that like he's a rag doll. "Get dressed, Egypt," she says, "and make yourself useful." She's at the door, boarded over where there used to be glass, one hand on the latch, the other cupped around the back of Aidan's head. "Just going to stand there all night, are you?" she says between gritted teeth. "While your neighbours burn to death?"

An ugly silence stills the room, and then a sudden percussion of roaring and crackling, a rattling of windows as night air rushes into the cabin along with the smell of burning creosote. She slams the door behind them; George bays at the ceiling. Ray turns back to the window.

"It's spreading to the next house."

Which house? Is it coming here? Egypt takes a step towards him. It's the flatness in his voice that is keeping her here in the cabin, stopping her from running after her mother; it's part of the nightmare that clamps her throat, sandbags her limbs. She can't escape the monster.

Make yourself useful.

"They need every set of hands out there." Her own have grown all thumbs; she struggles with the buttons on her coat.

Years ago, while out on the water fishing, father and daughter witnessed sparks from a passing train ignite the roof of the Allens' place. In less than a minute, Tanner Reid, a fireman with the city who lived a few doors along, was organizing the Allen brothers into an efficient firefighting machine – hands passing buckets down to the water and back up to Tanner, who had stationed himself on the roof next door. Neighbours rushed to help. Her dad rowed for his life, his neck and arms all cords of sinew, his shirt limp and sticking to him, but by the time their boat touched shore, the flames were already out.

A shiver runs through her as she wills him to move. Could be his sleeplessness has sapped his energy. The shadows render him cadaverous, like Death himself, standing watch at the window.

"You ever find your grandparents?" he asks without turning around.

"Yes."

"You tell your mother?"

"No."

"Good girl."

"Are you coming?" Hand on George's collar, she pauses at the door. "Dad?"

The fire is a theatre of roiling flames, a dozen open-throated monsters bellowing at the sky, thundering through her bones. The taste of sulphur in every mouthful of air. It's like running into hell. George bolts for the woods. An ordnance of embers, some the size of tin cans, pop and zip across the night to land on the icy snow, or neighbouring buildings. Three or four mini-fires flank their dam. And then she's stumbling in darkness, the wind cramming sooty, choking smoke in her eyes, her nose, her throat, through the pores of her skin. On her knees, coughing, eyes streaming, and the wind changes again. Now she sees the outline of the Byrds' house, shimmering through a ground-to-roofline blaze of witch-fire yellow, as if the house were no longer sure enough of itself for straight lines. The moon and stars have disappeared. Heat pours over her. Her lungs are going to shrivel, her ears will split and peel from her head.

"Out of the way," she hears, just as a cannonade starts up from the burning house. Gunfire. Who's firing, she thinks, and in the next instant is tackled and slammed to the ground. She's winded. Dazed. The body pinning her all muscle and hard angles. *Matt?*

"Ammunition. It'll be spent soon."

Joey Payne. Egypt struggles to push his weight off her, but Joey has flattened and spread himself like a flagstone, his weight even and immense. Bullets whiz over their heads.

"You're okay. I won't let anything harm you. Or anyone." His earnest admission delivered into her hair. She gives up, a whimper in her throat. Why must Joey Payne be her saviour?

"I have to go." Tears run down the sides of her cheeks and into her ears as the wind blankets them in smoke again. "I have to find . . . I have to find my mother."

When the wind swirls and uncovers them, a burly arm reaches down to drag Joey up to standing. "Your aunt's place," a sledgehammer-wielding man says.

The Mullinses are five doors down from the Byrds. Egypt cranes her neck to look. The flames are spreading quickly. Too quickly. The man shoves an axe at Joey's chest and lumbers towards the fire. Joey turns to glance down at Egypt, but she waves him off. Blood is thicker than a crush. Or it should be.

Where is her mother? Aidan? She gets to her feet and scans the clutches of onlookers gathered at the edge of heat, coats and shawls pulled over their nightclothes – the elderly, mothers holding children, children holding babies.

Men and women have formed a line from one of the sand bunkers Tanner Reid constructed; another small group stand braced on the ice, swinging axes. Matt amongst them. She laughs aloud in relief, feels the bands constricting her chest scissored away. Even the sight of her mother running frantically along the shoreline – her jerky, spastic movements as she slips on her bum, then on her face, scrabbling to secure her footing – cannot shrivel the gladness in Egypt's heart.

She joins the line passing sand buckets, and while it is already clear that no one can get near enough for the sand to have any effect, her head and arms are soon a blur of full one way, empty the other. Along the line, frustration and panic are building. She can feel it in the touching of hands, the clanking of buckets.

Several loud cracks sound, and a spray of sparks across the night sky heralds the collapse of the Byrds' roof. The line of firefighters wobbles and then breaks as the sudden updraft sucks the air from around them, rippling their clothes as if it might tug them into the flames. Egypt throws herself to the ground as embers shoot skyward with the heat, dance in the air and then spit off into darkness. *Stand up*, she commands her legs, but she's so drained, so bone-achingly tired, and it's hard to focus on anything but the flames themselves, their sucking, roaring energy.

A triumphant shout from the water – the ice-breakers have wrestled the stirrup pump into place. The line of bucket-passers realigns itself to run between the Bairstows' house and Myrtle Todd's place, on the other side of the Mullinses' house, the marsh monster's old lair fast on its way to becoming a firebreak. Like a dull bass in the background come the thuds of axes on wood, the concerted grunts of men swinging in tandem.

"Stand back," they shout to those hovering nearby, to each other.

A groan as the house leans off its axis, an air-shifting thwump as it folds in on itself, scattering building debris and random household items.

And then her eye is drawn to Ray, standing at the edge of the firelight, staring, hands in his pockets. The cast of yellow and orange distorts his features. He's laughing and then he's crying and then he's laughing again. Another crack rends the air as the house next to the Byrds' surrenders to the heat, discarding walls like a spent flower shedding petals. They tumble towards the water, hissing steam and exploding on impact. Egypt turns and runs for safety.

When she looks back, Ray has disappeared.

Chapter 28

Matt lifts the mug of lukewarm tea to his lips. Someone has laced it with rum. He doesn't remember how he came by it. Ditto the sandwich in his other hand. Even how he came to be sitting on someone's kitchen chair at the edge of the gathered crowd. His hands are black, his eyes dry, skin tight across his face. It's as if he can still feel the flames inches in front of him. He balances the sandwich on his leg, peels back the top layer of bread. Egg, perhaps. Or cheese. He has no appetite. Bends to scoop some freshly fallen snow and lifts his hat to brush it through his hair, wipe at his face. Trying to part the fog in his brain, trying to remember the sequence of events that led him here. To this moment. Did he black out? Every muscle in his body tugs and twitches.

The snow that began falling sometime in the night has obscured the peripheral debris, smoothed over the footsteps down to the marsh and the scuffle of mud at the water's edge. The flakes melt before they can touch the still-smouldering ruins. The smell of burnt chattel arrives in waves. The smell of charred wood. Charred lives. From the piles of ash and blackened debris, puffs of tarry smoke emerge; here and there, a glow of orange coaxed by the wind, a pocket of heat.

He coughs as if he might choke, lungs screaming. A fireman lumbers towards him in his long coat and stiff boots. Matt sees the man's lips moving but hears nothing. He nods he's okay but he's trembling, nerves taut as a sprung trap wire. Holds up a hand as if to ward the man off, and the fireman lumbers away again, melting into the crowd. He wants to shake off the people who come by and squeeze his shoulder, pat him on the back. Wants to lay his stiff and aching body in the snow, let the gently falling snow – or is it ash? – wash the smell of smoke from his skin and blanket him, render him anonymous, another soft mound in a melting wintry landscape. But every time he closes his eyes, he sees the back of Stan's jacket disappearing into the billowing black smoke. Feels again the jolt through his arms and shoulders as the handrail snapped and the stairs gave way. Or was it the floor above him that disintegrated? Left him hanging in mid-air. He draws a long, shaky breath. It feels like someone ripped a huge scab off his heart.

"Anything you could tell us about what happened here tonight?" A policeman has materialized in front of him. The place is crawling with uniforms now. "Matt Oakes, right?" He glances at his notes for confirmation. "I understand you were in the Byrds' house when the fire started?"

You understand nothing, Matt thinks, searching the crowd for Joanna. He needs a clear head, time and space to reason out what he should and shouldn't say. Which lies will bear up under investigation.

"I live there." *Lived.* After nearly five months at the same address – the longest he's stayed any place since leaving Winnipeg – he's homeless again.

"You were a tenant."

He wonders who's been talking. How much the police already know about him.

"And what exactly were you doing when the fire broke out?"

Broke out. As if it had been caged somewhere all along, waiting to escape. "Listening to the radio. We were sitting at the kitchen table listening to the radio and having a nightcap."

"We?"

"Stan Byrd and myself."

"What time was this?"

"Around midnight, I guess."

"Listening to that jazz, were you?"

Matt stares up at him from under the brim of his hat.

"Reception any good out here?"

"The city's just over there." Matt indicates with his chin.

"Drink a lot, did he, Mr. Byrd?" *They're looking to make this easy for themselves*. Matt runs a finger over his cracked lips; tastes blood and smoke.

"Now and again." *More than he could handle*. Not that Matt blamed him. Anything to keep the boy in the acid vat at bay, with his outstretched arm and melting flesh, his voiceless scream. And when he'd had a skinful, Stan was less inclined to growl at Matt, and the two of them could pretend for a while that they were friends.

"Knock the lamp over, did he? Candle? Or was it a cigarette?"

"I thought you were here to ask me questions." Surely it can't be that easy? Keep mum about what he saw and let Stan take the blame. Or maybe it can. He can feel his heartbeat thrumming in the hollow of his throat. He needs to inch his way carefully into the lie. Someone else could have been awake at midnight. Looking out the window. Others might have heard the sounds of breaking glass, running feet.

"I'm trying to establish how the fire might have started."

Matt watches the policeman's pencil moving across his notepad, then turns in his chair to gaze at where the Byrds' place used to stand. What's left won't be worth sifting through. Smart, whoever they were. Or whoever sent them. The broom handle they used to break the window will be nothing but ashes. Likewise the lighted balls of rags lobbed in afterwards. No rocks left behind to tell a different tale. No brass lighters. *Arson is nearly always impossible to prove*. His father's words. He'd come striding through the front door of the house Matt was putting the finishing touches to. The sanctuary he'd built to harbour his mother from his father's ill will, his alcoholic ruin, the vitriolic anger he'd hauled back with him from the trenches. Matt was planning on giving her the key on her birthday, just a week away, but his father, having grown suspicious of his son's activities, had begun spying on him, leaning on building suppliers and contractors, some of them army veterans. Vernon Oakes strode in wearing his spite and his hobnail boots. They echoed through the empty rooms, gouging the floors at every turn. "You think you're so clever, don't you?" he sneered at his son. "Think you've got all the answers. That your shit doesn't stink." He took his brass trench lighter from his pocket and flicked it in Matt's face. That night the house burned to the ground. When, the next day, Matt confronted his father, the older man grabbed him by his lapels, pulling him closer than they'd been in years. For a souse-bucket, he was surprisingly strong. "Don't think I don't know where you got your money from. *Son.*" More snooping. Matt should have known better than to hang onto Earl's timber mark and certificate. Keepsakes are only for those with a clear conscience. Or had he browbeaten the truth out of Matt's mother? Vernon spat at his feet, pushed him away. "You disgust me. You're a fraud and a cheat. Someone needs to teach you what it means to respect the dead. If you'd been on that battlefield, if you'd seen what I'd seen, had to do what I've done –" But Matt was already walking away. "Go on, get out of here. And if I ever see your face round here again, I'll turn you in."

The policeman's pencil has stopped. Matt licks his bloodied lips. Clears his throat.

"Stan was waving his hands about." Not a lie.

"He was drunk, then?"

"He was pretty animated. We were talking politics."

"And then?"

"And then his hand shot out and he knocked the lamp clean off the table."

"An accident waiting to happen, these places are." His pencil scratches across the page. Scratch, scratch. Fingernails on a blackboard. "You should hear the fire chief going on. Death traps, he calls 'em."

"It could have happened anywhere."

"Yeah, sure."

Matt slides his eyes over the policeman's polished leather shoes, the sharp creases down the middle of each pant leg.

"I'm guessing it took hold pretty quickly."

He nods. Flames raced across the floor to lick at the curtains, set them swaying. The cabin filled with oily smoke. In less than a minute, the fire was curled around the ceiling.

"And did you attempt to put out the fire yourself?"

"Of course. We tried smothering the flames with cushions from the couch, but it didn't help much." Stan was next to useless. "Farrells," he kept shouting, flailing his arms. "It's the Farrells, back for their pound of flesh." He was pretty drunk, now that Matt thinks about it. But the Farrells were Stan's Achilles heel. He'd been obsessed with the idea of their coming back for revenge, had been waiting for something like this night ever since he pushed the kid back down into the acid. But whether it was the Farrells who set the fire or men hired by them – or someone else entirely – Matt couldn't say. He never got a look at the one guy, only heard his feet pounding down the path, disappearing into darkness. The slower one he tackled to the ground.

Such a shock when he turned him over. Earl Todd's waxen features looming up out of the darkness. He nearly yelled out in surprise as his mouth flooded with the taste of the river again, brackish, metallic. He hocked up and spat, wiped his mouth on his sleeve.

"Who the hell are you?" he growled, shaking his quarry for looking like the past, for looking like a dead man, for sending Matt hurtling back to that day on the river when Earl Todd's body had reared up from between a jam of logs the two of them had spent days and weeks salvaging. Earl Todd minus his eyes and lips. In fright, Matt had leapt back, lost his balance and plunged into the swirling black water. The shocking cold of it rendering his arms and legs useless. As he whirled and sank, tugged this way and that by the currents, he worried about the logs, about possible deadheads in the water – which was more than likely what had done in Earl Todd in the end – thrashing about until his fingers locked around something hard. A primitive crawl at the base of his brain told him what it was before he dared open his eyes to look. The old-timer's arm. He recoiled, tossing it away in horror, but the dead man's skin slid off into his hand instead, a cold, rubbery sleeve. And then he was under again, swallowing mouthfuls of water, water that tasted like death and felt like it, too, an icy hand pushing down on his head. He was disoriented and panicked but knew if he didn't get a grip, if he didn't calm down, he'd end up in the same watery grave as Earl. And so he urged his body to relax, muscle by muscle unclenching himself, trusting the water to carry him to the surface, where he could take a breath and grab for a log. When his strength returned, he pulled himself along, hand over hand until he reached the bank and scrambled onto shore. The river having delivered its message, the logs closed up around Earl, trapping him. The riddle of his employer's disappearance now solved, Matt looped a rope around his decomposing body and pulled it from the water. It was while he was sitting around the fire he'd lit to cook himself some supper and savour what was left in Earl Todd's flask that his plans began to change, that greed began to take hold.

Matt has had plenty of time since then to wonder what direction his life would have taken if he hadn't found Earl's timber license that afternoon while moving the old man's body. Who Matt Oakes would have been if he hadn't become Earl Todd. If he had acted differently that day. Heroically. Instead of following his own markers back to where he'd buried Earl's body deep in the bush and then carefully removing them one by one as he made his way back to the river again.

"So then . . . So then," the policeman repeats himself, louder, aware he's lost Matt's attention. "So then you called for help?"

"I ran outside." *Grabbed the gun.* He's sure he grabbed Stan's shotgun first, laid across the table where he'd been cleaning it. He uncurls his fingers, still feeling the imprint of the trigger, the heft of the freshly oiled stock clutched in his palm. *So where's the gun now?*

"You ran outside." He's tapping his pencil, losing his patience.

"There's a series of metal triangles set up on posts every hundred yards or so. One of the residents here is a fireman."

"Reid, we know; someone's talking with him now."

Someone's talking with Reid. Of course. And how much does Reid know? How much can he divine?

"And so you sounded the alarm."

He did? It's possible. He stretches out his fingers again. Nods.

"And Mrs. Byrd? Where was she this whole time?"

"Asleep upstairs." Has he talked to Joanna yet? Matt can't read the man. Stan went to wake her, get her out of the house. But then he tripped and knocked her off balance. She tumbled down the stairs. The stairs. He feels weightless, like the moment they gave way beneath his feet. A ribbon of cold through his stomach. He looks up into the policeman's face.

"Where are they now? The Byrds?" But he can't, he won't, wait for the answer. On his feet, he begins pushing his way through the crowd, mumbling apologies, asking to be excused. So many people. The entire community, it seems, huddled shoulder to shoulder in the unfeeling light of early dawn. He makes his way to the front in time to see two firemen disappear inside the smoke-blackened remains of the Mullinses' cabin.

He stands with the crowd as everyone watches and waits. Mothers holding their children's hands, wives with their heads on their husbands' shoulders. Somewhere between the crowd and the doorway, Max and Zadie Mullins lean into each other.

The first of the firemen emerges, carrying a bundle in his arms. *How do they decide who leaves first? Do they draw straws?* He steps over the rope the fire marshal has used to cordon off the gutted homes, and a corner of the grey blanket he's carrying slips, revealing a child's foot. A pause in the silence a man could fall through, and then Zadie Mullins' keening cuts through the air. She sinks to her knees as the second fireman, carrying another grey-blanketed bundle, steps over the threshold. People part to let the men and their small charges through. Eyes follow them as they walk with due reverence along the path and up the hill to the waiting coroner's van. Some minutes later, the two firemen, their passage made awkward by the empty stretcher they now carry between them, make their way back down the path and along the waterfront, once again disappearing inside the Mullinses' fire-blackened house.

As Matt looks away, he catches sight of Laura in the crowd, her face pinched tight in the grey dawn.

Chapter 29

"Be an angel. Go downstairs and put the kettle on."

"Like some cinnamon toast with that?" His fingers walking up her spine. "Jam?"

"And scrambled eggs. In plenty of butter." Laura smiles into the dusty pillow.

"A couple of strips of bacon."

"You're making me hungry."

"And you make me –" Matt curls one arm around her shoulders, hands cupping her breasts, slides his knees up the bed and tugs at her hips so that they're spooned together. She leans back into his embrace, his hardness, the delicious heat of him travelling through her skin, her muscles and sinew; warming her bones. Her ragged soul.

"It's fun playing house with you, Mrs. Fisher." Lips nuzzling the back of her neck. "How much time do we have?"

She turns to him, to the window with its view of the outside world, and kisses his dry lips. "Never enough." The inchoate shadow of the tree in the front yard stretches its hazy grey across the bed. Sinking back into the pillow, she closes her eyes, wishing the world away. Any moment now, the yellow-orange of the street lamp will pierce the gloom, set the tree with its gnarl of pointy branches in sharp relief. Stabbing at her. *Get up, get going*. Laura rubs her toes under Matt's legs to warm them, threads her legs through his. Such a gift, having him here with her today, to be able to drink in the essence of him in daylight, to be able to take their time. Their usual arrangement is more clandestine: he waits outside Mrs. Pendlebury's in the alley until dark. She signals with the kitchen light that the coast is clear, and he slips inside. A furtive coupling in the dark and then she leaves and makes her way home. By the time she returns the following morning, he has let himself out again. It's both exhausting and exhilarating. She feels young again. Alive. Hums to herself as she cleans Mrs. Pendlebury's bedpan, sings out loud – her voice a rusty creature in need of practice – as she washes her flaccid old-lady limbs, clips her gnarled and yellowed toenails, washes and combs her brush of fine white hair. She smiles at strangers, smiles at the darkening ceiling.

But now, as if happiness must always have its antidote nearby, a darker thought creeps in. *What if this is a prelude to the end? A farewell lovemaking.* Now that the inquest is over, all that holds him here in Hamilton are her arms and the sanctuary of Mrs. Pendlebury's bed. By its very nature, this arrangement can only ever be temporary. As the days draw longer, it will become more difficult to hide Matt's comings and goings from the neighbours. As for today's outcome, she has yet to ask. Matt has spoken little at all of the fire, and she hasn't pushed him, admiring the way he compartmentalizes his life. There's no messy spillover of emotions the way there is with Ray, who has trouble drawing lines around anything. Matt was so anxious to lose himself in her when he showed up today that she held her tongue, reluctant to trail the spectre of death into bed with them.

"It's almost dark out. I should get her supper ready, before she wakes and starts fretting."

"What if she's already awake?"

"Then I'll tell her she's been asleep for hours. She's easily confused."

"She could have heard us."

"She hears things all the time. I'll slip a little whiskey in her drink."

He sighs a long and deep sigh that Laura feels all the way down to her toes. "I could do with a little whiskey myself."

She stills. A frisson of excitement, of unease, scuttles across her skin.

"How did it go this afternoon?"

"Hell."

"Who was there?"

"Everyone."

She presses her lips together. *Ray. Riling emotions. Setting everyone against each other.*

"No," he says, reading the fret lines on her forehead. "Noticeable by his absence. But Egypt was there, in the front row, chewing on her fingernails."

She glances sharply at him.

"Don't worry; she was penned in by Joey and the rest of the Paynes and the Mullinses."

"And Joanna? How was she?"

"Not good."

Laura nestles her head into the crook of his shoulder. "Still staying with her sister?"

She feels him nod.

"Still insisting the Farrells had something to do with it?"

"Uh huh."

A gust of wind pushes the bare branches against the window. Tap, tap. Laura counts to a hundred before framing the next question. Wills all traces of Ray from her voice. Whispers, "Do you ever think that she might be right? That maybe it was arson?"

"No."

She waits for an explanation. When one isn't forthcoming, she adds, "You said yourself you'd come back, if it was your child. The night of the beating? That first night –" She should leave well-enough alone he has been tense and preoccupied leading up to this date, and that it's finally over must be an enormous relief. But now that the subject has been opened, it isn't so easy to let go. There are too many claggy and unanswered questions. She licks at her dry lips. "You asked me, *If someone had played God with your child.* Remember?"

He doesn't answer.

"It's just that it caught so quickly. And there's nothing left. Of the Byrds' place, anyway."

"An expert on fires now, are you?"

She's taken aback by his sharp tone.

"No, of course not."

"Because it had been burning for some time before you arrived to save the day."

"Hey, hey, what's got into you?" She raises herself up on one elbow.

"The fire was an accident. I'm so sick of people . . ."

"What? Sick of people what? Has someone said something?" *Did they mention Ray's name at all?* It's what she really wants to ask, what she deep-down fears. That Ray might have started the fire, wanting to get to Matt, to her.

"No. Don't worry about it. It's nothing. I'm just . . . I'm sorry, okay. I didn't mean anything. I'm tired. It's been a tough day."

She strokes his arm, her hand travelling his rib cage till her fingers touch the bedclothes on the other side. She pulls him tight, tears pricking behind her lids. She wants so badly to believe him. Wants to believe it was an accident and nothing to do with Ray.

"It's okay," she says. "Stan was a friend of yours."

"No, he wasn't. He was a miserable son of a gun, but he didn't deserve to die. And Joanna didn't deserve to lose her husband and her home. And she didn't deserve to be treated with such contempt on that stand."

"Because she believes it was the Farrells who came back and set the fire?"

Matt rubs his hands through his hair, makes to pull it in frustration. "They grilled her. Counsel for the Coroner assured her she wasn't on trial and then proceeded to browbeat her as if she was."

"Do you think the jury believed her?"

"The jury saw a hysterical old woman trying to protect the reputation of her dead husband. Of course they didn't believe her. They ruled Stan's and the kids' deaths as accidental."

"Accidental." *So Ray gets away with murder.* There's a snarl of emotions behind her breastbone, blocking her breath. "That's all they had to say?"

"They made recommendations for fire safety."

Which is understandable. Three people have died. Two of them children. She searches Matt's face for something else he's not saying. "And?"

"Fire safety, or the whole community should be condemned."

"*Condemned.* They said that? And you kept it to yourself all afternoon?" She sits up, hand on her chest, trying to keep her voice under control. "You didn't think I might want to know that? To know that a bunch of biased do-gooders on a coroner's jury have just levelled a gun at my home, the community where I'm raising my children?"

He sighs and closes his eyes. "Because I knew how you'd react. Maybe I was giving you a reprieve."

"Or giving yourself one. Fire safety recommendations. And of course nothing's going to be good enough is it? And where's the money supposed to come from to pay for it? The city? Not likely. Fire safety recommendations! And I just know how everyone's going to react. Al Bairstow will be after calling meetings till everyone's sick of the sight of each other, but nothing will get done, nothing will change, it never does. So that's it. It's over." She throws her hands up in frustration. "The city's won. They'll drive us out before you can count to ten. The bastards. Joanna's got it wrong. It wasn't the Farrells came to set the fire, more likely some councillor hired a couple of thugs and gave them a pack of matches." *Hired Ray?* "Oh my God!" She clamps a hand over her mouth, the possible truth of what she's said like a rude shove in the chest.

Matt pinches the bridge of his nose and says nothing.

"I know, I know, I'm sorry. I'm upset. I know it was an accident. Stan was drunk; he knocked over the lamp, like you said." But she's shaking her head. "It's just that you don't realize how convenient this whole thing is for them."

"And you don't know that it'll come to anything. A month from now they'll have forgotten all about it and everything will go on as it was."

"No, it won't. They've been shuffling the papers on this western entrance plan for years." She lies back down beside him, but her body is rigid with tension, her mind racing.

Matt lies very still, eyes closed. So silent that she wonders if he's fallen asleep. When eventually he speaks again, she startles, his voice shattering the air. Shattering her world.

"Maybe it's time I was leaving."

"Leaving? Now?" She reaches for the blanket; pulls it to her chin. Curls her toes against a dull aching in her belly. *So this is it*. "For good, you mean."

"Yeah. I've been thinking of moving on for some time."

How cold the room feels now. How pinched and mean, with its faded wallpaper and threadbare curtains, the dresser packed with musty bed linens – she snooped once, her first week working here. Mrs. Pendlebury's marriage bed. When she could still climb the stairs. The crooked cross on the wall above the bed, and the picture on the nightstand of the Pendleburys in their younger days, posed in the front yard by a much smaller tree.

An icy cavern has opened in her chest. She can feel herself falling through its bottomless shaft, nothing to grab onto. "But I'd miss you so much."

"Then come with me."

Oh, her poor heart, clanging in her chest. She breaks into a giddy laugh. "And where would we go?"

"Fort William?"

"Not far enough."

"North Bay?"

"Too north."

"East or west?"

"West."

"Not Winnipeg."

"Farther than Winnipeg, much farther." She's giddy at the prospect. "The West Coast."

"Land of towering cedars and Douglas firs." He squeezes her hand. "The lady knows what she wants."

"Crashing rivers and mossy banks. The wide blue stretch of the Pacific."

"Eagles."

"Salmon."

"Seals. And killer whales."

"I'm picturing you in a beaver hat, chopping wood and hauling water."

"Not so different from how I live now. Minus the silly hat."

"Good." He turns on his side to face her, hand holding her at the hip. "Now that's sorted, when do we leave?"

She kisses the soft skin of his mouth, his eyelids, his cheeks with their prickle of beard, the cleft of his chin. "And where does Aidan fit into your picture?"

"We'll bring him with us."

"And Egypt?" Nursing a broken heart and a murderous grudge against her mother.

"We'll wait till she's finished school and off on her own, teaching."

And then what? She'll be doing what she did before. Running away with a man. A man who entered her life with a lie. *If you can't do it above board, Laura, there must be something shameful about it.*

"I'll leave a forwarding address for Ray, shall I?" Her voice has flattened out. "Or just wait till he tracks us down and dismembers us in our beds."

"He doesn't have it in him."

"I don't know what he has in him these days. I don't know the man anymore. It's as if something's missing inside. I don't know where he's been these past years, who he's been living with, but something's happened to change him. He's always been edgy. But now, it's as if his soul has been ransacked." *Tell me you weren't responsible, Ray. Please.* "Sometimes I wonder if he hasn't made a deal with the devil."

Chapter 30

The Carpenter barn is cavernous, too drafty and isolated for a midwinter gathering, and so the Owls' clubhouse has been pressed into use. Just when it seems they can't possibly fit another person inside, the door opens again and a wave of shuffling starts up until the newcomers, plus the food they have brought as an offering, are accommodated. Nods and greetings are exchanged, hats and mufflers removed, throats cleared, noses blown. A bottle of whisky makes the rounds among the men: moonshine or the real McCoy, no one much cares. Anything to gild the next couple of hours, inoculate them against emotions that might spill over. The women fuss over the food table, whisk away empty platters, consolidate picked-over bowls of potato salad and coleslaw to make room for newly arrived biscuits and last year's boysenberry jam, turnip cobbler, scalloped potatoes and carrot cake; they straighten the tablecloth and brush crumbs into cupped hands. Beneath the rise and fall of careful conversation, someone starts keening.

Egypt tenses. Glances in Zadie Mullins' direction and then away. The walls pulse. Someone needs to jam the door open a smidgen, let the fresh air circulate. The clubhouse was never intended to hold more than a clutch of kids, on top of which the boy-smell that has always hung like a damp cloth inside the place – of marsh water and playing outside, of dried-up frogs' eggs and boy-sweat and farts and stolen cigarettes – has been obliterated by the smoky, acrid stink of burned things. It wells up even over the aromas of freshly baked bread and sausage rolls. It's the same smell that, when you get too close, oozes from Zadie Mullins' skin, as if she has become part of the collateral damage.

Laura appears at her elbow. "I think you should take Mrs. Mullins out for a walk around the marsh. And when you come back, you can check on your brother."

"Why me?"

"Because I said so. He had another nightmare last night. Wet the bed this time. I don't need to tell you what that was like, stripping sheets in the middle of the night with your father snoring his head off downstairs."

"You weren't happy when Ray wasn't sleeping, now you're complaining because he is?"

"I'm just saying, I don't have spare sets of sheets lying around, that's all. I had to wash them out and spread them to dry and try and not disturb your father at the same time." Egypt rolls her eyes. "But when I need consideration from him, he just slinks off and does his own thing. So I need you" – she tilts her head, her eyebrows lift in warning – "to keep an eye out for your brother's welfare."

"And Zadie Mullins? I have to look out for her welfare too?"

"Put yourself in her shoes, would you? For that matter, put yourself in anyone's shoes for a minute and stop being so level selfish all the time."

Egypt turns from the sight of the Mullinses' meagre belongings corralled into one corner – items they were able to rescue from their ruined home, plus necessities people have donated, like bedding, a pot and some dishes, cutlery – but just as she opens her mouth to protest, Joey heaves into view, elbowing his way through the crowd of mourners. He lifts a hand in greeting, his face a twist of hope and resignation. She pockets a couple of fairy-cakes. "For Aidan," she says when her mother glowers at her; stuffs another whole one in her mouth the minute Laura's back is turned. Reaches for a couple of sausage rolls. A devilled egg.

Outside, the sun sits high in an azure sky. *Deceitful*, Egypt thinks, eyes watering from the glare off the snow and ice, the biting wind. She leads Zadie in the direction of the bridge, away from the ruins that flank the Mullinses' old house. Pronounced unsafe by the fire marshal, the house is roped off, but that hasn't stopped the morbid and the curious from snooping. Egypt has stood at the threshold herself long enough to take in the charred rafters, the gaping hole where the stairs used to be. Her hands in her pockets find the fairy-cakes. She waits until Zadie isn't looking and then picks off the buttercream topping and pops it in her mouth. Breaks off a piece of fairy-cake, squishes it and repeats the sly hand-to-mouth transfer. Licks her lips. Sugar thrums through her veins. Already she's pinching off the next mouthful. Zadie, her face muffled in a dun-coloured scarf, appears oblivious. By the time they turn around at the bridge, the fairy-cakes are done, nothing but crumbs in Egypt's pocket. She startles as her fingers light on something cold and damp. The devilled egg. She squeezes its rubbery coolness. Zadie seems much calmer now – that, or she's frozen stiff. Egypt turns aside and slips the whole half-egg – plus pocket lint, fairy-cake crumbs and a long, wiry hair from her mitten – in her mouth. She chews slowly, savouring the tang of mayonnaise. Flushes the hair from her teeth with her tongue.

"Would you like to go back now?" she says, still turned away – to look into Zadie's eyes is to invite in all her pain. "They're probably missing you." Maybe someone will have brought more fairy-cakes. Maybe Matt will have made an appearance. If he's still around. It leaves her hollowed out, imagining him hunkered down in a boxcar headed somewhere new, someplace he can shake off the ghosts of Stan Byrd and the kids he failed to rescue. When she took her seat across from him at the inquest on Tuesday, she thought her heart might fly out of her chest. He kept his eyes downcast, unwilling to meet anyone's gaze. He looked thinner, short on sleep, but she could have wept with relief to know he hadn't left town. Joey's clammy hand grasped hers as Matt solemnly recounted the tale of Stan Byrd's drinking and the spilled lamp, his voice robbed of its musical timbre. She was desperate to find out where he was staying, but he bolted the moment the verdict was delivered, and Egypt found herself trapped, commiserating with the Mullinses.

Insisting on the need to return to school, she fled the building in time to spot his quick, long strides taking him down MacNab Street. She ran to keep him in sight as he ducked down first Bold and then Caroline, where he turned left, weaving his way down streets she'd grown familiar with over the winter, accompanying her grandparents home from church.

And then he disappeared.

Egypt haunted the laneway down which he'd slipped, waiting for him to emerge from someone's back gate or hop over a low section of fence. After an hour he still hadn't reappeared, and she wondered if he was inside one of the houses – collecting payment for poached rabbits? fixing a sticky sash? – and walked around to the front and strolled down Caroline Street, past long porches and stained glass clerestories, past windows shaped like portholes and fitted with wavy greenish glass. But the net curtains and the shadows cast by the late-afternoon sun conspired to reveal nothing of his whereabouts. It was as if Matt had vanished into thin air.

She dashes ahead of Zadie as they near her house. "I'll just check on Aidan. Won't be a sec," she calls over her shoulder.

Zadie nods. Probably nods to everything these days. Sometimes it's easier to go along with everyone else's plans.

Egypt leans in the door. Hollers, "I got you sausage rolls. You hungry?" When he doesn't answer, she steps inside. There's no sign of Ray. "Where'd your dad go?"

Aidan shrugs. He's sitting cross-legged amidst a small battalion of lead soldiers: at once scout, rifleman, artillery commander, sound effects man and decider of who lives and who gets toppled on his side.

"Sausage rolls." She sets them on a plate at his feet. He pushes it away.

"George'll eat them if you don't."

"So?"

"You'll be hungry later."

"So."

"So don't come crying to me." One well-aimed kick would send his soldiers sprawling. How is it five minutes ago she was feeling sorry for him?

The door clicks shut. She turns to see Zadie, shucking off her coat and her rubber boots. Unwinding her scarf. *What does she think she's doing?* Egypt watches in mild amazement as the grieving mother walks in uninvited and sits on the floor in front of Aidan – even crosses her legs to mirror his.

Back in war land, Aidan is oblivious. His lips are moving: battle commands or curses on his sister's head? When she leans in closer, he clams up. Whatever Zadie Mullins is hoping to get from her brother, she'll be disappointed. He lives inside his head these days. Laura refuses to talk doctors, says he'll come around in time.

Zadie nudges a soldier. Aidan watches as she plucks a sniper and positions him behind a man on the run. He makes a countermove. Zadie's eyes flicker over the battlefield strewn with rocks and pebbles and clumps of dead marsh grass. Her fingers hover and then retreat. Egypt shrugs. She could interrupt, clear her throat, step on a rogue warrior, or she could tiptoe out and leave them to it. She starts towards the door and then catches sight of George licking his chops. Nose lowered to the empty sausage-roll plate, he sends a long, pink tongue across its surface. The plate jumps and clatters along the floor. Just as she lunges for him, he throws himself at the door, head back, bark-howling. Beneath the din, she makes out the sound of knocking.

"It'll be someone looking for you," she says, addressing Zadie over her shoulder and grabbing the scruff of George's neck. She pulls him back to open the door. Stares in open-jawed astonishment. George's tail bats against her legs.

Her grandparents. Stephan and Lily Aiken, standing on her stoop in their winter hats and Sunday coats, a shopping bag between their feet. Suddenly she's as light as air: one puff and she'll blow away. She releases George and he bolts for freedom.

"Well, I never," her grandmother says. "It's you." She turns to watch the dog disappear behind the Shackletons' goat shed. "Au revoir, George." She faces Egypt. "Hello, Evelyn."

"Egypt, Mother." Her grandfather clears his throat and brushes the front of his coat. "The girl's name is Egypt."

Her grandmother clasps her gloved hands together. "I like Evelyn," she says, her voice strident in the sharp air. "Evelyn is a good, wholesome name."

"But it isn't her real name."

"Well, obviously not." She allows a small smile. "At least some things are clearer now."

Egypt's eyes dart from one to the other, a hand to the flush rising at her throat. She's not who they were expecting. So why are they here?

"You were going somewhere?" Her grandfather indicates her coat.

"I just got back."

"And is your mother in?"

"She's at the wake."

He nods. A look of relief passes over her grandmother's face. "Would it be all right if we came in, do you think?" he asks.

Would it?

"We have some explaining to do." Her grandfather's face softens. "I think we all have a little explaining to do."

She steps back to let them enter. Follows their gaze as they take in their surroundings – dirty dishes by the sink, laundry spread out to dry on the backs of chairs, an empty plate in the middle of a floor littered with lead soldiers, river rocks and grit and, now that she's looking, clusters of dust and George's hair. A pair of Ray's socks, balled up. *Doesn't anyone pick anything up in this house anymore?*

"Drafty in here, isn't it?" her grandmother says, looking the windows up and down. Both hands clasp the handles of her handbag, which she holds in front of her legs like a shield. "It's a wonder you don't all have cricks in your necks."

"I didn't take anything that day," Egypt starts to say, but her words come out spastic and jumbled, her mouth not her own. She shrugs off her coat and licks her lips, glares at the back of Zadie's head, willing her to leave.

"We've missed your visits. Sundays haven't been the same, have they, Mr. Aiken?"

"Not the same at all."

His voice. Always so monotone and careful. And that's when it hits her. *I think I know what you're doing here*. Somewhere along the way, he must have guessed who she was. Some common feature or gesture perhaps. She turns to check Aidan hasn't snuck up behind her. For now, he appears still engrossed in his game, the two old people at the door just two old people at the door.

"Does he know who we are?"

Egypt shakes her head.

"Well, everything in good time," her grandmother says, but Egypt can read the disappointment in her face.

"I don't know how he would react, on top of everything else that has happened."

"Whatever you think is best," her grandfather adds. He turns his hat with one hand and brushes it with the other. Her grandmother pulls at the fingers of her gloves, one by one, inching them from her hands. Egypt wonders whether she should offer to take her grandfather's hat. But then where would she put it?

"So," her grandmother says, folding and refolding her gloves, perhaps regretting removing them, "secrets will out, eventually."

She nods and then, finding her voice, says, "Ray told me." They would have asked eventually.

Her grandmother's mouth crimps in a thin line. "In all these years, your mother never mentioned us?"

Egypt shakes her head.

"What did we expect, Mr. Aiken? She never even showed to her own sister's funeral." Egypt is beginning to regret the devilled egg, the sour taste of mayonnaise etching the back of her throat.

"She came to see us a few weeks ago," her grandfather says.

"She did?"

"Only because she needed money. Your grandfather fixed her up with a job looking after an elderly lady from the parish."

"Mrs. Pendlebury?"

"She told you, then?"

"Only about the job."

"She was always a secretive one, your mother."

Egypt wishes a magic hand would reach in through the window and pluck her away. Her breathing has grown so shallow her head feels spinny. Her grandfather reaches down by his feet for the shopping bag, which he lifts and sets carefully on the table.

"We brought you both something," he says, holding the bag open while her grandmother removes two brightly wrapped gifts: one that threatens to dwarf the kitchen table, the other no bigger than a box of matches, but no less compelling. Dressed in their bold paper, the two gifts eclipse their drab surroundings, like swatches of colourful fabric in a room full of serge. Carefully, her grandfather folds up the bag and slides it into the deep pocket of his overcoat.

"This is for Evelyn," her grandmother says, handing her the smaller package.

"Egypt," her grandfather corrects.

"Egypt." She waves a hand in annoyance. "What kind of a name is Egypt, anyway?" she mutters, half under her breath, and Egypt understands that she hasn't quite been forgiven for her deceit.

Prolonging the sweetness of anticipation, she turns the box around and around in her hands, fingering the thick, daring paper, the exquisite white bow that cinches the neatly folded ends in perfect alignment. She would leave the gift just as it is, wake up to its promise tomorrow morning, and the morning after, and the one after that, but even Egypt's limited experience with gifts has taught her that beneath the wrapping paper and bows lie other subtler expectations.

"Go ahead, open it," her grandmother urges. "If you don't like it, we can exchange it for something else."

"Oh no, I wouldn't –"

"Shh, Mother, let the girl take her own time."

Egypt's fingers tremble as she tugs at the ribbon and the paper unravels to reveal a smooth green leather box fastened with a metal clasp. Inside, nestled on a bed of ivory silk, a tear-shaped golden yellow stone on a silver chain. A dark streak through it, like a spill of ink, the eye of a tiger.

"It's . . . beautiful." She looks up into her grandmother's eyes and down again at the necklace. Gloria will have something to say, or snarl at. "It's the most beautiful thing I've ever owned. I don't know how to thank you."

"It's a topaz. A semi-precious stone. Hold it up against your neck. Look, Mr. Aiken, how it sets off her hair and her eyes."

"Allow me," her grandfather says, taking the necklace from her and stepping behind to drape it around her neck. She pulls her hair to one side so he can fasten the clasp and then fingers the stone as they pause to gaze at the wonder of their gift, at the wonder of her. But not for long. Curiosity has gotten the better of Aidan, who has at last left his game and Zadie Mullins to investigate.

"Hello, young man."

Aidan stares up at the two old people. "You're the lady from church who gave us the coins, the church with the Christmas cookies."

"What a wonderful memory you have."

He leans back against Egypt, his forefinger rubbing back and forth across the edge of the table.

"It's for you," Egypt says, indicating his gift, and his finger ventures onto the tabletop, looping daringly close to, but never quite touching, the box.

"Is it my birthday present?"

"It's your birthday?" Her grandmother pulls out a chair and sits leaning forward so that her face is on a level with Aidan's.

"Last week," Egypt interjects.

"And how old were you last week?"

It burns Egypt to watch her grandmother raking every inch of her brother, devouring him. Already she can feel their own tenuous connection slipping away.

"Six. It was my birthday and the next night there was a big fire." Egypt's eyes dart to Zadie, sitting still as patience.

"That must have been very frightening for you."

"I helped carry the water."

"You did not." Egypt rolls her eyes, but no one is paying attention.

"I did too. And then I went to rescue Darius and Efron, but they were burned in their house. They were my best friends."

Zadie, face buried in her hands, has started to rock. Egypt considers clamping her hand over Aidan's mouth before he says anything else.

"She's their mom," he whispers. Egypt nudges him from behind.

"You must miss them terribly," her grandmother whispers back.

He inches closer and out of Egypt's range. "Do you believe in ghosts?"

"In ghosts? Who's been filling your head with nonsense about ghosts?" Smiling, she reaches out an arthritic hand to brush a lock of hair from his eyes, but Aidan shies away and retreats to the other side of the table. Her grandmother brushes down her skirt and folds her hands together in her lap.

"They're not very safe, these houses, are they?"

"Lily," her husband says, putting a finger to his lips and nodding to indicate Zadie's obvious distress. To Egypt's surprise, he approaches the grieving mother. "My wife and I are deeply sorry for your loss," he says, and bends towards her, reaching to touch her on the shoulder before changing his mind. He straightens and stands still an awkward moment, turning his hat in his hands, but Zadie doesn't respond. Knees pulled tight to her chin, head tucked in, she's trying to make herself disappear. She may or may not have heard him; may or may not be crying.

"Well they're not, are they?" her grandmother whispers crossly when he rejoins them at the table. "The newspapers said they should be condemned."

"The newspapers exaggerate everything."

Her grandmother smiles and Egypt feels suddenly small.

"Newspapers are in the business of selling newspapers," her grandfather says, his salt-and-pepper eyebrows lifting. "You're wise to cultivate a healthy cynicism."

"Cynicism, Mr. Aiken, is the province of men, not young ladies."

Egypt has one eye on Aidan, who has climbed onto a chair and is leaned over the table, working a grubby finger beneath a flap of wrapping paper. "I'm not being cynical," she protests, her cheeks aflame. "I was at the inquest." *Oh, why does Zadie Mullins have to be here?* Curled up in the middle of the floor, holding her breath, her shattered heart. "If you only read the headlines, you'd think that was the case, that the jury wanted the whole community gone, when the truth is their first recommendation was that we be given better fire protection."

"The truth, Evelyn, is that no one's thought this through. You have no water mains to speak of, and even if you did, how do you propose to get a fire truck down here? Perhaps it could grow wings and fly?"

"Lily, please. You're –"

The sound of ripping paper precedes Aidan's tumble to the floor. The chair clatters behind him.

"Oops-a-daisy, there we go." Her grandmother has scooped him into her arms and settled him on her knee before anyone else has time to react. Aidan is too surprised to cry. "Are these okay?" she asks, rubbing first his knees and then his elbows. "And this?" She rubs his head.

"I think someone would like to open his present now," her grandfather says, and Aidan, needing no further encouragement, shuffles quickly from the old lady's lap.

He rips at the remainder of the paper to reveal a cardboard box bearing a picture of a train engine curled around a bend of track and hurtling out of its frame towards him. *The American Flyer.* Above and inset, three pictures of railway workers at their respective tasks.

"*The Toy for The Boy,*" her grandfather says, making his voice fit the proclamation along the bottom of the box lid.

"The toy for the boy," Aidan repeats. "That's me," he says, smacking his chest.

"I think you'll find it's still very much Mr. Aiken too," her grandmother says, one eyebrow raised. Aidan looks at her and back at the train.

Mr. Aiken pulls the lid free. "It's a windup train," he says, addressing Aidan as if he were the only person in the room. "More practical than the electric ones. You can take it anywhere; you can even play with it outside if you like, though I'd suggest staying away from the water."

"Trains don't go on water," Aidan says.

"That's right, they don't." He reaches into the box and hands Aidan the shiny black locomotive. "We're going to link this," he points at the locomotive, "to the passenger cars and the caboose. And then we'll wind it up and take it for a test run, what do you say?"

"Okay."

"Just like you, I lived close to the railway tracks when I was growing up. Closer. My father was a station agent for Canadian Pacific Railway. We lived in the rooms above the station." Click, snap, click, snap. He brushes his hands together with a little flourish. The American Flyer commands the table, pulsing with store-bought newness. "It was the highlight of my day when the train came through."

When Egypt was younger, the kids in the area used to hurl sticks and rocks at the passing trains, hoping to dislodge a few bricks of coal, or sometimes just for mischief. Egypt joined them more than once. They hid out in the bushes. These days, the bushes provide cover for itinerants who board the trains heading out of town, to the gold mines at Kirkland Lake or towns and cities rumoured to have work.

"They didn't have train sets like this when I was a boy. Not out on the Prairies. My father whittled one from wood for me. It wasn't even painted, but it had wheels that turned."

"He still has it," her grandmother says.

"But it's a battered old thing. I would have given my right arm for an American Flyer."

Aidan caresses the shiny black engine and its green cargo and passenger carriages.

"Go ahead," he pats Aidan gently, if a little stiffly, on the shoulder. "Don't be afraid to touch it, to get a feel for it. It's yours after all."

Suddenly, Zadie is on her feet and moving with purpose towards them.

"These" – she leans over Aidan's shoulder, waving a fistful of soldiers – "belong to my boys." She stabs him with a pointy finger, shocking them all into silence. "You are nothing but a common thief. A criminal," she continues to shout from the doorway, yanking on her coat and boots, "with criminal blood running through your veins." The door slams, shaking the cabin.

Her grandmother is the first to recover. "Aidan. Aidan? Look at me." She tries to hold his hands but he squirms away.

"She took my soldiers."

"Let her have the soldiers. They're obviously more important to her than they are to you."

"No, they're not." He tries to kick at her. "Darius gave them to me for my birthday. They were my birthday present and she took them."

"We'll get you some new soldiers."

"I want those soldiers."

"How about we go to the Eaton's downtown? We can go in the car. Does that sound like fun? To go for a ride in the car?"

"Now?" Egypt asks, but Aidan is already nodding yes. One disaster averted, another in the making.

"Can I sit in the front?" he asks.

"And we'll stop for ice cream on the way back," her grandmother declares, pulling on her gloves as though the matter were already decided.

"I don't think this is a good idea, Lily." Her grandfather is shaking his head. "Not today. It's too soon."

"Ice cream," her grandmother says, ignoring her husband, "for Aidan's birthday."

"Ice cream," Aidan repeats, wiping his cheeks on the back of his sleeve.

"It's too cold for ice cream, Aid." Now she sounds like her mother.

"It's never too cold for ice cream, is it?" Grandma Lily cajoles.

"Never."

Eyes lit up, standing with his skinny-boy chest against the table, he is almost his old self. How difficult to resist, to play the heavy, to watch his face take on shadows again. And because she, too, is anxious to escape the cabin and the discomfiture Zadie's outburst has precipitated, Egypt feels her resistance start to give.

"I'm not sure. Maybe I should leave a note for Mom, let her know where we are." *And who we're with.* The last thing she feels like is ice cream.

"You worry too much. We'll be back before she even knows we're gone."

Egypt has only ever walked by Crawford's, peered in the windows at the soda dispenser, the patrons seated knee to knee on the shiny chrome counter stools, tucking into cherry pie and slurping on Coca-Colas and cream sodas. Though it's difficult to see all the way to the back from the street, she reckons the King Street confectionery must be three times the size of Brunts, the store in the community. A bell sounds their entrance musically. Aromas of cinnamon and freshly baked pastries, cocoa, coffee and apples swirl around her head to weave through her hair, the worn threads of her coat, seep into her pores. She runs her eyes across the merchandise: scores of bottles of pop and juice, jars of brightly coloured candy, tins of tea and coffee and cookies decorated with scenes of horses and dancers and ships and bouquets of flowers, all set in gay relief against the dark polished wood of the floor-to-ceiling shelves; myriad cakes and pies in their glass cases, baked to perfection and sliced to reveal their creamy layers, their moist and glistening centres.

Aidan, his pockets filled with new soldiers, spins around slowly and then stares upwards at the giant ceiling fans with their dark blades, rotating slowly on long chains.

"It's winter," he says. "Isn't everybody going to get cold?"

This sets off laughter amongst the staff: two women in long black skirts and old-fashioned high-necked blouses and white pinafores, and a moustachioed gentleman in a crisp white shirt, a starched white apron folded and tied across his waist.

"The fans are running backwards," the man in the apron says, indicating with his finger. "They're pushing the warm air back down."

Aidan stares until he loses his balance, then he clambers onto one of the stools and folds his hands together on the counter.

"I think the young man would like a sundae," their grandfather says. "A birthday sundae. The biggest you have."

Egypt opts for one scoop of chocolate and has less trouble finishing it than she imagined.

Halfway through his giant ice cream sundae, Aidan sets down his spoon, spins around on the stool and steps off.

"I want to go home."

Egypt is not surprised, is already pushing back her dish, ready to leave.

"But you haven't finished your ice cream."

"I want to go home now." In his quiet, determined voice, his posture – chin up, arms at his sides – Egypt sees a glimpse of the man he will become. A lump rises to her throat.

"A small detour," her grandfather announces. They are on King Street, approaching the church at Queen. He makes a left-hand turn. Egypt tenses. They've been gone ages.

"We should be getting back."

"We just have to drop your – Mrs. Aiken off at Mrs. Pendlebury's."

"She'll be wanting her dinner and a bit of a chat," her grandmother says into the back seat. The sun has dipped behind the buildings, rendering her in silhouette, a shadow speaking into the shadows. "We knew your mother was going to be tied up with the wake today."

So they already knew she wouldn't be home. Egypt stares out the window at the row of eerily familiar porches and stained glass clerestories;

a porthole window set beside a door. Its wavy glass. Greenish. The car slows to a stop and a sudden dawning sets off a rush of noise inside Egypt's head. Matt and her mother. His disappearing act the day of the inquest. She doesn't realize she's being spoken to until her grandmother reaches into the back seat to stroke her face.

"Oh, you poor thing, you're crying. Whatever's the matter, child?"

"Nothing." She wipes her nose with the handkerchief her grandmother gives her. "Nothing at all."

"Keep it." Her grandmother pushes back Egypt's hand with the handkerchief. "I want you to know, this has been one of the happiest days of my life," she says, "spending the day with you lovely children. Will we see you in church tomorrow, Evelyn?"

Church? Egypt can feel her head slowly emptying down her spine and into the back seat.

"Never mind. If you're not feeling up to it. But you must both come for Sunday dinner. Roast beef and all the trimmings."

A fresh spate of tears spills down her face. "I'll try, but I can't promise anything." She feels numb, so worn out it's all she can do not to lie down and die a little.

"Any Sunday you want to visit then. Any day you like for that matter." Her grandmother's voice sounds disembodied. Faraway. "That goes for you too, Aidan. Ask your sister to bring you. Or come yourself if it suits. We live not far from here, at 47 Robinson Street. You can remember that, can't you? 47 Robinson Street. Just by the intersection of Robinson and Queen Streets." She blows a kiss into the back seat and steps from the car. "Bye-bye."

At a nod from the old man in the driver's seat, Aidan leaves Egypt alone in the back and climbs into the vacated passenger seat. He doesn't wave at the woman he doesn't know is his grandmother, though she keeps her arm in the air until they round the corner and disappear from sight.

Egypt picks her way down the path to the boathouses, trying to conjure what she will say to her mother about this afternoon.

Aidan walks ahead, hands in his pockets. He doesn't turn when she calls his name.

"Are you listening to me?" She jogs up to him so they're walking abreast. "You can't say anything to Mom about today. Do you understand? Nothing. Not about where we've been or who we've been with. Understand?"

"Why?"

"You wouldn't understand."

"Make your mind up."

"Don't be so cheeky."

"Mom doesn't like those old people, does she?"

"What makes you say that?

"Christmas Eve. You told me not to tell then."

Her grandmother is right about his memory. "She'll be very angry with us for going off with strangers."

"She'll be angry with you, you mean."

"No, with both of us."

"You're the oldest. You're supposed to know better."

"That's so stupid. Anyway, they're not strangers."

"Who are they?"

"Guess."

"I don't want to guess."

"Yes, you do. Go on, guess."

"The King and Queen of England."

"No, stupid, a proper guess."

"That was a proper guess."

"No, it wasn't. Guess again."

"No. I don't want to play your stupid game anymore."

"It's not stupid."

"Yes it is." He's close to tears. "I'm telling Mom." He begins running.

She catches up to him, grabs him by the arm to make him stop. "They're your grandparents."

"You're hurting me."

"Did you hear what I said?"

"I don't have any grandparents."

"Yes, you do. *We* have grandparents. And you just met them. Grandpa Aiken and Grandma Lily."

"So why didn't you call them that?"

Because I've only just come up with their names.

"How come they didn't say anything?"

"Because I asked them not to. I told them you couldn't handle such information right now, that you're too delicate." The look he gives her reminds her she's behaving no better than Ray did, telling him this momentous news as if she's doing him a favour when in fact she's dropping a bomb on his small world.

"Oh, buddy, I'm sorry." She bends down and hugs him. He really is so small and vulnerable.

"Don't cry, Egypt. Please don't cry." He tries to pull away. "Your snot's going in my hair."

She holds him at arm's length. "We stick together on this one, okay?"

"Okay."

Laura is home. The air in the cabin blue and sparking off her hair.

"What went on here this afternoon?"

"What do you mean?" But it's obvious. The box is sitting on the table. Dishevelled. The lid rammed on haphazardly. Surrounded by scraps of discarded wrapping paper. Laura has been on a rampage. Retrieved the balled up paper from the stove. Pulled the train from its hiding place under her daughter's bed. Though how long did Egypt honestly expect to be able to keep it from her, to keep anything of what went on here today from her? Certainly not as long as Laura has managed to keep Lily and Stephan Aiken a secret. Matt Oakes. Her secretive mother. Hiding grandparents and lovers.

"For a start, where have you two been all afternoon? And who was here with you? Why was Zadie Mullins so upset? She was in a real state." Egypt glares stonily at her mother and wonders which, if any, of the questions she should answer.

"And what is the meaning of this?" Laura taps the box with her ragged nails.

Egypt fingers the neck of her blouse and the pendant slips out of sight. "It's a train set. An American Flyer," she says, reading the name on the box. "It doesn't have any meaning. It's a toy. A *toy for the boy*," she says, amazed by the flinty tone her voice has acquired.

"Don't get smart with me, young lady. Where did it come from?"

"The store. Eaton's possibly."

Aidan stares at his sister, wide eyes in a pale face.

"Aidan? Who brought you the train set?"

His eyes don't leave his sister's face. "She told me not to say anything."

"She told you not to say anything about what? What are you two hiding from me? Out with it. I mean it."

"The old people from church gave it to me."

"What old people? What church? When was he in church?"

"Grandpa Aiken and Grandma Lily. I'm sorry, Egypt." Tears are running down his face.

Egypt stares out the window at the gunmetal-grey water. *The gloaming*, Ray calls this time of day. Barely a ripple breaks the surface. "Your parents were here," she says. "We went to Crawford's for ice cream. They invited Aidan and me for Sunday dinner."

Laura's face is so bleached of colour it's as if her features have been wiped clean away. Only her eyes remain. Hunted. "You have a lot of explaining to do, my girl."

A laugh bursts from Egypt; a raucous sound that leaves ground metal in its wake. She stabs a forefinger in her chest. "*I* have a lot of explaining to do! Me? That's rich, that is, Mother."

Laura turns away. "We'll talk about this later."

"So you always say. But the truth is, we never talk about anything in this house."

"There are reasons for that, Egypt. Reasons you know nothing about."

"You have no idea what I know and don't know."

"I know no one is going to be playing with this train set." Laura scoops the box up under her arm and marches over to the porch door.

"What are you doing with it?" Aidan cries out. "That's mine."

"I'm getting rid of it, that's what I'm doing with it." And before Egypt can move her legs to stop her, before Aidan can reach his mother, Laura opens the porch door, walks out and dumps the train and its box over the railing and into the water. She steps back inside and closes the door.

"Not another word, Egypt. I mean it." She glares in turn at her children, finger held in the air before her. "I don't want to hear a peep from either of you."

Aidan stares out at the patch of darkening water until the last rays of the sun disappear and he can no longer make out the place where his train went down. Egypt lies in bed that night fingering her pendant, bitter exchanges with her mother running through her head and keeping her from sleep.

Chapter 31

Aidan's Junior I class lines up in alphabetical order outside the door of the clinic. A strong smell of antiseptic seeps out from under the clinic door. Will Green is absent, so Aidan stands between Mary Fine and Everett Griffin. The clinic is in the basement of the Strathcona School, where it is so cold you can see your breath and the goosebumps on Mary Fine's legs, each bump sown with a fine, pale gold hair. She sniffs, and Aidan puts his fingers to his own nose. It feels cold and wet, like George's. Everett is bigger than most of the boys in Junior I and wears round bottle glasses. They make his eyes too big for his face, like eyes that belong on a bug. When he turns to Aidan, his whole body lumbering around, Aidan glances away and pretends to be interested in a chart pinned to the wall by the clinic-room door. The chart shows the human body as if someone had sliced it in half from the top of the head down to the toes. One diagram reveals the front half of the body and another the back. All the parts of the body are shown in different colours. After he stares for a minute, breathing in the antiseptic smell, Aidan's tummy begins to feel light and fluttery. He shifts his gaze to the floor and the T-bar on Mary Fine's red shoes. Her knee socks are white. Aidan wonders how they stay so clean.

"Hands," Nurse Critcheley says when he's in the clinic room and standing in front of her. He holds them out, and she takes them in her own and checks them front and back. "When did you start biting your nails?"

"I don't know."

"I don't know what?"

"I don't know, Nurse Critcheley."

"Good boy," she says, her eyes studying his face. "Go and wash your hands in that sink over there – make sure you use lots of soap. And try and keep them out of your mouth.

"Do you sleep well at night?"

Her voice seems to float through the back of his head.

Sleep.

He dries his hands on the scratchy white towel hanging next to the sink. Some mornings he feels as if he hasn't slept at all, though he knows he must have dropped off at some point because he finds his mother is no longer in the bed, or Egypt is shaking him awake. This morning, George licked his face. He's been trying to stay awake in case Darius and Efron visit him, but he knows he can't tell Nurse Critcheley this, as he has learned that grown-ups don't like it when children talk about dead people, especially dead children. *Even dead dogs*, he thinks, remembering the day Egypt took him to Manny's ice-fishing hut.

Darius and Efron usually appear during the daytime, but the last time they were so faint he could see through them, and although Darius thought this was funny, he could tell that Efron was scared. Aidan was scared too. He doesn't want his friends to disappear. They make him feel brave; they egg him on to do things, like wear his dad's hat and take his pocket knife and carve his initials into the wall behind his bed.

The first time he saw them, they were playing in his room, arguing over whose turn it was to hold their truck. Aidan knew the truck; it was a green and brown TootsieToy, with one missing white rubber tire, and the paint was all scratched at the front where the boys had repeatedly driven it into rocks and through mud piles. Darius was saying that as he was oldest, he should have it longest, and Efron kept saying how it wasn't fair. Same as ever. Aidan couldn't see any sign of the truck – maybe it had been lost in the fire, or maybe they'd had to leave it behind in the winter vault, where they waited for burial – but he was so glad to see them that he didn't care. Even though if it was Aidan's truck, he would have looked after it and kept it nice and new looking. If it ever had looked new.

Darius and Efron are not quiet. Aidan wonders why other people can't hear them, they are so loud. Sometimes yelling their heads off. If Aidan wants to yell with them, he has to go into the forest where his mom and his sister don't want him to go alone, and there he can yell, because around the house he has to be quiet and not even mention their names. No one mentions their names, and if they see Aidan, or Darius and Efron's mother and father, they go quiet and make an extra effort not to say their names.

George sees them. He steps around them, which is how Aidan knows that George knows they're there, unlike most other people, who charge right through them. Efron says that when that happens, it gives him headaches.

Aidan touches his head. He's never had a headache. He doesn't know how to answer Nurse Critcheley's question.

"Any nightmares?"

He blinks. "No, Miss Critcheley."

"Wetting the bed?"

Aidan glances towards the door at the large and colourless shape of Everett Griffin visible through the frosted-glass insert. Crosses his fingers behind his back. Shakes his head.

"Anything else I should know about?" Her voice, warmer, soft and rounded, sets off a buzzing inside his head and chest. The buzzing spreads to his mouth and then his tongue; even his teeth begin to tingle.

"No, Miss."

She parts his hair and pushes his head this way and that, her bony fingers traveling across his scalp, seeking out nits.

"Open wide," she says, then slips a giant wooden lolly stick in his mouth and pushes his tongue down. "Say aahh."

"Aahh." He feels it as a rumbling in the back of his throat. When the stick is removed, the taste of wood stays in his mouth. Suddenly, an ice-cold hand plunges down the back of his neck. Aidan has to catch his breath.

Next she wants to see his teeth, after which she fills in a card and hands it to him to take home to his parents. He recognizes his name on the piece of paper, but the rest of the words may as well be scribble.

"Don't forget to give that dental form to your mother," Nurse Critcheley says as he reaches for the door handle. He waits. His mother does this to him. Calls out her dos and don'ts even after he's reached the path or, skates on and laced up, is headed into the middle of the frozen lake. He wants to be certain that Nurse Critcheley won't say anything else once he opens the door; that the secrets he's been thinking about won't float out the clinic and follow him back to his classroom.

Afternoon is art class. Although he isn't very good, Aidan doesn't mind art class. It's easier to talk in art class than in most other classes. All talk is about visiting the dentist.

"There's this drill. Sounds like screaming."

"There's lots of blood."

"You have to sit in a big black leather chair."

Aidan picks up a paintbrush and runs his fingers over the bristles, the bristles over his face. He likes Monday afternoons best because that's when Junior I has music. Then, he tries standing as close as he can get to the piano so he can feel the vibrations from the notes thumping through his feet and chest. The way they break the air – poof, poof, poof – around him.

Monday mornings aren't as much fun, in part because his mother doesn't have any pennies to give him and so he can no longer line up at the teacher's desk to make a deposit in his school penny savings account. He isn't the only boy in class not to have pennies, but that doesn't stop his face from growing hot. Every Monday morning he has to listen to his mother mumbling how she could do with that savings account right about now and how the school should be thinking about how to give students their money back and not be taking it from them all the time. But he can't explain all this to Miss Swinton. It's too many words. He'll start off fine and then he'll get something wrong or mixed up. His sister yelled at him this morning when he was talking about the ice fishing, that he never gets anything right and that he should just shut up. But she wasn't even there anymore, so how would she know if he was right or wrong?

"You're such a pain," she screamed. "I wish you'd never been born."

His mother had said nothing.

He drips some red poster paint into a puddle of black, swirls it around and proceeds to paint a series of dark lines on the sheet of paper Miss Swinton handed him to clip to his art board. "Watch your fingers," she always says whenever she hands out the papers, "those bulldogs bite."

He concentrates hard on his picture and doesn't notice until the four girls at his table begin to giggle and point that he has streaks of dark paint all over his hands. Even though Miss Swinton makes jokes about bulldog clips, she lines all her pupils up at the end of art class to check their hands for paint. A lot of school seems to be about standing in lines. Anyone with paint splashed on their hands at the end of class gets the ruler across their palm. He wonders why the soft part of the hand is called a palm but doesn't know who to ask. His sister is clever, but she always gets so cross with him. *Because because* is her favourite answer.

The girls at his table have handkerchiefs they spit into and use to wipe off the paint before they have to line up. Mark Barnes, sitting at the table with Aidan and the four girls, looks down in dismay at the daubs of red and green paint on his hands. Aidan looks at his own hands and then hides them under the table. The girls giggle and turn away without offering to lend their handkerchiefs.

And then, ten minutes before class is to end, Aidan watches fascinated as Mark Barnes mixes up a swirl of mustardy-yellow paint and begins slowly and deliberately painting the palm of his left hand. He completely covers the red streaks and the green, and then begins filling in the rest of his palm before moving on to his fingers and thumb. When he is finished painting his left hand, he looks up at Aidan and grins. Aidan grins back and grabs the biggest, fattest paintbrush and dips it in the thick mustard-yellow mud. The girls with the handkerchiefs suck in their breath and clamp their hands over their mouths. Their eyes widen and roll.

Aidan feels a rush of giddy giggles busting up inside of him. Mark Barnes is slowly painting his right hand with his now-yellow left hand. His tongue is sticking out from between his lips and he hasn't once looked up to see where Miss Swinton is. Aidan is surprised by how cold the paint feels on his skin. It sends a stream of cool up his arm and into his shoulder. He keeps one eye on Miss Swinton as he begins covering up the brown splashes on his hands with mustard yellow. She is still making the rounds of children's pictures with her box of coloured pencils, drawing red stars on the best pictures, blue on the second best, yellow on the third and green on the fourth.

He has just finished painting his right hand when she turns to their table. Mark Barnes holds his yellow hands beneath the table. The girls are pink in the face, and Susan Croft looks as though she might cry. The girls each get red stars though Aidan thinks this is unfair because only Carolyn Manners' picture is original. Her friends just copied her with a strip of blue across the top of the page and a strip of green across the bottom, a corner of yellow for the sun, with long rays pointing down at a lollipop tree with red apples next to a house with a chimney and a swirl of dark-grey smoke.

Aidan's own picture shows a bunch of giant eyes and wonky fish swimming at the bottom of the lake. Along with a toy train. Except it doesn't really look like the picture he had in his head when he started. Make a picture of your favourite day. It isn't his favourite day, either, but he doesn't know how to paint hockey, and Darius and Efron keep disappearing and he doesn't know how to paint that either. And even if he did, he senses he would get into trouble because he's not supposed to even talk about them, let alone see them and play with them anymore. They've gone for a long sleep because their bodies were put in the winter vault after the fire. In the spring they will plant them in the ground. He learned this from his sister, who carefully explained everything to him the day the Mullinses had the awake party. The same day the old people from church, who are really his grandparents, though it's supposed to be a secret, came to the house and gave him the train engine that his mom threw in the lake. He cried all night over the train engine, but his mom didn't even say she was sorry and told him never to mention it or his grandparents again or he'd get what for. He wouldn't have even met his grandparents if he'd been allowed to go to the awake party, which didn't work anyway because Darius and Efron never woke up. He hasn't said anything to anyone, but he thinks that the awake party had the exact opposite effect – maybe because he wasn't invited – because it's been four days now – five if he includes today, which isn't over yet – since they last visited. And so he's been trying to stay awake at night in case they stop by.

Miss Swinton brings the ruler down sharply across the palm of his hand three times. It feels like fire.

"Your left hand," she says, but Aidan keeps it hidden behind his back. "Your left hand, Aidan Fisher. Or do I have to hold it out for you?" He has a sensation of wanting to pee in class, and when he goes to squeeze his legs together, some of the other kids start to giggle.

"Be quiet, all of you," Miss Swinton barks. "Or you will all hold out your hands." She's red in the face and her eyes look wild, like the eyes of a trapped animal. She has sweat on her upper lip. Mark Barnes is already snivelling.

He waits for his sister after school, but when he sees her leaving with that Gloria girl from the fancy house on George Street, he turns around and heads for home, keeping back several yards behind Andy Dummican and the hockey boys. Andy Dummican and the hockey boys don't live in the boathouse community, but in winter they come over to Cootes Paradise with their skates and sticks and store-bought pucks and play against the boathouse boys. Sometimes there's a fight.

Aidan's hands are sore. Three cracks of the ruler on each palm and then Miss Swinton scrubbed his hands under the hot tap until he thought his skin would come off.

Over the lake, the sky is the colour of a day-old bruise. The sun peeks through and lights the boys so that they all seem to be glowing as they walk towards the darkness. They don't turn around, but Aidan knows they know he's there, following them. He walks on the edges of people's gardens or wherever there's a scrap of grass or dirt so that his shoes don't make a noise, otherwise the hockey boys will get mad and put him in a headlock. His mom put taps in his shoes so the soles don't wear out. Whenever he hits a paved surface, they go tip-tap. If the ground is dry, he can make sparks by hitting the hardtop in a certain way. He tries walking on his toes. Then his heels. He wishes his dad were here. He doesn't much know what to say or do with his dad when he's around, but he can tell that other people are scared of him. He knows he wouldn't get any trouble from Andy Dummican and his bully friends if his dad were here.

His dad isn't like other dads, not like Darius and Efron's dad, who works at Greening's Wire. At least, he did until the fire, but now he doesn't go into work anymore; he stays in the Owls' clubhouse all day with their mom and holds her hand and washes her hankies and makes her cups of tea. If Darius and Efron went to talk to their mom and dad, maybe they wouldn't be so sad all the time. He hopes they come and see him again. He likes being with Darius and Efron because he is exactly in the middle of their ages. He is no longer the youngest, nor does he have to be the eldest, and so when he's with them, he doesn't feel as if any part of him is sticking out; it's like he's protected on all sides.

The hockey boys have stopped at the top of Dundurn Street, where the houses finish. Aidan should have kept a bigger distance between them; now it's too late to turn around and head down Jones Street, they'll catch him up and he'll be in worse trouble for running. He slows until he's almost at a standstill. When he's within spitting distance, they swagger over and surround him.

"Not so tough without the Mullins brothers, are we?" one of them says. Another puts him in a headlock and pulls him backwards so that he's looking up at the bruising sky. Then Andy Dummican steps forward and makes a show out of picking his nose and holding his finger out to show everyone his booger, the biggest booger Aidan has ever seen – wet and slimy and green, with a fleck of dried blood at the end. He wiggles his finger and the booger swings back and forth like a conker on a string. It stretches in the middle like a yoyo until the end threatens to break off and drip onto his shoe, or the ground. He reaches over and wipes it down Aidan's cheek.

"Boathouse baby going to cry?"

Aidan tries to shake his head, afraid if he opens his mouth a whimper will escape.

"Then we'll have to do something about that, won't we boys?"

Chapter 32

Egypt removes the pan from the stove and ladles soup into a bowl. She sits, chases the mixture with her spoon, stirs it and lifts a mouthful to her lips. The beans taste burned – caught on the bottom of the pan when she ran outside and down the path the rain has made slick, thinking she'd heard Aidan's voice. Oily clouds rolled in shortly after school let out, obscuring nightfall. Almost six o'clock and the sky is black as pitch. Her anger hovers on the edge of fear. Maybe Ray's taken him off somewhere, which is a worry in itself. If he'd fallen ill at school, surely someone would have crossed the road to the normal school to let her know. Or maybe – her mind strays to the ice, unstable and deadly now that temperatures are on the rise. And there are currents, even in the marsh. But he knows better. It's been drilled into him. Still. He's so small. Anything could have happened. She could kick herself for not coming straight home, for traipsing after Gloria instead. Seduced by vanity.

"Mother's finished her painting of you," Gloria announced as Egypt hurried from the cloakroom, fastening the buttons on her coat, mittens between her teeth. "If you'd like to see it." Green eyes flashing with mischief. Or was it malice? Egypt crosses her arms, suddenly self-conscious. Sweat prickles at her hairline. She pushes away the soup bowl, the smell of burnt beans. At least there had been no Philip, with his immoderate attention, his double-edged remarks. But it would seem that once again Gloria's invitations carried an ulterior motive.

The moment they stepped over the threshold, Gloria put her finger to her lips. "Mother likes to present her work herself." Then she slipped off her shoes and waved her hand, indicating Egypt should do likewise and follow her down the hallway to the back of the house.

Inside the studio, the air was shockingly cool. The girls' breath whorled in front of them, marking their trespass. Egypt's heart fluttered high in her chest. Dust motes danced in the fading light. Mrs. Henry had been there recently, yesterday, or this morning possibly, adding her final flourishes. Or perhaps the smell of paint and turpentine was always this strong. It made her lightheaded.

A covered canvas sat on an easel to one side of the room. As Gloria stepped towards it, Egypt flushed, remembering the way Mrs. Henry had lifted the cloak that had graced her shoulders, revealing her nakedness, and stepped back to appraise her. How quickly Philip had barged in with his tales of gambling and drinking the night away, trailing the stink of cadavers and vice. How could the painting be of her nude? Even a purple trapezoid nude? She hadn't been naked nearly long enough for Mrs. Henry to even set down broad strokes, let alone the details of her skin and shoulders. Her breasts.

Gloria picked up a corner of the cloth. "Ready?" she asked, and Egypt felt hot and nauseous. At first Gloria lifted the protective cloth slowly. Egypt could make out nothing distinct – a blur of beige. A stirring of disappointment in the pit of her belly. Perhaps that was all she was to the Mrs. Henrys of this world. Indistinct. Unformed. Beige. Then, "Ta da," Gloria yanked the cloth away and Egypt's heart began clanging against the walls of her chest. The entire canvas was taken up with her face. How alarming to be confronted with herself like that, bewildering to see herself larger than life, larger than the canvas itself even. Her hair at the temples spilled off the edges and into the darkening studio, the cleft of her chin barely grazed the base of the canvas. Lips, eyes, nose, the mole by her lower lashes – they were all most definitely Egypt, but Egypt in a way she'd never seen herself before. She raised her hand, drawn to touch this face that was both hers and not hers, and let it drop again, too frightened to break the spell the image was casting. The picture glowed, a life of its own. As if it were drawing all the light left in the room and shining it back out. How achingly vulnerable she looked. More naked than any nude Mrs. Henry could have painted. How had someone she barely knew managed to capture a side of Egypt she had never revealed? Not even to herself. It was like looking inside her soul and finding a lost and frightened child.

Egypt recrosses her arms and shuffles in her chair, trying to shake the feeling the painting has given her. Steals a glance at the clock. Her coat hanging reproachfully from its peg by the door.

Wind buffets the cabin, rattles the windows, a splatter of rain startles, like someone throwing pebbles.

Drafty, isn't it? It's a wonder you don't all have cricks in your necks.

Five more minutes and she'll put her coat on. She pulls a schoolbook from her bag, pages through it distractedly. *Where would Ray have taken him? To Manny's? Downtown? Or any one of dozens of places between.* The clock ticks obscenely loudly. She should be out looking for him. Or should she? As long as she sits at the table, he is merely late. The moment she pulls on her coat, lights a lantern and steps outside, it signifies that he's lost. And what if the moment she leaves, Aidan wanders home looking for his supper and finds the place empty? How will he feel? She could leave a note. *Out looking for your sorry backside.* Would he be able to read it? There is also no telling when her mother might return from work – the hours are long and unpredictable at her new job; the old lady she fetches and carries for cantankerous and forgetful – and Egypt will then be stuck trying to invent a lie as to where she's been and why that was more important than walking her brother home. It isn't as if he's never walked home by himself before. He knows the way blindfolded. He could do it in his sleep.

The rain grows more insistent, drumming on the roof. As long as he's somewhere warm and dry. As long as someone hasn't taken him. The bogeyman. To drown out her thoughts she starts up humming.

George gets to his feet and slinks towards the door, where he stands with head lowered, a low grumbling issuing from the back of his throat.

"It's okay, boy. It's just a storm."

Lightning sheets the sky, leaving a momentary imprint of silhouetted rooflines in the window. Thunder cracks directly over the cabin and Egypt leaps from her skin. Warm air moving in. Or God pointing his finger, blaming her.

And there's Ray, slamming the door behind him, cursing the rain. George whimpers and slinks under the table. Egypt can't decide if she's grateful to see her father or not.

"You look like you just saw your own ghost," he says, stamping his feet and shaking out his hat. A sodden cigarette hangs from the corner of his lip. "Don't tell me you're afraid of a little thunderstorm?"

"I'm worried about Aidan."

Ray shuffle-slides on the rag rug across the floor to the stove. Stirs the soup and raises a ladleful to his lips. "Smells burned."

"Probably your cigarette," she mumbles.

"What?"

"He hasn't come home from school." She tries to check her impatience. "I think he might be missing." The last word comes out almost a whisper, her throat suddenly blocked.

Ray pulls a bowl from the shelf. Rummages for a spoon.

"Did you hear what I said?"

"He'll be off with his mates somewhere; he's a boy."

"What *mates*? The only kids he ever hung out with died in a fire, in case you'd forgotten."

"How can I forget?" He hurls the ladle and throws his arms in the air; wheels on her, eyes wet with fury. "The way you go on, anyone would think I had something to do with the damned fire."

"How am I *going on*? It's the first time I've ever said anything." This is why her mother so rarely broaches anything with him. He's like a volcano set to blow. She lowers her gaze to her geography book. Canada in effete pink, the United States a more substantial green. Verdant. Fertile. "No one thinks you had anything to do with it."

He kicks the rug to the door and stalks towards her, grit crunching beneath his boots. She flinches as he reaches to unhook the hurricane lamp that hangs above the table, making it swing wildly. The light flutters, chasing shadows up and down the walls.

"Get your coat on," he snarls. "And bring that dog of yours if you think he'll be any use."

But George is unpredictable in a thunderstorm. If he runs off, it could be days before he returns. "He should stay here," she says, glaring at her hands, willing them steady enough to light a second lamp. Snapped out of her inertia, she's giddy, lightheaded and also grateful, despite his outburst, that he's taken charge.

Outside, the rain flays at her skin, the wind so fierce it both knocks her over and pins her in place, sucking the breath from her lungs. And yet how much better it feels to be outside doing something than staying inside fretting.

Ray heads right, towards the remains of the burned properties. Maybe he thinks Aidan could be hiding out in the Mullinses' house – the only building still standing. Or that he ventured in there, curious, and is now trapped, pinned by a fallen timber. He could be unconscious. Ray lifts the lamp before him to locate the rope the fire chief secured around the perimeter and steps over. Egypt stumbles after him, turning her ankles on a mess of charred debris and blistered paintwork. Glass crunches under her feet, nails scratch at her legs, splintered wood.

Ray disappears inside, taking with him the comfort of his light. Despite the obvious danger and risk to other kids who might be tempted to play in it, the community has been reluctant to start clearing the site, dismantling the precarious walls, the half-burned roof. Perhaps because the Mullinses are still around. In Gloria's opinion they'd be better off packing up their things and moving somewhere that doesn't remind them so painfully of what they've lost. Before storming off, Egypt had replied that she didn't think anyone would need reminders of the fact that they'd lost their children and that the Mullinses likely had no choice but to stay where they were. They had no money, and wasn't it typical of someone whose family had plenty of money to not understand how limited the choices were to people who didn't. Secretly, she wishes that the Mullinses would move away – and she probably isn't alone in that – Zadie's behaviour is growing more unpredictable and alarming, and it's becoming a chore to try to avoid her all the time. What will things be like when the weather improves and she is out and about more? Is able to waylay Aidan more often.

Of course! That's where the little monkey will be. She hollers to Ray and then waves her lamp in the direction of the Owls' clubhouse. Wacky Zadie will have lured him over there with the promise of returning the lead soldiers she stole the day of the wake. Or at least letting him play with them. She can almost see the two of them seated across from each other on the floor, engrossed in a game of war, having lost track of time.

But Max and Zadie Mullins are alone. The bitter stink of wet burned things, of desperation, wafts out the door Max holds open. In less than two weeks, he has aged a decade. Silver flecks his hair and the bristles of his five o'clock shadow. Zadie glances briefly in her direction when Egypt mentions Aidan's failure to return home from school. Adding, almost apologetically, that he could have come home and gone out again, but that it would appear now, as it was edging close to seven o'clock, that he was most definitely missing.

"I'll come with you," Max Mullins says. "Two sets of eyes are better than one." Obviously he hasn't caught sight of Ray yet. Zadie, sitting cross-legged on their makeshift bed, throws him a doleful glare, but Max squares his shoulders, lifts his chin. He pushes his feet into a pair of rubber boots, is over the threshold and pulling the door shut behind him when the keening starts up in the back of Zadie's throat.

Such a raw, wounded sound. So achingly lonely. Egypt watches anxiety twist at Max's face, at a loss as to how to arrange her own. He's torn. How quickly his spine loses its certainty. He stares out at the storm and back at his wife, climbing to hysteria.

"It's okay," Egypt says, stepping back. "My dad's helping." He nods, regret and relief playing equally across his face.

Lightning streaks across the sky again, another crack of thunder. Drawn to the water, storms often get caught here, circling around the head of the lake. When she was little, Egypt used to huddle by the window with her mother when a summer storm woke them, watching electricity paint the sky. Counting the number of strikes. Sometimes it would be over an hour before the storm moved on.

As if by unspoken agreement, Ray and Egypt pick their way to the water's edge. What fearful shapes her mind conjures from the flickering yellow light cast by her lamp, how monstrous the shadows of rocks grow, the spiky arms of bushes and last year's weeds clinging fiercely to the bank. Her heart lurches and skips, imagining scraped knees and twisted limbs, shanks of tousled hair. His face, so pale and still.

When Aidan was born, Egypt was both surprised and terrified by how quickly and how fiercely she came to love him: almost from the first kick of his feet, the way he gurgled and punched the air with his tiny fists, as if beating his way out of the grasp of some imaginary foe and into her heart. Egypt never shared such thoughts with her mother, who, watching her watch the baby from a distance, from the corner of her eye, said that he was just trying to pass wind. In turn, Egypt watched her mother change him and bathe him and sing to him. His vulnerability made her want to wrap him in armour, steel-plate his heart and soul. She'd helped out when asked, but mostly she'd held back and watched, nursing and shepherding her own feelings into a fierce little pebble that sat tucked behind her breastbone. When he learned to walk and then to talk and began expressing himself and his independence, she began to relax a little, and though his care more often fell to her, she found she didn't worry so much. He had enough Fisher blood running through his veins that he could take care of himself.

To a point.

The wind carries Ray's voice back to her, hollering her brother's name. "Aidan," she whispers. "Aidan." Louder this time. "Aidan!" Something loosed in her chest. A coil of grief. "Aidan! Aidan, where are you? Aidan!" How freeing to holler, to let it out there. Let the rain mingle with the tears on her cheek. Makes her feel stronger somehow.

She follows Ray along the shoreline, stumbling over rocks, slipping on patches of ice, calling her brother's name till she fears her throat will bleed. She changes hands often, burying the one not holding the lamp in her pocket, though there isn't a chance of warming them on this night. And then her lamp dies, plunging her into total darkness. She shakes it, feeling the kerosene shift and slosh around. Must be the wick. Sodden or run out.

And then, through the glaze of rain, she spots a lantern approaching Ray. Max Mullins, perhaps? Not until she's almost upon them is she able to make out the height and gait of the shadowy figure holding the lantern: Frank Sugden. A neighbour who lives in one of the larger cabins. *What's he doing out here?* Offering his affinity with their loss? Frank Sugden lost his son swimming in the bay when Egypt was a girl. She remembers walking to school with David Sugden, and then, the following September, he wasn't there. He was always such a funny kid. Loud, a daredevil. A lot like Aidan.

The two men begin making their way back to the Fisher cabin, Frank Sugden glancing over his shoulder every few steps to make sure she's following. Ray trudges along, head bent, almost dragging his lamp. Egypt's heart stutters in her chest. She'd run but her legs will barely move, she can scarcely feel them. *Aidan*. Her head thumps. *Aidan Aidan*, a mantra, willing him safe. Her eyes and nose stinging, the rain pelting her in the face. She screams into the wind, voiceless, just a tearing at her throat. *Come on legs, come on, move*.

Frank Sugden and Ray confer at the door before the neighbour moves off, back to the warmth and comfort of his own cabin. He knows this story, what comes next, the pain, the recriminations. How did people move on from such tragedies? The Mullinses were stuck in a holding pattern of grief. They had Stan Byrd to rail against. But what did you do if you had no one to point a finger at? How did you cope if you only had yourself to blame?

She follows her father inside, cold streaking through her stomach. His face as he peels off his wet clothing is unreadable.

"Your mother won't be best pleased with this turn of events." She waits for more, feels hot tears rolling down her cheeks. He levels his gaze at her. "You must have opened your big mouth at some point as it seems your brother's taken himself off to your gran's."

"He's what?"

"You heard. He's at your gran's."

"Frank Sugden told you this?

"Your grandfather called the operator, asked to be put through to anyone who had a telephone down here. And that would be the Sugdens."

"So is Grandpa Aiken bringing Aidan back?"

"Is he 'ell, the lad's staying the night."

"He isn't coming home?"

"That's what I said, isn't it? Your grandfather's run him to the doctor's for a once-over – hence the phone call. He would have driven over here otherwise and told you hisself."

"But he wouldn't have brought him back?"

"How the hell should I know? Sugden wasn't exactly flush with details. Said the lad got lost a few times making his way over there, so now they've got him warm and dry and fed, he's staying where he is for the night."

The little imp. All her careful strategy, weeks of courting their attention, and he just wanders over in the rain and usurps her place, gets himself a bed for the night. *And cocoa and cookies and a bedtime story, no doubt.*

"She'll play hell, your mother will, when she learns where he is. What did you go telling him for? That was between you and me."

She rounds on him in a fury. "You're mad at me because she might be mad at you! I'm not the one at fault here. And anyway, I didn't tell him. They just showed up here one day unannounced. And you know what? She hasn't said anything at all about you telling me. She doesn't even know. Your precious secret is still safe." She has to take a breath. Lowers her voice. "Not that it was much of a secret anyway; you only told me out of spite."

"It was time you knew. But you better get your story straight for when your mam walks in here wanting to know where he is. Hey, where d'you think you're going?"

"To see Aidan." She's pulling her wet coat on again; it hangs cold and heavy on her shoulders, like some sodden pelt she's tasked to carry.

"You're not going anywhere; you've got your mother to deal with."

"You deal with her."

"I have places to be."

"Me too."

He turns on the charm. "Come on, girl, it'll be better coming from you. Bit of comforting from her daughter."

Egypt glares at Ray. "Actually, it won't. You ever consider that she might appreciate you sitting and facing things for once instead of running away all the time?"

"You'll catch your death," he yells as she slams the door and braces herself to face the night.

Chapter 33

Laura is sitting on the edge of a kitchen chair, arms folded, legs crossed, mouth pinched tight, a deep frown line between her eyes. He's made her a cup of tea.

She sniffs at it. "What's this?"

"A drop of brandy. They say it's good for what ails you." She looks at him sharply. "For shock."

"Don't," she growls as he reaches out to touch her shoulder. He flinches as though struck.

"You carry brandy with you now?"

"Aye." Brandy, whiskey, hooch. Who knows what Red's peddling these days? *There's no more money in liquor*, Doyle says. He's onto something else. Decks of snow. Morphine. In small white pills. Papers of cocaine. Heroin. Scares the hell out of Ray. But sometimes it's the only way to be with Doyle. Grows him that inner layer of skin he can hide out in, but the pain afterwards is worse than any hangover. Like his bones are trying to push their way through his skin. And it's not him. The booze is still Ray Fisher. Louder, brasher, willing to take more risks than maybe he should, but at least it leaves him still recognizable to himself.

"You should drink your tea."

She does. He senses her relax as the liquor takes effect.

"That feel better?" He reaches out to touch her shoulder again. No response. Rubs her back. All ribs and vertebrae, thin as a potato peeling. "It's not like they're planning on hurting him or nothing, is it? Probably just want to spoil him a bit."

She's silent, jaw moving, chewing on the inside of her lip. Her nails are bitten to the quick, her knuckles raw. Slowly eating herself away. The ends of her hair all chewed. He can't remember the last time he looked so close.

"He'll be back tomorrow. Bright as a button."

"I should've been here."

"Aye. Work's work though." She doesn't say *you. You should've been here*. As long as she doesn't say he should've been here.

And suddenly, she's screaming about the kid. He's trying to explain. Her arms flailing. He wraps his around her to hold her, stop her hurting herself, quiet her down. And then he smells it in her hair. It. Him. On her skin. She's been doing it with him, that piece of shit from Winnipeg. It's like he's been punched in the gut. He tries to calm his voice so he can ask her about work, ask her where she's been. His arms are locked around her, bands of steel. His muscles screaming his arms are so tight. She tells him she was waiting out the storm, waiting till the weather broke; it's a long walk in that kind of rain. Her eyes look huge and wild. Waiting till the storm moved on. Waiting in his bed, waiting with the stink of his seed all over her. Coming in here with her skin flushed and her eyes bright. So bright. That shite in bed with his wife, his hands all over her, fucking her. His wife. His. He sees red again. Screaming. But the noise is coming from him. He opens his eyes. When did he close them? There's a trace of blood at the corner of her mouth. *Oh God. I've hit her*. His hand shot out and connected with her cheek. Already he can see the bruise forming. Her cheek reddening, swelling. Her eyes weeping. Tears. She's crying. No noise comes from her throat. Those eyes, staring at him. A look of pure, cold hate.

"Sorry.

"Sorry. I'm sorry. Sorry sorry sorry sorry sorry sorry. I'm sorry, forgive me." On his knees, the linoleum cold and hard under his bony bones, all skin and bone. He's sorry. He'll do anything.

"Get out, Ray."

Anything but that. He can't leave, can't turn his back on them, on his house. Anything but that. He needs her. Egypt and his son. He needs the house.

"Get out and don't come back."

The look in her eyes, the coldness there, cuts him to the core. Hurts worse than all his days and nights in prison. All those days and nights where only the thought of returning to her arms kept him alive, kept him going when they hurt him. Hurts worse than having his heart slowly torn from his chest. Hurts worse than the sticks, the hands holding him, the gag between his teeth, the black place he went to.

As soon as day breaks, he takes the Sugdens' sledgehammer from where Frank leaves it leaning against the side of the house and marches over to the Byrds' place. Glass crunches, wood splinters beneath his boots. He takes a swing at the walls. They wobble. Another swing before they buckle. The house twists in on itself and Ray wades in, sledgehammer swinging, not caring what he hits or if he gets hurt. Swinging madly until the place falls down around his ears. Has to leap out of the way when a roof timber topples near him, the air from the whumph as it lands on the growing pile of debris knocks his hat from his head. He picks it up. Sledgehammer raised over his head. Smashing. Smashing. Doesn't stop until the house is dust and splinters.

Chapter 34

Egypt wakens to unfamiliar light and traffic noise, the swish of tires in the rain, morning commerce in the city. She stretches her arms and scissors her legs the width of the soft bed. Buries her face in the pillow and giggles. She's drowning in roses and lavender. Bath salts. Her grandmother laughing as she tipped a sinful amount under the open taps, hot water gushing into the claw-footed tub, filling the bathroom with clouds of scented steam. When her grandmother lifted the sash window a fraction, steam rushed out through the gap to join the night. Egypt sank up to her shoulders in blissful heat.

Emerging half an hour later, pink-skinned and smelling like a garden in June, she donned the ruffled cotton nightdress her grandmother had left out for her, plus a faded pink chenille dressing gown and a pair of slippers, and floated downstairs. Her sodden clothes had been hitched to the ceiling on the drying creel in the kitchen.

"They were your aunt's," her grandmother said when Egypt asked to whom her night attire had belonged. "She had your height, height you both got from your grandfather."

Egypt glided towards the dining table, where her grandmother indicated she should sit.

"Sticky toffee pudding and custard," she announced, placing a steaming bowl in front of her. "My mother used to make it as a special treat for me when I was a little girl. It'll warm you through."

"How else am I like her," Egypt asked, fingering the soft ribbon threaded through the ruched-cotton neckline.

"She was a brave young woman, like yourself, not afraid to strike out on her own, to have an adventure."

"You think I'm brave?"

Her grandmother folded her hands together on the table and leaned back in her chair. "You set out to find us, didn't you? That took courage."

"And Aunt Anne-Marie? How was she brave?"

Grandma Lily smiled, though her eyes looked faraway. "She went to war. She signed up for the Red Cross and she drove an ambulance."

Sticky toffee pudding, a hot bath, a bedroom of her own. Egypt could get used to such luxury. To say goodnight and be able to close the door, to shut out the world and be alone in this room, truly alone. But there was also a sadness to being alone in her dead aunt's room. Anne-Marie Aiken, a relative she would never have the chance to know. She examined the walls before slipping between the covers, trying to learn something of this dead aunt. A framed petit point of purple and white flowers over the bed, her initials, A.M.A., in the bottom right-hand corner. A handful of books on a shelf: *Jane Eyre*, *Pride and Prejudice*, *Wuthering Heights*. A surprise: Jules Verne's *Twenty Thousand Leagues Under the Sea*. A clue perhaps to the explorer she would become, venturing off to war. Who else had she been, this young woman, only two years older than Egypt when she died?

She slips into her clothes, which are waiting in the bathroom, cleaned and ironed. When she arrived last night, Aidan was asleep, his door ajar. She pushes it open slowly.

"It's only me."

He stirs, opens his eyes, a wan face lost in the mound of pillows propping him up. A worn teddy bear is tucked in the covers beside him. They make a droll pair.

"Whose is the bear?"

"Grandma Lily said it was Mom's when she was a little girl."

"It suits you."

He screws up his nose. "It smells old and dusty. I threw it off the bed, but Mom put it back this morning."

"Mom was here? When?"

"You were sleeping."

"She came this morning?" *She must have been in some state; it's barely gone seven thirty.* "And how was she?" On the bedside table sits a tray with his breakfast, a half-eaten boiled egg and toast soldiers, picked over.

"She was crying, and then she sang me a song."

"She didn't say anything?"

"I dunno. I fell asleep. Like what?"

Egypt steps over to the window and draws back the curtains. More rain.

"How are you, anyway?" She pats his legs through the bedcovers. "Feeling better?" He shrugs, produces a small cough, a dramatic sniff. Then another.

"So what happened yesterday? Why didn't you come home?"

As he tells her the story of Andy Dummican and his bully pals, she looks around her mother's old room. It's bigger than Anne-Marie's room, the same flowered wallpaper, similar rugs by the bed, the bedside table matches the one in Anne-Marie's room, but all surfaces are clear of sentimental reminders. Perhaps reading and petit point weren't her mother's thing. Too tame.

"How you even remembered the way is amazing."

"I only got lost once."

"But why come all the way over here? It must have taken you ages."

"First I walked back to school and the janitor shooed me away. And then it started raining so I ran into the park, but I didn't know where you were, or Mom or Dad, and then I remembered Grandma Lily saying I could come over anytime and so I did."

She raises her eyebrows, indicating the bed, the room, the breakfast tray. "And landed on your feet, so to speak."

He pulls the covers up over his smile.

"You should tell your teacher."

"Telling makes it worse."

"So you're just going to let a bunch of bullies rule your life?"

"I might tell Dad."

She laughs. Squeezes his toes through the blanket. "Not as dumb as you look, are you?"

"He'll scare them."

"No doubt."

He coughs again, a chesty wet sound. She puts a hand to his forehead. Clammy.

"And do your plans include school this morning?"

He shakes his head.

"You do look a bit pale." A day in bed won't hurt.

At the top of the landing, she pauses to stare out at the back garden. Through the drizzle of rain, a riot of yellow daffodils and pale tulips bob their heads. Green shoots break the surface of leaves, the lawn coming back to life. She starts down the stairs, the smell of freshly baked bread making her stomach rumble. The clatter of dishes from the kitchen, and then her grandmother's voice.

"It's for a few days, that's all."

"A few days!" Her mother. Still here then. "First it was overnight, now it's a few days! What changed in the middle of the night?"

"The doctor is coming later this morning."

"The doctor! Again! And who's paying for that?"

"Don't be ridiculous, Laura."

"He doesn't need a doctor, he needs his family."

"We are his family."

Egypt sits down carefully on the step, fearful of making it creak and giving herself away. She strains to listen over the drumbeat of her heart.

"You didn't even know of his existence until a few weeks ago."

"Whose fault is that?"

"And Egypt. Are you going to keep her prisoner here too?"

"She's free to come and go as she pleases."

"Like I was, you mean?"

"They were different times, Laura."

"*Different times*. You'd bring in anything just to suit your argument, wouldn't you? What was it? The war? The suffragette movement? Someone threw themselves under the King's horse at some racetrack, women got the vote, started showing their ankles in public and somewhere along the line absentee grandparents evolved the right to take their grandchildren away from their mothers."

"We didn't take him, Laura. He came to us, remember?"

"Oh." A bloody scream of frustration in her mother's throat that makes its way through Egypt's bones. "That doesn't give you the right to keep him."

"Shouldn't you be getting to Mrs. Pendlebury's?"

"She can wait another five minutes."

"Her bladder can't. There'll be a wet bed waiting for you."

"Fine." The sound of a chair scraping back. Egypt leaps to her feet, the stairs creak.

A heavy silence drifts up the staircase.

"We'll let you know what the doctor says."

"Goddamn right you will."

"There is no need for that kind of language in this house. We didn't raise you to take the Lord's name in vain. But that's what you get when you live with riff-raff. I just hope for your sake that you don't use that kind of language in front of the children."

"For my sake? What is that, a threat?"

"You're being melodramatic again, Laura."

"You're enjoying this, aren't you? Well it won't last. The scales will fall from their eyes soon enough, and then where will you be? All lonely and bitter again."

"Don't you go quoting the Bible at me."

"Oh, go to hell, Mother."

Chapter 35

Laura is sitting on the bench in Victoria Park closest to the model school, her eyes trained on the throng of children milling about the entrance, anticipating the bell. A few are still in the park, dragging out a game of Red Rover. Aidan isn't among them. Her father has promised to bring her son to school this morning. He's already missed three days, in addition to spending the entire Easter weekend with her parents. She scans Strathcona and Locke Streets, even casts a glance down Lamoreaux, but there is no sign of them. Maybe they're coming in the car. Aidan will be teased. He hates being singled out and ribbed. Hasn't learned to laugh it off, or give as good as he gets. Like his father in that way, which is strange when you consider Ray has been a presence in his life for all of four months. She plans to make his favourite – pigs in a blanket. She wants tonight to be like old times, just the three of them. But Egypt has grown mulish, has barely exchanged a word with her mother since Aidan decamped. Blames her, no doubt. And Aidan will not only ask where his dad is but will be brimming with all kinds of awkward questions about his grandparents. She needs to extract her mother's versions of events from him first.

A familiar movement out of the corner of her eye draws her gaze to Egypt, slouching towards the normal school. She has her grandmother's slightly stooped way of walking. Funny that Laura never noticed before.

She'd tell her to straighten her spine and walk taller or she'll be bent over as an old woman, but Egypt will only ignore her, exaggerate her slouch. Same as if she mentioned how nothing good will come of her friendship with that anemic-looking Henry girl, bending her ear now as they take the steps and disappear inside. They're too unevenly matched. Chalk and cheese. She can't imagine what they find to talk about.

The monitor stands on the steps and rings the bell. There is still no sign of Aidan, or of her father's car. The children file inside, taking their chatter and laughter. When the door closes behind them, the silence rings in Laura's ears. A red-winged blackbird calls from a neighbourhood tree, seeking a mate perhaps. A baby cries. At the King Street end of the park, a trolley trundles by in a grind of metal on metal. By quarter past nine her feet are numb, the bones in her backside aching from the cold, hard seat. She runs her fingers over her bruise. What a picture she must cut: *Battered Woman on a Bench*. It could be why they're keeping him away. Briefly, she contemplates stomping over to Robinson Street, hammering on the door, extracting an explanation. But listening to her mother make excuses will only enrage her further. Besides, she's late for work.

She walks quickly to King Street, to the butcher's shop and the greengrocer's where Mrs. Pendlebury keeps accounts, or her absent son keeps them for her. Or maybe even her own father keeps them, for it seems as if Laura's father is behind everything these days, his purse strings choreographing every step she takes. She keeps her head averted, her bruise towards the back of the shop, but can feel Mrs. Cartwright's eyes boring through the scarf tied under her chin, through her skull. Mr. Cartwright will look anywhere but Laura's face. With Matt in mind, she orders half a dozen more eggs, a piece of chuck, makes a point of mentioning Mrs. Pendlebury's increase in appetite.

"That's good to hear, Mrs. Fisher," Mr. Cartwright says, his voice booming, as if to cover his wife's indiscretion. "Must be the stimulation of having someone around. Your father tells me you read to her."

Laura smiles thinly. She reads for her own sanity. Mrs. P. always nods off after a couple of paragraphs. But there's her father, rewriting her life again. It's like being stalked. She adds a couple cans of Campbell's oxtail soup. The less time she spends bent over the stove, the more she can spend in bed. Smiles as Mr. Cartwright's eyebrows lift a fraction in surprise.

Matt is gone by the time she arrives. Even when Laura leaves for work early, hoping to catch him still in bed, to slip between the sheets with him for a few minutes to warm her blood, harness her strength for the day, he is always gone. The bedspread pulled smooth, sheets tucked into tight hospital corners, as if he'd never been there. She pulls down the bed linen and lowers her head to the pillow, where the scent of him lingers, breathes in, pulling him deep inside her, runs her fingers across the sheet, the indentation of his body that he smoothed away. And yet even after these rituals, jealousy skulks the corners of her happiness, and she frets that he spends his nights elsewhere. He's young and handsome; she's seen the way women preen when he's around (Egypt hung on his every breath), the way they push the hair back from their necks, track him with their eyes. He's a liar – not a very good liar, but still.

They fought about her jealousy once. She a pantomime of harsh whispers, exaggerated facial expressions and spastic arm movements, he all folded arms and stony silence. She stalked over to the bed, reached beneath and pulled out the chamber pot, the contents of which slopped over onto her fingers. She couldn't raise her eyes to look at him but felt his cold stare, at her, at the pot filled with piss that sat on the floor between them like a scold.

She squirms in embarrassment remembering that day, and yet for her, the chamber pot has become the litmus test of this nameless thing they have together – she doesn't dare call it a relationship, a courtship. If he doesn't empty his bladder here, he doesn't love her. *Love. Get a hold of yourself, Laura. Take this affair for what it is – a bit of fun, a lark. Savour the confines of this illicit bed. As work is finished on the Mullinses' new cabin, Matt could move on any day.* Laura gives herself a slap on the face. *Is it really love you want from him anyway?* Surely he's just a crush, a distraction from the humdrum of her days, the pain of losing Aidan. *Roll your sleeves up, woman, get to work.*

Mrs. P. has, as her mother predicted, wet the bed. Laura opens the window, heats up water, manoeuvres her into her bath chair, washes and fits her into a clean flannel nightie, socks, slippers on her feet. If Mrs. P. weren't such a frail old bird, Laura's job would be impossible. She tucks a blanket around her legs and wheels her to the window. Sponges down the rubber sheet, boils the bedding, wrings it out and hangs it in the backyard. All before she can even think about food.

She's setting up the ironing board in the kitchen when Matt slips in through the back door. Her face is flushed, hands red and sore from lye, from wringing out sheets. She runs them through her hair. The steam has made it frizzy.

"You're early."

"Tell me you're pleased."

"Did anyone see you?"

"I ducked between the sheets on the line. You look like you had a rough day."

She presses her lips together to stop them from trembling.

"They never showed, did they?"

She shakes her head. She has to fill the kettle and light the stove before she can trust herself to speak. "I don't understand why they would keep him from school so long except to spite me. They always made such a big deal out of education."

"Maybe he's still sick."

"I can't get near enough to find out. Whenever I go over there he's sleeping, or he's in the bath, or he's at the doctor's. How many times does he need to see the damn doctor? I saw him the morning afterwards, and he was fine. A little overwhelmed with all that had happened, maybe, but there was nothing wrong with him." Waving her hands about, she catches herself on the iron. Cries out. It's a glancing burn but enough to unfasten her tears. Matt folds his arms around her and she rests her head on his chest. "It just feels like they're keeping him from me."

Tenderly he kisses her hair, her neck, the bruise on her face; his hands soothe the tension in her back, ease the kinks in her neck, the tightness in her shoulders. As she lets herself relax into him, more tears bubble up. He pulls her tighter and strokes the hair back from her face.

"You should go over there and take him back. Stop letting them push you around. Stand up to them. Walk in there and take him away. He's your child."

"I know. I know I should. Believe me, I've done it in my mind's eye a hundred times, but whenever I make a move to actually go over there it's as if my legs suddenly don't work, and I feel so tired, so utterly physically incapable of getting myself there, as if there are weights attached to my arms and legs."

"What are you afraid they'll do?"

"Stop me. Turn him against me. Call the police. I don't know."

"Call the police and say what? You haven't done anything wrong."

"I know, but they have this way of making me *feel* as if I've done something wrong – like I've been a bad mother. A bad daughter, a terrible citizen."

He pulls back and takes her chin in his hands. "You're none of those things."

"It isn't rational, I know, but neither is my mother. Once she gets her teeth into something, she won't let go. I've kept her grandchildren from her – and she's going to punish me for that."

"Then you need to appeal to her sense of reason."

She leans into him again, wraps her arms around his back. "She's never had one – at least not where her children were concerned. And now her grandchildren. Aidan ... All she ever wanted was a boy. I don't want to think about the lengths she'll go to –"

The back door crashes into the kitchen wall. They leap apart as Ray barges into the room, red-faced and shouting. She's a whore. He's low-life pond scum, a wife-stealing piece of shite.

Matt stalks towards him, fists clenched. "You're a wife-beater. You can't get much lower than that."

"And you're a liar." Ray's eyes seek Laura's, his mouth turned down in a snarl. She has to fight a rising panic. "You want to ask your precious boyfriend what really happened the night of the fire? Thinks he's pure as the driven snow. Mr. Old-Man-Byrd-got-drunk-and-knocked-over-the-lamp, did he?"

"What's he talking about? Matt? Ray? Ray, I want you to leave. Now." She's surprised to hear her voice shaking. Lifts a hand to her mouth and finds she's trembling all over.

"I can't understand what you see in him, Laura. Not your type."

"And I can't understand why someone hasn't laid you out before now." Laura can hear Matt swallowing his rage.

Ray smirks. "I saw you. I saw you catch one of those blokes who were running. And then you let him go. Explain this to me, Laura," he says, his eyes never leaving Matt's face, "Winterpeg here lets an arsonist go and then never breathes a word of what happened to anyone. What's it all about, eh? Who are you protecting? You tell me. Tell her."

"The fire was an accident."

"So they say."

"What are you accusing him of? Matt sounded the alarm."

"I sounded the alarm. He was busy."

"You're full of it, Ray Fisher. It's just another one of your tall tales, and I'm sick and tired of them."

"On my brother's grave, Laura. I'm telling the God's honest truth."

"So why wait until now to say something?"

"Because he knows no one would believe him," Matt spits.

But it isn't that. Laura has known Ray for far too long not to understand that while his emotions might be all over the place, his actions are more calculated. Ray the opportunist, always on the lookout for the better deal, the better angle, the best bang for his buck. She puts a hand out to steady herself against the wall.

"She believes me. I can see it in her face."

Laura turns away. She can see Ray that night, standing at the living-room window. *It's the Byrds' place*. Like he knew for sure. When all that could be seen from the window were the reflections of the flames cast on the water.

"He's lying through his back teeth." Matt pulls his hand through his hair. *Another tell?*

"I know what I saw."

"Word is you barely know your name. You want to take it easy with the moonshine. Or is it narcotics you're messing with these days?"

"Matt, please, stop taunting him."

Ray's smirk is now a grin. "Yeah, Matt, please, stop taunting me."

Matt lunges. Chairs topple as Ray crashes backwards into the Welsh dresser, Matt's hands around his throat. Dishes hit the floor and explode. A cry issues from the other side of the house. *Mrs. Pendlebury. Oh my God.* Laura rushes into her room to find her on the floor, having slipped from the chair. Nightdress up around her waist, shit stains down her legs, on the nightdress, the chair, the rug. The stench nearly knocks Laura back out the door. She tries to pull the old lady up onto the bed without gagging or soiling her own clothing. The noise from the kitchen has grown murderous: scuffling, grunts, a thud, more pottery breaking, cursing, the sounds of fists and boots. When she backs out of Mrs. Pendlebury's room, the two men are a blur of limbs and hair. For someone so small and wiry, Ray is a fury with his fists. But he's tiring. And Matt has the advantage of height. A knee to Ray's face sends him sprawling, and Matt lays into him with his boots, kicking him over and over in the ribs.

The sight of Ray helpless on the floor, hands over his face, is too much. "Stop. Stop it!"

Matt doesn't hear her, or doesn't want to. Laura steps forward, tugs at his arm.

"Stop it. Now! You're killing him." She thumps him on his back. "That's enough."

He turns and she sees how winded he is, his lip bloodied. "What was I supposed to do? Just let him at me? Let him at you?"

"You didn't have to beat him within an inch of his life."

"Make your mind up what you want."

"I just want him to go."

"You heard the lady." Matt pokes at Ray sprawled on the ground with his boot. "Go on, go."

Ray's breathing is ragged. He tries to rise but can't manage his arms. Breathing through clenched teeth.

"Go on, *mate*. Get the hell out of here."

Ray mumbles something into the linoleum.

"What's that?" Matt hisses. "I can't hear you." He kicks him again.

"Stop that. Stop that now!"

Ray winces. Coughs. Can't seem to pull breath into his lungs.

Laura kneels by his side, ear close to his mouth, trying to make out his words. "He can't breathe. You've broken his ribs."

Ray screams when they lift him into a chair. His breathing noisy and laboured, a gash above his eye. Laura pulls an embroidered napkin from a pile in the dresser drawer. He flinches when she presses it against his face.

"What are we going to do with him?" She glances around in despair at the destruction of Mrs. Pendlebury's possessions. And there's the old lady herself to deal with, still sitting in her stink.

"Throw him out."

"He can barely stand."

"You're feeling sorry for him?"

"He's hurt."

"He's an animal."

"*He's* an animal?"

A sharp rap at the front door interrupts their exchange. They glance at the door and then at each other.

"Who's that?"

"How should I know?"

"Don't answer it." Another rap, louder this time. "They'll go away."

"All the neighbours will be out on their stoops."

This time the door shakes in its frame. "Laura! Laura! Are you in there?"

"Oh God, my father, this is all we need."

"Don't let him in."

"I have to."

He knocks again, rattles the door handle. "The police are on their way. Laura! Can you hear me? Are you all right in there?"

"He thinks I'm hurt." She rushes towards the door, then back to Matt. "You have to stay and help me explain what went on here."

"Did you hear him? He's called the police."

"You didn't start this. You were just defending yourself."

But Matt is already making his way to the back door. "There are vagrancy laws in this city. And I don't need any run-ins with the police."

The back door closes behind him as Laura's father pushes past her into the house. "What on earth is going on here? The neighbours told me they heard shouting. The sounds of a fight." He takes in the broken ornaments, the toppled furniture, pictures askew. His gaze lights on her face and she puts a hand to her yellowing bruise. Then he spots Ray slouched in the chair. "Mrs. Pendlebury is in her room I take it?"

Laura rushes after him, shards of glass and china stabbing at the soles of her slippers.

"I'll deal with you in a minute."

"It was Ray, he just burst in here and went crazy. I don't know what's wrong with him."

Her father stops at the door to Mrs. Pendlebury's room but doesn't look at her. "Do you think I was born yesterday?"

"He was like an animal."

"Would you like me to repeat back to you what the neighbours heard? I thought not." He slips through the door and closes it with a gentle click.

When he comes back out, his face is a mask of calm. Unreadable.

"How is she?"

"As you'd expect: terrified."

"I should see to her."

"You'll do no such thing. Mrs. Pendlebury has suffered enough trauma for one day."

"But she can't manage."

"It's a little late to be expressing concern. Your mother will take over from here."

"No."

"It isn't up for discussion."

"But looking after Mrs. Pendlebury is my job."

"Not anymore, it isn't. As of this minute, consider yourself out of work."

"You can't do this."

But her father's face has changed again, into one of professional civility. He reaches out his hand to the first of the two policemen in their navy uniforms and shiny black boots who are suddenly filling up the hallway.

Ray's progress through the house and down the front steps is slow. She follows them to the door of the wagon, as much to put distance between herself and her father as anything else.

"Is he going to be all right?"

"Someone will look him over at the station, ma'am."

Ray beckons her closer.

"Why's he running scared then?"

"Who?" But she knows.

"It's just a couple of bluebottles." He smirks with his eyes at the policemen holding him up on either side.

"Knew there was something crooked about him the first time I clapped eyes on him."

"You're a fine one to talk, Ray Fisher." But the words feel half-hearted.

"Takes one to know one."

Her father is waiting for her at the front door. "You can clean up the mess you made now."

"So I still have my job?"

"Whatever gave you that idea?"

"Then clean it up yourself. I don't work here anymore, remember?"

"Never did take responsibility for your own messes, did you?"

"I'll clean it up if I still have my job."

"You're not in any position to negotiate, Laura. You were given a position of trust and you abused it. Worse! You are without shame. Using this house to conduct your sordid affair. And with some other spineless waste of humanity."

"I have to work." She clutches at his arm, but he shakes her off. "I have children to support."

"Not if I have anything to do with it, you don't."

Laura backs away, stumbles over her own feet. It feels like someone has strapped a lead weight to her chest. "Meaning?"

"I'll have my lawyer draw up the papers by week's end. He'll be in touch."

"Papers?"

"Your mother and I are assuming custody of Aidan. As of now."

She glares at him, tears burning her eyes. "You never planned on giving him back, did you? You set this whole thing up."

He raises an eyebrow imperiously. "I arranged for you to get caught cheating on your husband with another man? You ascribe to me powers I have no hope of possessing."

"I'm his mother."

"You're not fit to be anyone's mother."

"How dare you!"

"You're two steps from the poorhouse."

"Not as long as I still have a roof over my head."

"Exactly."

"What the hell is that supposed to mean?"

"You won't win this argument, Laura. I can assure you, the courts will be on my side."

"I want you to tell me what you mean by *exactly*."

"Nothing."

"Liar."

"You'll find out soon enough."

She steps towards him, reaches out to pluck at his jacket. "You know something, don't you? You know something about the boathouses. About the city's plans. You and that friend of yours, that Thomas McQuesten."

"I'd like you to leave now, Laura." He takes her by the arm, his grip so firm he is pinching her skin. With his free hand he pulls her coat from the cloak stand by the door, pushes it at her. "You've done enough damage for one day."

Chapter 36

Someone is nudging him in the back of the thigh. He lifts his head and groans, stiff as the salvaged boards he's lying on, his head as thick as the bottom of a bottle of bootleg. Another nudge. *Leave me alone*. He pulls his legs closer to his chest, curls his fingers around the stock of Stan Byrd's gun. My *gun. Finders keepers*. Draws the barrel closer. Again the nudging, and now a small hand groping at his pocket. He knocks it away, alarmed to encounter fur, something cold and wet. A hot tongue bathes his hand. A tail knock-knocking both wall and incline of the narrow lean-to. *Dog*. Matt laughs aloud in relief. Panting, George scrabbles his way further in until he's flopped down alongside, his rabbit-coyote-bruised-grass scent an overpowering but welcome respite from the ashes-and-burned-chattel stink Matt had to inure himself to last night.

"Been rolling in your dinner again?" In response, George bathes his face with his long, pink tongue.

Quickly Matt wraps the gun in burlap, stuffs it down the edge of his sleeping platform and backs out of his makeshift quarters on his hands and knees. His wrists and knuckles throb, reliving the terrain of Ray Fisher's weaselly face. His arms ache, shoulders, back, knees. Even his toes. George follows him out and barks, thinking it's a game, front legs lowered in a play bow, rump in the air.

"Another time, old buddy, I'm sore as a kicked you-know-what," he says, rubbing the dog's head and giving him a playful push.

"That's what you get for sleeping outside this time of year."

Egypt. He looks up to find her smiling down at him. Smirking? Maybe it's a trick of the dawn light, her halo of saffron sky. Or the fact that she's standing over him. Powerful. As if she's grown an inch, a backbone. Or did Fisher get in a couple of shots to his head? He stands, dusting himself off, his leg cramped, the one he slept on, the other jelly-like. And he's cold to his core. Sleeping under a roof these past six months has made him soft.

"You should see the other guy."

"Eh?"

Her eyes flicker with menace before her face resolves into a picture of equanimity. His imagination? But something has definitely changed; she's more collected, more grown-up than he's ever known her.

"Something my dad used to say when he'd been in a fight."

Nausea blooms and subsides. He rubs a hand across his face, feeling for bruises. He wonders if she knows about the fight. If Laura told her or if it's written on his face. *Matt Oakes is a lying piece of scum*. He'd seek his reflection, but he's afraid of what he might see. Or not see. On top of everything else, he left Laura alone yesterday to defend herself. *Coward. Liar. Thief*. He glances over Egypt's shoulder in the direction of her house. Wonders if Ray Fisher is up and crawling about or whether they threw him behind bars.

"You must be hungry."

He shrugs. Lightheaded, now that she's mentioned it. No dinner last night, just a vigil from the bushes on the slope, watching for Laura through the lighted window of the Fishers' house.

"I'll bring you something," she says, and is gone before he can protest.

Down at the shoreline he crouches to splash water on his face. Stands and faces the Byrds' site. His promised rebuild hasn't progressed much beyond what is taken up by the lean-to. Time he has, it's materials that are in short supply. Most of what was salvaged from the burned properties, plus Myrtle Todd's firebreak cabin, has been used to cobble together a home for the bereft Mullinses. He's scoured every backyard from here to the dockyards for lumber, broken packing crates. Tried his luck at the market. But people are looking to burn anything other than coal, and every scrap is guarded zealously. He has to rethink his ambitious plans, or maybe they just don't matter anymore. He's burned his bridges here. Joanna has no reason to return. She'll live out her days with her sister in Stoney Creek; it was only ever Matt trying to assuage his guilt. *Fuck. Looking for any reason to stay on, to stay near Laura.* He should leave. Try his luck in Kirkland Lake; there's work at the gold mines. He's talked to others headed out there and some who've already done a spell. Competition is fierce, you have to watch your back, watch your tools. Fights every night. Men are desperate, conditions crowded.

Egypt has returned, bearing a lukewarm cup of tea and a bowl of oatmeal that she calls porridge.

"*Sticks to your ribs*, as my mother says." Sharp eyes regarding him.

"How is your mother?"

"Not hungry, among other things. That's her breakfast you're eating."

"Then she should have it." He thrusts the bowl back at Egypt, but her hands remain at her sides.

"Believe me. She's in no mood for food."

He considers this. "She knows you brought this over? For me?"

"No."

He picks up the spoon; the oatmeal is congealing.

"Oh, and you don't have to bother returning those." She nods to indicate the bowl and the mug, which he has set down on a board at the mouth of the lean-to. "Consider them a gift."

"Thanks."

"They're chipped anyway. And the bowl has a hairline crack."

"And the spoon?"

She shrugs. "Who counts spoons?"

He stoops to pick up the mug and takes a long swallow of tea. He's tense. Wants to be alone to eat, mull over his options, how best to approach Laura, but he's waiting for Egypt to settle herself on a make-shift seat somewhere, begin the awkward task of drawing him out with a chain of meaningless prattle. He's irritated already.

But maybe the new Egypt can read minds because she's hitching her satchel on her shoulder, taking her leave.

"See you around," he calls at her retreating back. "Thanks again."

She lifts an arm in response.

In through Mrs. Pendlebury's back gate. But it's someone else in the back-yard, pegging laundry on the line. White-haired, stern-faced, a dowager's hump. Seeing his confusion, her mouth puckers. She holds a damp towel bunched at her chest.

"If you are who I think you are, you'd better make yourself scarce, young man."

Her nose. Something in the line of her jaw. "Are you Laura's mother?"

"*I mean it*. Or I will call the police. You are trespassing."

Matt doesn't wait to be told twice.

There's no answer at the Fishers'. He waits, knocks again, calls her name and taps on the door while pushing it open. Laura is sitting at the kitchen table, head in her hands.

"You okay?"

She doesn't look up.

"Mind if I come in?" He's in already, closing the door behind him. He hasn't crossed this threshold since Ray Fisher showed up at the beginning of December. It looks familiar and yet different from the way his memory has shaped it. Smaller, shabbier. The stove is out and the place is cold. He sets his hat on the table, crouches by her chair and gently pulls her hands from her face. She looks wretched.

"You get any sleep at all?"

She shakes her head.

"None?"

"Maybe an hour or so." Her voice is raw and gravelly. He fetches a glass of water, which she drains.

"Have you eaten?"

"Not hungry."

"I'll get us some fish, cook you a hot meal."

"No." She pulls her hands from the table, hugs herself. "You should leave."

"I just got here."

"That's not a reason." She lifts her blanched features to his.

"Maybe not, but I'm staying."

"Maybe I don't want you to."

He holds out his hands and she shakes her head.

"He's taken Aidan from me."

He stands, his legs beginning to cramp. "Who has? Ray?"

"Oh, for heaven's sakes."

She's upset, he should leave before this escalates into something he'll regret, but there it is, that hold she has on him. He can't leave; he can't even make it to the door. Laura Fisher, with her sharp little face and her work-roughened hands. Her dangerous husband. Why her? She isn't at all like the women he thinks he's attracted to. The women he met across the length of his travels, women who surprised him with their flirting, with their hunger and need, with the guile by which they slipped him food from their larders and liquor from their men, the way they kissed him and pulled him into their beds. She'd seemed so prickly that first day, her face creased in a scold, a foil to her striking daughter. He took it upon himself to try to make her smile. And then laugh. Quickly it became less a challenge and more a need in him. His day lifted when he felt he'd brightened hers. And then one fateful morning, a still moment of grace in her ablutions. Aidan was untying the skiff, sorting the bait, and so it was Matt who stepped back into the cabin for the boy's forgotten fishing pole. Unaware of his presence, Laura stood before the wash basin and dipped her hands into the water, bent to splash her face. Matt put his hand out for the door, but something in the curve of her back, the spill of early morning light on her arms, nudged a childhood memory and he found himself caught at the threshold by the intimacy of her gestures, her long, graceful fingers; by the way she held her eyes closed, the towel at her throat. She reached for a hairbrush to tame her fly-away hair and caught him staring.

"Pears soap reminds me of my mother," he said, but she turned away, attacking her hair as if it were a wild animal that needed taming, and he realized the words had never left his mouth. He lowered his gaze and reached for the door handle, but fate had already set its course: the door to his heart had opened a crack, and Laura Fisher had slipped inside.

"My father took him away." She chills him with a stony look. "Remember him? Tall, older gentleman who showed up shortly after you laid into Ray."

"Of course I remember."

"Well?"

He turns from the table and walks to the window, stares out at the strip of muddy yard beside the house, the neighbours' flopped-over daffodils. "He deserved it."

An exasperated sigh. "Back to Ray again, is it? Tell me why, then. Why did he deserve it? Because he objects to being a cuckold, or because he spilled your ugly secret?"

His ugly secret. And all the lies compounded on top. Whatever made him think he could keep it at bay?

"What was that about, anyway? What exactly did Ray mean? You swore to me the fire was an accident."

"I didn't actually swear . . ." he mumbles, half-turned towards her, but it's a lame response and he despises himself for letting it grace his lips.

"Maybe not to me, but you took an oath when you got up on that witness stand." Her eyes are wet, her mouth a slash of anguish. "Who does that, Matt? Tell me. What kind of man keeps quiet about something this wicked? It's morally beyond the pale. It's evil. People died in that fire. Children burned to death. And then when someone points the finger, you beat him within an inch of his life." She buries her face in her hands. "I don't even know who you are."

My father. He closes his eyes, can feel the kicks and punches pulsing through his veins, his murderous desire, his murderous need to pull Ray Fisher apart with his bare hands. To string his wiry body between two points, to take a stick, a rock, a gun. No one has gotten under his skin the way Ray Fisher does, no one since his father. Vernon Mayfield Oakes. Is that who he has become? Was it inevitable? Bred in the bone? He'd moved half a continent away, and kept on moving, to be out of the sphere of that man's influence. Not the man he knew as a young boy. The gentle man with the belly laugh, the one who played softball with him in the summer and took him on the Red River when it froze over and taught him to skate, to shoot a puck. The one who buttoned the toggles on his coat when he was small, ruffled his hair before pulling on the toque his mother had knitted. Not that man. But the monster who returned from war. The one with the gunpowder fuse who forced everyone to tiptoe around him, afraid to say the wrong thing, look the wrong way. The one who goaded and belittled. Matt had been eleven when his father left to fight and fourteen when he returned. Four years crouched in Europe's mud, stooped in the trenches, four years of killing had warped Vernon Oakes and turned him into a vile and violent alcoholic. He'd lied about his age, about the ages of his five kids, and been sent off to a war he was too old to fight in. Trying to keep up with men almost half his age, trying to prove himself among them. Why? The reasons had never been clear. Certainly not for his serviceman's pay, which, he'd heard his mother complaining to each of his married sisters, barely covered the wages she had to shell out to replace him in the store. Eventually, his infirm mother had stepped behind the counter herself. Maybe his father had been living a lie, holding it all together until the war snapped something inside and it was impossible to control anymore. Maybe Matt is just like him. Maybe it took Ray Fisher to bring him to this point, to make him into an animal.

"Not that man, I swear."

She folds her hands together, elbows on the table, as if in prayer. "Please tell me Ray was lying."

He places his hands on the back of the chair across from her. Matt has rehearsed this moment a thousand times in his head, even since before Ray Fisher opened his mouth. He can't explain why he kept quiet about the night of the fire, why he took that road, any more than he can say why he left Earl Todd's body in an unmarked grave in the bush. Stole his identity and his timber license and spent the rest of the season burning Earl's timber mark into salvaged logs and selling them as his own. His actions can't be undone just as they can't be properly explained. He can tell himself it was because he wanted to stop the cycle of retribution. But that would be gilding the truth. Until he comes clean, Matt will always be looking over his shoulder. He pushes his fingers through his hair before reaching for his hat on the table.

"Yeah," he says quietly, "he was lying."

Chapter 37

Mr. Mitchell casts about the room before fixing his glass eye on Egypt. "Where is Miss Henry?"

Egypt shrugs. "No idea." Unusually, Gloria has been absent for more than a week.

"You might want to tell her that young ladies who treat their studies with indifference will never amount to anything."

Tell her yourself, she thinks. It's not her job to be running after truant students, and Gloria's house is the last place she feels like visiting. But when Miss Summers, her rosewater scent clouding the air, approaches her with a similar request, adding that as a friend of Gloria's, she would likely be a far more welcome presence at the Henrys' door than someone from the school, Egypt feels her resolve slipping.

"The housekeeper refuses to pass on any information. Nor have we been able to speak with either parent." Miss Summers plays with the string of pearls around her neck. Egypt fingers her own necklace, the tiger's eye topaz that rests below the hollow of her neck. Tries to picture herself wearing pearls, wonders how they feel. If she could borrow her grandmother's set. If her grandmother still remembers her existence.

"Gloria has always been an exemplary student, which is why I – we – are so concerned. Her name has been put forward for a teaching position at the model school this fall." Egypt stares out the window at the bare-branched trees in the park. *April, May, June, July, August.* And where will she be teaching this fall? Where will she be living? Where her mother? Aidan?

Monday morning came the drone of diesel engines north of the canal, grinding their way into everyone's peace of mind. *Bulldozers*, Mick and Joey, both puffed up with self-importance, told her when she returned from school, though the term was unfamiliar to her. They hurried her along to the site. Her feet caked in heavy mud, Egypt felt herself grow still inside as she took in the two machines with their tall vertical blades in front, their shanks of steel pinned together in continuous tracks. Land laid waste behind them, their blunt noses pointed at the greening banks of the sandbar: *there, we're headed there.* No tree or hill could stand in their way. No boathouse. No community. Her whole world was suddenly upside down.

"So you see, her behaviour is highly unusual, and we'd like to get to the bottom of it. As I'm sure you would, too."

Egypt stares at Miss Summers with her pretty bob, her soft-grey cardigan. Her brother has been absent from school for over two weeks, but no one has been around to the Fisher house to check up on his whereabouts.

"Have I told you how much better your performance has been this term? Mr. Mitchell and I have both remarked on your progress. And the minister at All Saints is delighted to see you in his congregation again."

Egypt had planned on explaining her absences over the winter as more a brief abdication to another denomination, a testing of different theological waters, so to speak, than an outright renunciation of her moral and religious duties. But procrastination had become a habit: as long as no one was reprimanding her for not being in the church she was supposed to be in, she couldn't see the point in bringing the subject up. Now doesn't feel like the right time.

Miss Summers laces her delicate fingers together and fixes Egypt with a smile. "You're going to make a fine teacher."

"Maybe she's sick," Egypt says. *Maybe she's moved to Paris, to Constantinople; maybe she's been whisked away by Prince Charming.*

"Between you and me," Miss Summers lowers her voice and leans a little over her desk, "I don't think Gloria has many friends she can count on, do you?"

Egypt's cheeks tremble as she smiles back at her adored Miss Summers.

Ray is waiting for her outside the school. Her stomach does a swimmy somersault. She hasn't seen him since her mother threw him out.

"Hey there, Little Sphinx."

"Hey yourself." She prays Miss Summers isn't watching at the window. She manages a smile, though it's hard to look him in the face. His skin is the colour of ash, his eyes bloodshot. If possible, his sour, unwashed smell has grown more rancid.

"I thought I might have missed you. Maybe you'd slipped out the back way."

"I was talking to my teacher."

His hands won't still. Hands that hit her mother. She's hypnotized by them: in and out of his pockets, twisting the end of a cigarette, lighting it, removing his cap, mussing his hair, stroking his chin. If she'd known he was waiting for her, would she have slipped out another way to avoid him? Crossed other people's gardens till she reached Dundurn and made her way to Gloria's from there?

"Where you off to?" he asks as she sets off down Strathcona, walking quickly to draw him away from the school.

"I have an errand to run. A favour for someone."

"Hey, slow down, would you? Your old man's an old man now." He sounds winded, his chest a wet rattle. She stops to let him catch up.

"Your teacher, eh?"

"Sorry?"

"The favour."

She presses her lips together.

"You're a good lass." He coughs, winces.

"You okay?"

"These headaches, you know."

She doesn't. "Are you getting enough sleep?"

He laughs, which makes him cough again. He's camped out on Manny's floor. "It's bloody killing me, I tell you, your mother's a cruel woman."

Cruel. She can't look at him. Starts walking again, eyes down, marking her feet on the pavement – *step on a crack, break your mother's back. Or smack her across the mouth, eh, Ray?*

"Mould creeping up the walls and rats chewing on me shoes at night. God knows there's nowt else to eat there." Egypt can't recall seeing Ray eat anything since the pork chops he made such a deal of the night he barged his way back into their lives. It seems to her he lives on air and hand-rolled cigarettes.

"Wait up, doll." One hand on her arm, the other clasped around his middle. She wants to pull away but something in his face stops her. "Couple of cracked ribs." He shrugs as if to say it's nothing.

You should see the other guy.

"Maybe you should go to the hospital."

"Nah, you know me and hospitals."

"But –"

"I'm all taped up." He pats his middle delicately, as if this proves it.

"You okay to walk?"

"I'm right as rain, lass." Licks his lips, gives her a sly sideward glance. "Punctured a lung, he did."

"Who?" But now that she's asked, Egypt isn't sure she wants to know.

"Your mother's boyfriend."

Matt? "She doesn't have a boyfriend." Matt broke her father's ribs? Punctured his lung? Why is it Egypt only ever gets half a story? She steers Ray across the road and into the park towards a bench before her legs give out.

"You're getting better though, right?"

"Six months, the doc says."

"To live?!"

"To heal." He touches his ribs again.

She's shocked, more at the idea of Matt Oakes getting angry enough to inflict that kind of damage on another person than at Ray being his victim. He probably deserved it.

"Don't chew your fingernails."

"Sorry." But the minute she takes her fingers out of her mouth she feels like crying.

"Hey, hey, less of that. I hit him back good and proper, don't you worry."

"You make me worry." She wants to run him a hot bath, like the one at her grandparents' place, shave his graying bristles, feed him a hot meal, burn his stinking clothes.

"I wanted to talk to you about something."

"I thought we already were talking."

He produces a grubby envelope from his inside jacket pocket, pulls out a well-thumbed letter. "You heard about this, yes?"

"What is it?" She tries to keep the irritation from her voice, tries to drive the image of her mother and Matt from her mind, to rise above her feelings. He's made his choice, and Laura's taken leave of her senses. No wonder her grandparents are holding onto Aidan.

"It's an offer from the city."

"An offer?" *The bulldozers.* She takes the letter from him. "This is addressed to Manny."

"His is one of the houses in the way, see?" He taps the second sheet, a mimeograph of child's scribble. It takes a moment to determine it's a crude map, scratched out by some civil servant who might have glanced at the area once while passing by on the bridge, but who knows nothing of the lives lived there and obviously cares less. Crude boxes indicate the homes sitting in the path of the Longwood Road extension and the planned Low Level Bridge: Manny's, the Sugdens', the Smiths', Beareses', Flowerses' – dozens of them. The city's plans will cut a swathe through Cootes Paradise, eliminating a good three-quarters of the properties there, half of the total community. Joey's house is in the way too. She feels a frisson of anxiety. At the thought of losing Joey? Or the idea of undiluted Mick? "The city has put offers in on all the houses along both sides of the canal and those across from us that run upside the marsh."

She glances at the date on the letter. Sent a week ago. They are moving fast, not anticipating any opposition.

"You're going to have to find somewhere else to live when Manny sells up."

"It's not just me, kiddo. It affects all of us, don't you see? But with what the city'll pay us for the house – look what they're offering Manny –"

"Sixty-five dollars." It sounds like a lot, but how long will it take someone like Manny to fritter away sixty-five dollars? How long will it take Ray?

"I should get a lot more for *The Salty Mare*."

"But *The Salty Mare* isn't in the way of the bridge or the new road. They're not expropriating our side."

"Not yet. But it's going to happen soon enough, just you wait. I saw them drawings your mam cut from the paper. That McQuesten fella's got big plans for the area. And we'll have us a nice little nest egg. Enough to move away and start again."

"We?"

"We. The four of us. We can be a happy family again."

She forces a laugh, a bitter eruption of disbelief. *But you were the one who destroyed this family when you left*. "Aren't you forgetting something?"

"Huh?" His face is lit up with this new daydream. She has to look away.

"Mom never wants to see you again."

"She'll come round. As soon as she sees the opportunity here."

"I'm not so sure." *When hell freezes over* is what she'd said when Egypt suggested that she would take him back the way she always did. *Though God knows why*, she'd spat at her mother. *It isn't as if you love him, is it?*

"You'll see, my little Sphinx. She always comes round."

"Not this time."

"Well then, that's where you come in."

"Oh no." She makes to slide down the bench, back away. "Not a chance."

"Come on, for me?"

"I'm not playing go-between. I'd like to keep my head in one piece."

He pats her leg and then leans out, elbows on his knees, cracking his knuckles. He clears his throat. "What happened . . . between me and your mam. You know I'm . . . I've got myself in a spot of trouble. I'm in a bit over me head." And suddenly he's weeping. Face buried in his hands, he's scooped up some of her hair. Egypt gives it a tug, but it's caught fast between his fingers and his face. And so she sits there, tied by her hair, feeling both scared and exhilarated by his wracking sobs, his ragged, shallow breathing, and at the same time made hugely awkward by his breakdown. If she reached out to touch him, would he stop? Would she have to hold him? She scans the park, holding everyone at bay with the power of her wishing, praying he will finish before someone walks by. When his emotion is at last spent, they are both quiet. She watches a man walking his dog in the distance, allows herself to wonder a while about his life, the house he lives in, the family waiting for him when he and the dog return home. Or not. When eventually she opens her mouth to speak, it's to find her voice has deserted her. She's on the edge of tears. Toes at the grass with her scuffed shoes, hands tucked under her legs. Takes a deep breath.

"Dad?" Her voice so soft he doesn't hear her. "Ray?"

He sighs and takes his hands from his face, releasing her hair.

"Why did you stay away so long? If you love her so much, I mean?"

He wipes his eyes with his sleeve, chews his lip. A woman crosses in front of them, shopping bags in her hands, a harried look etched on her face. He waits until she disappears down Florence Avenue.

"I spent a few years inside," he says suddenly, too loudly, and clears his throat. "Got caught up in a fraud racket."

The tattoo. She pictures a dark cell, a barred window set high in the wall, the smell of rising damp and mildew. "Where?"

"Detroit."

She nods her head, trying to feel nothing and at the same time wishing she were far away from this park bench and the path Ray's words have taken. Would give anything to be striding up to Gloria's front door, bantering with Philip, whipping her clothes off for Mrs. Henry, returning Martha's withering glances. However must her mother have felt? "She doesn't know, does she?"

"It's not the kind of thing that goes down well in a letter."

"But if she'd known –"

"Things would've been different." He cocks an eyebrow at her. "You reckon? Then maybe you know something about your mam that I don't."

He's right.

She sighs.

He takes her hand in both of his. "Now you see why I need your help."

"How? By putting in a good word for you? Believe me, it's too late."

"You're friendly with that Oakes fella, you could do some digging around for me, find out what he's hiding."

"Hiding?" She pulls her hand free.

He looks around and leans towards her. "You remember the night of the fire?" he says, his voice so freighted her heart quickens.

"Not really, I mean not much. It's all a bit hazy." Not a lie. A little more than a month and the fire has become a collage of fragments that lurk at the edges of her sleep, or surprise her during long classroom hours: a burst of roaring flames, heat, the smell of blistered paint and burning hair. Ray standing at the edge of the flames.

"It wasn't an accident."

She glances at him sharply. *Please don't say anything more.*

"No worries, it wasn't your old man started it." Though he's smiling, there is something cold and troubling in his eyes. "But that Oakes fella knows more than he's letting on."

"Look, I have to go." Egypt has to steady herself on the edge of the bench before standing.

"No problemo, kiddo, you get off." Back to his old self already. He stands and fishes in his pockets. "Hey, wait up," he calls as she turns away. "How are you and your mother getting by these days?"

"Meaning?"

"What you doing for money?"

"Burning it to keep warm, what do you think?"

He palms her a roll of bills that he has tucked under his outstretched hand, like he's purchasing contraband. Egypt looks around to see if anyone's watching.

"Next time you see your brother, buy him an ice cream from me, will you?"

"Of course."

"He's a rum'un, little scamp."

"He is," she agrees, counting. "Chip off the old block."

"I hope not, lass. For his sake."

"There's sixteen dollars here," she says, looking up. "Where'd you get it?"

"Does it matter?"

"Yes."

"I worked for it."

"Honestly?"

His mouth twitches. "There's some might quibble about the honest part."

Despite her misgivings, the crawling sensation in her belly, she smiles. And in spite of the grubby feeling engendered by Ray's transaction, she isn't in any position to refuse the money. "Thank you," she says, folding the bills and tucking them into the waistband of her skirt. A *spot of trouble*, he said. Meaning what, exactly? But the time to ask has been and gone; Ray is already walking away.

Martha opens the door, starts to close it and then changes her mind and invites Egypt inside. The half-smile on her lips never makes it to her eyes. She disappears down the hall and into the recesses of the house, leaving Egypt standing in the vestibule in her coat and scuffed shoes.

The grandfather clock chimes a quarter to five. Egypt waits, the silence thick as syrup. And though she can see the minute hand as it clicks into place, still she jumps when the clock chimes the hour. Her feet grow numb; her hands are cold. A door closes upstairs and she thinks she hears Gloria's voice. She clears her throat and stamps her feet. Silence descends again, suffocating. Just as the clock finishes chiming a quarter past, Martha reappears bearing a tray.

"I have better things to do with my time than wait on silly young girls who get themselves into trouble." She holds out the tray to Egypt and narrows her eyes. "It's always the quiet ones you have to watch." Egypt catches a whiff of ammonia from Martha's hands. "Take this upstairs. You know which room is Miss Gloria's."

The wooden tray is surprisingly heavy. She glances over the contents: a glass of milk, an unappetizing-looking plate of mashed potatoes and overcooked cabbage, and a bowl of skinned-over rice pudding. Invalid food. She doesn't need to touch the bowls to know that the food has been sitting around for the better part of an hour. For Gloria's sake, she musters a withering glance.

Martha never flinches. "Get a move on," she snaps, "before it gets cold."

Gloria turns her head at the sight of the tray. Egypt is forced to try to find room for it on the dresser. Eventually, she opts for the floor.

"Miss Summers is anxious to know how you're doing," she says, straightening.

"Then you'll have to tell her I'm just peachy," Gloria says in a flat, bored voice.

"She's upset you haven't been in touch with anyone at the school." Egypt struggles to keep her eyes on Gloria's face, pale against the hill of flowery pillows behind her head, but they keep returning to the bandages wound around her wrists, long fingers interlaced across her stomach.

Gloria lets out an impatient sigh. "You care too much for Miss Summers and what she thinks. You should live your own life."

Is that what you're doing?

"When I get out of this bed, Mother is taking me to Paris for two months, possibly three."

"What about graduation?"

"I'm going to need a whole new wardrobe." Gloria has yet to meet Egypt's glance. "I'd let you have some of my cast-offs, but they probably won't fit you."

Egypt's eyes flick to the bandages again. The pink freckles on Gloria's skin. The way Philip reached out but didn't quite touch his sister's arm that first day. *It's wonderful to see you again, Glo. We have lots to catch up on.* She can almost feel him now, hovering over his sister and her troubles. It's on the tip of her tongue to say something, but she's afraid of what Gloria might say or do. "They've offered me your job," she says instead. "At the model school," she adds when Gloria doesn't respond. "Not that is was your job, really, it was just that they had you picked out for it and now they've changed their minds. Well, Miss Summers has." She folds her arms across her chest. She feels lightheaded. Philip in the room, stealing her air. "They didn't think you were interested anymore. I don't suppose it matters now because you won't graduate. Not if you're in Paris." Her voice trails off. Gloria is smoothing over the embroidered edge of her sheet with her fingers, her face tight and pale. Egypt licks at her dry lips. What was she hoping for? Congratulations, or a flare of temper?

"Take the tray with you when you go, will you?"

Egypt's cheeks are still blazing when she reaches the foot of the sweeping staircase. She could just leave the tray there and walk out the door, but in the gloaming, someone might trip. And she has unfinished business in this house. Balancing the tray in one hand, she flicks on a bank of light switches and then ventures down the well-lighted hallway in search of the kitchen.

No sign of Martha, but nestled on a low settee in a nook across from the pantry is Mrs. Henry. Her feet are tucked under her legs; a book lies askew on the floor, next to an empty glass, as if tossed there. Or perhaps it slipped off her lap. Her jaw is slack and her head at an angle that suggests she's asleep. But then Egypt hears her name.

Mrs. Henry pats the seat beside her. "Come sit."

It's a question of what to do with the tray first. She dithers in the hallway while Mrs. Henry urges her to sit again. "I didn't hear you come in." She speaks softly, as if afraid of waking someone.

"I came to see Gloria. She didn't want her dinner," Egypt says, once again left with no choice but to set the tray on the floor.

"Of course. Very good." Mrs. Henry frowns at the tray and its bland offerings. Then, as if remembering her manners, "School is treating you well, I trust?" Her voice swings so high at the end that Egypt expects to hear it crack.

"Yes. Gloria's teacher wanted me to –"

"Ah, yes, Gloria's teacher. Persistent, isn't she? *Miss* Summers." She leans heavily on the title, and Egypt realizes too late that Mrs. Henry is drunk. After all the fuss of seating herself on the edge of the settee, it is harder to excuse herself from the situation. "The woman knows nothing of the trials of raising a daughter. How does your mother manage, Egypt?"

By secrets and lies. "Oh, she just takes it day by day, I suppose."

"Day by day," Mrs. Henry repeats, her head slumping forward.

Is she passed out? Egypt leans across to check if she can hear breathing, then rises to leave.

"Exsanguination." The word uttered like a sigh.

"Sorry?"

"Exsanguination." Mrs. Henry lifts her head. Her face is bleary. "That's a thirty-dollar word, isn't it?"

Egypt feels a prickle of anxiety. Sits back down.

"Do you know what it means?"

She shakes her head.

"To drain of blood. That was me, you know. When I gave birth to Gloria. My blood draining out. The nurse told me afterwards she'd never known anyone survive such blood loss." Egypt is horrified. Not only at the details, but also at Mrs. Henry's impropriety. The room blurs as her eyes fill. She doesn't want to hear anymore. Why her? Why does she have to be the one pinned here by Mrs. Henry's breakdown?

"That's my little girl up there. My only child. And you see how much he cares?"

He? But it isn't her place to ask.

Mrs. Henry's face is a wasteland of pain. "Mr. Henry's first wife died, you know. Philip's mother."

Egypt swallows and gets to her feet. She has to leave before she hears something they will both regret. "I have to go now." But Mrs. Henry reaches out to stay Egypt with her hand.

"You'll be wanting your picture, I suppose?"

Not anymore. What she wants it to be gone as far away from this house and this family as possible. But in a surprisingly steady manoeuvre, Mrs. Henry is now standing and straightening her clothes. She threads her arm through Egypt's, leaning on her. "Come with me," she says.

Together they make their way to the addition at the back of the house, Egypt's anticipation curled to a tight ball in her belly. Dusk has chased light from the edges of the studio and twilight is ushering in a grey-scale of shadows. She wants to draw out this moment before the reveal, but Mrs. Henry shakes her arm free and wobbles uncertainly towards the easel perched in the centre of the room. She grasps the edge of the cover and Egypt holds her breath, envisioning the painting and easel crashing to the floor.

"Ready?"

"Ready." But she isn't. When Mrs. Henry tugs the cover free, Egypt's heart flip-flops all over again. The chaise is recognizable only from its colour, a blur of cloak, a block in place of her head. One perfect and disturbingly lifelike breast, the other a chalky triangle.

"You like it?"

"It's . . . very nice." A long and low ache in her chest. She glances around her for the other painting, the one of her face. Her soul. Where is it? Did Mrs. Henry paint over it? Or it is stacked behind her somewhere with all the other dozens of canvasses?

"Marvellous." Mrs. Henry claps her hands together. "I knew you'd love it."

She wrestles the painting from the easel and then steps with it over to the wash-up area where she keeps her palettes and brushes and pulls a large piece of brown wrapping paper from a roll mounted on the wall. It puts Egypt in mind of the butcher's shop. "I shall wrap it for you and you shall take it home." Egypt wonders how many people ever stand up to Mrs. Henry. A different kind of bulldozer, perhaps.

"We'll have to postpone our date, I'm afraid," she says, cutting string and winding it expertly around the packaged painting. With the act of doing, she seems more composed, more in control of herself.

"Our date?"

"We could reschedule for the fall perhaps, after I return from Paris."

Egypt is still confused. What date?

"You were going to take me to the boathouses. To paint, remember?"

Better hurry then before Tommy McQuesten and the parks board huff and puff and blow them all down. Obviously Mrs. Henry doesn't recall her son's flippant response. But then, why should she? She's rich. It's no skin off her nose whether those already struggling to make ends meet keep their homes or not. But between the fire and the expropriations for the Longwood Road extension, it is already happening. Maybe Aidan is better off staying with their grandparents. At least 47 Robinson Street isn't in danger of being destroyed. Or towed across the bay to someplace else.

Egypt carries the painting home. Almost. She pauses at the top of the path down to the boathouses and then walks into the middle of the High Level Bridge. She leans over the iron railing. Three times the painting bounces off the rocky sides and once, as a gust of wind catches it, it's briefly lifted up again before crashing into the canal. It floats out into the bay where the water swells and dips, stirred up and swollen with spring runoff and the waxing moon. Egypt watches until the moment when it simply disappears.

Chapter 38

"Egypt. How wonderful to see you." Her grandmother is wearing her church smile. "Come in, come in," she says, pulling the door wide and gesturing with her arm.

Egypt's feet remain firmly planted on the stoop. "We came to see Aidan." She indicates the scruffy piece of rope in her hand, looped around George's neck. "George misses him."

"What a lovely idea," Grandma Lily says. But her face doesn't match her words.

"We can stay in the yard. We're a bit muddy."

"Garden, dear. Yard makes me think lumberyard. Barnyard, stockyard."

"Aidan is allowed outside, isn't he?"

"Of course he is."

"Good. I just haven't seen him at school, so I was worried he might still be sick."

Her grandmother's pale blue eyes regard her a moment. "Come in through the gate, Evelyn," she says before closing the door.

Egypt commands George to lie at her feet. They face the door to the mudroom. When figures appear silhouetted behind the glass, he paws at the ground and whimpers. The moment the door opens, George is up and bounding towards Aidan, who takes the stairs two at a time, squealing at the sight of his four-legged friend. George jumps up, paws on Aidan's shoulders, and bowls him over.

"Oh, do be careful," Grandma Lily calls from the doorway, but her complaint is drowned out by George's barking. Boy and dog roll in the grass, Aidan helpless with laughter, unable to thwart George's enthusiastic licking.

"Stop it!" he cries, rolling into a ball. "Uncle!"

"Egypt!" Her grandmother rushes down the steps and into the garden. In her hand she holds a toy train identical to the one her mother dumped into the marsh. "Call your dog off at once."

"It's okay, Grandma. They roughhouse all the time. They're having fun."

"It doesn't much look like Aidan's having fun to me."

"But looks can be deceiving, can't they?"

Her grandmother sets the train down in the grass, then clasps her hands as she straightens and gathers a smile. "How is your mother these days?"

"Angry. Unemployed," she adds, wanting to know more but afraid to ask. A *money issue*, according to her mother. But Egypt suspects it has more to do with Matt and her mother's affair. And everything to do with her grandparents.

"She has only herself to blame." As Egypt suspected. "Your mother never did consider anyone but herself." Her grandmother bends to snap the shrivelled yellow heads from a clutch of spent daffodils. "And how's your father? He's had some troubles, hasn't he?"

"I wouldn't know about that."

"No, of course you wouldn't." She cups the back of Egypt's elbow, offers a conciliatory smile. "You're managing all right out there, are you? I can always put a care package together for you."

And have her mother throw it in the marsh? "We're managing just fine."

"It's no trouble."

"We don't need any help, thanks."

"Aidan says everyone does lots of fishing out there."

"He's a born fisherman. Did he tell you that?"

"He did. He told us about all the hunting and trapping, too. All the strange things you eat. Muskrat and raccoon and Canada geese and deer. Even squirrel."

"People have to do what they have to do, Grandma."

"But isn't that poaching? It's illegal, isn't it?"

Before Egypt can respond, her grandmother has slipped her arm conspiratorially though the crook of her elbow. "You know, I'm so glad you're here, Egypt; you can help me out because I'm in a little bit of a bind today. The thing is, I need to pop over and see to Mrs. Pendlebury, and Mr. Aiken is out at a meeting."

"You mean Grandpa Aiken." Her face aches.

"Your Grandpa Aiken, of course, that's what I meant. All this name changing, I can't keep anyone's straight these days." She pats Egypt's arm. "I'd like you to keep an eye on Aidan for me while I'm gone."

Aren't you afraid I'll run off with him?

"I won't be more than an hour," she says, releasing Egypt and deadheading her way back to the mudroom.

"I'm taller than George now."

"You've been taller than George for a while." But it's true, he has had a growth spurt. It must be all the roast beef dinners he's eating, all the milk he's drinking. In her eleventh summer, Egypt grew so much so quickly that she was left with reminders in the form of wavy silvery lines across the tops of her legs. *Stretch marks*, her mother said when she saw them, and laughed.

"When you have babies, you'll get them all over your belly."

"I'm never having babies."

Egypt's stomach growls.

"What did you have for dinner last night?"

"Pork."

"Any leftovers?" she asks, already halfway up the mudroom steps.

Inside, there's a neatly folded pile of new Aidan-sized clothing laid out over the back of one of the dining-room chairs. A blazer on a hanger hooked on the back of another. A *school uniform*. On the table sits an old cookie tin, similar to the one her mother uses as a sewing kit, and atop that, a spool of canvas tape and an indelible pen. Egypt pops the last piece of pork in her mouth and wipes her greasy fingers on the inside of her skirt before picking up the white sweater from the top of the pile. Emblazoned across the chest is an enormous crest: a boar's head, mouth open, tongue lolling backwards in the wind, like George's when he's running. On a banner beneath, the words *VELLE EST POSSE*. The rest of the pile reveals three shirts, two pairs of pants, one navy sweater with a single dun-coloured stripe at the neck and two around the cuffs and waistband. A couple of ties.

And alongside an inside seam on each item, fastened with impossibly neat stitches: a name tag.

She refolds the white sweater and places it back as she found it.

"How's the new school?"

Aidan casts a sidelong glance her way. "They told you?"

"I saw your uniform inside. Nice name tags. Whose idea was that?"

Colour leaches from his face. "It's so you don't get your stuff mixed up with the others'."

"A. *Aiken*. Interesting. I thought your name was Fisher, same as the rest of us."

He stabs at the lawn with George's stick, pulls a large divot free and stamps it back down with his boots. New boots. New coat. New boy.

"Where is this school?"

"Westdale."

"Westdale?"

"Grandpa takes me in the car."

"What's it called?"

"Hillfield."

"And were they ever planning on telling us you were going to Hillfield?"

"I don't like it there." Stab. Stab. Stab. The soft lawn is quickly turning to mud.

"I'm not surprised."

"Everyone ignores me. Grandpa told me not to tell anyone where I came from."

"So what do you say when someone asks?"

"They don't. I told you. Everyone ignores me."

"That's tough, buddy." She could just take his hand, open the garden gate and go home.

"It's okay. It's kind of like being invisible. Like Darius."

"And Efron." He must be still talking to them. No wonder everyone ignores him.

"Efron's gone."

"Oh." She leans over and pulls him into a bear hug but he squirms away. Picks up a ball and throws it inexpertly for George. It lands with a muffled thud in a freshly turned flower bed. They watch mutely as George charges after it, flattening daffodils and snapping the tops of newly sprouted bulbs – tulips or hyacinths, Egypt can't remember. He lays out his long body in the bed and commences chewing the ball.

"You never did teach him to bring stuff back, did you?"

"I thought that was your job."

"I thought he was your dog – isn't that what you always tell everyone?"

"Okay, he's your dog." Aidan's voice sags along with his head.

She ruffles his hair. "He's our dog. He loves us both."

Aidan sets his train in the grass and drops pebbles he's pulled from his pockets into the hopper coupled behind the proud, shiny black-and-green locomotive. "There's some white ones too."

"Sorry?"

"White trousers. It's like a whole other uniform I have to wear. White trousers, white shirt and a white jacket." His mouth is turned down, his brow crinkled with worry; he's like a little old man. "Mom says I just look at white clothes and get them dirty. Grandma Lily is going to be mad at me all the time."

"No, she isn't. Why do you have white clothes?"

"Cricket."

"Cricket?"

He nods vigorously and she can see it is taking all he has not to cry. Whispers, "I don't know what cricket is. But Grandpa says I'm too small for football and hockey and rugby and that cricket's a good sport for me, and that he used to play it when he was at school. But I don't even know what it looks like." He holds his hand up as far as he can and lets the last pebble go. More a small rock than a pebble. It falls fast, misses the hopper and hits the train, glancing off the side and taking a piece of shiny black paint with it. "I thought cricket was a bug."

George returns with the ball and drops it at their feet. Egypt bends to pick it up. Wipes George's spittle off in the grass first.

"You're supposed to rub it on your bum."

"What?"

"The ball. The bowler rubs it on his bum before bowling."

"The bowler?" She turns the ball around in her hand. The smooth oxblood leather now marred with George's teeth marks. She fingers a loose thread – he's even split the stitching. "So this is a cricket ball?"

"Uh huh."

"Yours?"

"Grandpa's."

"How is he?" Laura asks the minute Egypt opens the door.

"He's fine. They're feeding him well; he has new clothes." She pauses. "A new train." Laura raises an eyebrow. "He's grown an inch."

"He's grown an inch in two weeks? That's impossible!"

"Half an inch then. He looks taller, anyway. They had pork for dinner last night," she says, placing a small waxed-paper packet on the kitchen table. "Leftovers, if you're interested." She flounces into one of the chairs and leans back on two legs. "They're sending him to a private school."

"They are what?"

"Hillfield."

"Hillfield!"

"It's in Westdale. It's not too far."

"I know where it is." Laura strides to the window by the sink. Her hands grip the edge of the wooden counter. "I don't know what game they think they're playing, but he won't be happy there."

"He's pretty lonely. But he was lonely before. He'll make friends eventually."

"Hillfield is all sports and academics."

"I thought that was the point of school."

"Yes, but your brother is . . ."

"Is what?"

"He's a dreamer. He'll be miserable."

"So he's better off with bullies and kids who have to be dragged to class? That will make him happy, will it?"

Laura pinches the bridge of her nose. "I don't have all the answers, Egypt."

"Obviously. Are they rich?"

Laura turns and glares at her. "What?"

"Grandma and Grandpa. Are they rich?"

"They're comfortably well-off."

"So a senior accountant's position pays well?"

"I have no idea how much money your grandfather makes. In my day a child wouldn't have dreamed of asking. But your grandmother has a trust fund from her parents."

"And you walked away from all worldly goods to be with Ray. How romantic."

"I don't need your sarcasm right now, Egypt."

"I'm not being sarcastic; I'm just trying to understand who you are."

Egypt leans back in her chair and folds her arms across her chest. Laura sits down across from her daughter.

"Please." She's trembling. "I know I haven't been able to give you much in the way of new clothes, new shoes – it pains me to see you in the same things day in and day out, your shoes worn down at the heels – but money – your grandmother's money, at least – came with so many strings and conditions. It always felt like there was an anvil hovering just above my head."

"*Your* head?" Egypt can feel her heartbeat in her mouth, pounding through her teeth. She can taste the nails on the lid of her mother's coffin. "What about your sister's head?" she says deliberately, drawing out each razor-edged word. "What about Anne-Marie?"

Egypt watches her mother, the way her hands finger her throat, chasing the flush rising there. A whimper and then she buries her face in her hands. "I should have realized they would tell you."

"So you're blaming them?"

"No, no." She shakes her head. "Not at all. It's my fault." She pulls a handkerchief from her sleeve, wipes her eyes, blows her nose. "I shouldn't have kept my family from you. Your family. I've known it for years, but I went down this road so long ago that it just felt like too much work to undo it all."

"It was too much work?"

"It sounds terrible, I know." She reaches across the table but Egypt hides her hands in her lap. "I'm not proud of myself. I was just so angry and stubborn. I told myself I was protecting you from my overbearing mother, but the truth is, I was punishing them. I never thought about the consequences to you until it was too late. Aidan came along and I didn't know how to extricate myself from all the lies. How to own up to what I'd done without hurting everyone, you especially. So I said nothing." She lifts her gaze. "I know you probably can't forgive me," she says, her eyes beseeching. "Not now at least, but please believe me Egypt, I am very sorry. I should never have kept your family from you. Especially your aunt. She adored you so much."

Egypt's throat aches with the tears she's trying to hold back. "She adored me? So she knew me?"

"She knew you and she loved you. She would pick you up when she walked in that door and she wouldn't put you down until she left."

"She came here?"

"I needed her. I needed her help when your father would do his disappearing act and – this was long before I got the job at Hand & Company – there was a flower seller in the market who would hire me on for a day or two. Petra, she was called. She knew your father from when he used to set up his tonic stall. She took pity on me – on us – and would pay me for helping her out at the stall. It wasn't easy to have you with me. Certainly not once you were crawling. And once you learned to walk, I needed eyes in my elbows. Anne-Marie would look after you here."

"And your parents never knew?"

"They thought she was doing charity work with the poor – which wasn't exactly a lie," she adds, almost to herself. "I made her swear not to breathe a word to anyone. I told her –" she breaks off as fresh tears make their way down her face. "I told her I would never speak to her again, never let her over this threshold if she told them about you."

"And then she went to Europe and left you behind."

"She died from –"

"I know how she died," Egypt snaps. She can see Mick spastic with anger, feel the heft of the marble column beneath her hands.

"I suppose they told you I never went to my own sister's funeral."

"They mentioned it."

"And now you think I'm heartless."

She's been thinking it for some time. "I don't understand why you didn't tell me I had an aunt, even a dead one. You could have waited till I was older. Five, six. Aidan's age."

"And you would have accepted it then, would you?"

"Yes."

"The way Aidan has accepted his friends' deaths?"

"That is completely different. He's lonely. He misses them. And everyone brushes his feelings aside as if they're not important. They shut him up or ignore him."

"Who does?"

"You do. We all do. I was standing right here when Grandma Lily did it. He asked her if she believed in ghosts and she practically laughed in his face. He still talks to them, you know."

Laura throws her arms out in exasperation. "I know nothing, Egypt. I've had no contact with him for days. They won't let me see him. They won't even answer the door. I waited outside the house for hours. Eventually, my mother threatened to call the police if I didn't leave. The police, for heaven's sake."

Egypt pushes back her chair and pulls on her coat. "You still haven't answered my question. Why didn't you tell me I had an aunt?"

"I thought I was protecting you. It seemed pointlessly painful to resurrect my sister with you just to tell you she was dead. It didn't seem fair."

"Fair to who? Me or you?" Without waiting for a response, Egypt whistles for George and slams out the door.

Chapter 39

Jimmy Jar has risen from the bottom of the lake. On the end of someone's anchor. Eels for eyes, catfish sucking on his ribs. No more ice to keep him down. Jimmy Jar with his ragged lips and his howling. He's brought the police and they're crawling all over the place like bluebottles. Picking and chewing. The first day, Ray wears a groove in the linoleum with his pacing, checking and rechecking each window. He wants to leave, run away, hide, to get as far away as possible, but he needs to keep an eye on what's going on. He needs to keep an eye on Jimmy Jar. On the second day the bluebottles return and begin moving from house to house, licking the ends of their blunt pencils and scratching things down in small notebooks. *Where was Ray Fisher that night? Where is Ray Fisher every night? Have you seen his hands? Have you checked his fingernails, where they're bleeding? In the lining of his pockets? The soles of his shoes? Where did he get those shoes? That big stick?*

They'll be here soon with their questions, their skin smelling of soap and cold-water shaves. Ray slips out Manny's back door and unmoors the skiff. Tosses a rod in the bottom of the boat – someone comes after him, he'll make out he's fishing. Pushing off, he oars down the canal and out into the bay and past Carroll's Point, his unhealed ribs screaming, headed for the downtown. He can't let them pick him up. He can't go back inside. Can't let them find out he's been locked up stateside or it'll be all over.

Can't do that again. Thrown in with all the hard-heads, the nutbars, the throat-slitters. He hasn't the wits to survive this time. Would rather take his chances with Doyle. As long as he stays away from the white stuff. He just needs a break. One horse. One time. If he could cobble a decent wager together. His luck hasn't been so great lately. Not losing, but not winning anything either. Coming out even.

He's breathless, trembling with fatigue by the time he ties up at the wharf at the foot of Bay Street. Benn Kerr's old stomping grounds. King of the rum-runners. Except rum-running has had its day. Now it's all white powder and pills that make your head crazy. Manny told him the coppers fished Kerr out of the lake a couple years back. When the ice thawed. He remembered thinking how the lake was a lousy keeper of secrets. Now it's puked up his. He walks away from the wharf, crawls inside a dry-docked boat, curls up beneath an old tarpaulin and waits until the burning in his ribs subsides, waits until long after dark has settled, endlessly drifting asleep and waking to his heart skip-skip-booming in his chest.

Sleep in his eyes, a crick in his neck, he's hungry, thirsty, needs a cigarette, a drink, a flutter on the ponies, his head examined. He's sick. Sick and tired. Why is it when the road forks, Ray always finds himself on the slippery path? The wrong side of the tracks, the law, Red, his own family. Hands to his sore chest: the wrong side of a beating. Why is it some men get to be heroes? The right choices? Or the right chances? Time and circumstance he feels have shoved him up against the edges of his. And so this is it, the shape of his life. He can almost see the path and where it will lead: running, scrounging, running again. All he asks is that he be allowed to stay in one place long enough to watch his son grow into a man. He stands and dusts himself off. *One foot in front of the other* as his brother Malcolm would've said. *One foot in front of the other, bro.* One chance, that's all he needs. One chance. To undo a couple of wrongs. Start from there.

The streets are deserted. Ray heads to the market.

It's well past nine. Gone are the dancing bears, the musicians, the monkeys. The fruit and vegetable sellers are packed up for the day, likewise the itinerant traders of ribbons and thread, of coffee, tea, flour, salt, pots and pans: some finishing up suppers of fish and chips, wagons loaded, horses hitched. While the trucks pull away in an eye-watering haze of oil and gasoline, Ray empties his head of worries and approaches the horses, rubs the backs of his fingers down their velvet noses. Back in his market days, horse-drawn wagons were the rule, and sometimes when he was after a quiet moment, he'd slip inside the livery stables on Market Street, choose a sleepy-eyed cold blood and stroke its massive neck, lean his head against its shoulders, taking in the animal's warmth, the scents of hay and dander, of steaming compost. Ray should have been born a country boy. *You blow your breath up a horse's nose, it's like you're talking to him.* A farmer told him that once. They talk back, puffing clouds of vapour from their flared nostrils, jingling their harnesses as they change their resting feet, shake off the collywobbles, snatches of green-field dreams and buckets of oats.

When the oil lamps are extinguished and every last seller has cleared out, the place falls eerily quiet, the province of rats until midnight or so, when the first of the wholesalers trickle in. As business picks up and oil lamps are lit, chasing away the cold and shadows, Ray wanders the aisles between farmers and agents, grocers and hucksters shouting prices and weights, searching out those who might be short-handed. Lends a hand here and there shuffling bags of potatoes, carrots, boxes of turnips. Keeps his hat low and his eyes down. By daybreak he's earned himself enough for a mug of tea and a bacon sandwich at Barton Lunch.

He's waiting for the papers. Pages of the first edition already propped open behind plates of ham and eggs, fragrant stacks of buttered toast. Condensation streams down the windows, obscuring a grey dawn. His bones scream in agony, like someone's rubbing the ends with sandpaper. He ekes out his skinny meal, rolls a skinnier cigarette, takes mouse bites, smokes, sucks on the fatty bacon, smokes, tongue probing the bottom of his mug for crumbs. Sam behind the counter fills up his tea again, waving away the payment Ray doesn't have. *What happened to last night's money? Or was it the night before?* His stool shakes as a broad back and shoulders, leather patches on the elbows of his jacket, lowers himself next to Ray. He smells of onions. Shakes open a paper. Ray, hardly believing his luck, his dismal lack of luck, reads along, eyes straining across the page till they come to a halt at a block of heavier type: "Body found –"

"Hey, I know you, don't I?"

Ray leaps from his thinning skin, slopping his tea. Afraid to raise his eyes.

"Ray Fisher. There's a face from the past. What you up to these days?"

Death. Destruction. Raise your face, or the voice'll only get louder.

"Keeping yourself out of trouble?"

By the hair of my chinny chin chin. Manages a grin. Something passes across Mountain Man's eyes. He must look a fright. Flesh bagging on a skull.

"You're not still peddling that tar-coloured cure-all you used to bottle up back of the butcher's stalls, are you?"

Shakes his head. *You should see the new stuff. Pure and white as the driven snow.* Where'd that come from? That voice in his head. That woman's voice.

Broad shoulders shake with laughter, though Ray gets the tingly feeling his neighbour doesn't really want to laugh, doesn't want to be sitting here anymore, sitting next to the living dead. "Took a lot to get that stuff down as I recall."

You should try the new stuff. On second thought, scrap that. You'll never look back. You won't be able to get enough. You'll take more and more till your head blows apart and it starts trickling down your nose. And still you'll want more.

"Happens all the time. Seen it myself." His breakfast-mate's ruddy face turns grey and then puce. Did he say something out loud?

"Seems to me you might be needing some of it yourself, mate. You look like shit. Smell like it too." Rises from his stool and is out the door, leaving his paper behind.

Ray snatches it up and, hands shaking, glances down the page again: *Body found in Burlington Bay.* Scans the lines beneath it. It isn't him.

They've identified the body as belonging to a Nicolas Bridges. The article declares Bridges was a known bird handler. *Known.* Missing under suspicious circumstances since November. The police will likely conduct raids on known cockfighting rings. Ray doesn't know if he should laugh or whimper. Jimmy Jar is still at the bottom of the lake. His ragged lips still sealed.

Chapter 40

"This is Ray Fisher's house, isn't it?"

"It's still his house, yes." Laura glances in dismay at the trail of muddy boot prints the two policemen have tracked across the floor. That they appear to be familiar with Ray doesn't bode well.

"He around?"

"As far as I know."

"As far as you know." The constable doing the talking lifts an eyebrow. He is slightly wall-eyed. Laura averts her gaze. "He does live here, doesn't he?"

Laura's answer is drowned out by the noise of a diesel engine spluttering to life just outside her door. Or damn near close enough. Every day the bulldozers and steamrollers draw nearer. Like giant mechanical insects on caterpillar feet, grinding and flattening, ripping up trees and shrubs, dragging them away. Already the shape of the Longwood Road extension is nudging at the banks of the canal. The fields that flank the community reduced to mud, studded with stakes. Scraps of fabric flap in the breeze. When construction begins on the new bridge, the noise will surely be worse. "He comes and goes," she repeats, louder.

"Just get you out of bed, did we?" Wall-eye casts a disparaging glance at Laura's attire. Laura follows his gaze. The hem of her dressing gown is hanging down. When did she catch it? And on what? One of her slippers sports a dribble of egg yolk. Cooked, she decides, bending to get a closer look.

"And the last time you saw him was –?"

Being bundled into the back of a police vehicle outside Mrs. *Pendlebury's.* "A few days ago." She shuffles to the sink to sponge off the egg yolk.

"So he's done a runner."

"He's around."

"I can't hear you, Mrs. Fisher."

"He's around!" she shouts, irritation finally getting the better of her.

In two strides he's standing beside her. "How do you know he's around if you haven't seen him for days?" His voice rasps in her ear. "Think carefully before you answer, Mrs. Fisher, you wouldn't want me to write you up as an accomplice now, would you?"

She stops wringing out the cloth and takes a step back before turning to look him in the eye. "An accomplice to what?" An instant headache grinds between her temples.

"Any firearms on the property?"

"No."

"Traps?"

"No."

"Do you keep fighting cocks?"

She sighs. "No." Folds the cloth and hangs it over the edge of the basin.

"Stills?"

"Stills?"

"Equipment used in the illegal distilling of alcohol."

"What do you think?"

The constable stares hard at Laura. She flinches as a plate hits the floor and shatters.

"Whoops." His associate kicks the pieces aside. Knocks her one remaining matryoshka doll from the shelf.

"No," she says, her face pricking in the beginning of tears. *They're looking for a gun in a tea canister? A still between the cushions on the couch?* She feels vulnerable in her nightclothes.

"What do you know about cockfights around here?"

"Nothing."

"Married to Ray Fisher and she knows nothing about cockfights, eh, Barnes?"

Barnes snorts his disbelief and pulls open the door to the back porch. The din from outside is suddenly inside, the cabin throbbing with it. Wall-eye is at the stove, removing the ring burner covers and peering inside. "There's illegal gambling going on down here, Mrs. Fisher, moral depravity, and we intend to flush the culprits out, round them up and lock them away." As if on cue, an engine close by cuts out. "So," he adds in a more menacing tone, lip curled in contempt, "I suggest if you see that husband of yours around, you let him know that it'll be a lot easier for him if he turns himself in. Because we'll be back." He raps the top of the stove with a billy club. "And we're going to keep coming back till we've cleaned this place out."

The door slams behind them. Laura stoops to pick up the pieces of broken plate and hurls them, cursing. Her teeth throb from clenching her jaw. And now the tears; *the first respite of the weak.* Her mother's voice again. *Damn her. Damn both of them.* Her father has been true to his word. She's stared at the letter from his lawyer so hard and so often it's a wonder she hasn't chased the words clear off the page. *The child is too old to be sharing a bed with his mother.* Undeniably. But seeing it in print makes it sound so sordid and sorry. Can she provide for him? She'll manage somehow, she always has.

She stations herself at the window from where she can see her neighbours – those who survived May's expropriation purge – gathering their dignity and wrath. She girds herself; they'll be knocking on her door soon, trailing their dented pride and stories of broken crockery and busted doors.

Sure enough, a meeting has been called. A forum for hysteria and finger pointing. Laura cringes. *Ray.* His name on everyone's lips. An excuse is halfway out of her mouth but Al Bairstow stops her with a frown. She is one of the handful of survivors who can still call Cootes

Paradise home: those who can (and must, in Al Bairstow's magisterial view) stand up and be counted. She cannot hide behind neighbours who no longer exist.

Years of talk and rumours and in the end it was a quick and dirty amputation. In less than two weeks, fifty-seven boathouses were gone; fifty-seven families vanished with them. Absorbed into the city, or hopped the rails to someplace else, their lives spent in this semi-wilderness only memories now. Some had their houses towed across the bay to the north shore or Burlington Beach. Others walked away with little more than the clothes on their backs, expropriation dollars burning holes in their pockets.

What still surprises Laura is how quiet the place is, once the steam earth-shovels have been parked, their engines shut off, and the men digging and raking and calling instructions to each other are done for the day. Eerily quiet. It's amazing how much noise fifty-seven families made going about their day: kids playing, fathers fishing and gutting, the old folks working the gardens, mothers scrubbing and stringing laundry out to dry, chickens, goats, pigs. A cacophony of background noise whisked away. And those who remain speaking in hushed tones behind their hands, closed doors, treading quietly on the docks, dipping oars gently into the water, as if making noise might rouse the powers that be, remind them that their task is incomplete.

Every morning for two weeks, relief workers walked into the community bearing pickaxes and sledgehammers. What couldn't be carried away to be used somewhere else was burned in place; a scrim of acrid smoke hovered over the marsh for days afterwards. Laura swears she can see it still, taste it in the air.

People file into the Bairstows' place. Al Bairstow raised the first shack here on Cootes Paradise and over the years has often taken on the role of community overseer, styling himself as unofficial mayor of the place. He stands at the stove and raises his hands to quiet everyone.

"Ever since that body showed up in the marsh, the police have been breathing down our necks."

Here we go. Laura picks at the skin around her fingernails, sucks at the tiny trails of blood that well up.

"And they're being egged on by the newspapers."

"Wouldn't be surprised if they didn't plant that body."

"I'll bet they started that fire."

"There'll be evictions next."

"That's what worries me," Al says. "We need to stick together on this."

"We need a lawyer."

Laura squirms, recrosses her legs and glances at the door.

"What we need is a plan," Al rejoins.

Just like the talked-about plan for fire protection that came to nought. And the plan before that, for whatever it was. All Al really wants is more meetings. Laura needs action. She makes her excuses and gets to her feet.

Back at the cabin she straightens and sweeps up the debris, wipes the policemen's boot prints from the floor, changes into her one decent dress, applies lipstick and adjusts her hat in the mirror.

She walks purposefully past the cemetery and down Dundurn Street, across the bridge and into Westdale. Midday in early June and the sun is hot, her head throbbing beneath her hat. The school relocated to Colonel Ainslie's former estate last year, further along Main Street West than she remembers from childhood. Or is it all the new buildings she has to pass, the brittle basket of hope she carries, that make the journey seem that much more onerous?

Their voices reach her – the carefree, impatient yells of boys playing ball – before the imposing ivy-covered east walls come into view, long clay-coloured playing fields stretched behind and dotted with tiny moving figures. Her insides twist as she draws closer and the figures transmute into boys tall and short, then thin and burly, now crested with heads of brown, black, blond, red and shades in between. Stripped to their shirts, tails flying free of their pants, sleeves rolled up. Those engaged in less vigorous play, or off by themselves, slope around the edges and between the trees, still in their school sweaters. She scans the loners, her heart now a fist in her throat, and squints at one or two of the smaller figures before dismissing them. He could be inside still, at detention, writing lines. *I must not talk to myself in class.*

As she reaches the edge of the school grounds, a boy carrying a football hurtles by, pursued by a knot of chest-heaving grunts and thundering legs. The pack charges upfield after its quarry, dispersing after a shout and a whistle from somewhere. She starts again with the loners, the groups of twos and threes. No Aidan. The lacrosse game in the far corner yields nothing either. The football players slap each other's backs as they straighten their shirts and pull ties from their pockets, call across the field – *Nice block, Farnsworth. Call that a tackle, Oils?* – anticipating a bell that starts to ring. A master standing on the steps. Boys start towards the building. *Where is he?* She would recognize her son's carriage anywhere. His fox-like gait. Has he become a stranger to her in just two short months? A sultry wind whips at her eyes; the playing fields blur and quiver. She shouldn't have come. Perhaps he's ill again, or her parents have taken him away early on summer vacation, sent him to another school as a boarder, someplace far away from her lousy mothering.

And suddenly there he is, trotting towards her. She can hardly contain herself, her heart so full she feels it might burst through her chest. She stumbles towards him, arms out at her sides. He stops. She dashes the back of her hand across her eyes.

"Silly me. I couldn't see you out there."

He holds up the ball in his hand. "I was bowling. One over and three outs." He's glowing all over, her little glowing cricket-playing boy. She aches to scoop him up and bury him in kisses, a yearning that chokes the back of her throat and reaches through her heart and all the way down into her toes. A few of the boys have slowed their advance. They jostle each other. She can feel their eyes on the too-wide brim of her hat, her cheap dress, her stick-thin legs.

"You look happy! And healthy!" She clasps and unclasps her hands in front, rubs them on her dress, clasps them again.

He glances at the school and then back at his mother.

"How's George?"

"He's good. Still wild about rabbits."

"I miss him."

She fixes him with a bright smile. "I'll tell your sister to bring him by for a visit, shall I?"

He nods. Looks down at his feet.

"Come on, Fish," one of the boys calls, "you're going to be late."

His eyes flicker over his mother and then away. He palms the ball from one hand to the other. The ball makes a soft thwucking noise on contact with his flesh.

"You heard your friend." Laura's smile wobbles on her lips. "You don't want to end up in detention."

His mouth twitches; he seems on the verge of saying something. "See you, then." He raises a hand as he walks away.

Chapter 41

Egypt picks up the eraser. She starts with the frog, a creature so unrecognizable she had to write *FROG* next to it so that the kids would understand what it was she'd drawn. Next, the arrow curving down the blackboard towards the tadpoles, far easier to execute. Another arrow, followed by the eggs, a cluster of circles and dots to which she'd added a layer of shading.

"'Bye, Miss," three girls chorus at her desk.

She raises her eyebrows at their impish faces before giving them what they want. "'Bye, ladies."

They shriek and jostle for the door, their giggles ringing off the pale green plaster walls, shoes slapping the terrazzo floor as they run down the corridor. The boys she refers to as gentlemen, though most are neither. With the classroom empty, she kicks off her new shoes, which pinch, erases *THE LIFE CYCLE OF THE FROG* and begins chalking up tomorrow's spelling list.

The door squeaks on its hinges. Miss Summers leaning in.

"How are you?"

"Fine."

"The children?"

"They're keeping me on my toes," she responds, and wiggles hers, embarrassed to be caught with her shoes off.

"Staff meeting Monday, don't forget. I know it's still a couple of months away yet, but any thoughts you might have regarding decorations for the nativity play would be welcome. Have a think over the weekend."

"Will do. Thank you."

"Oh," she gives Egypt one of her winning smiles, "there's someone waiting outside for you."

George, chewing at a troublesome dewclaw, though he scrambles to his feet as soon as he hears the door open, yipping as she descends the steps, his whole body wagging furiously. Pushes his muzzle into her legs, nipping at her arms and waist as if he hasn't seen her in a week.

"Ready?"

He barks and bounds ahead and then returns to hurry her along before dashing ahead and repeating the cycle. Along with a paper package tied with string, she carries the leash from Grandma Lily looped in her hand, reluctant to tether him just yet. They walk along Florence and up Dundurn. York Street is a mess of construction and so Egypt cuts down Jones Street and through the cemetery. Once past the war ramparts, the vista opens on her left and she can see clear across the fields to the dark sickle-shaped scar of Longwood Road and the new Low Level Bridge that divides the community, a road Egypt must now cross in order to reach her mother.

She calls George, stays him with her hand. Cars travel fast along this new route into the city, and since York Street was closed for grading on Monday, traffic has easily doubled over last week. George is alert, ears pricked. Egypt fastens the leash to his new collar, binds it tight around her hand. Could be he's spotted a rabbit in the distance. George tugs at this new restraint, bites at it till she scolds him. He has to get used to it. York Street will be out of commission for months while the old High Level Bridge is dismantled and its replacement erected. She'd never forgive herself if he was clipped by a car. Never forgive her mother for having to come.

Laura is bent over the patch of front garden, snipping off the remaining green tomatoes.

"What, are you expecting frost already?"

Laura turns and straightens, smiling at her daughter. Egypt sees at once that her mother is transformed. Eyes bright, cheeks flushed. She holds George's face between her hands and kisses his long nose. George licks her face in reply. "I thought you might like to take them for your grandmother," she says. "She could put up a chutney with them."

"Don't you need them?"

Laura turns away without answering, a smile on her lips. Her whole body is a smile. Unease fishtails through Egypt's stomach. Since moving in with her grandparents, she has made a point of visiting her mother weekly; visiting her even when there are other demands on her time now that she's a teacher, with lessons to prepare and homework to mark. Visiting her when she'd rather be anywhere else: just a girl out walking with her dog. Until now, Egypt has shied away from examining her reasons. Her grandparents haven't asked. She's here to soften the bite of Aidan's absence. She brings goodies from Grandma Lily: cheese and fresh-baked biscuits, sometimes a slice or two of boiled ham, which Laura takes from her without protest. Egypt fingers the string around the care package as she follows her mother and George inside, unsure now whether to hand it over.

Laura busies herself setting out the tea things, filling the kettle. She may as well be whistling. She won't meet Egypt's eye.

"You look well," Egypt says, eventually.

Laura tucks her hair behind her ear, suppressing a smile. "Thank you," she says. "I feel . . . I've had some news."

"From Ray?" Egypt's cheek trembles, because even as she utters his name she knows Ray is the last man on her mother's mind.

Laura glances at the door that leads onto the dock. "We could sit out if you like, it's still nice and warm."

Egypt shakes her head. "I don't know how you can stand it out there, with all the traffic. And the smell of gasoline. The cars seem to be heading right for the house. It feels so threatening." She remembers when the Longwood Road extension and the Low Level Bridge were first finished a little over a month ago, just days before she moved in with her grandparents and Aidan – *it's closer to school, I can keep an eye on him* – and how at night, the beams from the headlamps pierced the cabin windows to slide across the walls like searchlights, probing. Word is that when the new High Level Bridge is finished, it will sit ten feet lower; a series of street lamps along its length will shine through the night. The city further trespassing into paradise.

"Did you bring that for me?" Laura indicates the package in Egypt's hand. She begins untying the string when Egypt hands it over. "I thought we could share it."

"But it's for you. Grandma Lily says –"

"I'm leaving." Laura sets the half-opened package down in the middle of the table.

"Leaving?" Egypt finally understands what, besides a sense of filial duty, a sliver of guilt and some cheese and boiled ham from Grandma Lily, has been bringing her here these past Fridays. And it isn't to see if her father has shown up. Because in a way, she has always understood that Ray's presence in her life was temporary, that he would leave again. No, it's this: her mother's pronouncement that she's leaving.

"A letter came the other day." Laura plucks an opened envelope from the odds-and-ends shelf, her fingers fluttery and nervous.

"Oh?"

"From Matt."

"Matt." His name a distress in her mouth.

"I'm going to join him. The plan is to move out west."

"Out west. Where out west?" she asks, unable to summon a more collected response. She's dismayed by the pounding in her chest. Who knew her heartache was still so raw, still quivering just beneath the surface?

"Somewhere in the Gulf Islands, they're a handful of islands between mainland Vancouver and Vancouver Island."

"And you're going to live on all of them?"

Laura picks up the care package and sets it on the counter by the sink. "Matt used to work out there with a man by the name of Earl Todd.

You remember Earl?" she says, over her shoulder. "He was from around here. Maybe not. He left when you were very young."

She remembers Myrtle Todd. Earl's mother. Matt's *grandmother*. Her own mother seems to have forgotten that before there was Laura and Matt, there was, briefly, Egypt and Matt. He spoke to her first, up on the brow of Burlington Heights with the wind blowing through her hair and the train rushing past, and she led him into the community. She draws a finger across the table, across the coating of grit the construction leaves in its wake each day. "When are you leaving?"

"It's best this way. You don't need me anymore." Her mother is fussing with the cheese, dividing the ham onto two plates. "Look at you. A grown woman, a teacher. Children in your care. You don't even need this roof over your head anymore."

"I didn't ask why, I asked when." Egypt cringes at the petulance in her voice. Not Miss Fisher's voice. What would her class think of her?

"Tomorrow."

"Tomorrow! What about Aidan? He's hardly grown-up, is he? He's still a child. Doesn't he need you?"

Finally, Laura turns around. Her eyes are wet. "Do you see him here, Egypt?"

"Does he know you're leaving?"

"Not yet."

"Not yet. So you were planning on telling him sometime before tomorrow?"

"I was hoping you'd give him this for me." She produces another envelope, this one sealed, Aidan's name printed carefully across the front.

"A letter – you're not going to make me give him that are you? You're not going to see him? Your plan is to tell him in a letter. A letter I'm going to have to read to him." Suddenly she's yelling. "That's so cruel. You have to tell him to his face."

Laura's mouth crumples. She dashes her arm across her eyes and turns away. A sob issues from her throat. "Then I'd never leave."

Egypt stares out the window at the approach of cars, the way they seem to veer to the right at the last possible moment. She glances up at the slew of mud and machines on the brow that is York Street, and then around her at the frayed and sagging couch, the worn pine table, the mended chairs, the hodgepodge of crockery on the odds-and-ends shelf. Viewed from behind, her mother seems so frail, her shoulders insubstantial.

"What are you going to do with all this stuff?"

Laura collects herself, wipes her nose and eyes and turns with a grateful smile. "Nothing much I can do. Leave it for the neighbours to pick over, I suppose. Unless there's anything you want," she adds.

"What if Ray comes back?"

Her mother shakes her head.

"You never know. He was gone six years last time. It wasn't his fault he couldn't get back here to be with us."

"It wasn't his fault? Oh, Egypt. How do you think people end up in prison? Through doing good deeds and paying their bills, playing with their children?" *She knows then. Perhaps she's always known.*

"Do you think something might have happened to him?" Egypt asks, moving to the window and staring hard at the slick surface of the water. "To Ray," she adds when her mother doesn't answer. Other questions prickle in the air between them.

"Your father has simply caught a train to the next get-rich-quick scheme."

"You really believe that?"

"I do." Laura steps up behind her daughter. Egypt feels her mother's fingers in her hair, stroking. She draws a strand back from her face and tucks it behind her ear. "He's always had the uncanny ability to go through muck and come out smelling of roses."

Ray-talk. Her mother even does a half decent Mancunian accent. But Egypt isn't so sure about the roses. Luck only holds out for so long. *I'm in spot of trouble. A bit over my head, to be honest.* Why hadn't she probed further? All that talk about prison and his feelings. He was clearly in the mood for confessing.

"If there's anything you'd like to have as a keepsake, or something that might be useful to you, you should take it now."

Egypt lifts her hands to her mother's to release them from her hair and turns to face her. "So this is it? The end."

"I wouldn't be surprised if squatters moved in, there are a lot of homeless people about. But the city won't be far behind them. It's only a matter of time. They have their minds set on this property, on their great north-west entrance, and whether they have the money to develop it right now or not, the fact remains they want us out. Even in these dire times. Everyone will be gone eventually. This place is doomed."

From the odds-and-ends shelf to her right, Egypt lifts the remaining matryoshka doll, chipped from a policeman's spite. "Can I have her?"

"Good choice," Laura says, taking Egypt's face in her hands and kissing her on the forehead. And then on either cheek. "Better hide it from your grandmother," she whispers into her hair. "Or she may steal it back from you."

"The nesting dolls belonged to Grandma Lily?"

"They were her favourite gift from her father. He brought them back from Russia for her when she was a girl. I took them to spite her."

"Then I will treasure her all the more. But in private."

Egypt walks around the shoreline until the road disappears from her periphery vision and she is facing Paradise. A breeze rustles through a patch of last year's bulrushes. A muskrat breaks the surface of the water and stares at her a moment, as if surprised to find her standing there, before diving back down again. A lull in the traffic, and Egypt feels the landscape around her pushing up through the bones in her feet, humming along her synapses. This landscape she's grown up in: swimming in the marsh and trolling the canal for pike, piping the devilled eggs for the community picnics, the long tables with their clash of edge-to-edge tablecloths. Skating and ice-boat races in the winter, the flat white landscape studded with ice-fishing huts.

"So long," she whispers, squeezing her eyes shut like a camera, capturing the image in her mind forever.

Whistling for George, she turns back in the direction of home.

Project Bookmark Canada

Trek Canada's literary trail with a visit to *The Fishers of Paradise* Bookmark plaque in Hamilton, Ontario, along the waterfront Desjardins Trail, under the second rail bridge. [*43.279036, -79.890625*]

Here, you can read a passage from page 188 of this book, in which Egypt and her brother, Aidan, skate from Cootes Paradise into the Desjardins Canal.

Project Bookmark Canada exists to mark our stories in our spaces, by placing fiction and poetry in the exact Canadian locations where literary scenes are set. Discover other Bookmarks around the country at *projectbookmarkcanada.ca*.

Acknowledgements

While this novel is based on historical events – the boathouse colony at Cootes Paradise did exist, and the City of Hamilton indeed waged a "war on the squatters" – I have taken liberties with certain facts and, with the exception of Thomas McQuesten and his family, peopled the story with characters from my imagination. All actions and dialogue attributed to the McQuestens are also entirely of my making.

Researching a community largely relegated to the margins of society was a challenge. In addition to combing through microfiched newspaper articles, I leaned heavily on Strathcona Reunion Committee's *Strathcona Remembers*, edited by Murray W. Aiken, and also Nancy B. Bouchier and Ken Cruickshank's "The War on the Squatters, 1920–1940: Hamilton's Boathouse Community and the Re-Creation of Recreation on Burlington Bay" (*Labour/Le Travail* 51 [Spring 2003]: 9–46). Professor Bouchier also provided me with a CD of early images of Cootes Paradise and the Dundas Marsh and shared information about their research on the area and the stories they collected of people who played there during their childhoods, which proved invaluable.

For insight into the vagaries of fire and the firefighting resources available to an isolated volunteer firefighting force, many thanks to John Wiznuk, retired chief of the Saturna Island Volunteer Fire Department. Thank you also to Ian Middleditch, a.k.a. Dr. Daylight, for a glimpse into some of the more nefarious logging practices of yesteryear. For input on early drafts and her unparalleled enthusiasm for this book and for Ray Fisher in particular, I will always be grateful to my dear departed friend Elaine Shirley. I miss you and I wish you were here. I wish I could show you the Project Bookmark Canada plaque. Sylvia McNicoll, thank you for all you do for writers, for always being there for me and ready to talk about writing, grants, blurbs, publicity, hair, recipes and why dogs rock. For comments and encouragement on the first edition, I owe thanks to Bill Schermbrucker, Sylvia McNicoll, Ellen McGinn, Gisela Sherman, Jim Bennett and Athena George. And to John Terpstra, for whispering that in 1930 Thunder Bay wasn't Thunder Bay.

In November 2013, within minutes of *The Fishers of Paradise* winning the Kerry Schooley Award for the book that best represents Hamilton, Noelle Allen of Wolsak & Wynn offered to bring out a reprint edition, and two fairy godmothers pulled me aside and asked me what I knew about Miranda Hill's Project Bookmark Canada. A heady night. Noelle Allen and Miranda Hill are my book heroes. To qualify for a Bookmark, *The Fishers of Paradise* needed a traditional publisher. Without Noelle, there would be no Miranda and no Bookmark in my world. Enormous thanks to the City of Hamilton for both site permission and generous funding, and to the Hamilton Public Library for cheering in my section. I am grateful to all the volunteers, donors, partners and supporters that make Project Bookmark Canada possible. Special thanks to Marijke Friesen for the beautiful new cover and book design, and to Emily Dockrill Jones for all her commas and for letting Ray chunter on in Mancunian.

And last, but never least, a huge shout out and thank you to Ian Warren, for being so supportive and willing to embrace change, and for always having my back. Here's to it always being like a sleepover.

The British Columbia Arts Council provided a writer's grant for this project, for which I am grateful.

RACHAEL PRESTON is the author of three novels: *Tent of Blue* (Goose Lane Editions, 2002), *The Wind Seller* (Goose Lane Editions, 2006) and *The Fishers of Paradise* (self-published, 2012), which won the inaugural Kerry Schooley Award for the book that best captures the spirit of the city of Hamilton.

A native of Yorkshire, England, Rachael Preston has a master's degree in English Literature from Queen's University and also studied at the Emily Carr Institute of Art and Design. She has taught creative writing in Ontario colleges and universities. For two years she chaired gritLIT: Hamilton's Writers' Festival. In 2001 she was nominated for the Journey Prize and in 2006 she won the City of Hamilton Arts Award for her contribution to the arts.

Rachael now lives in Departure Bay, Nanaimo, BC, with her husband, Ian Warren.

Visit her website at http://www.rachaelpreston.com.

Zimmerman
Mount Nemo
Tansley
Appleby
Nelson
Lake Medad
Freeman
Burlington
Port Nelson
Waterdown Sta.
Aldershot
BURLINGTON BAY
Hamilton Beach
Rock Bay
Carrolls Point
HAMILTON
GRAND TRUNK RY
HAMILTON BEACH
BURLINGTON BEACH
CANAL
BEACH ROAD